ITALIAN BLOOD
BRITISH HEART

ROBERT ROSSI

ISBN 978-1-79846-227-0

For Dennis Donnini, VC.

19 years old and less than 5 feet tall, this boy was a mountain of a man.

He was the youngest soldier in the Second World War to be awarded the Victoria Cross, the highest and most prestigious award for bravery in the face of the enemy.

This novel is dedicated to his memory.

To Joe, Olivia, Sophia and Hollie

They are the future.

"We don't receive wisdom.

We must discover it for ourselves."

Marcel Proust

PART ONE

ITALIAN BLOOD

THE BALDINI FAMILY TREE

Dino and Vittoria Baldini

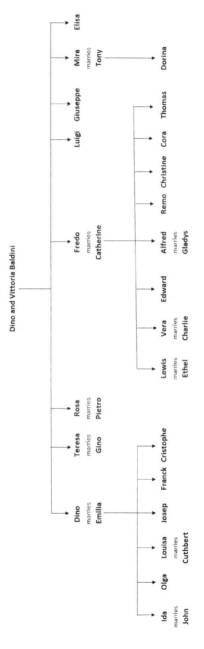

Chapter 1

1897

It was on the evening of his big sister's wedding when sixteen year old Fredo made the decision to leave the land of his ancestors and make his fortune elsewhere.

The late September sun was setting behind the mountain opposite and there was a slight chill in the air. The wedding had been a joyous affair. Most of the residents of the village of Montecino high up on a hilltop in the Apennines had attended the obligatory Mass at the local church of San Paolo. The lavish feast had been in the small garden in front of Fredo's parents' house.

Everybody in the village enjoyed a feast, especially when music was part of the festivities. Today there had been three accordionists who alternated in their choices of traditional songs. The locals never tired of singing them.

Dino and Vittoria Baldini were so proud of their daughter Rosa who had found love with a boy in the village of the same age. Rosa was eighteen years of age and her new husband Pietro was just one year older. Her parents were delighted that she hadn't been chosen by one of the elderly men who lusted for young virginal brides. It wasn't uncommon for men in their thirties to marry girls ten or fifteen years younger.

The wedding reminded the elderly couple of their

own bliss when they married more than thirty years previously. Nothing much had changed in the village. Dino and Vittoria's family were typical. They relied on the land for their survival. Years of toil showed on their faces and constant sun exposure contributed to layers of wrinkles.

By the time the sun set the guests had left. Despite the festivities they still had their daily chores. Chickens needed coaxing back into their enclosures to avoid prowling foxes having their own feast during the night. The harvest was in full season and an early start was necessary in the morning to milk the cows. Later corn required threshing and grass and hay from the wheat fields had to be gathered to sustain livestock during the winter. In between the villagers still had to find time to delve into the woods to collect firewood in advance of colder days and nights.

Fredo caught a glimpse of Rosa crying whilst leaning against a tree in the garden. He grabbed a blanket which was lying on a table. Husband Pietro was nowhere to be seen.

"*Rosa, siediti. Che cosa c'e, Perche piangi*? Sit down. What's wrong, why are you crying?"

Rosa sat motionlessly, she didn't say a word.

"*Rosa, Rosa, dimi dai,* Tell me, come on."

"*Niente, niente, va via, lasciami in pace,* It's nothing, go away, just leave me in peace."

"*Se la voi cosi!* Okay, if that's the way you want it." Fredo arose and headed for the house.

Fredo's parents were nowhere to be seen.

'*No doubt mamma is already at the pozzo washing the cups, plates and cutlery,*' thought Fredo. '*I must see if I can find Pietro.*'

Fredo walked down the mule path towards the

communal *pozzo* where the women of the village did their washing, clothes during mornings and dishes in the afternoons. He saw that mamma was on her own. She wanted to finish so she could return home before darkness fell. *"Non ritorna tardi*, don't get back late"*, she yelled at Fredo who nodded and carried on down the mule path.

He was aware of every crack in the *pozzo*, the u-shaped concrete structure built against the wall in the village square. This was where all the villagers did their washing. When the water inside needed re-freshening it was the duty of the younger boys in the village to re-fill it from the fountain spout of perpetually running water fifty yards away. He had been told that the water at the spout never stopped running, summer or winter. Nobody in the village knew its source. *"From the higher mountains above the village,"* they were used to saying.

Filling the *pozzo* was the enjoyable job, especially in summer. The boys had fun splashing around and cooling themselves in the midday heat. When the boys extracted the plug in the corner of the *pozzo* the locals were delighted at the temporary relief from the stench of rotting water quickly dissipating into the ground. It was also the boys' duty to repair the cracks which appeared from time to time. Constant threshing of sheets and clothes against the concrete ledge continually caused damage. Periodic maintenance was routinely necessary.

Fredo was one of eight children. Big brother Dino was named after his father. The family tradition was that the eldest sons were always named Alduino, Dino for short. Two years previously Dino had left Montecino with his stock of plaster cast statuettes and the last the family knew was that he was working in the port area in

9

Hamburg in Germany. Within a short time he had discovered that moulding and painting statues of saints which had become the traditional craft skill in the village couldn't provide a sustainable living in the city. So he gave up his hawking lifestyle. He sought and found permanent employment as a dock labourer with a steady wage.

Fredo's sister Teresa, the eldest daughter, was already married with four children and she lived in the village. His other siblings were two younger brothers Luigi, ten years of age, Giuseppe, aged nine and two little sisters, Mira seven and Elisa, just two.

As Fredo walked towards Teresa's house he thought back to her wedding six years earlier when after an identical day, of Mass, feasting, singing and dancing in what was supposed to have been a joyous day, he was recalling that just before sunset Teresa and husband Gino had been arguing so forcefully that *babbo*, his dad, had to intervene and restore some order.

Since Dino's departure, Fredo assumed the role of the responsible son. He was tall with gangly legs making him appear more mature than his years. He diligently obeyed his parents and as a child he rarely caused any concern or created any mischief. He was reliable and trustworthy. It was his job to find out what was happening.

Tonight there were other thoughts on his mind, *'same thing happening today, maybe it's normal that couples argue on the night of their wedding.'*

He arrived finally at Teresa's house. The door was locked and he peered through the windows. There were no candles flickering inside. He decided to turn back.

'Teresa and Gino seem so happy now with their four young children', thought Fredo as he tracked back

home.

"*Buona notte, buona notte,* Good night, good night." He exchanged greetings with villagers locking up for the night.

In the evening twilight the paths had emptied rapidly. Fredo paused at a bench in the village square near the church. He noticed the remnants of the celebration confetti which were thrown when Rosa exited the church earlier with Pietro. The air was still warm. He glanced around at the nearby houses and most were in darkness. He reflected on the day. '*I wonder if those who left are really making money. They gossiped all day about them. Were the streets in Scotland and in America really paved with gold? Dino gone. What about me? What do I want? Shall I go too? What about mamma and babbo? Who will care for them? And my brothers and sisters too?*'

Half an hour passed before he decided to saunter homewards. He knew his parents would wait up for his return before they bedded down. He walked past the *pozzo.* There was no stench tonight. The boys always re-filled it before a wedding. He contemplated on the shrine to Our Lady by the *pozzo.* '*Which villager sculpted this beautiful statue?*' He had never thought about asking anyone. '*And who ensures the holy water is always topped full?*'

He ambled past the only four storey house in the village. Mr Passerotti was leaning out of his first floor window smoking a cigarette, "*buona notte*", he said. Fredo looked through the window space on the ground floor of the house. In between the bars he saw two huge bulging eyes piercing the darkness and staring directly at him. Clearly Mr Passerotti's cow was not yet ready for sleep.

Soon Fredo was home. Before entering the house he placed his hand on top of the external oven in the garden. It was still only slightly warm from the cooking earlier in the day. He checked that the fire had been extinguished fully.

Dino's house in Montecino was one of the larger houses in the village. It was in the middle of a terrace of four houses directly on the mule track which wound its way higher up in the mountains to the next village Lama, an hour's trek away. The house was symmetrical, the entrance between two small rooms on either side, about ten feet by ten feet each. In one room Dino kept hutches for his thirty or so rabbits. Occasionally he let them loose on the gravel and earth floor. The more the rabbits were able to exercise themselves the tender the meat when they landed on the kitchen table. In the other room Dino kept his gardening tools, scythes, forks, spades as well as old bits of furniture and some old crockery, in fact all sorts of bric-a-brac. Nothing was ever thrown away, everything would be useful one day.

On the second floor up a very narrow staircase via a half landing was the main living area where on one side there was a small kitchen sink and sitting area in front of a small fireplace and on the other side Dino and Vittoria's bedroom. Upstairs on the top floor Fredo slept with his younger siblings in one room and the opposite room was now reserved for Rosa and Pietro.

Outside the main door on the other side of the mule path was the small garden, twenty feet long by twelve feet wide. A vegetable plot occupied half of the garden. Despite being season and weather dependent, most years the family were relatively self-sufficient.

In one corner of the garden, beside the chicken coup, Dino had built a stone hutch with a flue to the outside and this served as the external oven for bread making and roasts. Particularly flavoursome were the rabbit and chicken roasts. In another corner he had constructed a crude shed which was used as the family toilet. A large, sturdy plank of wood with a circular hole cut out and subtlety placed over a piece of ground which fell away into a now dried up stream, served sufficiently for the family's needs. One of Fredo's additional chores, especially now that the eldest son was longer at home had been to ensure that there was no excessive build-up of excrement lying in the stream. In winter, fortunately, the running waters of the stream automatically flushed the foul debris away.

Further down the mountainside about five hundred yards away from his home Dino worked a large field where his two cows grazed. Here a barn provided a home for his cows as well as storage of hay, wood and manure for the vegetable plot. In the field there were several plum trees, a hugely abundant fig tree and a couple of cherry trees. Surrounding the field Dino had planted grape vines, which additionally served as a crude but effective barrier boundary for the cows should they stray.

The Baldini family were typical of most families, hard-working and self-supporting as long as they maintained the strong work discipline which was determined by the changing seasons. Most families had a multitude of children, not only to satisfy the local priest who was glad to see his faithful flock increasing, but also essential to work the land from an early age to assist the family's healthy survival. Particularly so in the cold winter months where so little grew in the soil. Work was never ending. Even during the hot days of summer thoughts of preparing for winter were never far away. Younger boys were often absent for days accompanied with their mules, stocking up on logs and hay to maintain ample warmth in the home during winter.

Life indeed had to be earned. Babbo Dino didn't own his house and he owned no land. The medieval feudal system was still alive and well in rural Tuscany. The Porchetta family owned the land which Dino farmed, including his house. The Baldinis lived rent free but the family were required to donate half of everything they produced to their landlords. The Porchettas were outsiders. They had arrived in the region from Naples two hundred years previously after amassing a significant wealth from favours given to the Spanish viceroys when they ruled there. They owned several hectares of land around Montecino and their luxurious villa within the city walls of old Valbona down the valley in the municipal town was one of the most decadent.

**

When he arrived home Fredo plodded upstairs and through the candlelight noticed his parents in the living room.

"Babbo, why was Rosa crying tonight? This was supposed to be a happy day."

"It was a happy day," interrupted mamma.

"Yes, but she shouldn't have been crying. I'm going up to see if she is all right," Fredo said making his way toward the door.

"There's nothing wrong, stay here!" mamma said in a raised voice.

Fredo could see a tear swelling up in mamma's eyes.

"These are grown up adult things," said babbo. "No need to concern yourself with Rosa," hoping that Fredo would drop the subject.

Fredo walked out and ventured to go upstairs. "Don't bother," shouted babbo.

"Rosa, Pietro!" He knocked on the bedroom door. Fredo heard nothing. He waited a few moments. *'Maybe this is the wrong time to knock.'*

He pressed his ears to the door. *'Was there anybody inside?'* he thought. He wasn't sure. He and Rosa were close and he knew that she wouldn't mind if he saw her half naked. Slowly he slipped the door open and peeped inside.

The bed lay unruffled. Fredo could smell the freshness in the room. *'Mamma made sure everything was beautifully clean for tonight.'*

Fredo was deep in thought as he trudged back downstairs.

He strolled back into the living room and sat on the chair next to mamma. Not a sound, the silence deafening. No doubt his younger siblings were already asleep upstairs. Five minutes passed, babbo and mamma seemingly in deep meditation.

'This is sure unusual,' Fredo thought. Babbo and mamma always had something to say.

Every day the village was awash with something interesting. News always spread like wildfire. Somebody ill, somebody injured, a cow dying, a diseased rabbit, a poisonous snake, even ghosts in the forest. *'But tonight of all nights when babbo and mamma should be in a happy mood, they are silent and sombre,'* Fredo mused.

"*Babbo, mamma, basta, basta, che c'e?* Enough, enough, what's wrong? Something's happening tonight and I don't know what. Where are Rosa and Pietro?"

The silence continued. A few moments later babbo finally raised his head.

"Weddings are always great days," he said, "but the

nights afterwards are always difficult."

Fredo observed that tears were streaming down mamma's face.

"*Via, dai,* come on, tell me," Fredo said as he sat closer to mamma and stretched to put his arm around her shoulder. "I remember too the night after Teresa was married, you were both sad."

Dino looked over at his wife sobbing and nodding her head. '*Now it was time Fredo knew the truth. He is sixteen years of age now and he needs to know about these adult things.'* Dino and his wife had debated several times previously about when to tell their son.

"Wedding nights are always sad for us poor people", started out babbo, "when our daughters are married." Babbo took time to extract a piece of old shirt from his pocket in case he wept. "We have nothing but our family, we don't own anything not even the house we are living in. We tend our fields and look after our animals but we have nothing." He shed some tears. "The Porchetta family own the whole mountain all the way to Lama. We poor peasants work hard every day to stay alive. We have to give Porchetta half of everything we produce for living in this house and for the right to work these fields. Those bastards, bless me father, and their families never give an inch. They live in their fancy palazzi mansions down in Valbona. But worse of all………….." by now tears were running down babbo's cheeks, "they still want our daughters."

There was silence again, meanwhile mamma was sobbing loudly.

Fredo couldn't resist interrupting, "What do you mean they still want our daughters. I don't understand, babbo, please tell me," Fredo was raising his voice in deepening anger.

Silence and more tears.

"Babbo, babbo, che, che!" Fredo was now shouting.

"Prima notte, prima notte!" screamed babbo in return.

"Che prima notte, non capisco! What first night I don't understand!" Fredo was shouting louder still.

"Fredo, when one of our daughters marry, *povera Rosa,* those Porchetta bastards, they have the right to sleep with our daughters on her first night. Pietro has no say in the matter. They are stealing Rosa's virginity in the same way that they stole Teresa's virginity, what animals!"

Fredo couldn't believe what he was hearing. "What, you mean this is what's happening right now!"

"Si, *poverino,* correct," mamma managed to speak through her tears.

"No, no, no, how is this possible nowadays, surely no," Fredo was struggling to find the right words.

"Yes, my boy, it's happening right now in the vestry next to the church. The priest is obliged to allow either Mr Porchetta himself or one of his sons to do as they please. Remember, they provide the funds for the church renovations. The Porchettas maintain that this is a small price to pay to ensure all the villagers are able to survive."

"Often they don't bother even asking for their share of the food," babbo continued, "but the villagers know that whenever the Porchetta come calling then we have to do as they say."

"Do the Porchettas take everybody's daughters on their wedding night?" Fredo asked curiously, still angry.

"Less and less nowadays, I think," babbo replied, a little more composed now that he explained the horrific secret to Fredo. "I suppose we have been unlucky."

"And what about Rosa, when will she return?"

"I guess later Pietro will bring her back home and console her. Pietro is a good man and he knew this was going to happen. I am sure in a few days all will be fine."

Fredo remained in shock for a few minutes, sitting back in the chair, eyes closed, sighing deeply whilst stroking his hands through his hair. Above the silence mamma's sobs continued. Again he tried to comfort her but he knew now that there was very little he could do. *'Better to let her recover in her own good time.'*

Eventually Fredo blurted out, "What about Don Alino, what is he doing about this?" Don Alino was the local priest for more than thirty years. He was in his sixties.

"Don Alino, what can he do? He has been a good priest and he knows everybody in the village. He has little option. Everybody takes great comfort and strength from him and he ensures, where possible, to keep Porchetta's victims secret. There is nobody else who we can help us. It happens everywhere. I know that Don Alino has argued many times with Mr Porchetta how repulsive this old custom is and why it still has to exist. Discretely Mr Porchetta always lets Don Alino know who the next victim is. I know he argues constantly with them. Sometimes he wins his argument and sometimes not. But we have little choice, we are all at the mercy of that hideous family. The people in the village are not supposed to find out which unfortunate bride is chosen and Don Alino ruthlessly stamps out any malicious gossip. Life has to continue as normal even to the extent that tomorrow morning mamma will drape the sheets out of the window. A few droplets of blood on the sheets will let everybody know that the marriage has been consummated." Babbo took a deep breath.

"This is barbaric, I can't believe it!" Fredo couldn't hold his anger. "Please, please tell me this isn't true." Babbo stared at his son and nodded. Fredo ruffled his hair again and still raging, blurted, "My wife will never go through this indignity, I can tell you right now, babbo. I will never let this happen to my wife."

"As you say, my boy. I agree with you." Babbo knew that many of the men in the village had felt the same at Fredo's age. "We have to last it out. Soon these old fashioned customs will disappear."

"Don Alino, what about him, why can't he do more?"

"By the grace of God, Don Alino does what he can. He's on our side. He turns a blind eye to all the children born before marriage in the village. Maybe you know, maybe you don't, but many couples here in Montecino live together before they are married, even have children. They when they do marry, they know full well that the Porchettas are not so interested. You see, the brides are no longer virgins. When children do come along before marriage Don Alino is only too proud to baptise these babies in the same way as any other in the church. Don Alino regards these parents just as worthy as those who marry first before having children. He makes sure that in the baptism records in the church, there is no reference whatsoever to the babies being born out of wedlock."

"So what! That doesn't compensate for this horrendous and barbaric thing, this archaic custom." Fredo said continuing to struggle with the whole *prima notte* concept.

"I know, son, no never." replied babbo, "Don Alino turns a blind eye here in the village but in the town hall in Valbona when they register the births they take a different view. It's people like Mr Porchetta and the other wealthy land owners who run the town hall. They make it perfectly clear on the birth records when the child is from unmarried parents, that these children are illegitimate. I am told that sometimes they don't even mention the name of the mother, only that of the father. '*Donna non maritata*, unmarried woman,' it says. It demonstrates how little respect they have for these young women."

Fredo stood up, gave his mamma the warmest embrace for many a year. He kissed her in the cheek and declared. "That's it. No way am I having my bride spoiled. I am leaving. I am moving away. I am going to America or to Scotland." He slammed the door shut. They heard him stamp his way upstairs.

Fredo crept into bed alongside his two younger brothers who were fast asleep. He lay there eyeing the ceiling and figuring out his future.

***

"Boys, boys, rise and shine! The cows need milking!" mamma gently nudged Fredo on his shoulder.

Fredo jumped up, grateful that mamma had awoken him from his bad dream. But not fully, he realised quickly that the nightmare of the previous evening's conversation was real.

Through the window he saw the daylight emerging from behind the mountain on the other side of the valley. Milking the cows was one of Fredo's daily tasks but he was glad that soon Luigi, even at ten years of age would be able to assume this responsibility on his own.

"*Luigi, andiamo,* Let's go."

Babbo insisted the cows be milked every day. If even a day was missed, he preached, it would reduce the quality and quantity of future milking. Fredo never really bothered to think whether this was true or not.

He just accepted that the daily ordeal was necessary. Fredo had drummed the routine into Luigi.

After being milked directly into small pails, the still warm liquid required filling into larger churns. Milk had to be heated to boiling point on an open fire to remove harmful bacteria. It was normally breakfast time by the time boiling was completed. Fredo loved his soggy pudding of stale and hardened bread from the previous day, dunked into a bowl of fresh newly boiled milk. This was his favourite breakfast.

The rest of the milk required to be bottled. It was Fredo's responsibility, after breakfast, with his sack of filled bottles, to do the rounds to preselected neighbours. He exchanged the milk for other produce, ham joints or fruit and vegetables which the family didn't otherwise grow. Sometimes he returned home with other necessities, hand stitched shoes, homemade shirts or trousers.

His rota was predetermined, identical each day. Fredo was aware how well his parents managed the financial side of the bartering process in their heads, who owed what and to whom. On occasion arguments developed between villagers, in which case Don Alino was asked to mediate, but most times everybody seemed content with their part of the barter.

Today on his round he couldn't help but think of the previous day's events.

'Che barbarita! Che vita! What a barbaric ritual, what a way to behave!'

'I cannot accept it. My wife will never be subjected to these violations, never mind any daughters that I have. I'm just not having it. Even this damned system of bartering is fruitless. There is no money to be made. It's no more than a hopeless existence.'

"Ciao, Fredo." He was taken by surprise as Vito jumped onto his shoulder. "Great day yesterday, no!" Vito exclaimed in an excitedly high pitched voice.

"Actually, it wasn't," replied Fredo struggling to keep hold of his sack of bottles from Vito's sudden gesture.

Vito and Fredo had grown up together and were inseparable friends. They helped each other with their daily chores, often they milked cows together and they killed and skinned rabbits together. Later that day they had planned to scavenge for any remaining porcini mushrooms in the forests. These fungi were a great delicacy and this was the one source of food which could be exchanged for significant money in the markets down the valley in Valbona. Most years the scavenging was well worth the effort. The problem, however, was that virtually all the men and boys of the village had the same objective in making some real money. Finding these valuable mushrooms was difficult and it was competitive, and often dangerous.

"Maybe this afternoon we'll catch some snakes instead," remarked Vito. He stated that for several days most of the villagers were returning home with empty baskets. "You should have seen the beauty round my dad's neck the other day, a real *vibera*, poisonous snake. He swiped it dead with his knife in one slice. In its belly we counted twenty one little ones. Imagine all those hatching into adults."

It was common to tangle with poisonous snakes on the mushroom hunt and the fathers of the village continuously reminded their boys what to do when confronted with these creatures.

"*Non ci vado oggi,* I am not going today, Vito," said Fredo, "I have other things to think about. I am scared of these damned snakes anyway. I just don't want to go anywhere near them."

"Tell me," Fredo wanted to change the subject. "Your uncle Pepe left for America about a year ago. Any news from him."

"Well, yes, he sent a letter back to my mum a few months ago. All seems to be well now but the voyage he said was unbearable." Vito continued. "For ten long days, he said, he was imprisoned in a wooden bunk in the bowels of the ship with little to eat or drink. If he moved away from his bunk, he said, there would likely be a bigger guy who would steal it. He said also that the ship constantly rolled from side to side and since he was in the bottom bunk he was regularly covered in vomit from the people in the bunk above. He said, never again, would he make the trip." Vito used every mannerism and body language possible to describe his imagined version of the event on the ship.

But Fredo couldn't fully understand. He had never seen a ship before. He knew that out there beyond the mountains there was a huge expanse of water and that somehow a structure of wood and metal was able to float its way to this other land, America.

'A bed one of top of the other,' he thought, *'I would love to see that!'*

"And what's Pepe doing now?"

"Remember, he used to spend the summers up in the marble mountains at Arni where he learned how to sculpt marble. Seems he has found loads of work carving statues for the church. He said they are building many new churches in the big cities in America."

The pair continued walking kicking stones as they proceeded along the mule track.

"Vito, I want to leave, I want to live in a more civilised place but I don't have any skills. I am useless with my hands," Fredo stated. "I am not going to waste any time up at Arni. Marble sculpture and all that stuff is not for me."

"What about England or Scotland?" Vito replied "Some of those men at the other end of the village, Vincenti and Guidi, they went to Scotland."

"Maybe Scotland, yes. I did know that a few of the men had gone there. And some of their boys as well. I intend to find out more."

Fredo had led a relatively sheltered life. His parents seemed content with their lot and they rarely complained. They had no great hopes for their children other than for them to continue their family traditions. The boys to work the land, find a nice girl from the village and bring many more children into the world, vice versa for the girls, find a local boy and for them to be at home cooking, sewing, bearing children and generally keeping the house in order.

But now Fredo had no intention of continuing the family tradition.

Chapter 2

1899

The last snows of winter had long disappeared and after a year of mulling over his future Fredo was ready. He had spent the previous year accumulating as much money as he could. Now that younger brother Luigi had been able to take over many of his routine daily chores, Fredo spent the summer crossing the Apennines backwards and forwards with his mule laden with illicit salt and tobacco. Over the regional border in Romagna he sourced salt and tobacco in bulk. When he returned home he batched his merchandise into smaller quantities and sold it at the Valbona markets. Fredo's saved all his profits, as much as he could.

For many years salt and tobacco were licensed products. Salt was an essential preservative for food and the shopkeepers who sold it were required to pay special taxes, a great money spinner for the public coffers in Valbona. Nevertheless tax avoidance was the order of the day in the town and the shopkeepers wasted little time in attempting to buy contraband salt. This meant an ample supply of customers for Fredo. Although illegal, he thought it was still worth the risk, figuring that the salt police would never stray high up in the mountains to stop his activity.

Tobacco was taxed too. On his salt forays Fredo had discovered where and how to buy much lower quality tobacco and sell it on as the genuine article. He had assessed that his biggest risk, which if caught, was the loss on any one single consignment. He knew the mountains well and he could outrun any local policeman, who usually were fat and stumpy. *'The police are corrupt anyway'*, when all alone with his thoughts in the mountains, *'I am skinny, they are fat, I can outrun them. If that doesn't work, then I can always bribe them.'*

Fredo was absent up to fourteen days at a time. He slept in the rough but his adventures were not without their dangers. In addition to the constant fear of meeting the salt and tobacco police, there were hungry boars and mountain bears in the wilds of the Apennines. A machete and a large knife, both readily available, were permanently attached to his belt. He had been reliably informed that the little bell around the neck of his mule would scare the boars and bears away. He hoped it was true. Fredo had no intention of inadvertently being a hearty feast for these predators.

At night there was also the prospect of scavenging wolves searching for food. Maybe, however, during these summer months, he assumed, there were many mountain hares and moles available to them. So he figured the wolves were happy to spend the night asleep just like him.

Meandering along the well-trodden mule tracks, he was never without a large and sturdy stick in his right hand to fend off approaching snakes. He comforted himself with the village tales that snakes had a very keen sense of hearing. And if any happened to be sunbathing on the flat stones of the mule path, they said, on hearing the bell of the mule, they would shuffle themselves back into the safety of the forest.

Babbo and mamma rarely approved of Fredo's activities. But they understood his motive for money. After numerous and heated discussions in the long winter months after Rosa's wedding, Dino and Vittoria had resigned themselves to losing their second son so he could find his fortune elsewhere.

Life for the villagers in Montecino as well as for the townsfolk of Valbona down the valley, had been turned upside down following the unification of Italy thirty years earlier, the Risorgimento, they called it. The Italian peninsula was formerly an amalgam of separate states. Valbona and its neighbouring villages had been part of the Duchy of Florence for centuries. Geographically the town was an enclave surrounded by two other states, Lucca and Parma. In their wisdom Valbona had been designated by its masters in Florence as a tax free zone. The town had no need to levy any taxes on businesses nor on its population. Consequently a great entrepreneurial spirit had emerged in the area. Fine silks and clothes and casted metals were produced for export. In addition the plentiful and huge forests of the high Apennine mountains within Valbona's jurisdiction provided the wooden logs which ultimately meandered down the Serchio valley on their way to the Republic of Pisa for the manufacture of its ships.

But all changed after unification. The town was no longer allowed to be designated a tax free zone, as the councils of the national government eliminated all the privileges from the people and power vested rapidly to influential land owners like Mr Porchetta. Many skills were lost as businesses floundered and slowly but surely the local economy regressed to be dominated by agriculture. The land owners smartly moved in to ensure that they obtained more than their fair share.

The local population became impoverished and for a great many, emigration was the only answer. America had become the emigration of choice for those with some degree of manual skill whereas it was England and then Scotland for the *contadino*, or farmer and for the *bracciante*, the agricultural labourer, very hard-working and diligent but with little sellable skills. Fredo and his family and indeed virtually all the inhabitants of Montecino fell into the less skilled category.

"*Me ne vado,* I am definitely going, *non ci sto qui,* I am not staying here." Fredo was determined. His frustrations became stronger as his mamma made attempt after attempt for him to remain at home.

"*Sei troppo giovane,* you're too young," she repeated. "*Non ti rivedo piu*, I will never see you again."

But Fredo always had his final say. And mamma usually cried herself to sleep. "*Mia moglie, quando la trovo, mai sera violata come Rosa and Teresa,* my wife, when I find her will never be abused like Rosa and Teresa."

Montecino and the outlying houses had a population of just less than seven hundred, about a hundred different families and Fredo knew them all by name. He had established that about two dozen of the menfolk, some with their sons, had emigrated to Scotland in the preceding two or three years. Only one had since returned, Leo Santi, who lived about fifty yards from the other side of the church.

"*Oh Santi, cinque minuti,* Mr Santi, five minutes please." Fredo asked as he chanced upon Mr Santi at the end of Mass of the first Sunday in Lent.

"Can you tell me something about Scotland, I want to go?" enquired Fredo offering Mr Santi one of his home made contraband cigarettes.

"Here we have bright sun and lovely food," responded Mr Santi immediately, "but in Glasgow, there is no sun. Instead there are splendid and beautiful new buildings, and there is a lot of smoke and soot, and horse shit in smelly streets. But best of all there are lots of people with lots of money. Are you interested?"

"What do you do?"

"All of us who have left Montecino, we are in the same business. You know, Fredo, we help each other, we have no skill with our hands, we just have our brawn and our brain. We obtain ice, salt and milk and we make ice cream. Some of us have a shop where we sell this, others have barrows where they walk the streets selling to the people," Mr Santi said with a sense of pride.

"But no sun means cold weather, Mr Santi, why do they buy ice cream," Fredo looked puzzled.

"*Bischero,* Idiot, the sun is still there. It's just you can't see it with all the smoke. It's still warm in the summer. Admittedly in the winter we don't sell much ice cream. We tried something new and now we are selling a great meal which the Scottish people love."

"And what's that, Mr Santi."

"Fish fried in pig fat. We also fry pieces of cut potatoes in the fat, they call them chips. The fish and potatoes are wrapped together in newspaper. This is their meal, they eat it directly with their hands."

"*Mamma mia!*" gasped Fredo, offering Mr Santi a second cigarette.

"Actually Fredo, I have returned home to recruit some more boys to come over to help us. We cannot cope with demand. There are so many opportunities over there, new factories, new coal mines, more ships being built. The Scots have lots of money and they love to spend a lot of that money with us."

Fredo's listened intensely, eyes wide open in amazement.

"And in ten years I will build my own house right here in Montecino on the top of the hill." Mr Santi pointed to the highest point of the village which had magnificent three sixty degree views up towards the Apennine peaks and down the valley to Valbona, two miles away.

"I will lend you one half the cost of your ticket, the other half you pay yourself. You pay me back when you work for me." Mr Santi held out his right hand in advance of a quick deal.

Fredo took one long and last puff of his cigarette, stubbed it out on the ground and placed his hand forward. "When do I leave?"

"I'll talk to Pippo, who sells the train tickets in Valbona. I'll give him my share of the money after you have paid your share, agreed."

"And one other thing," Fredo hesitated slightly. "*Prima notte*, you know, on wedding nights, please tell they don't have it on Glasgow, as well."

"Fredo, it's a new civilisation over there, I have never heard about it in Scotland, and trust me, I know a few girls. You will find out for yourself. Don't forget, fifty per cent."

The pair shook hands and they parted.

***

Two days later Fredo made his way down to Valbona. Downhill it didn't take that long. The mule path wound its ways through the chestnut forest for about a mile until it reached the little hamlet of Ronchi half way to Valbona. On his way he passed the little chapel of San Rocco where he paused for a few moments for reflection and inspiration. San Rocco was the patron saint of travellers, his parents had told him, and the locals consistently paused at the chapel for moments of prayer on their way to and from Valbona.

'San Rocco, please keep me safe in my new travels and keep my family safe too. Amen.' Three Hail Marys later, Fredo continued on his way.

The inhabitants of Ronchi were busy with their early spring chores, *"Buon giorno, buon giorno."* The locals knew everybody from Montecino who passed by.

The remainder of the route to Valbona was on the flat except for the crossing over the Corsonna river where the mule path descended to the water's edge. At the shortest crossing point between both banks of the river, strategically placed large stepping stones were safe enough to cross during the hot summer and autumn seasons. But now in early spring the waters ran like a torrent down the valley as they surged towards the larger Serchio river. The stones were deep under water. Thankfully the fragile bridge of wooden slats held together by woven rope was intact and Fredo crossed with little problem. Sometimes the ropes on the bridge hung loose and it was the custom to call on the closest house nearest the bridge on either side of the river to report the damage. It was the tradition that the occupants of the houses assume the responsibility to keep the bridge in good order. Nobody knew who had created the rule but everybody accepted it.

The town of Valbona was inhabited by about five thousand people, half of which still lived within its ancient medieval castle. The walls had survived many centuries despite numerous local wars and a few earthquakes. The rest of the population lived outside the town walls in the outlying districts. In the *Giardino* district two rows of elegant buildings had recently been built. On the ground floor across the length of the buildings there were shops and on the floors above, apartments. Today on the street, there were also a handful of stalls, one selling bread, another selling vegetables and fruit, one selling all sorts of crockery and another with a wooden plank overhead etched with the word, '*Viaggi, Travel*'. Fredo was heading there.

In front of the stall there were two posters. On the left hand side a poster, headlined '*Da Europa all'America.*' Fredo figured that the object in the image was that of a pristine looking ship gleaming on the sea. On the right hand side another poster headlined '*A Thomas Cook's Ticket,*' written on what looked like a globe of the world being held up to the sky by a man in uniform.

Fredo caught Pippo's attention immediately. "Oh Pippo. I assume Mr Santi has alerted you that I would be coming. I'm Fredo Baldini."

"Yes, of course. Sit down. Let me give you some details." Pippo flicked through some loose papers. "Actually in ten days' time we have a group of five going to Glasgow by train. The journey will take two days and we could add you to the group. In fact one of the passengers is Pamela Rinaldi, also from Montecino. She is just twenty years of age and her parents have asked me whether I knew anybody to chaperone her to ensure that she comes to no harm. You would be ideal."

Fredo sat attentively whilst Pippo sucked again on his pipe. "Old man Topolino is also on the trip. He's made the trip a hundred times. On the way over his job is to care for the ladies who are on their own. And on the way back, so they say, he brings back sacks of cash for the families of those who are earning good money in Scotland. Pamela really doesn't like him, thinks him a bit too personal, so it would be great if you could make it. Look there he is, Topolino, sitting on a bench over there. Go and talk to him."

Fredo strolled across the piazza and grabbed the attention of the elder man. Topolino explained in some detail what the journey would be like, what clothes and food to bring. Horse and cart to Pisa and then a train and boat for the rest of the trip. Up the Alps and through the mountain passes, stops in the big cities of Paris and London with a boat trip in between and then another train journey finally to Glasgow. He endeavoured to explain to Fredo the concept of a train of many coaches carrying hundreds of passengers. But the image of linked carriages propelled by a steam engine riding along metal rails on a dirt track couldn't be captured by Fredo. Horses were the limit of Fredo's imagination never mind the thought of coaches being pulled along by a contraption billowing out smoke.

'I am really looking forward to experiencing this train phenomenon', thought Fredo, the only image in his mind being that of a horse and carriage fit for just four people with the mayor of Valbona sitting inside.

Fredo returned to the stall and paid for his share of the ticket price. Pippo wasted little time stuffing the cash into his pocket. "I am sure Mr Santi will pop in with his half of the money in the next day or two. It's the same deal with all the boys. Don't worry, he sticks to his word. So don't forget to come back next week for your ticket."

Fredo trekked back home, his mind full of all sorts of plans and dreams. *'Trains, Paris, London, money, ice cream, pig fat, smoke and dirt, Mr Santi, strange places and strange food, this adventure will be scary and very exciting too.'*

But an overriding thought was continually uppermost, '*I am doing this for Rosa and Teresa, I won't allow my wife and daughters subjected to these abuses, these crimes. At least in this place, Glasgow, they don't do that sort of thing, so Mr Santi has told me.*'

Later in the day in Montecino Fredo met Pamela and she was so pleased he would accompany her on the trip.

Pamela explained her situation. "I am going to Glasgow to be married to my Gigi. He left two years ago. He started out with Mr Santi as a *garzone,* a manservant and dogsbody, but it didn't work out. In his letters he mentioned he worked eighteen hours every day doing anything and everything Mr Santi asked. Making ice cream was only part of it. He had to go to find the ice, he had to clean up the horse dung from the streets and sometimes even human dung too. Not very pleasant, he said, but Gigi managed to pay off some of his loan and he and Mr Santi parted company. He managed to borrow some more money from elsewhere to pay off Mr Santi completely. Now he is selling some form of water flavoured with various fruits. The bubbles inside sparkles the drink, he said, makes it fizzy. He says his life now is better than before and he's earning good money too."

Fredo wasn't too bothered about Gigi's experiences. Some of the stories he heard about Mr Santi's cruelty to his *garzone* matched Pamela's description to a tee. But now he knew there were no alternatives. Despite this he trusted Mr Santi, His instinct was telling him that his new life would work out successfully.

***

The trip was scheduled to leave a few days after Easter. On the previous Sunday Fredo's parents had organised a special lunch. The family were all present, Rosa and Teresa with their husbands and children. Babbo had invited Pamela and her mother and family. Don Alino had also been invited so they could all join in a family prayer wishing for a safe and healthy journey.

Don Alino was well used to these family gatherings when the young boys left. It was the tradition and the priest lapped up the hospitality.

Mamma had spent the previous three days preparing the meal while babbo managed to find a joint of lamb, the traditional meat for Easter. Lamb was rarely eaten at any other time of the year since it was difficult to obtain. It was sourced from farmers higher up the mountains in the Apennine pastures. Earlier in the week babbo had been gone two days to fetch the lamb.

Before the main lamb course, Mamma had prepared potato gnocchi with her special ragu and tomato sauce which were always well received on those special occasions. For dessert she baked several traditional rice cakes, cooked rice inside a flan of sweet pastry. She had also baked a Colomba cake, a treat reserved for special occasions. The cake, shaped in the form of a cross to represent the Crucifixion was another Easter speciality. Its recipe contained dried fruit to complement regular ingredients of flour, eggs, sugar and butter.

After the meal, Don Alino asked for a few moments of reflection and the group prayed together.

"My holy Jesus, bless this journey which Fredo and Pamela are undertaking, that they may remain healthy and safe, that they may reach their destination, and that when they return home fattened and rich, they may find their family here in good health."

Mamma couldn't hold her emotions back, "*Fredo,*

attento, molto attento, be careful, be very careful. *Ritorna presto,* come back soon." Babbo put his arms around his wife and within moments everyone enveloped themselves in a tearful group huddle.

However Don Alino stood back and watched. *'Always the same. Tears of sadness and tears of joy at the same time'*, he thought.

***

The sun had yet to rise on another glorious spring morning. Six passengers accompanied the driver on the horse and cart as it left Valbona. Three had tickets for Glasgow and three for London.

The cart wound its way uneventfully along the Serchio valley towards Lucca. Once before Fredo had been to Lucca. He was an infant so he remembered nothing of the town. The city walls appeared huge and inside there were throngs of people on the move carrying all sorts of merchandise. Some were carrying dead pigs around their neck, others lifting sacks of potatoes from carts and some sitting on wobbly chairs bending bits of metal. *'This must be the main market place,'* Fredo thought. The market was jammed packed with horses and carts. Horses were being re-energised with fresh hay and water.

Each of the passengers took the opportunity to relieve themselves in the nearby latrine which was nothing more than a trench dug at the side of the road. Before she crouched down Pamela eyed Fredo for assistance. Her message was clear. He extended his large cloak and it surrounded Pamela, amply protecting her modesty as she crouched down.

The group continued on their way and as they crossed the Pisan mountains, Fredo and Pamela were left awestruck at the panoramic view. For the first time they saw the sea. Down below beyond the city of Pisa lay a vast expanse of water.

"Is that the sea?" Fredo exclaimed. "What is at the end over there?" pointing towards the horizon. The sea seemed immense and unending. He was beginning to comprehend why a ship voyage to America could take ten days. In fact what he didn't know was that this was a tiny sea compared to the huge ocean which led to America.

Fredo noticed a multitude of crafts slowly moving on the sea. One specific area near a piece of land which was split in two by a river was particularly crowded. *'Just like bees flying in and out of the hive,'* he thought, *'that is the area where all the boats and water crafts arrive and depart.'*

In contrast Pamela was in awe of another aspect of the marvellous landscape. Directly beneath was a great city, billowing smoke from hundreds of chimneys slowly dispersing in the sky. In the distance she made out a church tower which was clearly leaning to one side. *'It must be frightening, looks like it could fall any minute. That must be the Leaning Tower. Maybe we might be able to get closer when we are in the city,'* she thought.

The cart approached what was left of the old city walls and made its way through the streets crossing the river towards the railway station. On its route it passed by the Leaning Tower. Fredo and Pamela stared in amazement that the tower was able to stand firm.

The railway station itself was nothing like Fredo had ever seen before. The entrance with eight huge archways was squeezed between two impressively high buildings with huge stone columns. Above the archways were further storeys of carved stone, one of them fronted by a huge clock. *'What a structure!'*

Inside the building Fredo finally set his eyes on the train. The excitement was beyond his wildest dreams. Huge carriages with metal wheels on metal rails. He couldn't wait for the experience. *'To be on a moving train.'* Now he understood why he could never have imagined such an engineering marvel.

Fredo ran to the front of the train where he stood in wonder at the engine, in an intoxicating atmosphere of smoke and steam, large funnels, hundreds of pipes and constant noise. *'The mules and mule tracks of Montecino are indeed a world away from this.'* He looked inside the cabin and peeked into the boiler to see where men were stoking coal into a huge raging fire. The next carriage, he saw, was filled to the brim with coal. *'This must be what powers the train.'* He recalled the small mine back home in Ronchi where families managed to extract coal to barter for their milk and grain. *'But the coal extracted in Ronchi were pebbles compared to the huge chunks I am seeing here.'*

The group from Valbona had a compartment all to themselves and as the train rolled out of the station, Topolino stood to announce his set of instructions.

"One, never stick your head out of window," he emphasised to ensure everybody understood. "You will get bits of coal in your eyes or worse, be struck by another train travelling in the opposite direction on the other track."

"Two, we must stay together at all times. The train is full. Some people are good, eager to help but others are dodgy and clever. There are many thieves and pickpockets. They will steal from you without you ever noticing."

"Three, always hold on to your bags and cases. Never leave them out of your sight. As I said there are many vagabonds on board. Be wary at all times."

***

By the following day, Fredo's fascination for the mechanics of the train had all but dissipated. There was little to do other than marvel at the changing landscapes. Excitement had transcended into boredom.

Topolino announced that soon they would be entering the great city of Paris. Here they would be required to cross the city by carriage to reach another train station. Outside the Gare de Lyon station Topolino summoned a carriage. Meanwhile Fredo and Pamela were amazed at the surroundings. There were beautiful tree-lined wide boulevards, elaborately decorated buildings, elegant ladies with umbrellas and horses and carts as far as the eye could see. In the near distance they noticed masses of workmen busy at work. Huge impressive mechanical equipment stood nearby.

"Why are they digging up the streets, Topolino?" Fredo asked.

"This is the underground railway which they are building, wonderful isn't it?" he replied.

Fredo looked at Pamela. "A railway under the ground, how is this possible? What about the smoke and steam?" They both shrugged their shoulders in bewilderment.

The carriage arrived at the Gare du Nord railway station and inside Topolino identified the train leaving in two hours for London.

"Paris is the most beautiful city in the world, but wild and dangerous. I need you all to stay in the carriage until I return," Topolino stated "I have some business to do here."

After Topolino left, Pamela whispered to Fredo, "Listen, back home I was warned that Topolino would leave the train here in Paris."

"Why do you think?"

"They say his only pleasure in life are his stops in Paris. Seems he has a lady waiting for him each time he visits. Wait and see, when he returns, his face will be flushed with happiness and satisfaction."

"Good for him, I suppose."

Pamela couldn't resist the temptation to venture into the street. "Let's have a little stroll outside," she whispered.

"Only ten minutes. We don't want to get lost."

They exited the station hand in hand and walked westwards for two blocks in wonderment and awe. Both felt exhilarated being side by side with elegant gentleman and ladies. 'I want to be like them one day,' said Fredo. "Me, too," replied Pamela.

After a few minutes in their private dreamland the pair headed back towards the station.

When Topolino returned Fredo noticed indeed that his face was flushed and that he was in a joyous mood. "I trust your business was enjoyable," he said. Topolino winked and gave him a wry smile.

Later the same evening, the train arrived at the port of Boulogne.

"Here we have to leave the train," said Topolino, "and board a ship to reach England on the other side of this large sea, the English Channel."

Fredo glanced ahead at the train tracks terminating right at the end of the dock and noticed the vast blue sea ahead. On one side he saw a ship *Le Pas de Calais* steam billowing out of its huge funnels. '*This must be what takes us to England."*

As soon as the ship started to move, Fredo felt the swaying. His stomach began to belch. He felt uncomfortable.

"Don't worry," said Topolino, "the crossing is only three hours and then we will be on dry land."

The choppy sea didn't relent. "You need to stay out in the fresh air," said Topolino. But fresh air made no difference. Fredo and Pamela held each other tightly on the top deck as the wind threatened to blow them over. One went and the other followed. They couldn't avoid it. They tried to comfort each other alternately as the contents of their lunch and breakfast lurched out several times. It wasn't just them who were vomiting constantly. Many passengers were experiencing the same, a lurch of vomit, a moment of calm, another sway of the ship and another lurch.

"Do we need to clean this up?" Fredo asked.

"No, don't worry, a huge wave will wash it away," replied Topolino laughingly.

At last land was spotted, the sea calmed somewhat and to Fredo's surprise the urge to vomit came to an abrupt halt. His stomach seemed to return to normal.

"It's in the mind, see, I told you," Topolino said annoyingly. "There's Folkestone over there. Told you. You see land and then you are okay."

In a short time the group were on board their designated train and on their way to the next destination, London. They were reinvigorated. There were new sights and new smells. Soon they would be in another huge city.

The terminus in London was reached. Goodbyes were said to the three remaining in the city but for Fredo and Pamela there was yet another coach ride to yet another station. Here the city seemed busier than Paris. The horses seemed to be smarter. They were amazed how the drivers managed to squeeze their carriages past each other without collision. They was little opportunity to marvel at the equally impressive city landscape.

"You have just seen two of the largest and most elegant cities in the world," Topolino stated. "Now our last train takes us to Glasgow where you certainly won't see the same elegance, but you will it enjoy more, because it's there where you will make your money, you will see."

As the train steamed through the green pastures of the English countryside Fredo and Pamela relaxed. They were less anxious. Soon they were reaching their final destination.

"What is Scotland?" Fredo asked, "is it a different country from England?"

"Yes, so the Scottish people say. But really it's just like Toscana and Romagna in Italy, different regions but one law which governs all," replied Topolino.

"Why are so many of us in Scotland?" he continued glancing to Pamela, "when maybe London might have been the place to be. It's the capital city, after all."

"A long story," sighed Topolino. "It was about thirty years ago when the first Valbona people came over. They were *figurinai*, moulders of plaster cast figures. You know, Fredo, your babbo and mamma made and painted those little figures when they were young, did your parents not tell you?"

"In those days they left Valbona by road and travelled on foot all the way. They walked and walked. On their way they sold those little *figurine*. In Italy they sold casts of Garibaldi, in France they sold casts of Napoleon and in England the casts were of Nelson. The funny thing was that the casts were all the same, it was just the paint which was different. The people they were selling to, didn't really know any better. Anyway, when they arrived in London they continued to make and sell what they could and they just kept moving north. They passed through the big towns of England, some travelled to the North West to Birmingham, Manchester, Liverpool and Carlisle and some travelled towards the North East to Leeds and Newcastle. The intention was to continue walking to the next big city. After Carlisle, the next big city stop was Glasgow. Here they were told that there were no more big cities so they decided to stay put. For the people who went east they reached Edinburgh. They were told that there were other cities further north, Dundee and Inverness. In their travels some of the men met and fell in love with lovely city ladies and their journeys ended right there. This is why there are little Valbona communities dotted all around the country and in some surprising places."

Topolino continued, "But the biggest group is in Glasgow. They realised selling *figurine* couldn't make them enough money, so they supplemented their income as organ grinders in the streets. But the more savvy started businesses selling ice cream in barrows in summer and roasted chestnuts in winter. And nowadays many see better opportunities opening shops, particularly as ice cream and fried fish merchants."

"That's why I'm here," interrupted Fredo. "I want to be an ice cream and fish merchant. I am hoping Mr Santi can help me to set me up. Then I want to meet a nice Scottish lady to marry and have many children."

"And what about your Gigi, Pamela?"

"I think, same story for Gigi. He started out selling ice cream and chestnuts in his barrow. He worked all the hours for his *padrone* boss but it didn't work out for him. He was just sixteen when he first went to Glasgow, they gave him all the dirty jobs. He did that for six years and then he returned home to Montecino. After we met, we agreed he should go back to Glasgow and try again, maybe get a proper job with the locals so we could have a more stable life together. From his letters he seems to have done exactly that. Now he works as a salesman, drives his own horse and cart selling flavoured water. The locals call it ginger."

As the steam train duly sped up the west side of the country Fredo noticed the vastly contrasting landscapes. On leaving London there was lush flat countryside, with picturesque rolling fields of varying pastoral shades of green separated by hedges in neat rectangular patterns. Then as the train slowed down to stop in the cities of Birmingham and Manchester he saw the industrial landscape of chimneys and long rows of houses all jammed together under a seemingly endless cloud of smoke and soot. *'This is where money is made.'* he thought. He observed that there was little colour, just black and grey. The people too were dressed in black and grey, in huge contrast to the empty green fields and colourful landscapes.

"Now we are crossing into Scotland," Topolino remarked excitedly as if they were about to enter a new land.

'Will this be any different?' Fredo thought. Soon he did notice the difference. The landscape was bleaker, hills filled with sheep and a distinct absence of trees. Some of the hills were still capped with the last of the winter snows. "We'll soon be there, we'll soon be there," repeated Topolino several times. The last part of the journey seemed never ending.

At last the train arrived into the suburbs of Glasgow. Topolino's description of the city was confirmed.

The first image of Fredo's new home was of chimneys, smoke, steam, soot and thousands of people on the move in horses and carts. Here too, everything was black and grey.

Just as in Paris and London, Fredo gaped in amazement at the huge concourse in the railway station and at the number of trains and platforms and the constant flow of people to and fro. It was as if the whole world had assembled right there within the huge building.

"A carriage will take us to Mr Santi's premises and he will make the arrangements for you to meet your friends and families," said Topolino. "Pamela, I do hope Mr Santi knows where you husband is since he is no longer his *garzone*."

"Yes, I am sure, Gigi told me to meet with Mr Santi, too, when I arrived."

"Follow me, everybody, there's money to be made in these streets. Fredo, one thing for sure, Mr Santi will keep you very busy."

The distance from the station to the Saltmarket, where Mr Santi had his premises was two miles. As the horse cantered along one of the city's main streets, Fredo felt the adrenaline rush. *'Here, at last!'* Despite the general grimness and greyness, the highly embroidered columns and large windows of the buildings on Argyle Street sparkled when the sun managed to break through the clouds. There were rows and rows of elegant tenements, shops at street level, houses above, most windows decorated with embroidered lace curtains. *'One day I will live in one of those magnificent houses above the shops.'*

A shop sign caught Fredo's attention. "Pieri's Ice Cream Parlour," written in bold lettering above the shop entrance. Topolino noticed him pointing to the shop.

"Yes, Freddie Pieri, there, is from Valbona too. A few years back he brought his family over. Now they are very happy. They live in the house upstairs from the shop. Very convenient, no?"

"What does Parlour mean?"

"The Scots stole our word. *Noi parliamo, we* speak. I suppose it means a place to speak. See, Fredo, we are already making a big difference here."

Soon they arrived at Mr Santi's. After dutiful embracing and kissing formalities were over Mr Santi organised proceedings.

The shop was twice the size of Mr Pieri's with display windows on either side of the main entrance. Inside were benches and tables of a dark rich wood and the marble tables were engraved in a fine gilding resembling gold, LS. "My initials," Mr Santi remarked proudly.

On either side of the serving counter there were window cases inside of which were platefuls of a variety of strange looking biscuits and cakes. "These are scones. They are usually filled with jam or cream." Mr Santi said pointing to most appetising of all the cakes. Behind the window case was a flat wooden slab with a hole. "Inside here we make the ice cream."

Behind the serving area there were metal containers of different shapes and sizes. "And this is where we boil water to make tea," Mr Santi continued.

Soon after Mr Santi motioned his guests to a table in the corner of the room.

"Sit down, my treat."

Just as they made themselves comfortable, a *garzone* arrived with a tray of cakes and with some glasses filled to the brim with ice cream. The glasses, with a circular base, were in the shape of a tulip with the tips of the petals leaning to the outside. The ice cream inside the tulip was covered with a rich and sticky red sauce.

"*Mangia, Mangia,* eat, eat. The Scottish people have sweet teeth," Mr Santi said. "The sauce is made up of crushed raspberries infused with lots of sugar. In the autumn in fields outside the city these raspberries are everywhere, growing wild, so they cost nothing. It's a great deal for us. We charge extra for the sauce."

"The *garzone* make the ice cream by hand right here on the premises," Mr Santi continued looking over to Fredo. "We source huge blocks of ice. The blocks are cut out from frozen lakes or ponds in the winter. We store it in the cellars below and it's packed in deep straw so it doesn't melt for a long time. Daily we chip away at the ice bit by bit and mix it with salt and sugar to make a cold and sticky fluid. Then we add milk. Wooden cylinders are manufactured for us. A knob is attached to the brim of the cylinder. The ice and milk mix are placed inside the cylinder which in turn is placed inside a box laden with more ice. The cylinder is turned as long and as vigorously as possible within the box of ice. Gradually this great stuff called ice cream emerges inside the cylinder and it's ready to sell."

"I assume that's what the hole in the counter is for, then," asked Fredo.

Mr Santi nodded and he continued, "Our *garzone* go out onto the streets with their hand carts to sell the ice cream. In summer it's a great business. Little kids, in particular, love our penny licks. We have a glass of ice cream always at the ready and for a penny they can lick the tip of the glass. The longer their tongue, the more ice cream they get. Here just like this."

Mr Santi picked up a glass to demonstrate before proceeding to enjoy the remains of the ice cream inside. "Just recently we started selling a new product which originated in America. They invented an edible container, cone shaped, where the ice cream neatly fits in. Basically our customers can now eat the whole thing, cone and all. Since we introduced the cone our business has tripled. So now instead of all those broken and stolen glasses, now we sell ice cream in ball shaped scoops inside the cone. Great too, that we can charge more and there is little mess. In fact parents love it for their children. Cones are safer, more hygienic, they taste good, too."

"Very exciting, when do I start?" interrupted Fredo.

"*Attento giovannotto,* hold on, young man, you need training first," replied Mr Santi. "It's not all good news. Some people won't come anywhere near this place. In some parts of the city, staunch protestants are determined to have our parlours closed down. They think we are corrupting their children and their teenagers. Ice cream is the food of the devil, they say. They are against anything which appears any way luxurious. It's sinful to indulge, they say too. It's serious, you know, they have even taken some of our Italian friends to court. All they see are kids coming in here to partake in the devil's food and they don't like it. They complain too that the kids are allowed to smoke too. Some even think we are running brothels. It's ridiculous! Routinely the police visit us to snoop around."

Fredo's gaze was transfixed on Mr Santi.

"But I don't think they will ever close us down. Despite the objections the poorer people continue to support us and every year our business keeps growing. When we manage to have the law changed we'll open on a Sunday as well. Then I know we'll have won."

"What about the winter time when it's cold," Fredo asked, "do they still eat ice cream?"

"In winter we sell ice cream only inside the shop, we serve meals too. Not pasta or anything we have back home but food which our customers like. Simpler food such as hot bowls of meat extract or plates of peas covered in vinegar. In addition to tea our drinks include hot lemonade seasoned with pepper. Increasingly also hot chocolate. Before Christmas we venture out into the streets. We build a brazier into our carts and we roast chestnuts in the streets if we can find enough of them. Sometimes it is difficult to source chestnuts so this part of the business is a bit of hit and miss. Nevertheless this keeps the money rolling but really it is in summer when we make our fortune."

"Now we have bigger plans which is why we need more *garzone.* Some Italians have started a new fast growing business and I have big plans to do the same."

"Some Valbona people have already struck gold. They have opened shops which sell fried fish and this is served with fried potatoes which are chipped into rectangular pieces. This work will be tougher but it's more rewarding financially. Fish arrives in huge boxes packed with ice. We cut off the scales and we remove the insides of the fish of all the intestines and rubbish. We slice the fish open and lay it flat then remove its bones. We dip the fish into a mixture of flour and water and toss it into a huge pan of boiling pig fat. The pan is powered by coal, so it means that our hands are constantly covered in a mixture of fat, coal dust and fish scales. Not very pleasant but it makes money," Mr Santi said rubbing his right thumb and first finger together. "And we can do this thing all year round! This is how we feed the population. The people here live in tiny houses, many living in a single room, so cooking and sleeping in the same place is not ideal."

"What about the potatoes?" Fredo remarked, still intrigued.

"We receive the potatoes in large sacks, we wash them by hand in water, remove the skin, cut them into pieces and put them in the same pig fat. Very efficient way to make a quick meal, same pan, same fat!" replied Mr Santi.

Fredo recalled back at home in Montecino in winter when he helped mamma wash and peel the potatoes at the fountain. His hands were always frozen solid after peeling just a handful of potatoes. The thought of doing this for a whole sack, he thought, how could he manage that?

"I am in the process of renting the shop next door here and buying the frying equipment. By the middle of June we will be ready to go. Then we start selling fish and chips. That is why I needed more *garzone* and you, Fredo, are here to help me do this."

Just at that point Gigi walked through the door and he ran to Pamela. They embraced for several minutes.

"Thanks, Topolino, for bringing my beautiful bride home safely," Gigi said.

Chapter 3

1901

Mr Santi's businesses had expanded to six other establishments across the city, five additional fish and chip shops and one additional ice cream parlour. Fredo, now aged nineteen was regarded as the senior *garzone*. He worked tirelessly, he was loyal to Mr Santi but this was at a price. He was occupied a constant eighteen hours daily, yet he was earning little money despite accommodation being provided by Mr Santi in a flat above his first business in the Saltmarket. Mr Santi explained he would be happy to lend Fredo some money in the future to set up his own business but Fredo considered this would have resulted in an extended period of reliance on Mr Santi and he wasn't quite ready for that.

Fredo had seen many *garzone* come and go. Some of the younger boys, aged anything from twelve to sixteen and mostly all from the Valbona area, had no longer been able to withstand constant grease and coal dust on their hands. They also found of the smell of hot pig fat obnoxious. The comparison between this grimy lifestyle and the open sunny pastures of the Valbona landscapes was too great.

"*Non ci sto piu,* I am not staying here anymore," was a common sentiment. "*O vado all'America o vado a casa,* I'm off to America or off home."

Even Fredo reflected often on where his life was heading. He wondered what was better. *'A life of servitude to the Porchettas or a life of servitude to Mr Santi in these awful living conditions.'*

***

As he awoke Fredo couldn't get the events of the previous day out of his mind. Whilst minding his own business serving his happy customers, out of the blue three irate teenagers had entered the shop.

"Gie us three fish suppers, ya tally bastard," shouted one of the group. Fredo ignored the insult and handed the first portion over, then the other two. "We've nae money, what you gonnae dae aboot it," said the tall one, obviously the leader of the group. The other two laughed, one of them flicking his cigarette end in Fredo's direction, the other throwing chips back towards the pan of boiling fat.

Fredo had never experienced behaviour like this before although he had been warned by Mr Santi about what to do in such circumstances. Without any thought he dipped a small saucepan into the hot fat and threw it towards the teenagers' faces. Whilst the screaming youths were scrambling into their pockets trying to grab anything to wipe themselves clean, Fredo ran past them into the street and blew his whistle. In quick time a passing policeman was on hand to restore order and march the teenagers to the police station.

'I hope they never come back,' he mused. *'I never came here to put up with that nonsense.'*

He thought again of Teresa and Rosa and his determination hardened. *'The miserable life of servitude to Mr Santi will end soon and I will make my own money. Remember why you came here, Fredo, to find a loving lady, to set up a new life in this land, a new family and to ensure my wife and daughters will always be treated with dignity, unlike my sisters.'*

***

Fredo found great difficulty sleeping at night. In a bedroom crowded with four or five other *garzone,* whom when not talking in their sleep, were continually releasing the previous day's effluent from their backsides. Inevitably he reminisced of back home. *'At least there I would be waking up to the sun streaming through the windows.'*

His life was tough in his newly adopted land. Glasgow was seen by some as the second city of the British Empire and employment was plentiful. The dockside areas were buzzing with activity. He had been informed that a quarter of all ships in the world had been built in the city. There were hundreds of small factories in the Saltmarket area surrounding the fish and chip shop which were involved in all sorts of activities, textiles, carpets, rope making, glass blowing, porcelain making and tanning. Furthermore the city lay on top of a huge coal reserve so nearby there were also several collieries. All this industry meant hungry men, hungry families and lots of money with which to buy fish and chips and ice cream.

However Fredo also saw the black side. Despite the recent completion of a network of sewers and a new electrified tram system which went some way to alleviate the obnoxious stench in the air from the heaps of horse dung which littered the streets, living conditions for the locals were still filthy and unhealthy.

Infant mortality was high and often little children dressed in rags without shoes came into the fish and chip shop asking for scraps. These were the little of bits of fried batter left over after frying. Normally these were dumped into a huge tin and collected for feeding to pigs. '*Same food for kids as for pigs*,' Fredo thought. When Mr Santi wasn't around he routinely gave the kids little bags of free chips. Problem was, he quickly sussed, they would return time and time again. But Fredo's conscience wouldn't let him stop.

The *garzone* were always in the firing line of Mr Santi's complaining tantrums. Fredo was the only one who pretended to listen attentively.

"Hopefully this year we won't have an epidemic like we did last year," Mr Santi said. "You know, Fredo, they blame us immigrants for everything which goes wrong, these protestant councillors. Firstly the Irish, who just happen to be catholic, well they have always been the brunt of their complaints. They declared that death wakes caused the diseases, open coffins in single room houses with numerous kids around too. They never approved of them having parties with all sorts of people arriving for a free drink. Then this time last year they blamed the sailors who were supposed to have brought rats into the city from overseas in their ships. Load of rubbish, that's what I say. Now they are blaming us. They think we've brought some pestilence over from Italy in our pasta. It's ridiculous! If there are any contagious diseases in this city, you only have to look at the living conditions of these poor people, and right next door to us."

Mr Santi continued. "Have you seen the state of the houses in which these councillors expect people to live?" He paused for a few moments. "Fish and chips might be the only balanced meal these people get. Can you imagine these large families cooking on their tiny little stoves in their tiny little rooms?"

"I bet you these councillors live in luxury. I'm sure

there are no fish and chip shops where they live," Fredo replied.

"They wouldn't eat our stuff anyway. We're just like the Irish, second class citizens."

***

On the day the Queen's death was announced a policeman rushed into the shop. "The queen is dead, the queen is dead," he said handing Mr Santi a handwritten poster. "You must all dress in black for a week and you must drop your blinds. In fact you must close the shop for two days."

Fredo was taken aback at the policeman's tone. *'In Glasgow everything is black, so what's new,'* he thought to himself.

"What do you mean, close the shop?" said Mr Santi.

"The council has stated all shops must close for two days, Sir. It's the rules. I'll be back if you are not closed," replied the policeman, becoming grumpier by the minute. He cast his gaze around the shop, gave a few tuts and left.

"I'm going to check this out, Fredo. Just stay here and watch the shop."

Mr Santi returned an hour later. "I think that copper is trying it on. The butcher next door knows nothing about this and neither does the jeweller around the corner. That policeman is typical of those who don't like us. They want us out, they think we are up to mischief in here."

The policeman never did return.

Meanwhile Fredo was anxious to change the topic of discussion.

"Mr Santi, next Saturday morning, I would like to go to Pamela and Gigi's wedding Mass. It's in St Mary's, just a mile from here.

"Yes, as long as you're back for lunch time," replied Mr Santi. "You know how busy it will be on Saturday. I think they are opening the new grandstand at Parkhead. Everybody will want to be there, so be back on time."

"Sure, Mr Santi," replied Fredo with some degree of despondency. '*Just a morning away from work and after all I've done for him*,' he thought to himself.

On the day of Pamela and Gigi's wedding Fredo walked the mile to St Mary's Church through Glasgow Green. The wide open spaces of the park were attractive, in contrast to the grimy city streets. He knew the park well. In his first summer Fredo had weaved his way through the pathways all day in an attempt to gain Mr Santi's favour by selling as much ice cream as he could, and certainly more than the other *garzone*. He had rung his bell and blown his whistle. "*Gelati, ecco un poco*, here's your ice cream." Little children had screamed out, "hey ma, there's the hokey pokey man, can we get a penny lick?"

In Glasgow Green Fredo noticed the healthy buds emerging on twigs in the trees. Then he heard the birdsong. *'I can smell the spring,'* he thought, *'soon the boys will be out again with their barrows.'*

The vast majority of the guests at the wedding were Italian from the Valbona region. Fredo made efforts to acquaint himself with as many guests as possible. He was keen to establish how their businesses were doing. The general view was clear. The fish and chips people made more money but the ice cream business, they said, was easier for families and less strenuous. It was noticeable that it was the Valbona people who were exclusively into fish and chips whereas ice cream parlours were predominantly run by Italians from the south of Italy. He couldn't work out why this was the case. But overall a general feeling of wellbeing abounded and some were already making new plans.

"Gigi, how are you doing selling this flavoured water," Fredo asked whilst Pamela was milling around making small talk with the guests.

"Not enough money and the hours are too long. Our living conditions are still little better than in Italy and we want to have children. I think next year we will be returning to Valbona, have our kids there and then I fancy going off to America to do something more exciting, maybe groceries, selling fruit and vegetables. They tell me America is better than here, you can earn real fortunes there." Gigi continued. "Here's a tip, Fredo, if you are thinking of staying here. My cousin Vincenzo in England in Stanley near the border, wrote to tell me they might be sinking a new colliery in a place called Errington. Might be a great opportunity. Some of our people here in Scotland have made it big in the coal towns. The mines bring jobs, they start new communities. It's too late for me. My patience in this country has worn thin. I have been here for too long. I made a few mistakes. Errington's near the sea, you should think about it."

"Think about what?"

"Jobs, families, they will build new houses and it's near the sea so the air will be cleaner." replied Gigi, "but you might need to hurry before somebody else moves to the area and beats you to it."

Fredo remained calm, reluctant to demonstrate any great excitement at the opportunity. "Can you give me Vincenzo's address, I will write to him."

***

Within a month Fredo was in Stanley. The parting of the ways with Mr Santi hadn't been pleasant. Initially Mr

Santi had insisted on an immediate repayment of all the money which was owed but after an evening of negotiation which gradually morphed into one of argument, raised voices and aggressive hand gesturing, Fredo made his promise to repay his debt with interest after he was established in Errington.

Mr Santi's parting comment before they shook hands was succinct. "Never forget your debt to me. If you don't pay I will make sure that you cannot return back to Montecino with dignity and your name will forever be tarnished."

***

The train crossed the river Tyne and reached the station of Newcastle. Fredo noticed the city's similarity to Glasgow. The river split the city into two parts. They were huge cranes in the distance along the river, and the grime from the chimneys was identical. Fredo had been informed that this was another area built on seams of coal underground. He knew that the combination of the large river, coal abundance which powered factories full of hard working men meant relative prosperity for the population and consequently also for both the fish restaurant and the ice cream parlour business.

The journey to Stanley on a local single carriage train was a short one. As the train reached the summit of Causey Moor, Fredo saw the town of Stanley nestled in a valley below. The scene was picturesque. There was some industrial activity, a few smoke stacks and several colliery wheels visible in the distance and a landscape of surrounding green pastures framed the town.

Vincenzo's temperance bar was barely a hundred yards from the station on the main street. He was there for all the trains which arrived from Newcastle that day.

He had no idea of Fredo's arrival time.

Later in the evening, the pair reminisced of old times back home.

"How come you are here in this small place, Vincenzo?"

"At first I wanted to go to America, but when I reached Genoa to board the ship, they told me I was too young to travel on my own, I was only fourteen. They simply refused to let me board. What could I do? I couldn't return home. I would have brought shame to the family. So I decided to come to England instead."

"And Stanley?"

"There are coal mines everywhere and across the hill in Consett, there is a huge factory which manufactures iron and steel for trains and ships. Business has been very good to me here."

"I see you just have ice cream," said Fredo gazing around to look for any evidence of fish and chips.

"This is a temperance bar but it's not alcohol we sell. We open on a Sunday as well. Here it's common for men to overindulge in their drink and the wives often force them to come to our place to sober up. You should see some of the drinks we make here to relieve their drunken stupor, a cream soda with egg whites and sugar, a ginger drink where we add a little bit of spice to water and sugar and then we have a drink made from dandelion leaves. Come, let's try some."

Fredo's palate had changed hugely since his arrival in Scotland. He enjoyed sugary sweets and drinks but nevertheless he found most of Vincenzo's concoctions disgusting. Only the cream soda was palatable.

"Currently we are trying something new with raspberries and blackcurrants. The fruits are free. We find them everywhere in hedges around the town at the end of the summer."

"Ice cream, a variety of drinks, and I see you have confectionery and tobacco too. I am impressed, Vincenzo."

Soon the two men were chatting about the opportunity in Errington.

"I can give you a bed for a few nights and I can let you have the use of one of my carts. Errington is about twenty miles away. Or if you want you can be my *garzone* for the summer," said Vincenzo with a twinkle in his eye.

Vincenzo's staff were mostly close family and Fredo was sure they weren't treated anything like the *garzone* in Glasgow. '*I might just think of your offer*,' he thought.

Early the next morning Fredo set off for Errington on the horse and cart. His route towards Durham city was straight forward, all roads led there. Colliery wheels dotted the landscape either side of the road at Craghead, Beamish and Sacriston.

The city itself was dominated by a huge cathedral, the likes of which Fredo had never seen before. The building, perched on a hilltop above the town, had squared shaped double towers at the front and a large more impressive tower behind. '*This church has been here a long time. Great location for warding off enemies,*' as he surveyed the cathedral's location surrounded all on sides by the river.

Fredo stopped briefly at a local tavern to refresh his horse. He needed to obtain specific directions before continuing his away across the rolling hills east of Durham. Even on the moors heading towards the coast, colliery wheels were seen everywhere. The villages of Sherburn, Haswell, and Shotton all appeared identical. Numerous rows of houses close to the colliery, their inhabitants no doubt providing the work force for the mine.

In Errington however the landscape was altogether different. There was no colliery wheel and there was no activity. A small hamlet surrounded a pretty green field, oak trees at each corner. The only buildings were the local church, several smart and tidy houses and two coaching inns.

Confused and slightly disconsolate, Fredo decided to enquire at one of the inns before embarking on his route back to Stanley.

The bar was empty, so the landlord behind was delighted to chat away whilst continuously cleaning the same glasses over and over at his counter. "Sir, there is no coalfield here, yet. A couple of years ago they sunk a shaft down near the coast. Maybe there will be coal here someday. I don't have a clue when that might be. But from the experience of the other coal pits sunk in the county I would say it's still a few years away."

"How far away is the nearest pit from here?" Fredo asked.

"In Seaham the pit has been going fifty years. It took them more than five years to extract the first truck of coal. The pit goes right under the sea, you know. I still don't understand it, why the sea doesn't flood the pit." The landlord paused for a few moments. "The locals here don't want another pit, did you notice the lovely green fields around? Seaham used to be like us many years ago, a quiet little village. Now it's no longer a village and it's dirty. Even the sand on the beach is black. Never mind though, the pit, if it ever does come, will be a godsend for my business. Miners are thirsty folk. When their shifts end I'll make sure they'll be delighted to spend most of their money with me here before they go home. Perhaps then I might be able buy my own coal mine."

On his way back to Stanley Fredo mulled on his future. *'I made a mistake to come here. They didn't tell me it takes years for a mine to open. What do I do now?'*

That night he slept very little. *'Do I go back to Glasgow, return to Italy, go to America?'* He recalled the day he bought his ticket to Scotland when he stopped at the chapel to say a little prayer to San Rocco. It was time for another prayer.

The following day Vincenzo and Fredo were chatting over morning coffee.

"It's a pity about Errington but I have a proposition for you, Fredo," said Vincenzo. "Up in Consett, where the iron works are, there has been an ice cream parlour on Front Street for over ten years. It's owned by Gino Coia. He, too, came over from the old country. He did very well in the business, he married a local girl and they seemed to have a great future up there. The iron works are growing and more houses are being built every year. But last year they lost two little kids, consumption I think it was, and just before Christmas his wife, Bridget, passed away whilst delivering their third child. In winter the snow and the frost claim lots of victims in the conditions up there. Gino says he's had it with England. Understandably he is in a state of depression and in the last few weeks his health has deteriorated fast. He's lost weight, and he has no more enthusiasm for his shop. He wants out and longs to return to Italy. He asked me if I was interested in buying his business."

"And are you interested, can you afford it?"

"Well actually, you being here is perfect timing. Do

you fancy running it for me? I'll organise everything. There is a flat above the shop so you could live there."

"I would love to, Vincenzo, but I still owe money to Mr Santi. I don't want be constantly in debt to you as well."

"Listen, let me fix that for you." Vincenzo went on. "It would be down to you, the harder and cleverer you work, the more money I make and the more money you make too. It will be win win for me, for you, for Gino and also for Mr Santi. What do you think?"

Without any hesitation Fredo shook hands with his new colleague. Within the hour he had purloined the cart again and he was on his way on the six mile journey to Consett.

Front Street was the main thoroughfare in the town and it wasn't hard to locate Coia's premises at the gable end of a row of single story shops.

The ice cream parlour was double fronted with two display windows separated by the entrance door. Mr Coia showed Fredo around. The sitting area was in the form of cubicles, four on each side of the large room. Within each cubicle was a marble table supported by iron cast legs. On each side of the table, sumptuous leather seats. The cubicle surrounds were made of a deep shade of oak wood and adorned with oval shaped inlays in symmetric patterns. The inlays contained small mirrors which were themselves decorated in a variety of kaleidoscopic shapes. The public counter and serving area was constructed from a huge marble slab with display cabinets at either end. Behind were a series of shelves and floor to ceiling mirrors which gave the appearance of a shop twice the size it actually was.

Fredo returned to Stanley enthused at the opportunity and he wasted little time in confirming to

Vincenzo that he was ready and willing.

Part of the deal was that Gino and Fredo would work in tandem until Vincenzo's purchase of the business was completed before the summer season was in full swing. Vincenzo duly paid the necessary deposit to Gino and he guaranteed a quarterly sum for the next five years. He wrote a letter to Topolino in Glasgow that on his future trips to Italy, he should divert through Stanley to collect the quarterly instalments. Topolino's task was to deliver the money personally to Gino in Italy.

Vincenzo and Fredo's partnership worked well. Fredo liaised directly with the suppliers for his deliveries and soon the offerings were identical to those in the temperance bar in Stanley.

Vincenzo, ever the innovator, was constantly trying out new concepts for his flavoured waters range. After midnight on an unusually warm summer night as the pair relaxed in the backyard of the shop together, they invented the brand name for their next best seller, a raspberry and blackcurrant cordial recipe infused with Vincenzo's secret list of spices. Vincenzo viewed his new drink as another health tonic and as a hangover alternative. They settled on the brand name 'Vinto'. Over a few beers the brand quickly evolved. From Vincenzo's Tonic to Vintonic to Vinto. They agreed that a deep shade of red was the perfect colour to replicate the combination of the colours of the fruits.

By the end of the summer, customers were coming as far away as Newcastle to sample Vincenzo's new health tonic. And the customers in Consett loved it too. Of all the hangover drinks which were available, Vinto quickly emerged as Fredo's best seller.

Fredo was making his mark in Consett. There was no shortage of customers. The ironworks had been established in the town to take advantage of the coal and ironstone pits which had been sunk fifty years before. Many small craft factories had been built solely to supply the iron works. The town bustled constantly with activity. Pubs and inns abounded too and it became evident to Fredo that the temperance bar would be just as financially successful in Consett as it had been to Vincenzo in Stanley.

However the pair have differing views on recruiting staff. Whereas Vincenzo was keen to maintain the Italian custom of recruiting from his extended family back home in Italy to work as *garzone,* Fredo's idea was to recruit locals instead.

"These *garzone* are apprentice dogsbodies," said Fredo. "I was once a *garzone* in Scotland and I didn't like it."

"But that's the plan," replied Vincenzo. "You work them hard for two or three years and then we allow them to go off and start out on their own."

But in saying this Vincenzo was aware he was being slightly disingenuous. He knew that in most cases the opposite applied. At the outset, yes, the *garzone* worked very hard in difficult conditions and with little reward. But many never made it, either returning back home or changing plans completely by setting off for America. The less willing or less ambitious *garzone* were concluding that all they were doing was transferring their allegiances from one feudal lord in Italy to another feudal lord in Britain. The streets may have been paved with gold for the owners and *padroni* bosses, they said, but not for them or their customers. In fact only those with a true spirit of ambition and enterprise, and these were few in number, were able to break out and build successful and profitable businesses.

"I would prefer to recruit my own people here locally," Fredo insisted.

"But all the boys in the town are in the mines and factories by the age of twelve, sometimes even younger. How are you going to find any boys?"

"Then I will recruit girls and women instead. There should be an ample supply and they will be desperate to earn a few shillings, I am sure."

Vincenzo peered over to Fredo, in slight surprise.

"But women, they must stay at home, look after the children, cook the meals, mend clothes, do the washing," said Vincenzo. "Here it's like in Italy, no difference. That's the way of the world."

"Yes, and be available for sex at all times as well, I suppose. You never put that on your list. No, Vincenzo, you may live in that world, but my world is different. My world treats all women and girls with more respect and dignity. I left Montecino precisely because they showed no respect whatsoever to my sisters. After what happened to them they were left with no dignity."

Vincenzo was puzzled.

"You know full well what I mean, Vincenzo, *prima notte*," Fredo angrily replied.

Vincenzo held up his hands in surrender, "okay, okay." He understood and had no need to respond. He acknowledged that in isolated cases the old tradition was still being practiced.

"All right, as long as you stick to our financial agreement, I am fine with it."

Chapter 4

1905

At twenty three years of age Fredo was making good money. For four years he and Vincenzo had worked well together in partnership. Both in Consett and in Stanley the coal mines were breaking new records of production every year. The iron works were expanding rapidly to cope with the increasing demands for iron and steel. Consett was regarded as the primary quality supplier of iron and steel across Britain and the contract for the construction of the tower at Blackpool ten years earlier had firmly established its world-wide reputation. From a village of barely one hundred people some eighty years previously the iron works and mines in the town were now employing over ten thousand men. And this was great for Fredo's business.

In contrast to the situation in Glasgow where religious affinity was split, in Consett the population was mainly catholic. For most there was a Sunday routine. It was family day, the obligatory attendance at church for Mass, then an ice cream treat before lunch at home. The ice cream treat was well established as part of local custom and it was only in the big cities, Newcastle included, where there was any protestant resistance from other shopkeepers who resented the so called *'macaroni catholics'* making money on the compulsory day of rest. There was no such resistance in

Consett.

And Fredo was well aware of catholic practices. He knew that during Lent a large percentage of his Irish catholic customers would be abstaining from the ice cream vice in the six weeks leading up to Easter. He needed alternatives to maintain his income stream during this period. It was during Lent when he had doubled his efforts in promoting the new Vinto tonic drink which had been developed by Vincenzo. Fredo had managed to convince most of his customers that as well as the perfect cure for hangovers, Vinto was the ideal digestion aid after a heavy Sunday lunch. He delighted in his success at figuring out new ways of promoting his wares. Nevertheless the heavy drinking habits of his customers occasionally did bother his conscience. '*Better that they give up on drink altogether than worry about hangover cures'.* But he came to realise that the addiction habit to alcohol was almost impossible to break.

***

During the year Fredo decided it was time to return home for a holiday to Italy to visit his parents. He hadn't seen them for six years and from their letters he gleaned that all didn't seem well. They were struggling. Farm life remained tough and he was homesick too. He duly made the arrangements with Vincenzo that during the four weeks of his absence his partner would manage the business directly.

Fredo purchased a suitcase with a special lock to ensure there were no prying eyes into his hard earned cash. His family back home would certainly value his gift. They would be able to invest in new implements for the farm, buy some new clothes and ensure more comfort. The case was never out of Fredo's sight during the journey. *'This will be enough to see mamma and babbo through a couple of winters very comfortably.'*

Nothing had changed in Montecino. As was usual the recent harvests had been hit and miss, some good years, some bad ones.

"Montecino has lost its soul, where have all the men gone?" Fredo asked his dad. "I see only women now."

"Just like you, my boy, they don't want to stay here anymore. They want to seek their fortune elsewhere. They hear all the stories from Scotland, they say many are making great money in these fish and chip shops and in America, well Da Prato in Chicago is continually demanding more *garzone* from Valbona to join him over there. They need more masons and sculptors to furnish all those new churches they are building."

"It's great for me too in England, I would like to bring both of you over soon."

"That's impossible. What about our animals, our crops, our grapes, we can't leave them."

Babbo continued, "Are you eating well? Who is looking after you over there? You know there are many women and girls here in Montecino who have no boyfriends. You need to find a wife soon. We like Angelina who lives at La Torre near the church. She is a very nice girl. She is always asking about you. Remember her?"

"Plenty time for that, babbo. I still haven't found the right one. Too much work, no time to play."

It was clear that the thought of his son's wife not being Italian had not entered babbo's head.

"Moglie e buoi dai paesi tuoi," babbo declared again. Fredo had heard the rhyming phrase often. Both Mr Santi and Vincenzo were used to saying it. Translated literally to English, the idiom declares, *'wives and bulls*

from your own people.' Spouses were to be found from within the Italian community and even better if they were found from the same village. Fredo had already become aware of Mr Santi's plan in Glasgow to have his children marry fellow compatriots from Valbona, and Freddie Pieri too also had expressed the same wish for his children. He figured too that when Vincenzo's children were at a suitable age he would be lining up appropriate spouses, within families with Valbona or Montecino blood.

Fredo had witnessed the spouse bartering process at first hand. Two years previously he had attended the annual dinner and dance gathering of the Italian community at a Newcastle hotel. He had seen it happening between courses, the bartering of future wives and husbands even as much as ten years forward into the future. And it was at the end of the evening when too much wine had been drunk, that irrevocable agreements had been made.

On one occasion Vincenzo had tried to explain that business and marriage were inextricably linked. His plan was to own multiple shops which would in turn be passed down to one of his children and then to another. He further explained that the in-laws too required to be Italian since transactions had to be done the Italian way, no written contracts or detailed formalities. Deals were to done on a handshake. Proudly he declared that a man's word was worth a hundred times more than a scrap of paper. "Lawyers, bankers, taxmen," he said, "I want to have as little to do with them as possible. They are scavengers, parasites, their only interest to steal your hard earned cash. Why give them money which you sweated to earn, and the banks, well, you only put money in just to take back out again. I prefer the Italian way."

But Fredo's mindset was altogether different. He had emigrated to Britain to become British, and eventually to become a naturalized citizen.

***

Holiday break over, Fredo arrived back home in Consett just before Whitsun. The sun shone from a beautiful blue sky. "This looks to me like the first day of a great summer. I can sense it," Vincenzo said as he handed the reigns of the business back to Fredo.

'Yes', Fredo thought, *'the town does look more attractive when the sun shines. Even the smoke from the iron works looks whiter than white today'.*

Fredo was now ready for the long haul. The money he was earning was good but he wanted more. With Vincenzo's approval he was ready to launch an alternative ice cream, adding cocoa powder to his ice cream mix, a new trend he noticed while on holiday in Italy. He had negotiated a deal with Vincenzo whereby for every cocoa infused ice cream sold he would receive fifty percent commission on the selling price. Fredo had convinced Vincenzo that sales of traditional vanilla ice cream wouldn't be compromised following this new addition to the range. "You do well, Fredo, we all do well", Vincenzo said, "and then we will launch this chocolate ice cream in Stanley as well."

That afternoon, a sign was attached to the front door. "Help needed, long hours, free lunch, inside and outside work, apply within."

To Fredo's surprise there were no shortage of youngsters who applied, mostly boys. He swiftly concluded that not all the boys in the town were destined to be miners. Physically some would never cope down in the bowels of the earth. He was searching for boys to tour the streets in the hand carts and for any girls who applied, to work inside the shop, helping to make ice cream, serve customers and clean up.

The following day Catherine Brown entered the shop. She was petite and her voice was softly spoken. Fredo showed her into one of the booths.

"I am here to apply for the job you have advertised on the door," she said. "I am ready to do any work."

"Tell me where you have worked before, Catherine, your experience."

"I have never worked before. I am the eldest of eight children. I am seventeen years of age and I have been helping my mum at home all my life. My two little brothers have polio and mum spends all the time she has caring for them."

"What about you dad, does he work?"

"Two years ago, you remember, there was the accident at the pit, where three people died. Well two of them were dad's pals and if it had happened just five minutes earlier he would have lost his life too, he was that close. Well for years, he's been forever coughing and after the accident they gave him a new job. Now he works above ground. But it hasn't worked out too well. He is classed as a labourer, so he queues up every day at five in the morning seeking work. Only once in a while do they need him so he doesn't work much. We need money desperately. We've many mouths to feed. As the eldest I need to bring some money home."

Fredo's heart was touched. Catherine started work the very next day. In little time he was amazed at the weight of the milk churns she was able to lift. Despite being small in stature she was as strong as an ox.

"That's too heavy, leave this one to me," Fredo butted in from time to time. "I don't want you getting injured, then what would your mum do?"

On occasions after lunch in the middle of the afternoon when few customers were around Fredo offered Catherine a cup of tea. "Time for a short break, just fifteen minutes now." He was conscious of the fact it wouldn't look good for business if he was seen relaxing with a worker, especially a female one. He had to remind himself regularly that he was the boss and that Catherine was a mere employee.

On this day Catherine felt relaxed enough to explain her family background. "My grandparents are Irish. At the time of the potato famine, we lost most of our family to starvation. They had been told of a new iron works which was opening here in Consett. That's the reason we are here. My grandad managed to hold down a permanent job and he worked at the works for over forty years. Sadly he passed away within months of his retirement and grandma only lasted just another two weeks. They say she died of a broken heart. On the other hand my dad has been in the pit all his life and my mum is a local lass."

Afternoon chats were more frequent and before long, Fredo was waking in the morning in excited anticipation to rush to work and talk with Catherine. He found their conversations about Ireland and Irish customs absorbing. Furthermore he was amazed of the commonality in Irish and Italian peasant traditions, particularly how multi-generational family life was sacred to both communities, how the middle generation worked the hard labour, how the aged cared for the infants and then in turn how young adults cared for the aged.

Religious traditions were common too. Baptism rites were identical whereby children were named after grandparents and baptised as soon as possible after birth. Often the family's favourite saint was immortalised in children's middle names. It was clear the influence of the church was an enduring factor. Godparents were deemed vital guardians of the child to ensure the continuity of the catholic faith throughout its life. Even matchmaking customs were similar. Traditionally the prerogative of parents was to find suitable spouses for their children.

Fredo was particularly curious at Catherine's description of the Irish wake after a death. He discovered it was a lively event in total contrast to the sombre funeral rites back home in Italy.

"When my grandpa died, my grandma insisted we maintain the traditional Irish custom. The last rites were administered by the priest the night grandpa passed away. The following day our family's Irish friends came to the house. After a series of prayers Grandma led all the women to the blazing fire in the hearth and she squatted in front of it. The women lifted their skirts over their heads, and I was told to sprinkle ashes over the heads of all the women. Then the death chant started. My grandma stretched her hands out to the fire and gradually her body started rocking to and fro, mimicking the tortures of the soul, as if exorcising evil spirits. The other women joined in the ritual and they too broke into hypnotic type chants. Then suddenly my grandma plunged forward, grabbed two handful of ashes, turned round and ran forward to throw the ashes out of the door. She believed that in his way she was exorcising the evil spirits barring the entry of grandpa's soul to heaven."

Fredo listened, almost traumatized, but he wanted to hear more.

"Then the wake began. My dad laid grandpa's corpse in the corner of the room and covered it in white linen. He had acquired several packets of tobacco and as each mourner passed by the corpse, women included, they offered their pipe to my dad. Seated by grandpa's head it was tradition that he fill everybody's pipe. After a few smokes, a few prayers, and a few silent murmurings, then the whisky was delivered. Wow, how the wake livened up, God rest grandpa's soul."

"My, my, Catherine. No way can our traditions compete with that. We take our corpses to the church for Mass and after that straight to the cemetery. No elaborate customs, no drinks, no food. Everybody is dressed in black from head to toe and little is said. Whilst it's usual for our women to weep for the rest of the day, this is one occasion when we men are required to hide somewhere and leave the women to mourn. I am not too sure of that scary evil spirit stuff."

***

Days and months passed and the tea breaks became the routine, regular as clockwork at three o'clock in the afternoon. Catherine's working day was long and after a time Fredo had become to trust her implicitly, and particularly so where cash was involved. She even had her own set of keys. It was her job to be at the shop promptly at five o'clock in the morning in order to catch the start of the early coal mine shift which started thirty minutes later. Her day ended about seven o'clock in the evening. Saturday, however was her special treat. While she was able to leave for home immediately after her afternoon cup of tea, her chats with Fredo were increasingly lasting longer.

Fredo was delighted with Catherine's work ethic. She worked much harder than many of the *garzone* with whom he had worked before. On good days he offered her a few more shillings as bonus. He knew the bonuses were well received and appreciated by Catherine's family.

Catherine was reluctant ever to take time off work, but during one tea break in the early autumn she plucked up the courage to pose her question, "I am so sorry, Fredo. I have to ask a favour from you. I would like a day off. I am the bridesmaid at my sister Jane's wedding. She is getting married in early November. It's on a Saturday, so I would be absent just half a day."

Fredo was slightly taken aback by Catherine's timidity. "Why, of course. No need for any apology. Not an issue at all. I can steal somebody from Vincenzo's staff," he stated.

"One other question, though, my dad insisted I ask you." A huge smile was painted across Catherine's face.

"Yes, tell me."

"Are you able to come to the wedding too? Mass will be in the afternoon and then we'll have some sandwiches and tea at the new miners welfare club. Will you come, please? My dad would be so pleased."

"I would love to be there. I have never been to an English, or should I say an Irish wedding. I assume the lucky groom is a local guy."

"Yes he is but I am sure it won't be as exciting as the Italian weddings you are used to, but ……"

"But nothing, Catherine. Listen, I really will come. You can't expect me to turn down an invitation from my favourite lady, can you? It will be great experience for me. Already I am looking forward to it. Please tell me what sort of gift I should bring, also what sort of clothes do I wear. I don't want to appear out of place."

"You are fine the way you are. You could bring along

one of your Italian cakes. Mum and dad would sure love that."

In due course Fredo made the arrangements with Vincenzo to ensure no business was lost while he was away. He also coaxed Vincenzo's wife to bake a panettone, a cake which Italians, by tradition, baked at Christmas time.

'It's not Christmas time, but what does it matter, this will be something different for Catherine's family.'

At the short nuptial Mass there were only about twenty people, mostly women. Catherine explained at the church that there would many more at the party later. The men needed to finish their shifts in the late afternoon, she said. They weren't able to afford the time off.

At the welfare club, although slightly timid initially, Fredo soon realised that most people there were his customers. He had little trouble comfortably joining in what soon became a feast of Irish singsong and jollity.

"I am so glad you came, Fredo," said Catherine's dad. "She speaks so highly of you and you treat her so well. I really appreciate it. I can't thank you more from the bottom of my heart."

"Catherine is a great worker, Mr Brown. You should be very proud of her as you no doubt are with all of your children."

"Thanks, just call me Edward." The two men exchanged firm handshakes.

Soon the festivities lapsed into a merry chaos. Men swayed and sang in unison to the sound of the fiddle being played in the corner by the only man who seemed to be sober. The ladies chatted away in groups drinking cups of tea whilst marvelling at the sublime taste of the panettone. The younger boys were crowded round the billiard table. Fredo had never seen a game like this before and he couldn't understand how the boys could become so excited about hitting three balls round the gigantic table.

Half way through the evening he spotted Catherine on her own. "It's time for me to go now. I need to lock up the shop. It's been a great experience and I have had a great time. Please give my thanks to your parents. They seem to be very busy just now."

"Let me walk you out, Fredo, my friend," replied Catherine, as she caressed the back of his hand.

As they said goodbye outside the hall Catherine leaned forward and gave Fredo a gentle kiss on one cheek. "Many thanks. It was wonderful you were able to come. I need to go back in now, have a good night."

As Fredo lay in his bed that evening, over and over he relived Catherine's soft and tender kiss. *'I can't wait to see her on Monday morning.'* He pondered whether this was the day that his life might be changing forever.

Chapter 5

1907

The eighteen months since Jane's wedding had passed very quickly and the respective businesses in Stanley and Consett had grown rapidly. Tobacco and cigarettes had been added to the range of items for sale. Fredo had even managed to convince Vincenzo to set up what was to be the first ever billiard hall in Stanley. And soon Fredo was opening one in Consett too.

During this time Vincenzo had returned home to Montecino to marry Anna, his childhood sweetheart. He brought her back to Stanley together with her younger sister Paolina. Another servant and assistant for the business from within the family, and help with the babies when they arrived.

"So you went back home for your bride, and you brought back your own staff with you," said Fredo jokingly after all the welcome formalities had been completed.

Fredo was astounded that the two little girls he last saw in Montecino had grown into such mature women.

"It is ideal, Fredo. We keep everything in the family, we all support each other and we all trust each other," replied Vincenzo. "This is it, we are Italian and we stick together. The other families do the same. Come on, let's lighten up, have another more drink!"

"Only joking. I know you're right. But I too, I have

some news I want to share with you."

***

The Italian community in the North East had grown hugely in the previous ten years. Not only were there ice cream parlours in the big cities of Newcastle and Sunderland but also in most of the outlying towns where thriving coal mining communities had emerged, Ashington, Bedlington, Wallsend and Blyth north of the river and at Gateshead, Blaydon and South Shields south of the river. Further south the Italians had also arrived in Darlington and Middlesbrough as well as in Crook and Bishop Auckland. Indeed the ice cream business had taken a solid foothold in the whole region and was dominated entirely by Italians. The immigrants were exclusively from two distinct areas of Italy, from the Tuscan hills in and around Valbona and from the valleys and hills surrounding Monte Cassino south of Rome.

The structure of the businesses were identical, a combination of '*back shop*' kitchen and miniature factory and the '*front shop*' selling a variety of ice creams, sweets, soft drinks and tobacco. Most shops had a '*sitting down*' area. Hot drinks and snacks were on menus in addition to ice cream. The majority of the businesses possessed hand carts where the more junior *garzone* or younger boys in the family would spend days on end selling their wares at the gates of parks, at street corners, outside working men clubs, outside schools, in fact anywhere where people were in transit and where they had a few spare pennies to indulge in a little luxury.

The ice cream parlours had become an integral part of every high street. Resistance to the '*ice cream vice*' had all but disappeared and the Italians were being

80

accepted and mostly welcomed by the respective communities. The days of penniless immigrants scrounging for donations in the streets as organ grinders or peddlers were over. Even the government assisted to secure the parlours' status as bona fide businesses. A new immigration law had been introduced two years previously that only those immigrants who could prove they were able to support themselves financially were allowed into the country.

However despite this shift in the public attitude full integration into the community was impossible for most. When it came to marriage, for example, some Italian traditions were being stubbornly retained. The immigrant families continued to search for spouses for their children from within other immigrant families. Mixed marriages with local lads and lasses were a rarity.

Consequently in the summer of the previous year Fredo had taken special care when writing the letter to his parents.

"Dear mamma and babbo, I hope you are both fit and healthy. And that the sun and rain are keeping the crops fit and healthy. What about Teresa, Rosa and the children? I have some bad news for you and some good news. Firstly I know that both of you were trying so desperately to marry me off to Angelina in the village or even somebody else from Montecino. But that didn't happen and I know how disappointed you might be when you read this. Nevertheless I know you will be happy if I am happy. Here in Consett I have found myself the most beautiful woman with whom I want to spend my life. She is called Catherine, *Caterina*, and I see her every day. We have known each other since April last year. We are so much in love and we plan to marry next year at Eastertime. It would be great if you both made a huge effort to come over for our big day and meet her. I know you will love her instantly. I will send you the money for the long train journey so no need to worry about that. I will establish Topolino's movements for next year and with any luck and if you find it more comforting I can make sure he accompanies you on the trip over. And another thing, Caterina is catholic, she is Irish and her family are all catholic, so we will have God's full blessing at Holy Mass. I will write again soon, keep well. Your loving son, Fredo."

Mamma and babbo found it difficult to hide their disappointment.

"*Che peccato,* What a pity, Fredo couldn't find a nice girl here," mamma said, a small teardrop falling from her eye. "Or even an Italian girl already there in England. There are so many families there, the Cecchini, Guidi, Rinaldi, Vincenti. *Dio,* God, why not one of them."

Babbo rose to comfort his wife. "The world has changed now, my dear. All the young ones, they want to explore new lands. There are great opportunities in England, in Scotland, in America. Look at the money they bring back, the money which Fredo gives us. Dino, too, he's doing great in Marseille. Don't forget he sends money back too. We could never have dreamt of that kind of money here. Do you really want Fredo's own family still to be under the thumb of the Porchetta? No, this is better," babbo continued. "Fredo is a fine boy, he works very hard, they tell me he is very loyal to Vincenzo and he is sure to make a great father. I know how Teresa's and Rosa's horrible experiences affected him. He is very sensitive and he will be a great husband, trust me, my dear. I feel certain that he is convinced Caterina will be a great mother and wife."

"Come on now, we have to prepare for a long and

exciting journey next year and for a great wedding. Let's see if we can meet with Topolino."

At that the couple embraced in tears of joy.

***

The date of Fredo and Catherine's wedding had been fixed well in advance, but as was typical the date was fixed to suit the needs of the business. They had wanted a spring wedding but it had become difficult for dates to work out. Easter Sunday had fallen on the last day of March and Fredo knew that business would pick up rapidly once Easter was over. April weather normally meant a significant increase in temperature and consequently more activity in the town. Another consideration had been that directly before Easter was Lent, the forty day period of fasting and mourning in advance of crucifixion of Jesus. Priests typically were not prone to perform marriage ceremonies with regular nuptial Mass during Lent. All in all the couple had settled for the middle of February on the Saturday before Ash Wednesday, the first day of Lent. Weather wise they had good fortune. After a frosty start, the sun had shone all day.

There had been an added complication necessary for discussion with the priest. Fredo had wondered whether it was in order for the priest to marry them when Catherine was displaying an obviously large bulge in front of her stomach. By the time of the wedding Catherine was seven months pregnant.

"Father, back home in Montecino, this horrible and obnoxious *prima notte* custom encourages our women into sex before marriage." Fredo had declared on the evening he met Father O'Sullivan. "There is little shame with pregnant brides, it happens frequently. The locals accept the situation and there is no stigma. Mostly they get to find out which girls will be chosen and subjected to this evil practice."

"Ah yes, *Jus Primae Noctis*, or *Le Droit du Seigneur,* is what we call it here. In Ireland the practice is supposed to have disappeared centuries ago although I do know of instances from our Irish friends here that occasionally the protestant landowners still abuse their privilege," replied Father O'Sullivan. "It's truly shocking, you know!"

"But in our case, of course, Catherine's dignity is unblemished. This was a pure accident borne out of a genuine love. I hope you can see your way to forgive us and sanctify our union in the normal way."

Father O'Sullivan explained, "I know the Brown family very well and already I have had words with them. They are convinced your intentions are honourable. They also realise that since Catherine met you, she has been a changed young girl. Her happiness and joy is there for all to see. Her parents are delighted with the marriage and I know they bear no malice at all towards you."

The priest continued, "Fredo, don't think for one moment that here in England we are all pure. It happens very frequently here too, pregnant brides I mean. Most times at the wedding the bride won't show yet, nevertheless it is a common occurrence. All too often the pleasures of the flesh dominate. Well our instincts sometimes are still somewhat primitive. Nevertheless it's very clear that in God's eyes to have sex before marriage is still a sin. But remember we are fallible human beings and Jesus did die on the cross for our sins. There is no shame in the eyes of the Lord, as long as conception has been the result of a genuine act of love. I only ask one more thing of you both, next time you come to confession, please be open and confess your sins fully."

***

Mamma and babbo arrived a week before the wedding and in little time they were treating the shop as their second home. Babbo was taught how to make ice cream and mamma continually insisted on snatching Catherine from her much reduced shop duties to teach her how to cook the Italian way. One of Vincenzo's *garzone* was permanently on duty to perform translations for the two ladies.

"Fredino," mamma said with the glint of pleasure in her eyes, "Caterina is wonderful, I am sure she will make you a great and loving wife."

She continued, "Now look here again, Caterina, I will show you how to make my favourite pasta sauce."

Catherine needed to rest her heavy lump and sat down at the table close to mamma.

"Fredo, can you buy garlic here?" Mamma's shrieked in Italian in a high tone over the general noise in the shop. "And what about celery and carrots, do you have any around. I cannot make my sauce without these."

The three old ladies sitting in the cubicles enjoying plates of hot peas looked up, shook their heads and plugged their ears.

"Mamma, a little less noise please. You'll scare our customers away. We have everything you need. I was in Newcastle two days ago buying everything we need."

Catherine gave a gentle, but happy smile. '*What have I let myself in for?*' she thought to herself.

Fredo and Catherine decided that their happy day would be celebrated at the same venue as Jane's wedding two years previously, the miner's welfare club in Consett. Fredo asked Vincenzo to be his best man.

There was no alternative and Catherine's sister Jane was her choice as bridesmaid. At the same time they invited Vincenzo and Jane to undertake the responsibility of godparents for the upcoming arrival.

"Absolutely, no problem," said Vincenzo, "be delighted on both counts."

But Vincenzo had another suggestion in mind. "What about the expectations within our community. Don't you think we should have a grand celebration in one of the big hotels in Durham or Newcastle? Many in the city are our distant relatives and they would expect to be invited."

"Exactly. Distant relatives are what they are. We don't need them. Instead we decided on the miner's welfare," replied Fredo. "Remember Catherine's father is a miner and he doesn't have much money. I really don't want them going to all that unnecessary expense. After all, remember Vincenzo, this is not really an Italian wedding, this will be an English wedding."

***

Whilst Catherine and her future mother-in-law were having great fun exchanging a variety of weird hand signals in the back shop during lessons in making homemade pasta, Vincenzo popped in to see Fredo. He was determined to ask once more.

"Let's go for a walk," he said.

There was a chill in the air and a freezing misty grey fog stubbornly shrouded the buildings in the main street. "At least we can't see that filthy smoke oozing out from the chimneys."

"How are your mamma and babbo with the arrangements?" asked Vincenzo. "Are they really content? They know that other Italians have had their big weddings in the hotels in the city."

"I told you before, my friend. Mamma and babbo are totally fine with it all. I explained to them in Italy a couple of years ago it would be like this. I told them my future was here in England. I always wanted it this way ever since I left Italy all those years ago. And now that I have found a great Irish wife, or I should say an English wife, my children will be English too. My ancestors may be Italian, but Catherine's family are English and since we are living here in England, earning our money here in England, bringing our children up here in England, it's only fair to Catherine and her family we start the whole process by having a wedding which is typical here in England. I cannot allow Catherine's parents to think we are in some way special just because we have more money or because we eat better food. Catherine's dad works seventy hours a week in those damn mines. Already her little brother is down there as well and he's only twelve. I really don't care what the other Italians think. A life with Catherine and with loads of children is exactly what I want. It will be great."

"Yes, I know. Actually now I really do know you're right. You are a great and loyal guy. You are like a brother to me."

"None of that soppy stuff. It's maybe time we talked seriously. About our partnership," Fredo continued, "we have worked well together and you have inspired me to earn some good money here in Consett. But you'll understand this situation cannot last forever. You cannot always be my *padrone*."

"I have been wondering for a while when we would have this conversation."

"That coal pit at Errington, the one I went to see about a few years back, it must be about ready to start recruiting for miners. I am guessing huge numbers of people will need to relocate to the area. And you know what that means, new pit, new people, new opportunity. I would love to be the first ice cream parlour there selling everything, maybe even fish and chips."

"You have always been so ambitious, Fredo."

"I heard also that the new railway connecting Sunderland directly with Hartlepool has been completed. And would you believe they are planning a new station at Errington. This will definitely help to bring lots of new people to the area."

"Then when the wedding is over, next week, you ought to get yourself over to Errington and see for yourself what is happening. If your parents are still here, no need to worry, I will look after them."

As Fredo and Vincenzo re-entered the shop, babbo was fast asleep in one of the booths. From the back shop they heard Mamma singing what seemed like her favourite Christmas carol. They squirted their eye brows at each other, thinking '*what's going on.'*

Dormi, dormi bel bambino, re divino, re divino, fa la nanna, bel bambino…………….. Sleep little baby sleep, king divine, go to sleep little child………….."

Fredo whispered to Vincenzo, "I told you, mamma's fine. She's already ahead of us, thinking of the future."

The following day he stuck a notice in the window of the shop.

"Closed Saturday for just one day, Family Wedding. Open as usual on Sunday."

***

The walk from the shop to the church was a short one. Previously Catherine had explained the traditions of the '*scramble*' and Fredo was still musing about it, slightly unsure.

"Watch, mamma, what happens now when we leave the shop, it should be fun."

Fredo stepped outside the shop into the street behind mamma and babbo. Instantly there was a huge roar of cheering and screaming from the thirty or so kids who had congregated around the shop entrance. The three walked along the street and the kids, mostly dressed in rags, some without shoes, followed in expectation.

"Babbo, give me the bags, now."

Fredo thrust his hands into one of the bags, grabbed a handful of coins, and as he swung his shoulder round he released the coins. Babbo noticed that the bigger kids were pushing the smaller ones away, so he grabbed one of the bags back, took a handful and threw the coins in the direction of the smaller kids. The kids pushed and jostled with each other. Within seconds every single coin had been pocketed and the kids scampered away in every direction.

"I hope none of those kids hurt themselves," babbo said.

For Mass the church was full, some of the parishioners standing in the aisles.

"You are obviously a very popular couple," Father O'Sullivan remarked after the Nuptial Mass and about to sign the register. "Rarely have I seen so many people here. It seems the whole town has come to share your joy today."

Fredo reflected on the stigma of a pregnant wife being married, *'all nonsense, all this thing about shame, all nonsense'*.

"And I welcome you back for the baptism of the child," continued the priest, "and the next child and the next after that too. May I personally grant you both

God's holy blessing at all times."

The reception was limited to close family and a few friends of Catherine's family. At the miner's welfare the festivities were in full swing within minutes. Edward, Catherine's dad, started the proceedings before anybody could relax in their seats.

"Just before we lose our minds on the beautiful liquid, I thought we should do something we should have done before this beautiful couple were married." Edward looked at the couple as they waited in wonder.

"As the old Irish saying goes, '*Marry when the year is new, always loving kind and true, when February birds do mate, you may wed, nor dread your fate, if you wed when March winds blow, joy and sorrow both you'll know*', and so it goes on and on. You chose your dates wisely, Catherine, Fredo," he said.

"Now, let's have a drink to our Irish hand-fasting tradition. Jane, can you hand me the cord, please."

Edward gestured to Catherine and Fredo. He took their hands and bound the cord crudely around them.

"As your hands are now bound together, so your lives and spirits are joined in a union of love and trust. May these hands be blessed today and may they hold each other forever. May they remain tender and gentle as they nurture each other in wondrous love. May they be healer, protector, shelter and guide for each other. On this beautiful day may God bless you both."

Fredo found it difficult to hold back his emotions to this wonderful surprise. He looked at Catherine and they kissed passionately.

The crowd erupted into a huge applause.

Later in the evening as the heavily pregnant Catherine was made comfortable in her bed. "I am glad that is over, Fredo. Our parents seemed to have enjoyed their cross cultural experience. What about a name for our little offspring. It's only a month away now."

"In Italy we usually name the first child after the father's parents, boy or girl, and then the second boy or girl after the mother's parents. What do you think, my dearest," as he gently leaned over to listen to the baby's heartbeat.

"Pretty much the same as in Ireland", replied Catherine.

"That's it, then, do we settle on Luigi if it's a boy, Vera if it's a girl, and when we have the next, it will be called Edward or Doris."

"And what about a middle name. Fredo after you if it's a boy and Catherine if it's a girl.

"Job done, agreed."

"Oh, by the way, exactly how many children do you think we will have?"

"You are still only nineteen, let's say twenty five years of bearing children, one every two years, how about twelve?"

"Oh no, dearest Fredino! I am not sure I could manage so many." Catherine slowly stretched over and kissed her new husband on the cheek. "Good night, sleep well."

The following month at the end of April, little baby arrived. The birth was smooth with no complications and the new mum and dad were elated to hear their little son's first cry. They called him Luigi Dino.

The following week at the Registry Office, after a long and painful five minutes spelling out Luigi letter by letter to a bemused registrar, mum and dad settled on its anglicised form, Lewis.

Fredo's parting thought on the day of the

registration was abundantly clear. *'Now that little Luigi has become Lewis, my family is truly British'*.

Chapter 6

1909

In the summer of the previous year Fredo and Catherine doted on their new arrival. Vera Catherine was born.

Business continued to thrive for the couple, Fredo greatly extending his influence in the town. For the third consecutive year at the miner's welfare he sponsored the local billiards tournament and a snooker tournament too, an increasingly popular sport. Prizes were modest, steak pie and potatoes for the family of the winning contestant and a free ice cream for their children. Contestants' kids had two shots at a win as the runners up prize was also free ice cream. The event was firmly establishing itself in the annual social calendar and the tournaments attracted increased numbers each year. The reputation of Fredo's business in Consett had never been higher.

But it was in the middle of February when events conspired to remind Fredo and Catherine of their fragility. It was a cold, but sunny day. In the town and at the Stanley coal pit nearby, life was proceeding as normal as it had done for over sixty years. Late in the afternoon the muffled sound of an explosion reverberated throughout the small town. This was the sound which locals, living above the coal seam, feared for every day of their lives.

A second explosion followed, much louder than the

first and flames started shooting into the sky. Townsfolk feared the worst and the women of the town raced anxiously towards the pit. All had the same thoughts in mind. Within seconds, a few arrived on the scene, then a dozen or so, then a hundred and then a thousand. The buildings at the pit head were as normal, no damage, but it was the smoke in the distance seeping through from below which realised their worst fears. It was obvious the explosion was underground.

The death toll was enormous. One hundred and sixty eight men and boys had lost their lives in what was the worst pit disaster in the North East coalfield. Twenty six men survived the ordeal, trapped in a pocket of clean air and they were brought to safety the following day.

A few days later as Fredo and Catherine were chatting over their breakfast egg roll, "Let's keep the blinds down for a few days. Today we should close the shop as a mark of respect. I want to help dig out the mass grave at St Joseph's. Half of the dead are to be buried there. These people have been great to me and I love them all deeply. I feel I need to be there. It's only right. This is the church where we baptised our two kids."

"I will take the kids to my mum and dad. The loss of Uncle Robert at the pit has hit my parents very hard." Catherine continued, "They say about sixty of the dead were boys under twenty years of age and a couple were only thirteen. Still babies. It's just not fair they have to die at that age. Uncle Robert was in his forties, how's Marjorie and their kids going to cope now?"

"Catherine, we can't let our boys work in these mines. The situation here is awful. What horrible lives these miners are forced to have. Imagine so many families......."

"Maybe it's time for us to move soon. That pit was sunk over sixty years ago. I think they still use picks and shovels to extract the coal. There are bound to be more heart breaking disasters in the future in these old pits. The pits give our families a chance of a good living but at what cost. And the country is still desperate for this damn coal, so they can't close them down. Maybe they will improve safety in the future."

"Yes, we should grieve with the locals for as long as it takes. But let's wait before we do anything. First we need to help your parents cope with Robert's death.

"And Robert's family too, of course," interrupted Catherine.

"Perhaps I should finalise that deal with Vincenzo and see if we can make the move to Errington. At least the new colliery there should have the most modern of equipment. We can start again there. In a month or two I will go back there to see what's happening."

***

Two months later Fredo was sitting with his pint of beer at the Liberty Tavern in Errington. The pub was situated at one corner of a triangular shaped village green surrounded on all sides by houses, shops and a church.

He spoke to the landlord in his best English, "Sir, what's the situation regarding the new pit here?"

"I am told there have been a few problems, and it is still not open. But construction of houses for the miners is well under way. In fact some are finished."

"Any idea of the number of miners they will have."

"They say between two and three thousand," replied the landlord. "That's as long as they can fix their technical issues. They have asked the help of some engineers from Prussia. There were two of them drinking here last week. They were proudly boasting that only Prussian engineers could solve the problems."

"Very interesting," remarked Fredo. *'I never heard of any of the people from Montecino emigrating to Prussia. I wonder where that is,'* he thought.

"And another thing. You know about these new contraptions, these days, airplanes, the engineers were telling me their country had finalised the development of huge airships. You know, huge balloons full of some gas or other, I can't remember what they called it, powering a carriage underneath which will be able to transport passengers long distances. One of them even joked that before the mine opens he would be able to fly here from Prussia on one of these airships. They say the journey here would then be just ten hours instead of the usual two days by train."

"I will believe it when I see it," replied Fredo.

Before venturing back home, Fredo decided to scout the Errington area. The contrast in the landscape compared to his last visit several years before was evident. Terraces of new houses were gleaming in the spring sunshine and the main thoroughfare in the village looked splendid with its blocks of new shops and apartments above.

However the experience was an eerie one. Everything so fresh and pristine, yet no people. *'It's still too early. I am wasting my time. I need to wait until the mine starts production.'*

Scouting trip over and slightly dispirited, slowly he trekked home to the hustle and bustle of Consett.

In the town the disaster at the mine in Stanley was gradually fading out of conscious memory, at least for those who had no direct family involvement. Life still had to continue, children still had to be fed and money still had to be earned. Already the routine stress of needing to survive, day by day, was replacing the emotional trauma from the disaster.

Other pits in the area were in full swing again and the vast majority of the survivors who lost their immediate livelihood at the Stanley pit found employment elsewhere.

Fredo's business too had returned to its usual levels, customers were beginning to smile again as they consumed their hot peas, egg sandwiches and ice cream treats.

"Little surprise for you," Catherine said interrupting Fredo's morning tea. "Little Vera has started to walk. Let her show you. Come on Lewis, help to show daddy what she can do."

Lewis, now aged two, jumped down from the table and held Vera's hand. He guided her a few paces to the door. Both turned round in unison.

"Come back to mama, Vera. You can let go, Lewis," Catherine said.

Lewis let go and Vera seemed to stagger as if she was going to fall.

"Come on baby dear," Fredo said in a comforting voice.

Slowly little Vera placed her right foot forward, then left foot, and within a few seconds she reached the table and fell into Catherine's waiting arms.

"Fantastic, my babies," Fredo stood up, kissed both Catherine and Lewis and wrapped his arms around his family in a warm embrace.

The kids scampered clear and he stepped back to finish his breakfast sandwich.

"Surprises not over, my dear Fredino," Catherine said in a huge beaming smile. "Child number three might be on its way too."

Fredo stood to attention immediately arms aloft. Another kiss to Catherine and another group cuddle.

"Wonderful news, I love you all so much, Catherine. Let's celebrate with a special meal tonight. Let's close the shop early. You can relax now. I'll cook the meal."

Since her marriage, Catherine's diet had changed considerably. She found it difficult to resist the new tastes in her palate. She loved the new flavours which were introduced to her, garlic, celery and wild mushrooms. She had been fascinated particularly by the annual mushroom hunt. Every year during September, Fredo and Vincenzo would depart together in the middle of the night well before dawn to hunt for mushrooms in local forests. Usually they returned before breakfast with baskets full.

At first, Catherine was unsure. After Fredo washed and sliced the dirty fungi to prepare them for the pot, tiny little white worms would squirm across the kitchen table. 'These will do no harm at all,' Fredo would say, 'Back home, nobody ever died.' He insisted the mushrooms were a real delicacy and a treat to be savoured. Now Catherine, too, looked forward to the bounty of the September scavenger hunt.

On Sundays it was Fredo's responsibility to cook the main meal of the day. His was always typical Italian fare. His favourite menu was a first course of minestrone, followed by a chicken cutlet, fried in egg and breadcrumbs.

"I managed to obtain a lovely healthy chicken from Mr Robson, the farmer up at Tanfield. You know him, occasionally he pops in with his six children for an ice cream treat."

A couple of hours earlier, in the back court behind the shop, over a small brazier, Fredo had deskinned the chicken and carefully carved out the meaty breast fillets for the family meal. The legs, together with the thighs and wings were for Catherine to use the following day.

'Pity about the eyes and the head and feet too. Mamma and babbo would have loved these. They always used to say that these were the best bits,' he thought, *'I can't really ask Catherine to use these.'*

Catherine knew that when Fredo offered to prepare a coffee after the meal, a serious conversation was looming.

"I think now might be the time for us to think about leaving," he suggested as he poured her a coffee.

"This is a real treat tonight. Coffee as well."

"We are still paying Vincenzo rent for this place and it will never be ours to own. We need to build a business for our children, don't you think?"

"Are you sure, my dear? We are doing so well here, we have money for food, we can make sure our children are clothed well, and my mum and dad are here too."

"Errington seems a great opportunity. I've been there three times already. Its look like the first coal will be drawn from the pit next year....."

"But it's so far away," Catherine interrupted.

"Already they have built rows and rows of houses for the miners. And of course, there's the beach, the children will love growing up at the seaside."

"Fredo, you must be certain this will work out for us. We will be sacrificing a lot to move away from here. I love it here. In any case we'll have to wait until after the baby is born. That will be next year."

"Please trust me. It will be fine," pleaded Fredo. "We need to secure our children's future, how many did we say we wanted, ten, eleven, twelve?"

Catherine stretched across the table and grabbed his

hand. "I know, I know that everything will be fine, I do trust you."

"I knew you would see sense. Together we'll make this thing work," said Fredo. "One other thing I almost forgot to mention. About the letter I received today. Mamma and babbo suggested it might be an excellent idea if my little sister Mira, came over to help us."

"Good idea, tell me again, how old will she be now, I forget."

"She is seventeen. I feel I need to be responsible for her after everything I said back home. I don't want any *'prima notte'* nonsense happening to her."

"Looks like it will be all change for us from now on." Catherine replied. "I might just be able to get excited about Errington too."

"In the next few weeks I will talk this over with Vincenzo," Fredo paused. "Oh….and I will make the arrangements for Mira."

That night their little family all slept well.

Chapter 7

1911

After several more scouting missions to Errington, Fredo had found the ideal site for his ice cream business. It was located in Station Road, the main thoroughfare in the newly named town of Errington Colliery, several hundred yards towards the coast from the ancient village of Errington.

Fredo pondered on how the colliery had changed the character of the area. He had viewed Errington as a quaint English village, a manicured field of green at its core, surrounded by several houses, a church and a couple of pubs. Beyond the green had been a small workhouse of about one hundred and fifty inmates, mainly the poor from the south end of Sunderland. The atmosphere then had been agricultural, with great serenity and tranquillity. Now a new town had sprung up, with the colliery dominating.

Further beyond and looking out to sea, more houses were being constructed. Fredo had already decided that Station Road would be at the heart of the town, where the locals would gather. There would be shops and other amenities.

The previous year when Fredo finally relocated, rows of shops on the main street with flats above were already built. Construction of two churches, a new hotel and a large school were in progress. Several rows of terraced houses, adjacent to the main colliery entrance, lay behind Station Road to the north. Along the coast with great views to the sea, more terraces were being constructed. The area was a throbbing place of construction activity with emerging new factories and high smoke filled chimneys. It was no longer a beautiful landscape of rolling green fields, but a fledgling industrial landscape of smoke, soot and dirt. However, Fredo knew that if good money was being earned by indefatigable miners and by workers in the factories, then it meant good money would be earned for his own little family too.

In the central section of Station Road Fredo had found the ideal spot. He occupied two adjacent shops, one double fronted and the other with a single front. Living accommodation on the second floor straddled both premises. In due course, he thought, and with a large family planned, he could extend to a third floor in the attic. Behind the premises, were small backyard courts leading onto a dirt track which allowed access for goods deliveries. He decided that the double fronted shop would be the ice cream parlour and the other smaller premises for his new venture, fish and chips. Fredo hadn't forgotten how successful Mr Santi's had been in Glasgow. Mr Santi had convinced him that feeding the population was more rewarding financially than giving it a treat from time to time. Furthermore, although fish and chips was dirtier and a more strenuous, there was no seasonality and no outdoor selling.

Relieved of the financial constraints whilst under Vincenzo's control, Fredo had taken the gamble to invest heavily in his new venture. The fish and chip business needed a large investment in frying equipment and Fredo sourced the funds from the growing Italian community in Scotland. The same Mr Santi and his contemporaries had reaped significant financial benefits from the big immigration from Italy. They had broadened their businesses into money lending and almost exclusively to their fellow emigrants from Italy, who had establishments in almost every industrial town in Scotland and Northern England. Fredo's gamble was a huge one whilst interest rates were high. **B**ut there was no alternative. Financial failure was unthinkable. He knew his standing in the Italian community would sink dishonourably if his new venture failed. Fredo's ambitious gamble simply had to succeed.

***

Fredo and Catherine settled into their new surroundings in Errington with their three children, Lewis, Vera and little Edward, also born in Consett. Fredo's sister Mira had arrived and rapidly she had become an indispensable member of the family. Living accommodation upstairs was certainly more spacious than they had been used to before. In addition to a larger sitting room area, they had a small kitchen scullery, an inside toilet and three bedrooms. During the first day at their new house, so excited were Lewis and Vera that they ceaselessly ran in and out of the rooms in a newly improvised hide and seek game.

"We can afford just one month to have everything ready," said Fredo. "In three months we need to make our first loan repayment, we're committed now. You look after the children and Mira and I will work morning to night to ensure everything is ready."

"Don't forget that in the first month you're talking about, we need some furniture for the house too, not just the equipment for the business," replied Catherine.

By the end of the first month the house upstairs was sparsely furnished, bare necessities only, a stove, table and chairs, a sofa, beds, drawers and a wardrobe. Downstairs the shops were fully kitted.

By spring they were ready. Initially business was lighter than expected. Already there were two thousand employees at the colliery and another thousand, he estimated, in the local craft businesses which relied on the mines for their livelihood. But Fredo was in no mood to panic. He hadn't yet a full ice cream season whilst his new fish and chips business was at least generating more income week by week. The family were still managing with no need for any full-time staff, Fredo himself in charge of fish and chips and Mira in charge of ice cream. Catherine helped where she could in between caring for the children. However Fredo knew from his previous experience he needed a presence on the streets to quicken the pace of his growth.

"Catherine, I think we need to advertise for staff to help us. We need to have our ice cream cart out in the summer. This will help promote our fish and chips too. We can't let Mira do that. This is a boy's job, so we need to find somebody here locally whom we can trust."

"Before we put a notice in the window, write to Vincenzo and Mr Santi. They might have somebody spare. Better, surely, to get a *garzone* with experience," replied Catherine.

***

Before long Fredo and Catherine were set into a daily routine. The shifts at the mine were twelve hours long and Fredo was there with his cart every day at the main exit gates, at six in the morning and at six in the evening. For the evening shift, while Fredo was away,

Mira and Catherine, between them looked after the shops. Customers didn't seem to mind Lewis and Vera scurrying around, whilst Edward slept comfortably in his box underneath the counter.

The cart was loaded with all sorts, ice cream, lemonades and Woodbine cigarettes. After their long shifts the miners were grateful of a fresh cup of lemonade to drink or a swig of ice cream to quench their thirst. Even though miners had no loose change in their pockets, Fredo's cart was a sight to behold after their long shifts in the darkness and dustiness of the pit. Fredo realised immediately that to sell anything the miners needed credit, time to pay. And grasping at every possible sale there was no time to write in his notebook which man bought what. Consequently he rapidly learned a technique to commit the necessary details to memory. When he returned home it was Catherine who maintained the 'tick' book.

"I am leaving it to you to ask wives and mothers for our money after they have received their wages at the end of week." Fredo knew the job of collecting debts was best left to his wife.

"Don't worry, dear. I told you many times before that these women are heaven sent, most of them give me what's due without even questioning the amount. It's only the odd one who has to go into the red book. Sometimes we need to give them more time to pay."

Fredo and Mira were continually kept busy. They had few moments of spare time and gradually the business became a focal point for the community. Catherine was the mainstay of the family. Since her father and brothers were also miners, she and the Errington women had much in common. This helped greatly to ensure that the unpaid debts were kept to the minimum. She understood how tough miner lives were. She had learned that from time to time even the women too, were forced to work at the mine to add a few shillings to the family coffers. Above ground there was always work available sorting out good coal from bad as well as shunting coal trucks along the rails from the pithead to waiting cargo trains.

It was only when the kids were fast asleep in their beds when Fredo and Catherine could properly discuss the day's events. Inevitably they finished off with an analysis of the unpaid debts. They also discussed Catherine's regular gossiping in the shop with the women of the town.

"I seem to inspire these women, I don't know why. They think I could be their role model of some sort."

"What do you mean, dear?"

"You know, all this talk about votes for women and equal rights. I think they want me to start a movement, like, what do they call them in London? Suffragettes."

"Yes, I've heard of them. As long as you don't break any laws and you are peaceful about it then that's okay with me. But you're not taking it seriously, are you?"

"No Fredo, of course not. I am not going on hunger strike or tying myself to any railings."

"By the way, some guys were telling me, did you know that in jail they are force feeding those women. How do they manage it? With tubes or pipes, I think. It's barbaric. Another example of man's power over vulnerable women. It's shocking."

Fredo briefly recalled to mind the abuse of his sisters Teresa and Rosa.

"You have to do what is right for you, Catherine. However perhaps it's better you concentrate first on our little family and our little business here. By all means give these ladies all the moral support you can. But we can't afford to have you at the police station or in jail."

"I really don't want to be involved in all that stuff, especially when we have three young children."

"Boys will always be boys, but our Vera, she is already three years old. Let's make sure that she and any other girls we have, are nurtured to grow up as strong independent women, so they won't need to rely solely on their husbands for their livelihood. Encouraging women to be strong and independent. That would be the best legacy which the suffragettes can leave."

"I agree completely. Let's go to bed!"

***

By the end of the summer, the family's new *garzone* had arrived. Mr Santi recommended and sent Tony Mucci, aged nineteen. Tony was one of several boys whom he had brought over from Valbona when he was sixteen. Tony was a second cousin of Fredo and he was delighted and keen to re-unite again with Mira, whom he knew well from the days when they ran through the fields trying to spot and catch harmless snakes. Mr Santi had considered that since Tony was part of the extended Baldini family anyway, it was only right he should send his smart young worker to Errington. Tony was equally happy to move.

Fredo was delighted to have another pair of trustworthy hands. Upstairs the house was already crowded with three adults and three children so there was limited space. He arranged for a mattress to be placed in the corner of the back shop. Fredo had already seen the living conditions of some of the *garzone* in Glasgow. Some had been living in dark and damp cellars with little light, so he figured it would something of a luxury for Tony to have a mattress in the corner of a warm back shop.

With Tony by his side, Fredo could now realise some of his bigger plans and he could keep the fish and chip shop open for longer. He was already looking at other premises in the town with a view to open a billiards hall. He was keen to build a reputation much in the same way as he did in Consett. Since no billiards hall yet existed in Errington, this seemed a good opportunity. He was planning that his new premises might become the meeting place for the youth of the town to eat, drink and play.

Tony, himself, understood the fish and chips business well. Mr Santi had taught him how to source his fish and other supplies including coal for the frying range. Coal, now, was right on his doorstep.

"Sleep all right," Fredo asked as he made Tony a hot cup of steamy coffee. "I am normally not so helpful at breakfast, you know. This is your first morning. You make your own coffee from now on."

"Great, thanks, the mattress was really comfortable. My first night in Glasgow was in the middle of winter on a wooden board with a single sheet. At the time I thought, *what have I done coming here,*" replied Tony.

He continued. "Fredo, in the shop you sell just fish and chips, nothing else, is that right? Up in Glasgow, Mr Santi introduced all sorts of other items to sell."

"In fact I was thinking of adding other things. Maybe you can help me now. What else sells in Glasgow?"

"Mr Santi sells other cheaper stuff to accompany the chips. They are very popular, especially for kids, pies and puddings, for example."

"Pies and puddings, what do you mean?"

Tony continued. "He has two types of pie, a mince pie and an ashet pie."

"What, a shit pie, a rubbish pie!" Fredo interrupted in amazement.

"No, not shit. It comes in a square shape. The ashet is the dish in which the pie is cooked at the bakery. Anyhow it's filled with bits of meat, kidney and various pieces of offal. You know what I'm talking about, same as all the insides of the animals we ate as children in Montecino."

"And what about the other pie?" asked Fredo.

"It's a pie full of minced meat. In Glasgow it's supplied by a bakery started up by another Valbona man, Dante Renucci, you must know him."

"God, yes, is that what he is up to now?" said Fredo with a grin across his face.

"And the pudding, tell me about that too."

"They call it a black pudding. It's the shape of an Italian *salsiccia.* Contains onion, bits of kidney and offal too. It's all blended together in fat and blood, mostly from pigs."

"Seems tasty," said Fredo. "And are these all fried in the same pan?"

"Yes, the only thing is, whereas fish needs a very high temperature, you can get away with a lower temperature for pies and puddings as they have already been cooked. So you are just heating them up."

At that moment Mira came downstairs and entered the back shop, with a huge, beaming smile.

"It's great, Tony, you are here with us." She said, giving him a gentle kiss on the cheek.

***

By the end of the year, all shops on one side of the mile long Seaside Road had been occupied. The coal mine had brought with it all sorts of support businesses, haberdashery, grocers, butchers, fruiterers and a pub on every corner. The brand new school on the main street had been completed, made of red brick construction in an impressive Baroque style with elaborately decorated moulded cornices. In contrast the surrounding streets the rows of colliers' houses looked indistinguishable. At various points in the town adjacent to the houses, there were tracts of land which were given over as allotments to the miners and their families. In this way people had the opportunity to grow their own vegetables, either for themselves or to sell to the local grocers.

Fredo, was in awe particularly of the craftsmanship of the school building which, he often remarked to his customers, would outlive every other structure in the town, such was its quality. He appreciated the intricate stonework and fine skills of the masons. He had been told that the imposing building was built to emphasise the importance of education, notwithstanding the town's large dependence on the mine for its employment and its future livelihood.

Occasionally when in need of inspiration Fredo walked from end to end along Seaside Road. His optimistic hopes for the future rarely wavered. He was convinced that the hustle and bustle he continued to see and the thriving nature of the community would provide the necessary financial security and safety for his family. And Tony, too, had now become part of the family.

.

Chapter 8

1914

The pit employed over four thousand miners and the town was a constant buzz. Despite the absence of cleanliness in the air, a sense of growing affluence pervaded. The early morning sea fret was no longer a fresh mist and even it was having difficulty breaking through the industrial grime. The air was generally covered with a cloud of soot which never seemed to disappear except on those crispy frosty cloudless mornings when the night frost somehow gobbled up airborne carbon particles. While the chimney stacks at the mine, in factories and in other buildings forever pumped out more and more smoke nobody in the streets seemed to bother. Children played aimlessly and effortlessly in the narrow streets, mothers and grandmas oblivious to their kids' potential decaying health. When the sirens sounded at the end of the shift the children ran to the pit gates in unison to meet the hordes of men streaming out of the gates. The kids searched whoever they knew to scrounge a lick of ice cream on somebody else's tab.

Fredo and Tony alternated at the pit gates with their cartful of offerings. And Tony too had mastered the mental skill of noting which miner took what and on which day.

"It's Friday, and despite it being warm today I bet

you takings will be less than on other days," said Fredo just before Tony left the shop for his four hundred yards stroll to the pit gates.

"Funny, isn't it, when they pick up their wages and have cash in their pocket, they rarely buy anything," said Tony.

"Yes, they have no problem buying on credit when they don't have cash. Yet on a Friday, it's different. It's obvious those tough miners' wives wear the trousers in their families. The women take charge of the money and woe betide the menfolk if there's a penny missing."

"That's okay as long as they are still happy to pay us for what's bought earlier in the week."

"Yep, the women are definitely in control. That's good for them and it's good for us too for we know we will be paid," Fredo declared.

"Men are brittle. Without these strong women to hold the fort, they would be straight down to the pub and we would never see our money. That's the way it is in these parts."

Tony smiled as he sauntered out and he knew he was in for an easy day.

The sirens rang aloud and the miners streamed out.

"Tony, *areet, wor lad*, when this damn war starts I hope ye eyeties are *wae* us," shouted one as he strode past the cart.

"*Whey aye man*, they will. Young Tony there, he's a canny lad," another replied.

"Stop shouting and bawling. Leave the man *alane*. Let's go, *am clamming for me bait*," yet another said.

Tony stood frozen to the spot. He wasn't sure whether they were happy to see him or whether they were insulting him. As expected, little was bought, although all of the kids present still obtained their free penny licks.

***

A few weeks earlier Archduke Franz Ferdinand, heir to the Austrian Empire had been assassinated in Sarajevo by a Serbian nationalist. The newspapers were full of details of the evolving diplomatic crisis. The major powers, France, Germany, Russia and the Ottoman Empire had declared their position and the British government was deep in mediation to avoid a conflict.

That night at their evening meal Tony aired his concern.

"What is likely to happen to us if they go to war," he asked Fredo.

"We Italians have always been at war. Remember our country is only fifty years old. Austria is our traditional enemy but maybe our leaders will leave us in peace this time. And in any case we are British now. Catherine is English and we have three young children born here. Nobody can touch us."

"For all our sakes, I hope you are right."

Later Tony had difficulty falling asleep. He thought back to the banter of the crowd earlier in the day. He was in two minds. *'Were they serious, were they joking?'* He was used to the odd derogatory comment from time to time, but this time it was different. The insults were hauled in unison, one after the other, he felt the potential threat of the angry mob. *'How easily the situation could be out of control,'* he thought. *Perhaps the banter might have been worse if the kids hadn't been milling around. Were the comments really serious?'* Nevertheless he remained anxious of the situation on mainland Europe. *'What would really happen?'*

From then Tony's post dinner discussions with Fredo

intensified and focussed increasingly on the political situation. Insults at the pit gates had all but ceased and customers in the shop continued to be relaxed. However each passing day the menfolk in the town were becoming more and more animated at the news reports. They were indicating they would be joining up immediately and take the fight directly to the enemy if war broke out.

"A couple of months on the battlefield and we will be back for Christmas," they were declaring so frequently that eventually it seemed to be morphing into truth.

***

Since the assassination, the British government was supporting Serbia whilst trying to mediate for peace. It allied with France and Russia. Germany on the other hand, acknowledging its historical association sided with the Austrian Empire. As the newspapers were accurately predicting, war was declared by Britain on its new enemies at the height of midsummer. It was to Fredo's and Tony's great relief that Italy remained neutral.

In the weeks following the declaration of war, the character of the town changed. Apprehension had replaced bravado. Menfolk were more downcast and the women were more anxious. At the notice board in the main street and at various strategic places in the town, outside the pit gates, at the post office, at the school a huge poster was affixed to walls. Nobody could miss it.

A man in a navy type hat and with a large black drooping moustache, finger pointing outwards, looked straight into the eyes of anyone close enough to read its contents.

"BRITONS! WE WANT YOU,
JOIN YOUR COUNTRY'S ARMY.
GOD SAVE THE KING."

Britain was still the only major power where army service was voluntary. It was clear that the poster was designed to touch the conscience of the country's men and boys.

Fredo soon learned the man in the poster was Lord Kitchener, who, in direct contrast to the opinions of those optimists who thought the war would be over for Christmas, had calculated and confirmed to Parliament that it might take more than a couple of years to defeat the enemy and win the war.

The family sat down for breakfast wondering whether the war would really be over by Christmas. Breakfast was the only time of day when the family were able to be together.

"We are in for a few years of hardship," Fredo warned Catherine. "So many young men here have signed up. And it's so worrying the number of boys I have been seeing in military uniform. These kids should still be at school."

"Their mothers are in despair, I can tell you that," replied Catherine. "We are so lucky, Lewis is only seven and Edward four. Hopefully and thankfully they might never see war."

The family felt that hope of the war ending before Christmas was daydreaming. It seemed an impossibility.

"More men are being mobilised all over Britain," said Fredo, "and the newspapers are spreading more doom and gloom. The whole world has gone war mad, Japan, the Ottomans have also declared war. Ships are being sunk, man to man fighting in Flanders, when will this thing end?"

"One of our customers has already received bad news," replied Catherine. "She showed me the telegram. It started '*Deeply regret to inform you....................*' She was in a state of absolute shock and hopelessness. She's lost her man and wage earner. She fears for her little one now. What will happen to her?"

At that moment a series of booms shook the windows of the shop. All went quiet for a few short seconds and then another boom.

"Oh God*,"* shrieked Catherine as she drew the three children closer to her. "What's that?"

Mira grabbed onto Tony's arms. *"O Mamma!"*

"Stay here everybody!" said Fredo immediately rushing out onto the street quickly followed by Tony.

Several men were running down Seaside Road towards the coast. Fredo followed them whilst the booms continued. "Tony, you stay behind, look after the girls."

At the beach a crowd of about thirty men stood aghast at the plumes of smoke further down the coast. They ascertained the scale of the events. In the distance out to sea they could see two, maybe three ships shelling the coast in the direction of Hartlepool, about ten miles away. It was clear shells were being fired back in the opposite direction, '*presumably from the defence battery*,' thought Fredo. The shells were missing the ships and exploding in huge splashes in the sea.

"Home, home everybody, families out," shouted one man. Within minutes they were scrambling back to their homes.

Fredo rushed back too. A group of women were in conversation with Catherine at the front door of the shop. "I think the war has reached us now. Ships are bombing Hartlepool. We need to get out. We might be next. Maybe they will bomb the mine. Get the horse and cart, Tony! We are going to the hills."

"But Fredo, are you sure? Hartlepool is a big town with ironworks and shipyards. That must be the reason they're bombing. And they've a couple of defence batteries. We should be okay, here. There's nothing here for them to bomb."

"Never mind, let's be ready anyway and see what happens next."

For the next hour, the main street in the town was a constant throb of men racing backwards and forwards, women crying in panic, whilst young kids carried on playing oblivious to the events.

When the noise of the shelling ceased, nevertheless chaos and confusion continued in the town.

"No need for panic!"

"Keep your bairns indoors!"

"Get out of the town!"

A group of men marched up Seaside Road declaring, "The ships seem to be leaving. They are moving away." Shouting and screaming stopped. Chaos over. A degree of calmness and normality was restored.

Later in the evening the rumour was confirmed. A rota system had been quickly organised by some at the shoreline to spy on incoming enemy ships which could endanger the town's safety.

In the following days the Hartlepool Mail described the events of the bombing. This had been the first attack of the war on the home front, it said. There had been three German destroyers which had deployed over a thousand shells on the town in just forty minutes. Over a hundred dead bodies had been recovered and there were more to be found, the reporters indicated. Dozens of houses had been destroyed or damaged. Pieces of shrapnel had littered the streets and embedded in the walls of buildings. It was reported that ships had also bombed Whitby and Scarborough although Hartlepool had been the worst hit by far.

During the following weeks many more young boys signed up. After the Hartlepool incident the Lord Kitchener poster seemed to have taken on a new meaning of its own. Every able bodied adult, man and woman, had a job to do. Either at the pits or in the army, there were responsibilities for everyone. It became essential for women, particularly, to work at the pits to replace the men who had signed up. The war effort needed the mines to keep producing.

For weeks on end after the Hartlepool bombing incident the shoreline was never empty. It just seemed appropriate, for anyone and everyone when they had time to spare, children too, to walk to the shore and watch out for any dangers at sea. Tony felt the same responsibility and on this day at the beach he was accompanied by Mira.

"I feel guilty. Business has collapsed since the war started and I have a lot less to do. I need to find work at the mine. But I really don't know how I could manage down there. In any event, they might not even want me."

"Never mind all that now. We need to tell them soon. In a few weeks I will begin to show. Then what will happen to us?"

"You know very well, Mira, I love you and I will always be with you. Fredo and Catherine will still need us, when this is all over, and we will need them too. I am sure all will be fine. Let me speak to Fredo, man to man."

"How do you think they will react? I am afraid. Babbo back home would certainly not be pleased if he knew."

"Yes, mine too. You know Fredo better. He's different. He's not the typical Italian who treats his wife as his servant. He demands little from her. Goodness, when Catherine is at the wash house, he prepares lunch himself and for the kids. I think he is more liberal. I am sure he'll understand. He doesn't even bother that we don't go to Mass."

"And Catherine, what about her," said Mira anxiously.

"I think she's a great one. She hardly ever sees her family back in Durham. She has dedicated her life completely to us. Remember we are the foreigners. She's a modern woman, moving with the times. She's fascinated with all those stories about the suffragettes."

"I do hope you are right, Tony. When this war is over, we can make a nice life here. We can have a big family of our own."

"Okay, first I speak to Fredo, I get a job at the pit and we marry next year. We settle here, have many more children and we have a great life together. Settled then."

"Fine, let's go. I am getting cold now. We don't want our little baby to get a chill now, do we?"

Their mood was more than jovial as they walked back home.

Tony wasted little time to speak to Fredo. The children were already sleeping whilst Mira was cleaning the work surfaces behind the counter. Catherine was mumbling as she swept the floor. "In winter they bring in so much muck on their shoes. Without the sawdust this would be a nightmare."

Only Mira acknowledged Catherine. "Yes, and the smell too. Once the horse manure is on your shoes……. You just can't avoid it."

Tony made for one of the cubicles. "Fredo, Catherine, can you come here a moment, I have something to tell you. Come on, you too, Mira, especially so."

As Mira cuddled up close to Tony, huge smiles etched across their faces Fredo guessed immediately. In almost telepathic motion, Catherine snuggled into her husband. She knew too. For several weeks they had recognised the signals. Only a few years previously they were doing the same things and acting in the same way. Holding hands behind the counter, disappearing together into the back shop, whispering together and most of all, the huge gleaming and beaming smiles when they saw one another.

"Come on, we can't wait." said Fredo. "When is the big day?"

"It's not just that. We will soon have another mouth to feed."

"O Dio" said Catherine, squeezing Fredo's hand tightly. He squeezed back in return.

Fredo gestured his wife to stand up and move out of the booth.

"Fantastic, wonderful!" he shouted. "Let's all have a drink."

"And what about the wedding?" Catherine said after the drinks had been poured.

Tony and Mira looked at each other in surprise.

It was Mira who responded. "Actually we never even talked about that. We were just so excited about the baby. Somehow we feel as if we are married already."

She paused for a moment.

"But yes, we will have to get married. We want our child to be baptised in the church and I don't suppose the priest will do that unless we are married."

"Old habits die hard", said Catherine. "I don't know about Italy, but here, having children before marriage is still taboo. People gossip. Some will think less of you. At least if you are married, then nobody bothers."

***

The following day the young couple visited the parish priest at Our Lady's Catholic Church in Errington Village.

Following the influx of four thousand or so miners into the area Father Donovan's parish had been transformed. It was no longer a small rural parish. Of course not all the miners were Catholic but nevertheless he had estimated that the church's flock had increased by about two thousand families and he had already set the process in motion to recruit another priest. Almost overnight Father Donovan's pastoral care too had been transformed. Whilst previously he cared for a congregation of conforming parishioners, now he was dealing with a variety of complex social issues which had been imported into his parish. He was seeing the effects of drunkenness, child neglect and poverty. In parishioners' homes behind closed doors he knew there was increasing abuse against wives and children. His role had become more councillor than priest. Frequently he resorted to questioning his own teaching too. Did couples really understand their responsibilities to their children at the baptismal font? Indeed were marrying couples really prepared for the responsibility of children at all? He knew that sexual relationships between youngsters before marriage was on the rise. And in addition he was experiencing an increasing number of mixed marriages, although he was thankful that in the vast majority of the cases, the couples were committing to bring up their children in the catholic faith.

But in his heart Father Donovan was a liberal. His belief was that in God's eyes, all his children on earth were equal. He was in no position to judge on the morals of his parishioners. He considered his pastoral care was best served by adopting a more compassionate and obliging attitude to his work.

"Of course, we will marry you before your child is born," said Father Donovan, "as long as you commit to continuing your love for each other and your new family to the end of your days."

"And what about our child," said Mira.

"What about your child?" Father Donovan replied. "It will be a member of our flock when it is born just like any other. Oh, and as far as the Church is concerned he will be legitimate, if that is what your concern is."

"All we need," continued the priest, "are your baptism certificates. This is the one real obligation I have, that you have both been baptised in the Church. There are some rules I still need to follow."

"We were both baptised in Italy," said Tony.

"Then you should write to your local church immediately and obtain a certified copy of your baptism certificates from your priest in Italy. Our Irish friends always do that. Parishes in Ireland quickly oblige."

"Maybe we could do this through the consular office in Newcastle," said Tony.

"As long as you are quick, I don't really mind how you manage it," replied Father Donovan. "Now, let's arrange some pre-marriage classes."

Later in the day Fredo helped Tony write his letter to

the priest at Montecino.

The following morning Tony was at the colliery personnel office.

"We are desperate for any help we can get," Mr Simmons said. "So many miners have already gone off to war and we are short of able bodies now. We need to keep producing. All the jobs above ground are done by women. You are a fit young man and we need you at the coal face. Don't worry, our guys will see you are well looked after down there. I can help you complete this form, if you like."

Tony was hoping for more gentle tasks above ground but he knew he was in no position to bargain. Britain was at war, after all.

"Another thing, Mr Mucci, or can I call you, Tony. Do you play a musical instrument?"

"I do, actually, the accordion."

"Slightly unusual in these parts, but that's great. We are starting a colliery band. All the collieries have a band and we think we have some great musicians here. Unfortunately some of them have signed up, but when they return in a few months, we plan to have some great days out in the summer playing with other bands. In July next year we want to inaugurate our band formally at the Durham Miners' Gala. I can count you in then, can I?"

"Yes, I am in, but first I need to get my head right to go down there into the bowels. My plan is to do this only until the rest of the miners return from the war."

"That's fine, let's get you your lamp now. When can you start, tomorrow morning?"

Chapter 9

1915

Mira and Tony were preparing their contribution for the family's Easter meal. Back home in Italy the tradition was for the eldest daughter of the family to bake the traditional rice cake, an indulgent treat after the fasting of Lent. Rice was boiled and sweetened and made ready for the oven in a pastry mould and covered with a lattice of leftover pastry.

"Six large cakes should do us. We could also try to sell some by the slice in the shop." Mira called over to Catherine, who were sitting at the table minding her own business.

"I am only doing this mining work until the war is over and because money is tight at the moment," said Tony. "The conditions down there are hellish. In summer it must be ten times worse. This is nothing like the open cast surface mining I was doing back home when I was a boy. It was fun then. But here it's serious, no slouching. There are targets to hit."

"Nevertheless, I am so glad you get to come home every night. Some of the mothers who come into the shop are desperate. They can't sleep at night. Their boys have gone and they hear little from them," replied Mira. "And the newspapers don't seem optimistic. They think this will go on for years. It's nine months since it started and they say we've already lost over twenty thousand men."

"That man Kitchener and all his stupid politicians, what a mess. Just as well Italy remained neutral."

"Old Mrs Bridges, you know, the old lady with jet black cropped hair, who comes in two or three times a week, she told me she has already lost two of her boys, only eighteen and twenty. They were so happy when they left, she said, marching proudly at the front of their regiment. And somehow they all thought they would be back before Christmas. Now they are gone, they will never come back. Poor Mrs Bridges, she is inconsolable."

Mira took out the handkerchief from inside her cuff and wiped the tears from her eyes. "Can you imagine, Tony, a boy of ours leaving for war."

"And what about our Lewis and Edward," shouted Catherine. "If this happens again I won't let them go. I'll handcuff them to me. They would have to drag me to the war as well."

"Oh, don't be so silly, Catherine. This can't happen again. If we've lost twenty thousand men, then so have the Germans. Even politicians can't be that stupid again."

"The awful thing now, the ladies in the town have started a sombre and horrible habit. Every morning as soon the postman is seen on his rounds the women knock on each other's door. They rush outside, stand there and wait. It's so crazy. If the postman passes on by without delivering any post, the women heave sighs of relief, knowing that at least on this day, there is no bad news."

"Even worse, when they do get an envelope with the fated telegram inside, they are frightened to open it. Have their boys died or are have they been just injured?

Seems like pot luck. Mrs Bridges received bad news twice while Mrs Robson, she was ecstatic, her seventeen year old son was only wounded."

"When will this all end, Tony?" continued Mira.

"Come on Mira, we have these cakes to finish. Let's get them into the oven. Then let me practice on the accordion the pit men obtained for me. We have our first session next Sunday afternoon."

**

The following Sunday, the colliery band had their first practice session, a trial for the Easter Sunday church services. They weren't aiming for perfection, only to avoid any embarrassment at the Durham Miners' Gala later in the year. Tony left the practice session early as he was reluctant to leave Mira for too long since, six months gone into her pregnancy, she was now heavily showing. Due to his long shifts at the pit he was also conscious of the long periods of time when Mira was left alone, although he was comforted, of course, that Fredo and Catherine would be at Mira's side at a moment's notice.

Tony and Mira's wedding date was still not fixed as the baptism certificates had still not arrived despite two more reminder letters. The consular office in Newcastle had offered little help. The bureaucratic process, it seemed, involved too many officials, too many signatories.

"Italy is still chaotic and disorganised," said Tony. "Let's visit the priest again. See if we can work something out."

However Father Donovan was clear and succinct. "We can't marry you without your baptism certificates. The sacraments form the basis of our whole christian life. We can't compromise, much as I would like too," he stated.

"Father, can we get baptised again, then. This way we can be married before our child is born," asked Tony.

"But you have been baptised already. The only way we can baptise you again if the first one wasn't valid. Baptism leaves an indelible mark on your soul. It has already been freed of all sin and you have already been welcomed into the Church of God. We cannot baptise you again, just for convenience, as this would invalidate its whole purpose. In any case both of you are no longer chaste. I know you love each other profoundly but in God's eyes, however, it makes little difference now whether you marry before or after your child is born. Eventually if and when you do marry, your child will be legitimised fully and it will be regarded no differently from any other."

Satisfied with the priest's little sermon the young couple rushed home. "Maybe those damned certificates will arrive this week. You know we should have asked Topolino to obtain them on one of his visits back home," Mira suggested.

"It would've made no difference. The priests in Italy would have refused to the hand the certificates to a stranger."

"I don't remember me having to get my baptism certificate when I married Catherine. Do you remember anything about that, dear?" Fredo asked.

"Remember, Father O'Sullivan in Consett was a close friend of the family, he came from the same village as my parents back home in Ireland. They left about the same time after the famine. Maybe he bent a few rules, or probably he just didn't bother. But that doesn't matter now."

Catherine continued. "With all this war stuff, do you think it would be good idea, Tony, if both you and Fredo both find out what you need to do to become British citizens. He and I discussed this the other night. You never know what will happen in the future."

"I think that would be a great idea for you, Fredo. You have already committed to Britain, but for me and Mira, we are still young, and we are both Italian. We might want to return home, who knows."

"Yes, you're right. As soon as the war is over I'll find out. I already speak English, I have an Irish wife, I have three children born here and I have a business here. I guess I can claim to be British now," replied Fredo. "Next time I see Vincenzo I will find out what he did."

Make sure you don't forget, then," ordered Catherine.

***

During the following weeks, the postman continued to deliver bad news to residents of the town, and Tony and Mira continued to wait for their baptism certificates.

The pit owners still needed every available body to fulfil its quota for the war effort. Tony found it tough. At the end of each shift, he delighted in taking a long, deep sigh and inhaling the fresh spring air which was warming by the day. Band practice was taking a back seat. The musicians were exhausted with work. Only occasionally did they meet. Their ambitious initiative to play at the summer gala had now worn thin. The men and women of the pit needed to spend more time with their families at home.

At the end of May Tony emerged from the hellish darkness into a beautiful early summer's day. He was surprised to see Mira outside the pit gates waiting for him. Her stomach appeared larger in her lighter fitting summer clothes.

"*Maybe the certificates have arrived at last,*" he thought.

"Hello Mira, don't kiss me now. I am filthy all over, Wait until we arrive home," he said. He noticed that Mira seemed to be in no mood for merriment.

"What's wrong? *Il Bambino*! No! No!" he yelled.

"No, no, Tony, nothing like that. Fredo read me the news this morning. Italy has declared war."

"What do you mean, I thought we were neutral."

"It's okay, okay, Tony," said Mira in an assured manner. "We are on the side of Britain, so everything will be fine."

"No, Mira, this is not good news. What happens now to me, to Fredo, to you, to our parents in Italy? Look here in Errington, more and more young men our age gone to fight. Boys of sixteen, seventeen even."

"Let's go home and talk to Fredo. He knows more about all this political stuff."

At home Fredo offered his take on the events. "During my lifetime Italy has always wanted to fight the Austrians for the lands around Venice and right round the coast to Dalmatia. Even the mountains in Tyrol as well."

"But we've had peace for over fifty years, why now?" asked Tony.

"Politics, politics, my boy. It's about machismo and huge egos. It's the scramble for Africa. That's why they sided with Britain and France. These stupid Italians want some of Africa too. I read it was part of the deal for siding with Britain. The British agreed to allow the Italians to have Eritrea, Somalia and Abyssinia for themselves. What for? The people in these countries aren't christians, they all live outdoors in huts and shacks and there is nothing there but sand and hot desert. No resources, at all. You would think after the unification all those years ago, we would have been glad to keep what we have, a beautiful bountiful Italy. But no, these *pazzi*, these crazy people. All they will do is send more young men to their graves."

"What about the King, can he not stop this?" replied Tony.

"No, *pazzo anche lui, Emanuele,* even he's a fool, King Emanuele. They think he's a great man after they took control of Tripolitania and won the Turkish war a couple of years ago." Fredo was fuming. *"Boh*, these land grabbers! What about us poor country folk? Why do they think all these people left, *Napoletani, Siciliani, Toscani, Veneti*? Half of our young Italian men emigrated so they could have the opportunity to work and earn some real money. America, Brazil, Argentina, Britain, this is where the smart ones have had to go."

"Calm down, Fredo," said Catherine. "The children are sleeping."

"All we have in Italy are our fields. We have flour for bread and pasta, we have tomatoes and vegetables. We depend totally on the weather. Look back home in Montecino, some years are good, some are bad. We Italians have little skills, we are all farmers. This is why we all end up making fish and chips or ice cream. Just you watch! In the future we will be only be famous for our restaurants, for our food, for our recipes. This is all we can do. The rest of the world, they are developing, manufacturing things, building machines, trains, even these contraptions flying in the air. Those brave miners in those horrible pits are earning more money than we could ever dream of back home. Yet all we want to do is venture into the desert to conquer nomads who just want to be left alone. What do they offer? God, even our farmers have more skills than these desert people. At least the British Empire is intent on developing their colonies, cotton, sugar, tobacco, building railways and infrastructure everywhere, and ensuring good futures for the local population."

"And in any case," as Fredo continued his rant. "I thought we were supposed to be siding with Germany and the Austrians, yet now we are on the side of Britain and France. *Boh*, typical of Italian politicians! What can we do with tons and tons of sand! Precisely nothing! This will just give us more headaches!"

"Well, let us all thank the great Lord," said Catherine trying to relieve the tension in the room, "that those stupid Italians, one of which, by the way, I have married have sided with Britain after all. I cannot even imagine what it would be like if they had sided with Germany."

Tony and Mira looked at each other speechless.

The young couple understood the potential consequences if Italy had indeed decided to declare war on Britain. They figured they would have had to pack their bags and be on their way back home immediately. Tony thoughts strayed back to the incidents the previous year when Britain first declared war. He thought also of all the young boys who weren't coming back to Errington. The locals would certainly not have been so courteous to their Italian neighbours if they were the enemy. Tony pondered only slightly what he would have to do. But fortunately there was no need for him to pack any bags.

The next morning whilst indulging in his morning luxury of coffee and bread, Fredo tried to allay any fears or anxieties.

"Italy is at war, but this has nothing to do with us.

We should carry on with our lives in as normal a manner as possible. Our customers are our friends and we are part of this community. There is no reason for us to fear anything. We are all on the same side. Tony, you should continue at the pit as usual. Catherine and Mira, do as you always do, continue to support our customers and neighbours. We haven't lost anyone in our family. According to the newspapers the British people are losing more and more brave young men every single day."

"Do you think there is anything special we could do for the families which have already lost loved ones," said Catherine.

"Excellent thought, let's mull it over."

***

Weather wise the summer was a scorcher. The Durham Miners' Gala was cancelled since there were so few bandsmen still at home and with that the practice sessions at the pit ended too.

Mira, with one month to go before the baby's birth, urged Tony to visit the consular office in Newcastle to find out how to hasten the arrival of the baptism certificates. Train services to the big city were efficient and regular. The return journey could now be completed within a day.

Outside the train station, Tony was astounded at the bustling activity in Newcastle's streets. Laden horses and carts meandering to and fro, housewives pushing prams, and children milling around, mostly without any form of footwear whilst trying to avoid the mess left behind by the horses.

He noticed smartly dressed gentleman in formal suits with hats shaped like a church dome and ladies in fine clothes carrying small umbrellas by the side.

"*Clearly,*" he said to himself, "*these people never venture down into the pits.*"

He was particularly struck by the elegantly painted carriages being dragged along by bedraggled and tired looking horses. On some streets similar carriages were running along railway lines powered by their own steam. "*The twentieth century has arrived here in Newcastle.*"

Tony came across a street musician with a long beard, hauling a long barrow with a huge organ. He was with a woman dressed in clothes of many different colours, in contrast to the other women he saw who mostly wore black. Alongside was a dog with shaggy hair and a pail between his teeth. Tony noticed that there were some coins inside. The man was singing a song badly, a song which Tony thought he knew and he hesitated for a moment. The woman ventured forward, '*bel uomo*, handsome man, *a penni per la fortuna,* a penny for luck, please.'

He stopped, "Italiani, si!"

At that moment the woman lunged forward and put her arms around Tony. "*Che bello, che bello, un baccio!*" How handsome, how beautiful, please give a kiss!"

Tony obliged and the three indulged in conversation for a few moments.

This organ grinder, Pino and his wife Desi, had been trolling the streets of Newcastle for three years, after several years in London. They were from the Lazio region near Cassino.

"*Molti italiani da Cassino in Newcastle*, Many Italians are from Cassino here in Newcastle." Pino explained, as he rhymed off a list of names which meant little to Tony. "*Le conosci*, do you know them?"

"*No, io sono di Valbona,* No, I am from Valbona."

"Okay," at that moment Pino looked at his wife and said *"Andiamo,* let's go," and Tony, wondering if he had insulted the pair, swiftly moved on.

The consular office was situated on the first floor on one of the new recently built impressive buildings in Grey Street. "*No expense spared for these people*," Tony thought.

Mr Morsiani was an imposing gentleman, impeccably dressed and he looked majestic behind his huge desk of solid oak. The air reeked of cigar smoke, which Tony found intoxicating.

"*Come ti posso servirle*, how can I help you?" The vibration from Mr Morsiani's deep and loud voice bisected the thick cigar smoke.

Tony explained his predicament. Uttering no response the consul duly stood up and ventured towards a chest of drawers in the corner of the room. He ruffled through his files and pulled one out.

"*Ah, Signor Mucci, da Montecino, nato 1892, di padre Antonio di Giuliano*." Mr Morsiani looked at Tony over his thick brimmed spectacles. He walked round the table to where Tony was sitting and held out his right hand. "*Complimenti, la leva vi chiama per la patria, viva Italia!* Congratulations, Mr Mucci, you have been called up to fight in the war, long live Italy!*"

Dumbfounded at the revelation that the consul even knew his father and grandfather's name Tony clasped his head in his hands. Suddenly the outcome of the proceedings had become clear.

Mr Morsiani stated he had been just completed identifying the locations of all the Italian males between the ages of twenty and thirty living in the area from Berwick in the north to Carlisle in the west and to Middlesbrough in the south.

"As an Italian citizen, you are obliged to go to war. There is no option. Otherwise you will be classed as a deserter," the consul explained, ignoring Tony's anxiety. "Don't worry, you will be trained to shoot and to defend yourself. You will also learn construction and engineering skills, so you can build homes for the Italian people whom we'll liberate from that evil Austrian empire."

Tony sat back frozen in his thoughts.

"In addition at the end of the war," Mr Morsiani continued, "and who knows it might be over soon anyway, our government will take back the acres and acres of land from all those fat and rich land owners. The lands will be returned to the people who fight with us to defeat the enemy. And the farmers whose sons emigrated will receive priority. In this way, we will build a new Italy and a self-sufficient Italy. It will be built by the people for the people."

Tony was showing more interest. "Does that mean Mira and I would be able to return home, possess our own land, our own house and our own fields? No more exploiting and unscrupulous landowners and the like?"

"Exactly. This is the commitment of our government at this time."

"Well, maybe fighting in a quick war just might be a better alternative to the horrendous conditions of the coal mine, especially if there is a pot of gold for me at the end." Tony said.

"You have to pack your bags and go soon, Mr Mucci. Our training camp in Cuneo in Italy is waiting for you."

On the way home, Tony tried to make sense of the day's events. His world and that of Mira and his new baby, had been turned upside down. The journey home flashed by.

Mira was waiting for Tony, as usual with a warm embrace and loving kisses. "Tell me, Tony, your news of today?"

Tony sat in one of the booths and relayed his conversation with the consul. Fredo heard it all.

"Boh, politicians! What do you mean, give you your lands back?" Fredo said angrily. "These people are conning you. Do you think these landowners will hand the land back, just like that? Don't you see, Tony, the landowners are the government. They never fixed it before, they will never fix it now."

"Tell me, do I really have an option?" Tony asked, holding Mira's hands.

"Of course, Tony, stay here in England." Fredo paused for a few moments, "but If you do go to war just make sure you come back. We will look after Mira and the baby."

That night Tony and Mira lay in bed restless and anxious.

"You might never see the baby, don't go, please, please! The baby is less than a month away."

"I have to or they'll take me by force. I could be jailed and then what. They know where I live now."

"What if we run away together? They won't find us," urged Mira.

"Mira, then what, we would be running away all our lives, no family to depend on and little future. I have no skills, Mira. What can I do?"

Mira couldn't stop crying.

"At least when I return we'll have a future. I will be careful, very, very careful, Mira. Please don't worry."

Tony stared at the ceiling and placed his left arm under Mira's neck. "Come closer," he whispered. Mira cuddled as he sought the warmth of her large bump.

Soon she drifted into sleep, and hours later he, too drifted into sleep.

The early morning sun shone through the windows and bathed the room in sunlight.

"Tony, Tony, I am wet below," Mira screamed.

"What, what……….what do you mean. What's happening?" Tony jumped out of bed and stared aghast at the damp sheets at the top of Mira's legs. "It must be fine, there is no blood!"

"No, Tony, I think it is happening. *Presto, presto!* Quick, quick. I can feel things in my stomach. This is it, Tony, *presto, presto*."

"*Mamma mia*, what do I do?" Tony strode to and fro struggling to get some clothes on.

"*O Dio, mamma,* quickly get Catherine here and then Mrs Rooney, two doors down. Now, Now!"

Tony barged in to awake Catherine.

She explained that Mrs Rooney was the local midwife always on hand to help the ladies in the town give birth. Catherine prepared the room and within twenty minutes Mrs Rooney was also at Mira's bedside, fully prepared.

"Now, go away, Tony, and don't come back in until we tell you," said Mrs Rooney.

"And you and Fredo need to keep the children busy today," interjected Catherine. "Tell them to be quiet, and nobody has to come in here, okay."

Tony obeyed his instructions immediately. He knew he had no more business in the room. Fredo assured Tony that Mrs Rooney was the best midwife in the town. Nevertheless he prepared him for any bad news, "Remember, Tony, sometimes they don't survive, when they come this early."

Fredo hastily grabbed some cardboard and a pencil.

He pinned the cardboard to the front door of the shop, "Closed until midday."

For the next two hours at regular intervals, Tony heard the screams of pain, *"O Dio, mamma, O Dio, mamma!"*

"Don't worry, Tony, this is normal. Remember I have been through this three times already."

They sat speechless. Lewis, seeing his dad sitting in silence, managed to convince his younger siblings to stay quiet too. He knew something important was happening and he waited eagerly for the new arrival as keenly as Fredo and Tony. He believed that somehow the baby was being delivered from inside Mrs Rooney's bag.

Suddenly the screams of pain went quiet. Momentary silence upstairs. And then a baby's cry was heard.

Tony jumped up, bolted upstairs and stormed into the room.

"There you are," said Mrs Rooney calmly holding a sheet with a little baby's head protruding out, "Tony, you have a little baby girl," and she bent down and placed her in Mira's waiting arms.

Tony knelt down beside Mira, kissed her forehead and whispered. "She's beautiful, Mira, tell me how you are!"

Mira looked at Tony, exhausted, "does she look like me or like you," and she burst into tears. "I did it, I did it, Tony, please don't go!"

At that moment Tony started sobbing too.

Catherine was unsure whether these were tears of joy or tears of sadness that he was leaving soon.

"Everything seems okay, "said Mrs Rooney. "She is somewhat small for a baby girl, but she is fine. I will return home and bring back my scales so we can weigh her."

"Will you return often to see me?" Mira said to Mrs Rooney as she made her way out.

"Of course, Mira, I will come back to see you every day. Later on, perhaps a few days a week, then weekly. Don't worry."

Tony and Mira duly settled on a name for their little one, Dorina, after Tony's mother Dora.

"Next time," Tony said, "we will name the child after your *babbo* or *mamma*."

Tony knew that soon he would be on the battlefield. He needed to spend as much time as possible with Dorina and Mira. But time was limited and he still had his job at the pit. Mira needed a few day's rest, and he had to be on hand to help Fredo and Catherine during the little spare time he had left.

Three days after Dorina was born Tony received his letter.

"You are required to board the train at Newcastle at eleven a.m. next Saturday morning. There will be twenty others who will accompany you to your training camp in Italy."

"Mira, I have just another four days with you then I have to go."

"Please stay with me, now, every hour, every minute, every second. You won't need to go to the pit any longer," Mira said.

"I will, I will stay beside you until Saturday."

"And when you are away, write to me every week, please promise me, Tony."

On Saturday morning at six Tony said farewell to his new family amidst floods of tears and he joined a group of four other uniformed young men from Errington who were also making their way to Newcastle train station.

"We are off to Flanders," said one. "Where are you going to?"

"Don't know yet, but I need some training in Italy first."

"Just as well you eyeties are fighting with us," another said, "or this would have been a difficult journey."

Tony nodded, *"Yes, what if Italy was on different sides, what about him, what about Dorina and Mira, and what about Fredo?"* The thoughts weren't pleasant ones.

At Newcastle station Tony met twenty other fellow Italians, six of which were also from the Valbona area and the rest from elsewhere in Italy. They burst into a chorus of *'Santa Lucia'* as they boarded the train together. Further along the platform Tony noticed that his new pals from Errington were part of a larger group of uniformed soldiers boarding the same train.

"Imagine," he said to one of his new friends, "look, we are all so happy and jolly going off to war together. I wonder if we will all come back together."

***

Back home in Errington, the family tried to make the best of their new reality. Tony gone, very few young men left in the town and the business providing much less income than before the start of the hostilities.

"Come on Mira, tomorrow," Catherine proposed, "we need to go to Durham to register the birth. Make sure you have Dorina well wrapped up. We don't want her catching any chills or infections."

The registrar was an elderly and stern looking lady, her frosty eyes glaring with menace over her spectacles sitting on the tip of her long nose.

"Baby's name, please, when and where born?" she demanded emotionlessly.

"We have had Doreen before, but never Dorina, is that e-e-n-a or i-n-a, are you sure?"

"Father's name, please?"

"Well, we're not married yet, but his name……….."

"What! Not married, then the baby is illegitimate, we can't have a father's name shown."

"But Tony, he is the father. When he comes back from the war we will get married."

"Sorry, Mrs……….." the registrar insisted, "what is your name again? Ah, Mira Baldini, that's fine," she said.

The registrar started scribbling on the big book on her counter, stood up and said. "Let me get you your certificate now."

Catherine and Mira examined the certificate. "Tony is not mentioned. And also what's this, the 'n' and 'a' are a scribble. It looks like Doris, which is not right."

"Don't worry, Mira, it's just a piece of paper. When Tony is back we will have it changed."

Mira shrugged her shoulders and decided to avoid any confrontation. She took the opportunity to feed little Dorina in the Registrar's Office before they headed back home.

***

At the height of the summer Mira received her first letter from Tony. He had safely reached the training camp. "*We start training tomorrow morning. It's very warm here. I miss my little baby Dorina very much. I hope you are well, my love. I'll write a longer letter tomorrow. Be back soon.*"

Four short love letters later Tony wrote that his thirteenth infantry division was being mobilised to the

River Isonzo in the mountains above the Gulf of Trieste in the Adriatic. Here his infantry, he was told, would be in combat with the enemies' fifth army. *"It will be fine,"* he wrote, *"our commander Marshall Cadorna, knows what he is doing. A huge kiss to my little Dorina. See you soon."*

Mira had already started taking some interest in the local newspapers to learn of the war's progress. "Fredo, can you buy The Times every day. The local newspaper has no news about Italy."

"My dear, there is very little news in The Times too, and it's heavily censored. I fear we may never know much until Tony returns home."

Mira's more immediate concern, however, was Dorina's health. She was feeding poorly and she was having regular bouts of coughing. Occasionally there had been blood droplets in the mucous of her tiny mouth.

"Catherine, can you ask Mrs Rooney to visit? Dorina appears to be sick, I think she must have a fever."

Mrs Rooney instigated daily checks on the baby. Increasingly her breathing was accompanied by whistling from deep inside her lungs.

"There is little we can do, Mira, but pray," Mrs Rooney said a week later. "I'm afraid there are many children in the town who have the illness. Consumption it's called."

"I don't like the look of this. What can we do, there must be something surely. What's the cure?"

"They say this is a disease which is spread through the air. You yourself must be careful too, Mira. Maybe it's due to all the coal dust and grime which is forever in the air ever since the pit came to town." Mrs Rooney continued. "I suggest every day you take Dorina a long walk into the clear atmosphere of the hills. Or even along the coast but well away from the mine. This might help your baby to recover and it might avoid you being infected too."

As Mrs Rooney was leaving she continued. "And keep Dorina away from the other three children in the house. We don't want them infected too, do we?"

For the next three days Mira kept Dorina in her room in the small wooden box which Tony had constructed before he left. She ensured Dorina was warm and cosy in her bed and she covered her with a light blanket.

Dorina's cheeks seemed to be regaining some colour so Mira decided it was time for those long walks. The five miles walk to the Durham moors was brisk. Occasionally along the way she wiped away the perspiration on her baby's body. When it was time to turn back she sat firstly on a stile in a field coaxing Dorina to take her feed. She fed well. But on the next day at the same time on the same stile Dorina wasn't interested. Mira's mood on the way home depended on how her baby fed.

A week after Mrs Rooney's first visit, Mira was up at her usual time and she stretched out to pick up Dorina. She sensed immediately something was amiss. She let out a huge scream, "Dorina, *o Dio*, Dorina, *o Dio!*"

Catherine came rushing in and the two ladies collapsed together flooded in tears.

Dorina lay stiff in her little makeshift bed. Her skin tinged a shade of blue and the women could no longer make out any breathing. Catherine had already prepared herself for the moment. She had seen the symptoms before in her own family, an older brother, an aunt and her little toddler, aged seven. None of them had survived more than a few weeks after the first spates of coughing.

"Mira, Mira, it must be God's will," she said. "We have to remain strong. We have other children to look after."

Mira sat on her bed aimlessly and distraught. "Let me hold her, please. I need to hold her."

Catherine lifted up the little corpse and placed her carefully into Mira's waiting arms.

"We need to let Tony know. Oh Tony, Tony, where are you?" Mira sobbed. "Tony, I need you."

***

Mira was never able to make sense of her tragic loss. Her days took on a never changing routine. First thing every morning she went to the cemetery, where she prayed for Dorina's little soul and for Tony's safety, then she returned to the shop to clean, serve and do anything necessary to help Fredo and Catherine with their children. She needed to keep busy. At the cemetery Mira had met many women in similar circumstances and she realised she wasn't the only one in a state of permanent suffering.

The weeks passed quickly, Mira increasingly in despair. Not only had Mira lost her little girl but she was no longer receiving any letters from Tony.

"What is happening in this stupid war," Mira asked her older brother. "Will Tony ever return, please tell me?"

Fredo had taken it upon himself to keep in touch with the bulletins which were pinned to the noticeboard in the main street every day. He was reading as many newspapers he could get his hands on. A couple of times during the summer he had met with other Italians, once in Newcastle and once in Middlesbrough in an effort to obtain some news from the Italian front.

He called his sister to sit beside him.

"It seems that our boys, the Italians, are fighting in the mountains above Gorizia where the Slovenes live. The Austrians want access to the Adriatic along the Isonzo river but the Italians are fiercely defending their position. They have been battling all summer along the river and Mira, I am sorry to say that there have been many casualties on both sides."

"But no news is good news." Fredo continued. "Tony knows nothing about what has happened to Dorina so he has everything to live for, so I am sure he will remain very careful. Be positive, my dear, and keep praying."

Chapter 10

World War 1 - Tony's Story

On the train from Newcastle Tony met up with Leo Badiali, an eighteen year old from Ashington, a coastal town north of the city. His family had the identical emigration story. Poverty in Montecino, his father Santino decided to follow the elusive trail to riches, firstly to Glasgow to be trained in the rudimentary skills of ice cream and fish and chips and then to Ashington, a town on the North East coast to set up on his own account. Ashington was another coal town, a booming town of Irish immigrants and exiles from the English countryside no longer able to sustain an agricultural living for their families. Leo too, spent much of his time at the gates of the pit with his penny lick glasses and variety of lemonades.

"Why, Leo, why are you here? You were born in England."

"My father insisted that I do my duty for the motherland. He is very strict."

"If only I hadn't gone to the consul that day, they might never have found me," replied Tony.

"Actually my dad registered my birth back in Italy. When the war kicked off he even went to the consul to make sure my name was there, silly old fool. He really thinks we are going to get some land after this is over."

On their way to the training base in Cuneo, a military

town on the Italian side of the Alps, Tony and Leo spent the time mostly chatting over their respective love lives.

"My dad would kill me if I became a father before marriage. Funny thing is he told me that my mum was pregnant when they got married. I was born a month after their wedding." Leo looked across to Tony. "I wish I could have had you as a pal when I grew up. I had nobody. I have to always do what my dad tells me to do."

"Well, Leo, you are my pal now. Let's stick together."

The pair changed trains in London and another group of Italians joined them for the rest of the journey. The train to the English Channel was full of soldiers, a dozen or so Italians and the remainder British soldiers on their way to Flanders. The high pitched notes of 'Santa Lucia' couldn't compete with and were drowned out by the merrier choruses of 'It's a long way to Tipperary.'

"We'll sort them out in Flanders, and if you eyeties can do your business, the German hun will be forever beaten." The maiden soldiers, mostly young boys, had little idea what was ahead of them.

At Cuneo, Tony and Leo were assigned to the 3rd Alpini regiment.

"Your families were from the mountains, Le Alpe Apuane, the Apuan Alps," said the arrogant Italian Corporal in his pigeon English. "The mountains are in your blood, you will both be fine where you are going. Your training will include learning Italian too. Dismiss!"

***

During their time at Cuneo Leo stuck close to Tony, training together, eating together and writing letters back home together. Soon they were on their way on a special troop train to the Dolomites in the north of the country where the mighty soldiers of the Austrian army were already lying in wait.

None of the boys on the train had been informed of the previous skirmishes with the Austrians on the Isonzo river. They had little idea that the mountain region of the South Tyrol had been in dispute for centuries. Many times in the past the area had been subjected to land grabbing by both sides. Local wars had resulted. They had no inkling whatsoever of the prevailing politics of a secret treaty in London earlier in the year, whereby, as part of the agreement that Italy choose to side with the British and French, it had been promised the lands inhabited by ethnic Slovenes at the northern tip of the Adriatic Sea. These were the lands crisscrossed by the Isonzo. Trouble was the Austrians weren't ready to yield these lands.

The boys were equally oblivious to the fact that the Isonzo river was already a conflict zone. Italian soldiers had been in hand to hand combat with the Austrians for six months. But their task this time was simple, the generals had said, to prevent the enemy from reaching the Venetian plains and Venice to the south and to push them back to the other side of the Alps. Several weeks previously, at the first battle of the Isonzo, despite having double the amount of troops than the Austrians themselves, the Italians hadn't been able to dislodge their enemy from high mountain strongholds. It had become clear to the Italian generals that fighting uphill against an enemy was severely disadvantageous and a horrendous number of casualties ensued. Two weeks later, following the arrival of more than a quarter of a million additional resources, and only after deploying more appropriate tactics in a second battle, were some of the mountain top positions recaptured.

This was the third offensive. Tony and Leo were ably trained and fully kitted. The aim was to take the region known as the Caporetto, an area of plateaus, ragged mountains and unforgiving terrain.

The boys were in a troop of a hundred soldiers, mostly young raw recruits. After two days trekking upwards on rocky slopes, in sharp contrast to the flat plains below, the troop reached a vertical face of rock about a mile wide and fifty yards high.

"We are close to the front. Over and above this rock face there is a plateau where our reconnaissance team has informed us, there are trenches we built in the previous offensives. We'll spend the night there," said the sergeant offering some encouragement to the boys in advance of the climb.

"We might have mountains in our blood," said Tony to an anxious Leo, "but we never climbed rock faces like these in Montecino."

The three more senior soldiers took command. They steered the climbing process ensuring that the group all reached the summit of the rock face safely.

The weather was favourable and for days previously there had been no clouds in the sky. Days were warm, however nights were becoming increasingly colder as the autumn air rapidly cooled.

With aching limbs, the troop reached the summit in good order and they quickly found the trenches which had been used in the previous offensive.

"Tomorrow we join the battle, we need to be tuned and ready. Our soldiers have already engaged near the river. The enemy's close. Remember your training and be vigilant at all times," said the sergeant. "Any danger, shoot to kill."

As day morphed into night the silence in the dark

was deafening. '*Eerily quiet*,' thought Tony. '*This is supposed to be a war zone*.'

Tony and Leo lay horizontal in the trench and they struggled to keep warm in the deep chill. They were engrossed at the beauty of the night sky. "Feels like you could stand up and pull down one of those stars, then throw them back," Tony said.

"What a magnificent sight," replied Leo. "Strange, you can hardly see the sky itself. I never knew there were so many stars. What an experience! I've never seen this before."

"In Errington, there's no way of knowing what outdoor life is like. Back home when I was a boy and we slept in the fields we would gaze at the sky recalling the good times, the feasts, the music. We would dream of beautiful women and of being in love." Tony paused for a moment. "But right now I am thinking of my Mira and our little Dorina. She has beautiful long black hair, you know."

"Lucky you."

"I will never leave them again, never."

Conversation ended and the pair fell into deep sleep.

Tony had no idea of the time when he awoke. He nudged Leo on his shoulder.

"Look, Leo, the colour of the sky!"

Tony scrambled up, climbed onto a wooden slat and perched himself up to glance at the golden ball, that was the sun rising from the east. It filled the horizon completely. He squinted and rubbed his eyes. Tony saw little, he was momentarily blinded.

"Let me up!" Leo held his right hand upwards.

A rounds of gunfire suddenly pierced the silence. Dramatically the world slowed down. Tony's legs gave way. Leo felt warm splashes of liquid on his face. His right hand was covered in blood. Then the dawning! Tony had been shot. There was no head attached to body. "Tony, Tony, no, no!"

Leo sprang up and grabbed his rifle but it was too late. More gunfire rained towards the trench, which was rapidly immersed in thick smoke. He thought he heard the muffled voice of his sergeant. '*Stay down, stay down*.' But Leo froze in the glare of the sun. Where was he, what was happening! He peered at the silhouettes of two soldiers armed with rifles. Further shots rang out, and Leo too, plunged into deep darkness. He was no more.

The battle raged on for less than an hour. The troop had been caught unaware and the surprise attack by the enemy devastatingly brutal. The young recruits hadn't yet shot their guns in anger. For the hundred young men, including Tony, their war was over before it had begun.

Chapter 11

1918

"Fredo, when will this war end," said Catherine. "They told me that one of those balloon like airships was flying over again yesterday, zeppelins they call them. I am afraid that one day they might bomb us again. Look at the damage they did last year when they dropped their bombs on Hartlepool. I pity these people. That was the second time the town has been bombed. I thank God we managed to shoot one down last year, but they keep coming back."

"Never saw it."

"They said it was flying high in the clouds. Nobody noticed it and they never heard it coming. The soldiers on watch could do nothing. Some people were killed after it dropped its bomb near the railway station." Catherine continued. "It's like an invisible killing machine. What can we do?"

"Well, very little from here, dear Catherine. All we can do is hope and pray the war will end soon, and that the new baby will be fine when it comes."

Catherine ignored the baby remarks. "We have lost so any men from the town. Do our generals really know what they are doing? The papers are talking of a million British dead. Can it really be so?"

"Then there must be a million Germans dead, a million Austrians, a million Italians, who knows." replied

Fredo. "We can only concentrate on our own little family, now that another's on the way."

Shortly afterwards at the end of spring Catherine gave birth to her fourth child, Alfred. 'No more Italian style names," Fredo declared the day of the birth. "We are British now, our livelihood depends on this community which has sacrificed so much. We owe it to them."

Indeed the business had become a focal point of the community. Catherine recognised virtually every woman in the town as a customer. It seemed that almost daily, she would hear of yet another casualty in the trenches.

"No family has been unaffected. Mine, we've lost a few cousins and uncles and poor Mira, at last, she can grieve. Your visits to the consul finally achieved something."

Faithfully every month for over two years, Fredo had made the trek to Newcastle to the Italian Consular Office to receive any updates about what had happened to Tony. The letters had dried up so soon after his departure and it seemed clear, and eventually to Mira, that Tony might no longer be returning. At the consular offices Fredo had studied the bulletins carefully, he had met other Italians in the city and he realised that Italy, too, had lost hundreds of thousands of men.

On his latest visit earlier in the week Fredo obtained the confirmation. The official record stated Tony had been lost in action during the last week of October of 1915, probably the twenty fifth, when the Italians had launched another offensive in the Caporetto, on what became known as the Third Battle of the Isonzo. His body was never found. This was the primary reason, the consul said, why details of Tony's demise had never been released previously. "They simply had to be sure," the consul insisted.

"*Typical Italian bureaucracy*," Fredo thought. "*Over two years to find out he never returned to his billets. Che pazzi! What idiots! In Errington it takes no more than a week or two for the poor women to receive their post.*"

When Mira received the news the coincidence was remarkable. "Twenty fifth of October," she gasped. "Precisely the date on which baby Dorina passed away."

Mira held the consul's official letter in her hands. "I cannot believe it, on the same day, I lost the two loves of my life."

Catherine put her arms around Mira's shoulder. "Maybe that's the way it was meant to be. They'll both be together in heaven looking down on us."

"No, no, I will never believe Tony is dead, maybe he escaped, perhaps taken prisoner. I won't believe it. Or he ran away to return home. He must be out there waiting until the war is over. One day my Tony will turn up looking for his little girl, and she won't be here. What shall I say to him?"

"Mira, he won't come back, you have to believe that."

"No, Catherine, no, he will be back."

Mira slowly made her way upstairs and Fredo glanced over to Catherine. "We need to keep an eye on her. I am concerned. The truth will soon dawn on her and it will hurt."

"Of course, I will. No need to worry. Now what about this letter we received from Dino."

As the eldest in the family, Fredo's big brother, Dino, had been entitled to inherit the rights to work the land in Montecino when their father passed away. Whereas

Fredo had left in his teenage years, Dino had returned from his adventures in Hamburg to marry his childhood sweetheart, Emilia, at the turn of the century. Within two years their first two children were born, both girls.

At the time a couple of families from Montecino had been seduced by opportunities available in Marseilles in France. Rumours were that there was a plentiful supply of work and as a bonus there was no shortage of sunshine in Southern France. Shipbuilding was booming in a city which was ideally situated on the main trading route between Europe and Africa. Local gossip was that these two families were making a great living in Marseille. Finally Dino, too, was seduced to emigrate for a second time and he took the plunge. He surrendered the land rights to his younger brother, Luigi, and he moved with his young family to the cosmopolitan city within two years of his marriage. In Marseille another girl and three boys were born.

"Dear Fredo............." the letter contained the usual list of family news, *"........for the war effort, Marseille has become a staging post for all sorts of troops, French from Africa, British also, before they are re-assigned elsewhere. Our eldest daughter Ida has fallen in love with a British soldier. He is from the Newcastle area. When the war is over, they want to get married in England. It would be great if you could help to look after our Ida until they are married. He would be keen to obtain work locally, even in the mine there in Errington. Maybe they could get married there too. I need your help, Ida insists on going. She is so young, only sixteen and I do hope this guy is serious. If you ever think he is not what he seems, you could send her back to us."*

"What do you think of this," said Fredo.

"Ida would certainly be able to help us," Catherine

replied, "I hope once this war is over we can get back to some normality."

"Well, that depends, how many of our boys from the town return safely."

"And, of course, it might be good for Mira to have another younger woman around. After all Ida is her cousin."

"Stop talking like a middle aged old lady. You are still young as well, Catherine, and in any case, it might never happen, young love can come and go very quickly."

Fredo replied to his brother. Ida would be fully welcomed in Errington despite her tender age. He took the opportunity to ask Dino for information on the war from the French viewpoint. Maybe the English newspaper reports were being manipulated, he thought. Fredo desired an alternative perspective.

Dino's return letter was very explicit. "*Here in Marseille we are far away from the action but we obtain lots of information from the British troops. The Allies and the Germans have been fighting for three years now in Flanders on the River Somme. They have dug themselves into trenches which stretch almost four hundred miles from the Swiss border to the sea. The trenches between the opposing armies are probably only fifty to a hundred yards apart. Seems that often there are periods of intense shelling when the two sides are focussed on capturing the middle ground between the trenches. Then it's retreat and back to their trenches. The middle ground remains. It's crazy warfare, men, boys, on both sides, losing their lives for little gain. They say the conditions in these trenches are awful. Conditions are cramped, wet, cold and ridden with disease. But the generals who issue the instructions, they stay back behind the lines in comfortable lodgings.*

If these generals were to experience life in these trenches, no doubt the war would be over by now. I just don't know, dear brother, when this madness will end. War is war. I know we have to fight to defend our rights and lands from invaders and evil tyrants, but not in this way. Lives aimlessly lost. Maybe somebody will see some sense soon. Who and how can we end this? Our leaders seem toothless."

"Dino is right," said Fredo. "In war, a nation needs strong leadership. We have to fight when we need to. Of that there is no doubt, but strong leaders should know when it's time to change direction or amend strategy. If there are no soldiers left when the fighting is over, then what really is the point? Maybe soon somebody will have the foresight to end this carnage."

Indeed the end did come soon later in the year. The German high command had informed the Kaiser that its military situation was hopeless and that there was no guarantee that their front could hold out much longer. In order to save face they had requested the Kaiser to call for an immediate ceasefire and an end to the fighting. After much negotiation and discussion on a train in a forest outside Paris on the eleventh hour of the eleventh day in the eleventh month, the British and French accepted the German surrender. After German financial reparations were decided a truce was agreed and an armistice was signed. The soldiers who survived in this war to end all wars were free to return home to their families.

Chapter 12

1920

More than a year had passed since the end of the war and the pit's workforce had been restored to pre-war levels. As the survivors returned to the town, the heavy price paid by the town's families was evident. However many never made it back. The vicar at the local church, St Mary the Virgin, had placed a notice with details of over two hundred who lost their lives in the conflict. On the notice he pleaded for moral and financial support to those who did return, so many with limbs missing, and particularly for patience and understanding for those who had suffered mentally. It was disturbing, he wrote, the sight of some returning soldiers, although not limbless, who were marching up and down Station Road, invisible rifles on their shoulders, and darting in and out of the shop doorways to take cover from passing ladies laden with heavy shopping bags.

"These poor souls have been unable to return to their normal lives," Catherine had noted after the pastor placed another bulletin on the notice board on the anniversary of the end of the war. "What do you think is wrong with them, Fredo?"

"They must have seen some terrible and horrific sights, arms and legs torn apart from torsos. They must have been terrified. And they were supposed to be back after a few months, remember. These politicians, I bet they never lost their limbs or their minds. Seems a huge waste to me."

"What can we do, is there anything?"

"I don't know. I think, treat them as normal as possible. Be kind, gentle and sincere when we talk to these poor souls." Fredo replied. "We should be courteous, ask what support they might need from us. Maybe we should tell the girls to give them an extra scoopful of ice cream. Or more chips than usual."

"Above all, Catherine, we should ensure all this is never forgotten, the dead, the injured, those who have lost their mind. Let's discuss this with the pastor and the priest to see what we can do as a community."

***

Fredo sucked deeply on his pipe before finishing off his morning coffee.

"It's great we have Ida with us," Catherine said. "She and Mira are working very well together, especially since the business is improving again."

"And great too," Fredo replied, "that Lewis has now learned the ropes and ably replacing Tony at the pit gates with the cart. He has learned so quickly. He has yet to turn thirteen. The miners love his boisterous charm and banter."

"Do you think our next child will also have the same boisterous charm?" replied Catherine.

"What Alfred, you mean."

"No, not Alfred, the next one, the one in my stomach." Catherine beamed, huge smile across her face.

It took a few moments for Fredo to register what his wife had said. He sprang from his seat and sprinted over to her wrapping his huge arms around her. "Oh, Catherine, fantastic, another little Baldini," and the pair embraced and kissed.

Fredo's thoughts jumped to accommodation. "We'll need to change a few things around here now. Soon there will be five children. With Mira and Ida, that makes nine of us in total. I'll have something built in the yard to provide us with an extra room."

Later in the day Lewis was presented with a list of requirements with which to enquire at the pit gates. Within days he had his tradesmen, bricklayer, roofer and carpenter. A week later the shell of the small extra room was complete. It was fully weatherproof well before the birth of the new arrival. There were no shortage of labourers who, in return, were granted free fish and chips and ice cream for their kids. No questions were asked regarding the source of the materials.

***

"It's taken nearly six years for our business to return to normal. We have more mouths to feed so we need to earn more money," said Fredo. "You've seen these motor cars in the street, Catherine. The pit owner has one and a couple of the managers too, what if we had a motorised cart instead of what we have now."

"Are you sure, you have no idea how they work," replied Catherine. "Can we afford it? Where do we buy one?"

"In his last letter Vincenzo in Stanley told me he bought one. He says they are great, easy to run. They can travel up hills with no effort and they are much more efficient. No need for horses and all that mess. It would mean we could sell at the Seaham and Hartlepool pits as well. This could double our income. We can teach Lewis to drive. We have to be able to make more money."

"I do hope you are right. I've always trusted in your

decisions."

"Vincenzo gave me the details of a place in Newcastle which specialises in building the carts. We can have our names painted on them. In fact our first cart should be in Lewis' name as one day he will own the whole business."

"Careful, Fredo, remember what you always said soon after I met you." Catherine said wagging her finger in his direction. "You said you hated the situation in Italy, where the eldest son inherited everything and the rest of the children nothing. Here in England you promised, all our children would share equally, including the girls."

"I got carried away for a moment, yes, you are right, the children must share equally. No special privileges for Lewis."

The following week Fredo was in Newcastle ordering his first motorised cart.

***

Mira's incessant workload helped her ease the pain of Dorina's death. Occasionally she seemed too distracted from her job, daydreaming of Tony's return, despite Catherine repeatedly urging her to face her reality. But very slowly smiles were returning and the Mira of old, warm hearted, jolly and very talkative, was returning. "You will never forget your first love, Mira, but you have to try to move on."

Catherine's watchful eyes weren't solely concentrating on Mira but more so on Ida. Her love, John Bolton, a former soldier from the Royal Army Ordnance Corps had been demobbed and resettled in Durham city. The couple's love affair had been rekindled. For over six months John had made his trip from Durham to Errington every Sunday to spend time with Ida. Typically they strolled around the town for two or three hours before John's return home. Catherine was burdened with responsibility. Even although Ida had turned eighteen she was finding it difficult to refuse Ida's requests to travel to Durham to visit John. Ida wanted to meet John's family, she had insisted. Eventually Catherine found some consolation. She convinced herself John was noble and honourable and that he had the best of intentions.

"The first time you go, Ida, why don't you take Mira with you? Thereafter you can go on your own." Catherine proposed.

She was relieved Ida agreed.

"Actually John suggested it too, that bringing Mira would be a good idea."

The ladies agreed the protocol. Ida's first trip to Durham passed without incident. "Yes," confirmed Mira later. "True love is in the air. Their relationship is genuine."

***

In the meantime, little Remo was born, a healthy boy weighing exactly seven pounds.

As was the norm, Mrs Rooney assisted at the birth. Initially she visited Catherine twice weekly to ensure the baby was growing healthily.

"Strange name, where's that from?" enquired Mrs Rooney.

"It's one of Fredo's many middle names," replied Catherine.

Two months on, however, Mrs Rooney became anxious. "Catherine, I am a little concerned, the baby has fever and diarrhoea. This doesn't look good. Is he feeding well?"

"Maybe a little less than usual, but I am not

particularly concerned."

"You heard of this Spanish Flu, I suppose," Mrs Rooney remarked. "All over the world in the last two years millions of people have died and they are still dying. I don't want to alarm you unnecessarily but we have to keep a close eye on Remo in case this awful virus has arrived at your door."

Mrs Rooney continued, "If, in the next few days you see any dark spots on the baby's cheeks or notice his skin turning a shade of blue, please let me know immediately." She was standing up to leave, "oh, and by the way, purely as a precaution, please keep the baby away from your other children. This flu is very contagious. Children are more susceptible than adults of catching the infection so you have to be careful."

Catherine couldn't bear thinking about another baby death. The memory of Mira's loss was still ingrained in her consciousness.

Two days passed. No need for any fuss. Remo seemed to be recovering. But on the morning of the third day Catherine noticed the fateful dark spots.

"Mrs Rooney, Mrs Rooney," she cried as she ran out into the street, "please come quickly."

Meanwhile, Fredo and Ida were apprehensive, fearing the worst. Remo lay in Mira's arms. He was finding it difficult to breathe. His fragile little body seemed to be turning blue all over. "Please don't go, my little baby, not again, please don't go, please stay with me, *Ave Maria,* Hail Mary." Mira's face was raining tears.

Mrs Rooney examined the child but she knew instinctively it was too late. There was little she could do. The room echoed in silence. After a few moments Catherine gently placed the baby into his tiny makeshift cot and kissed his little forehead. Indeed she knew too his short life was over. Remo's temple was ice cold and his body lifeless. The family slumped to their knees and prayed silently. Catherine extracted the rosary beads from the pocket of her dress and the family knelt together reciting the mysteries of Our Lady.

At the cemetery Remo's tiny wooden coffin was placed side by side with his cousin Dorina. "I'll arrange a plate just like Dorina's," Mira said. Two months previously Mira had affixed a silver plate on her headstone which stated, "Dorina, here lies a little girl who died on the same day her father Tony went missing in Italy, October, 1914."

The family had chosen the words for Dorina's plaque very carefully. Tony was missing. Mira was delighted that there was no indication of Tony's death. Now they needed the correct words for another plaque.

"Now I hope the two unfortunate little human beings can rest in peace together," Father Donovan said.

"And I hope, too, we'll never have to return here with any more tiny coffins." Catherine replied.

***

The end of the war had brought with it new legislation regarding immigrants and immigration.

"I have been reading in the newspapers, that soon I will have to register with the police." said Fredo. "Can you believe it, I have been here for over twenty years and I am still being regarded as a foreign alien."

"You mean all of us," Catherine said.

"No, just me, I believe. Listen to this from the Times, *'The 1919 Alien Restriction Act obliges foreign nationals to have an identity card and to register with the police to enable undesirables to be deported and to restrict where they can live. It is targeted at aliens to restrict employment rights and to bar them from public service jobs. It is targeted primarily at criminals, paupers and undesirables and it is illegal for aliens to take part in industrial action. The motivation is to end wartime labour shortages and to safeguard jobs for indigenous Britons.'*

"Surely you don't have to worry. You're not a criminal, pauper or an undesirable," Catherine said, "unless that is, there is something you don't want to tell me."

"You mean, you think maybe I am a spy, like that Mata Hari lady? I doubt it, my dear. All I do is sell lemonade, ice cream or some fish and chips. The only people I ever come into contact with, concentrate their lives on scratching a living in those awful pits. That hardly qualifies me a spy."

"But that's exactly what a spy does," Catherine said, "blends into their surroundings, no questions asked."

"Let's be serious for a moment," as Fredo inhaled on his pipe. "There are some very proud Italians who would never surrender their heritage but I am determined. I want to be British. I need to find out what's necessary to become a British citizen. Nobody can guess the future."

"But what about your children's heritage."

"I won't forget why I left Italy. One day, for sure, we can return for a long holiday, soak up the sun and lunch on homemade *pane e prosciutto,* bread and ham with some juicy tomatoes and a glass of lovely wine. But that's about it. My life is here with you and the children."

"Your whole life, don't you dare threaten me with that, Fredo," Catherine burst out laughing. He looked puzzled. "My dear, British style joke. Laugh with me, I am only joking."

"I definitely feel British now. I am becoming a British citizen. That's my decision."

"Fine and it's great you have come to a decision. Now you should go and check out if that brand new ice cream cart is finished. It's costing us loads of money and we need to find a lot more business to pay for it."

Chapter 13

1922

Post war Errington was typical of all coal mining towns. Pits had been obliged to ramp up production levels to rebuild the ravaged economy. There was plenty of work for new generations of young boys. Women and girls had mostly returned to domestic duties. In the town a revitalised sense of optimism pervaded. Meanwhile Fredo was intent on trying to understand the economic state of the day. Nobody else in the town had any inclination to read The Times so the newsagent was taken aback with a special order. One daily copy for Fredo Baldini.

Before the war the British Empire had been regarded as a superpower. It had been estimated that three quarters of a million servicemen had lost their lives in the war and nearly two million wounded. The conflict had caused a huge decline in economic production. Since so many able bodied men had signed up during the war for the armed forces, the country had to rely on the United States for its raw materials and food supplies. Factories whose production had been switched over for various munitions and military hardware had found great difficulties in re-establishing themselves. Now post war, the economy was stagnating and there was the need to pay off billions of debt to the United States. In addition war orders for military hardware had dried up causing further depression.

However Fredo was suspicious of the post war analysis by the economic experts. It didn't match the environment in Errington. His calculation was that production at the coal mine was appearing to be back to its normal levels. Furthermore his own personal economic situation was improving despite quoted doom and gloom stories of high unemployment in the newspapers.

Two years previously the government had passed laws forcing a reduction in working hours to a maximum of forty eight hours per week. Fredo's business benefitted. Instead of the mine operating on a two shift system six days a week before the war, it was now working on three shifts daily. Indeed, less working hours for miners but it meant that Lewis was at the pit gates three times a day instead of twice. The consequence was more income and more profit. The miners were spending more with Lewis and from virtually the same earnings. This went some way to help pay off part of Fredo's loan for the motorised cart.

Lewis, the strapping fifteen year old, was in charge of the cart and Edward, now twelve, was ever keen to help him. The teamwork operated well. Their patter optimised takings. "A tab and a pop, a hokey pokey, get it here."

Lewis had long gangly legs just like his father and he relished the fact that at shift changes, there were many young girls about his age waiting for their dads. He assumed the girls were there just to see him but in fact their mission was more specific. Their mums had drilled them well. The girls' job was to ensure their dads never put too much money on the tab. Furthermore on Fridays when the men were paid, the girls had a further role. A role as chaperone. Dads were not allowed to spend any of their hard earned wages at the pub on their way home. Pay packets were to remain intact.

While the boys were at the pit gates selling, Vera, as eldest daughter, was usually at home on domestic chores. Her work was ceaseless. Not only did she work at the counter but was always on hand to assist her mum and two siblings, Alfred, four, and Christine, just a year old. Catherine was slow to notice that Vera was establishing a reputation, the beauty at the café with her dark hair and olive complexion. When young lads entered the shop Vera's sweet smile beamed from ear to ear. But mum and dad already had other intentions for their eldest daughter.

Mira's interest in any new relationships had waned completely. Almost every day Mira found time to say a few prayers at Dorina's gravesite. At the same time she prayed for the miracle that one day Tony would arrive on the doorstep of the shop to restart his life with her. However whilst her heart constantly hoped, her head was telling her Tony was gone forever. Her principal delight was that the daily grind to the washhouse was no longer her responsibility.

At the washhouse the ladies of the town indulged in local gossip. Catherine liked to keep her linen and her kids' clothes spotless at all times. Good hygiene, she had concluded, was the best way to avoid her children contracting contagious diseases. As a result Vera was at the washhouse every day before lunchtime, and now she was taking Ida to help her improve on her English and accelerate her command of the language. The ladies in the town made the rules. Mornings were for daughters, evenings for mothers and elder ladies all to themselves. During these evening sessions the assembled mothers openly shared their family secrets including detail of extraordinary night time experiences in bed. The washhouse language in the evenings, Catherine knew, was too advanced and obscene, no place for still innocent young girls.

All the while Ida was busy preparing for her wedding to John. They decided to marry in the local church and Father Donovan was only too pleased to perform the ceremony. Emilia, her mother, was aware of Ida's long term plan and she had the foresight to ensure she took all her certificates with her, birth, baptism and confirmation, before she left Marseilles.

"It's great to see that the French authorities are more organised than the Italian ones." Father Donovan said to the couple at their first visit to the church. Father Donovan never examined the documents. He counted the three pieces of paper and nodded, "Yes, certificates in order," he said before handing them back to Ida. He never realised the certificates were actually in Italian, not French. When Ida later recounted the story of the documents with the priest, Mira fumed. "We could have given him any old document, even a false one. That old fool would never have known."

Meanwhile Fredo and Catherine were figuring out how to accommodate Dino and Emilia for the impending wedding.

"A week is a long time for them to be all cramped up in here," Fredo said. "We have little option but to find them lodgings at the Masons Arms up the road."

"Agreed," replied Catherine. "They can remain with us all day, but overnight they can sleep there. It's just fifteen minutes' walk."

"Job done. Another thing I need to talk to you about."

"I have something too for you. You go first, Fredo."

"You know the town has lost all those men in the war, over two hundred. The Vicar at St Mary's, Father Donovan and the pastor at the Wesleyan chapel have suggested we should convene to organise some sort of memorial to honour our dead. Since we have one of the biggest businesses on the main street, they asked me to be part of the group."

"What would that involve?"

"Well, we would need to find a suitable site and raise some money to fund the building of the memorial. Also we would need to gather a list of all men who died so we can arrange to have their names inscribed. What do you think?"

"What about Tony. Would he be included too?"

"Well, we must assume he's dead. Would he qualify anyway, being Italian?"

"Don't be daft, Fredo, of course, he would. He's from the town, isn't he? Some of those who died were born in Ireland, so what's the difference. In fact, as my dad loves to keep reminding me, Ireland is now a foreign country after all that Easter Rising and political stuff. Amazing, isn't it, that Tony is no more a foreigner than my dad now."

"You're right. Let's make sure that, for Mira's sake, Tony's name is on the memorial as well. Now what did you want to say."

"When I was in church yesterday I found out the parish has plans to build a new church right here in Errington. The old church in the village is too small to cater for the increase in the congregation. Our catholic population has ballooned. Maybe it's all that hard work which makes our men so lecherous!"

"So, what is it we can do?"

"Not a lot really, but they, too, need money to build the church. Most of it, Father Donovan says, will come for the Diocese's funds, and there will be additional collections at Mass. They will expect us to contribute more into the plate," replied Catherine, "and they'll expect us to have some money raising events of our own."

"Then we'll be able to save some money if we don't go to Mass," said Fredo with a sarcastic smile on his face.

"No, my dear, you will not miss Mass. And I do hope you are joking. We can't do that. We have to go. So many of our customers are catholic and they take their religion very seriously. And remember some of them owe us money. We need to be seen at church."

"Of course, I'm joking, dear! Don't worry, we will play our part in this as well."

"Everybody needs money these days. Talking about churches remember I told you about the earthquake in Valbona a couple of years ago. Well, Vincenzo has informed me that even they are appealing to us for any spare funds. They need to rebuild the Duomo, the main church tower which was badly damaged. It nearly collapsed. He also said that many of the houses in Montecino were damaged too."

"You haven't been back in nearly twenty years. Maybe you should think about returning soon. You never know, you might never see your mama and papa again."

"I'll think about it. If I do go, it has to be in October or November when the ice cream sales have tailed off. Do you think Lewis and Edward, between them, can manage and be left on their own?"

"I am sure. We girls can concentrate on the shop, no

bother. Lewis is a fine lad, switched on. Of course, he'll manage. The cart is safe in his hands. You would be gone for a short time anyway, only two or three weeks and the trains to Italy are faster nowadays, less than two days now, I think."

"But we were saving up to buy one of those automobiles, those motor cars. Up in Newcastle you see lots of them around."

"You can buy your motor car in a few years' time, your mama and papa might not be around in a couple of years. So you must go to see them instead. If Topolino is still around you should find out from him the best way and the best time to go."

"Next week, I will see Vincenzo and try to meet Topolino."

***

Fredo was shocked at the latest news from Vincenzo about events back in Valbona. The earthquake had caused great damage not just to the Duomo cathedral but to most of the buildings in *Valbona Vecchia.* Old Valbona was the part of town built in medieval times which had already survived many previous earthquakes. Its outer walls had survived every earthquake intact. They were built well, he said, designed to keep Valbona's traditional enemies out at all costs. The masons who had constructed the walls eight hundred years previously had done the perfect job.

Vincenzo commented that his own home in Montecino had somehow caught fire during the earthquake and was totally destroyed. However the Baldini family home, he was told, had remained intact and habitable. Most of the other houses in the village had suffered some form of damage. But the locals were resilient. They were accustomed to damaging earthquakes. When the aftershocks died down, they had started work on refurbishment and rebuild immediately.

"These people are robust," Vincenzo said. "It's in their blood, they expect these quakes every now and then. For them life has to continue nonetheless." Vincenzo paused for a moment. "Maybe the earthquake was God's revenge that so many of us emigrated. When I have made enough money I'll return home. I'll make sure the house I build will withstand any earthquake."

"You might want to go back some day, but I am staying here in England. All our kids are English and none of them speak any Italian. I won't forget what happened to my sisters, maybe the same happened to my mum, I don't know, and to all my *nonnas,* grandmas before that as well."

Just as the two colleagues embraced to say goodbye, Vincenzo remembered the prime purpose of Fredo's visit. "By the way, we never saw Topolino again after he left here with a sack load of my money two years ago. We don't know what happened. If you see him over there enjoying the fruits of our money, tell him he owes us. I will collect from him, for sure. And be certain to tell him that I'm serious. I will collect and more."

Vincenzo continued. "When you are in Newcastle to arrange your travel documents, go to Benny's in Pilgrim Street. He'll give you the name of the new courier."

***

In Newcastle Fredo had little trouble in obtaining the travel documents for his journey. On his way out of the consular office he picked up a bundle of pamphlets lying on a table with a photograph of a heavy boned gentleman on the front cover. Below the photograph there was a name in bold lettering, '*Benito Mussolini,*

Partito Socialisto Italiano." I wonder who he is, Fredo thought.

***

Dino and Vittoria Baldini were in their sixties and they laid out a huge welcome party for their prodigal son. The locals had tracked down a wild boar and the whole village had been invited to the feast.

After sixty hours of weary travel, and changing trains in the smoky cities of London, Paris and Pisa, Fredo was struck by the crisp freshness of the air as he stood on the platform at Valbona train station. He watched the local steam train slowly puff along out of sight to its next stop. He breathed a mouthful. He felt fantastic. His tired limbs seemed to have been magically invigorated.

Fredo hadn't returned to his homeland for over twenty years. When he left all those years ago, there was no railway between Pisa and Valbona, just dusty roads suitable only for carts and their horses. He had marvelled at the huge villa style buildings masquerading as trains stations constructed all the way along the line from Lucca. As he strode out proudly to the main piazza outside the station where Dino and Vittoria were waiting, he took another deep breath, *finalmente aria fresca,* fresh air at last. The three remained in a full embrace for several minutes before the cart was loaded and Dino's horse galloped away towards Valbona, three miles away.

The cart was deposited at the local stables in Ronchi, and the group embarked on the winding ascent towards Montecino on the *mulatierra*, the mule track.

"Nothing has changed here," he said to his parents.

"It will be some time before one of those motor cars can reach Montecino. Certainly not in my lifetime, Fredo, maybe not even in yours. So until then we have to carry on doing what we have always been doing, walk. Come on, Fredo, let's sing some songs on the way up."

Slowly the three ascended the mule track stopping occasionally for a break. As they passed houses adjacent to the mule track they delighted in hearing locals joining in on the singing.

"*Avanti, un vinetto,* sit down and have a glass of wine." The residents needed little excuse for a quick glass of wine.

After four house stops, and endlessly long tales of war and earthquakes to accompany their wine and coffee they finally arrived in Montecino.

Fredo immediately got a fix on the effects of the earthquake. Many buildings had damaged walls, some still had holes on the roof where tiles had broken free and in some cases Fredo noticed that houses had disappeared altogether.

"Our house suffered minimal damage," Dino said, "but look there at the Vincentis, their house was destroyed, all gone."

***

At the feast later in the evening Fredo had to sample every part of the boar.

"This is the tastiest meat I have ever had since…………..well since I was last here." He said tipsily after his third glass of wine, "and the wine, I never realised it was so strong. My head is beginning to spin. Let's have a song."

"Actually," said his mamma, "the wine isn't so strong. He's not used to drinking it any more. So look now, a few glasses and he wants a party."

"I know but isn't just great to have him back for a while?" replied babbo.

The following day Fredo strolled round the village to meet his pals of long ago. He listened keenly to the stories of tragedy, of men who never came back from the Isonzo. Gossip was that over a hundred from Valbona and its surrounding parishes never returned from the war. Just like the two hundred in Errington, Fredo thought, men and boys who were forced to fight for a pointless cause initiated by war hungry politicians.

"Babbo, what about those who did come back from America and England to fight in the war, did they ever receive the land which they were promised?"

"No, Fredo, as a wise old man, trust me, these politicians, they say one thing and then they do another. I despise them. They don't know what hard work is. These government people, they are only in it for the money. They talk, they talk and they talk more, meanwhile their pockets fill with gold. Do they really care for us, the poor people?"

"But this new guy, Mussolini, he's a socialist, so maybe it will all change now, surely." Fredo uttered. He anticipated that his dad's response was likely to be the same as his. He shared his dad's contempt for politicians.

"Socialists, communists, they are all the same. They blame anybody and everybody for the country's problems. Then to obtain votes they guarantee paradise, a land of milk and honey. You watch what happens now in this country. *Bimbo*, boy it's all about ego and power. When you return to England, you keep working hard and you provide for that wonderful family of yours. And make sure you fight all the way for real freedom and real democracy."

Fredo was keen to participate in the autumn harvest activities during his stay. He hadn't experienced any farming life since he was teenager. He relished, in particular, taking part in *la vendemmia,* the harvesting of the grapes, rolling up his trousers, removing his socks and plunging his feet into the barrel to squelch the grapes of its juice. Then there was the threshing of the wheat crops. He was thrilled to grab a long handed sickle to thresh away at the foliage, its grain later converted into flour for baking bread. He loved the traditions of the old days.

"*Attento alle vibere*, watch out for the poisonous snakes," Fredo was advised. But really he had no fear. He excited at spying one in the foliage. Momentarily he marvelled at its beautifully patterned skin. Then with a swoosh of his sickle, the snake was no more a threat. In its capture he realised he had lost none of his skills. Tradition was that for any man who strode into the village with a dead *vibera* around his neck, a glass of wine was offered at every house he passed. That night he staggered home. He never could recall where he left the carcass of the *vibera*.

On his gossip rounds Fredo learned of every death in the village since he first left. Tittle tattle of deaths, illnesses and diseases was normal but now the main topic of local conversation was the so called March on Rome by a certain Mr Mussolini, the story of which, was being reported at large every day in the local newspaper.

In the previous year's general election Benito Mussolini had been elected to the Italian parliament for the first time. He had been inspired by the communist revolution in Russia several years before and now his Italian Socialist party was making rapid advances. Since the war ended Italy had been in political turmoil. Factory workers had complained of their appalling working conditions. Union representation had swept through all the factories in the north of the country, particularly at the brand new Fiat motor car plant in Turin. Management had clashed heavily with unions who wanted total control of production along communist principles. The progressively volatile situation had led to a nationwide general strike. Many factories had been occupied by their workers. Chaos reigned supreme. Political assassinations were a common occurrence. In an effort to restore stability the government had banned unions. But the government strategy failed and turmoil prevailed. Violence in the streets had increased to such an extent that the government had no option but to declare martial law. The opportunistic Mussolini sought to use the turmoil to impose himself as the national leader. He was in prime position.

Having spoken at a huge rally in Naples indicating he wanted to rule Italy, Mussolini implored on his supporters to march on the capital and demand that King Vittorio Emanuele make him Prime Minister. Fearing that anarchy was about to take over his kingdom, the King folded under the pressure. The prime objective of The March on Rome had worked perfectly. The King duly sent Mussolini the telegram which appointed him Prime Minister.

All local gossip in Montecino inevitably finished with the politics of the day. This Mussolini had appeared from nowhere and now he was Prime Minister. Fredo couldn't help but notice that opinion in the community was polarised. To his surprise, views and opinions were being very strongly expressed. Mussolini had made an impact.

The themes were clear, "We need a strong leader,"

was one view. "He is nothing but a terrorist," was the other view.

But Fredo refrained from taking any sides. He prepared for his return back home to his family and for the upcoming wedding of Ida. *'An honest politician worthy of the job or yet another opportunist with all the right rhetoric to capture votes. We'll find out soon.'*

Chapter 14

1926

"Look, Fredo, little Thomas has started teething," Catherine smiled over to her husband as she stood over the stove making her morning porridge. "Go and see."

Thomas was only three months old. "Seems a bit early for that," replied Fredo, "early just like Cora."

Cora, their third daughter was already two years old and it was the job of bigger sister Christine to ensure that the lively Cora didn't bump her head against the furniture.

The Baldini household was a busy thoroughfare of comings and goings with seven kids ranging in ages from eighteen to just three months. Lewis and Edward were still in charge of the business. They divided their duties between ice cream and fish and chips, and they worked long eighteen hour days. It was Lewis who had discovered that playing music as the cart made its way around the town was attracting more customers. He had managed to attach a mini organ grinder to the cart and jingle jangle tunes alerted local kids that the ice cream cart was nearby. Dads in the town seemed to be unable to resist giving their children a few pennies for their ice cream. Mums were stricter.

The two elder boys were in charge of sourcing ice from the lakes on the moors. The previous winter had been one of the most severe across the whole of

Europe and they toiled tirelessly to bring back as much ice as they could. Conditions in the cellar were ideal. When covered with straw and sawdust the ice usually lasted until the following winter. The boys were also responsible for sourcing coal briquettes for the fish and chip range. It was vital that the range remained continually fired up during the whole day. Coal stocks in the yard were required to remain high at all times.

The highlight for Alfred, now eight years old, was the ride on the cart to the pit. Edward allowed him to sit on his knee to steer. Often he was teased and tormented by the other kids. They were jealous he had the privilege of driving the music machine and of course, that he was able to indulge in as much ice cream as he wanted, or so they thought. Compared to other kids at school Alfred was already aware at his tender young age he lived in more privileged conditions. Conversely his family circumstances made it more difficult for him to find and keep friends.

Big sister Vera was the second mother in the home. She was key in maintaining a degree of domestic structure and organisation in such cramped living conditions. In between her frequent trips to the washhouse and her front shop counter responsibilities she had found the time and resilience to become an expert in cooking. Her mum had trained her well, traditional Irish soups, stews and puddings while her dad never lost any of his enthusiasm for demonstrating his repertoire of traditional Italian recipes which included ingredients, pasta, olive oil and garlic, which were largely unheard of outside the family home.

Vera's attentions were beginning to stray elsewhere. She had her eyes on another emigrant from Montecino, Charlie Gonnella, who ran a small ice cream shop in nearby Seaham. Mum's intuition had been accurate. The relationship was indeed serious. Charlie had managed to enter the country by the skin of his teeth immediately before the government introduced the new Aliens Act. The government had been intent on restricting immigration unless the immigrants could prove they were financially self-sufficient. Vera's dad had known the Gonnella family well and he reckoned Charlie was a good man and well intentioned. Having met with him several times to give him general advice on the ice cream business, her dad had regarded Charlie as the perfect no risk option for his daughter.

Mira too had moved on after several years of torment. Finally she had become reconciled to the fact that Tony was no longer returning. Her natural bubbliness had resurfaced fully. She had started to smile again at the handsome males who came into the shop. Many young men admired the dark goddess behind the counter with the olive complexion.

Meanwhile, after their wedding, Ida had moved in with John at his home in Durham. Every Sunday the pair returned to Errington to spend the day at the café. Lewis and Edward listened attentively when John narrated exciting army tales from the war.

Edward's fascination for the army grew week by week and during school holidays, he was allowed to spend time with John and Ida in Durham. Whilst at home he was often seen around the house wearing John's military caps. For his fifteenth birthday John and Ida had arranged to make Edward his own special glengarry. Catherine noted that the glengarry was never out of his sight. It was always under his pillow when he slept.

John was an active serviceman in the Durham Light

Infantry and when his tour of duty stationed him to Upper Silesia in Germany, Ida returned to Errington to lodge.

"One day too I will join the army," Edward often said to his mum.

On one occasion Catherine was distressed, "Ida, can you please speak to John, for goodness sake, to tone down the army stuff, our Edward is obsessed," she said anxiously. "And Mira, come here, please tell Edward it's not all about colourful uniforms and battle hymns. Sometimes people die. Tell him about Tony. It's about time he knew."

She continued, "Fredo, please tell me it's all right for Edward to sleep with that glengarry under his pillow and that this fascination will pass."

"Let it be, dear, there is no harm, he's just a boy, the war is long over. These politicians are not stupid enough to start another one."

"We've seen enough heartache in our family. And in the town too. So many families homeless from that damned war. It was so cruel for them, the ones who lost their dads, the wage earners. The pit manager would then have taken away their homes, too, for somebody else. I wonder where these people are now, I do hope they are all right."

"Catherine, stop ranting back to the past. It's over now. We all have to move on and live in peace. We need to trust that all will be fine in the future."

***

Since the end of the war, business had improved steadily and the family survived well. But austerity prevailed in the country and as with all families in the town, they continued to regard every penny as a prisoner. At the table little food was wasted and clothes were passed down from child to child. Damaged clothes were mended when it was possible or as a last resort recycled into washing rags. Opportunities for making savings were never missed. The family were only too aware of the new loan instalments which required to be paid and on time. In the previous year, Fredo had finally bought his first second hand motor car. It was funded with a loan from the Anglo-Italian association, a recently formed credit union in Newcastle focusing specifically on the immigrant community.

***

Before another early morning ice sourcing trip the two boys were breakfasting with Fredo.

"Billiards," Fredo shouted out. "A Billiards Hall. What do you think boys?"

"What do you mean, papa?" answered Lewis.

"There are a number of billiard halls which have opened in Newcastle. It's an old sport which is becoming popular. Our Italian friends there tell me that they make great money with these billiard halls."

"Have you been inside any of them," asked Edward.

"Yes," replied Fredo, "It was mostly young kids up in Consett before. Listen to this, boys, we can rent a large room, buy a couple of tables and charge our customers by the hour. While they're playing, they'll get thirsty, then we sell them lemonade and ice cream. We'll open seven days a week, if we do our sums correctly, the hourly charge will pay for the rent and the cost of the equipment. Once the tables are paid for, it's profit all the way afterwards. If we find a suitable place nearby, then all we need is for one of us to be there every hour to collect the money."

"Sounds too easy, papa," said Lewis. "Let me work this one out. In the next few weeks let me talk to my school mates to see what interest there might be."

"I'll start looking around for some premises," said Fredo, "and boys, don't say anything to Catherine yet. She's content and happy these days, now we decided to have no more children. Seven's enough! I don't want to give her any stress at the moment especially at least until after little Thomas is walking."

Fredo continued. "By the way, boys, whilst you are at the pit gates, find out what is going on down there. There's a lot of stuff in the newspapers about unions and reducing working hours again. The government is involved. It seems that the country's mines are producing a lot less than they did before the war and they want to reduce miner's wages. Up here, I've heard nothing. Everything appears normal. The last I heard they were producing at record levels. I don't understand it. They say the country's production is less yet we seem to be buying in coal from overseas. Find out what the men are saying, if you can."

Just at that point Catherine interrupted. "Don't forget, tomorrow you have to be ready for the unveiling of the new war memorial. We have to close for an hour or two, you need to be there. Remember, you were one of those who sponsored its construction. Be ready in case they ask you to make a short speech."

"Oh, don't worry, my dear, all will be fine. I won't make the same mistake again."

Four years previously, Father Donovan had announced the building of a new catholic church in the town. A year later it was completed and dedicated to Our Lady. Fredo was a member of the construction committee, and he and Catherine were major players in arranging part of the funding for the new building. On the day of the inauguration of the building the

Archbishop and senior bishops of the Archdiocese attended. Out of the blue and as a prime fundraiser Fredo had been asked by Father Donovan to say a few words. However Fredo had meekly shaken his head, declining to do so. A stony silence in the proceedings had ensued before another parishioner kindly stepped in to continue with the ceremony. Fredo had avoided total humiliation. As a gesture of gratitude he had extended an invitation to the obliging parishioner to partake and indulge in a free meal at the shop for himself and his family. Later he had confessed to his wife he had lacked the confidence in making a coherent speech in his non-native tongue.

Catherine was keen to avoid another such embarrassment.

The formal unveiling of the Great War Memorial in the centre of the town graveyard was scheduled for the following day. The committee which had been formed by the local religious leaders to raise the money and to organise its construction, had managed to identify all two hundred of the town's brave soldiers who lost their lives. The committee members visited every single one of the town's homes, establishing details of names, regiments, when and where they fell and dates of birth. Fredo had convinced the committee to include Tony Mucci on the list.

The memorial service was a moving occasion. The majority present were women, most of whom had lost a husband or son. This time, Fredo, did pluck up the courage to say a few words in his pigeon English. He ended with a sentiment which carried its way throughout all the conversations. "May these brave souls rest in peace and may this never happen again, never again." Mira was delighted to see Tony's name carved in the stone structure.

***

Fredo and Catherine decided it was time to have a family celebration on Easter Sunday. Catherine had invited her parents from Stanley for the Easter feast. She had determined that the main course would be based on traditional Irish food whilst Mira would arrange a typical Italian dessert.

The previous week Catherine had toured the local butchers to buy the largest joint of ham she could find. On the day the succulent ham joint was accompanied with boiled cabbage and roast potatoes. Lashings of homemade gravy ensured a hearty meal for all. As a special treat for her parents she also arranged for a local baker to bake several loaves of bread each with a carving of three crosses on top. One cross was slightly larger than the other two. In accordance with the old Irish tradition the three loaves signified the three crucifixions on Mount Calvary.

Mira, meanwhile, had coaxed Christine and Cora to assist the baking of a Colomba Easter cake, which she had fondly remembered from her childhood, was regarded as a symbol of peace. It was baked in a shape of a cross. Catherine thought this particularly poignant so soon after the inauguration of the war memorial. Mira found little difficulty in sourcing the ingredients, including the almonds, of which she had an ample supply. Earlier in the spring the chocolatier, Cadbury, had launched its Fruit and Nut chocolate bar. The company's representative who had been in the shop a few days earlier plying his wares had left behind several packets of almonds so that customers could sample the strange nut inside the new chocolate bar. Few in Errington knew about almonds, never mind seen or taste one. In contrast Mira was aware of several dessert recipes which featured the Mediterranean grown nut.

From his contacts at the local brewery in nearby Sunderland, Fredo had obtained a special deal on a barrel of Vaux Maxim. He reckoned that the beer left over from their Sunday celebration on the Sunday could be sold covertly from underneath the counter during the following days.

"Don't worry about this, Catherine," he said. "I've been learning about the gangsters in America. The newspapers explain how they manage to sell their illegal alcohol despite prohibition."

The day was a great success. "We must do this more often," agreed Fredo as Catherine said goodbye to her parents.

In the evening Fredo sat exhausted in the corner of the room in a futile attempt to avoid the kids' noise and commotion. He filled his pipe. Meanwhile Catherine and the girls were chatting, washing the dishes and generally tidying.

"Papa," Lewis said. "Let me tell you what I have been hearing from the miners."

"Yes, please. I read so much stuff in the newspapers but it's all so complicated. It feels like something major is about to happen."

"You know, the miners are really angry," said Lewis, "they are annoyed they're being forced to work for lower wages. They are complaining the government is buying coal from overseas, yet they know that in some areas of the country production is being reduced. They don't understand it. That's why the unions and the government are involved, and in a big way."

He continued as Fredo listened attentively. "The union reps are updating everyone constantly on what's happening in London and the word is that they are up for a fight."

"You mean fighting in the streets."

"I don't think so," continued Lewis. "The miners are talking of a large scale strike. At some point they will refuse to work. And they think the whole country will back them. They really hate this government. They want that Labour guy back, the one who was the prime minister a couple of years ago."

"He'll get back if the country votes him back. That's democracy, my boy. Striking does nobody any good in the long term," Fredo said waving his index finger to and fro. "Governments have to do what's right for the whole country, not just for a special group of people, like miners. I'll bet that the Labour guy, Macdonald, I think his name was, if he was in power, wouldn't want a strike either. If there is to be a huge strike, there could be real chaos, anarchy maybe. That would damage any government in power and by default damage the population too."

"Yes, papa. If they do strike, there'll be less money in the town and that's no good for us, either."

"Common sense normally wins at the end of the day, or so we can only hope."

During the following week after intense negotiations between government, the coal owners and the unions, a strike call was called by the unions. The mines ceased production immediately and an array of industries followed in full support. Transport services came to an abrupt halt. Steel works throughout the country closed their doors. It seemed that overnight, all workers in the country had downed tools. At the Errington colliery, pickets constructed a barricade in front of the pit gates, a row of lighted braziers to ensure nothing and nobody could pass through. On the first day of the strike, Fredo and his boys walked to the pit to see for themselves. They were horrified at the threatening and violent behaviour when some carts and trucks tried to force their way through the barricade.

"Scabs, scabs," the striking miners shouted threateningly. Lewis recognised some of those shouting. He couldn't believe that the incessant foul mouthing was emanating from some of his customers, who on the previous days were gentle and harmless.

"That's the power of propaganda," Fredo said. "It can transform your demeanour from one day to the next."

The boys were frightened. "Let's go back home, papa." Edward said.

"Come on," whispered Fredo.

"It was propaganda that forced so many of our young men to sign up for the war," Fredo continued as they walked back. "Those young lives who never returned. What a mess! They'll be back before Christmas, they had said."

"It was the same for the Italians. Tony and some of his pals from Newcastle never came back either. The war broke up many of our families too. Even for those who did survive, they were never given the land they were promised. They cheated them. They fought for little, just to satisfy the pride of the politicians."

"What is propaganda," asked Edward.

"It's a new word. They use so often in the newspapers these days. It's how politicians influence the people to follow them. They use biased, exaggerated messages, sometimes even lie. When things go wrong, there's always somebody else to blame. Furthermore, they scare us by continually predicting doom and gloom. It's a form of nasty manipulation, not really democracy."

"That sounds complicated," said Edward.

"Complicated?" replied Lewis. "Basically what papa is saying, you don't have to believe everything people tell you, or everything you read in the papers. It's important that you learn to think and decide for yourself."

"Thanks, Lewis, don't believe in anything, now I am even more confused."

"Best advice is to trust mum and dad, believe in them. They are the only people who truly care for you. They are older, with age comes wisdom and life experience."

Edward remained confused, "Looks like with all that chaos we won't be taking the cart to the pit today."

"Actually, maybe yes," interrupted Fredo. "Later when their emotions have calmed a little, and some of the fracas has died down, the strikers might just need a few scoops of ice cream to cool themselves. In fact we could become their best friends, let's fill our tea urns. We go back down there and offer them cups of tea."

"What, free," said Edward.

"Yes, exactly, let's pretend to be good supporters of the strike. Then when they do return to work, since we were so kind to them they might just spend more money with us. While the strike is on we'll offer them free tea in the morning, and when we return later in the day with the ice cream cart. We'll give them a good dose of guilt. Hopefully we'll benefit when it's over. It's a form of propaganda, is it not?"

***

During the following days Fredo followed the newspapers very closely. Every day of the strike was costing him more and more money. He was concerned also at the cost of his continuing free tea exercise. But now there was no way he could stop, otherwise the propaganda strategy could backfire. His interest in the political dogfights rapidly waned. His own personal view was meaningless. All he needed was for the miners to return to work as soon as possible. He had his loans to pay off. Before the strike he had signed up for the rent of the premises where he planned to launch his new billiards salon.

Increasingly Fredo despaired at the newspaper reports and particularly so when he read of the derailment of the great Flying Scotsman in Newcastle. *'Now this mess really is becoming dangerous,'* he thought to himself. *'I certainly hope that was an accident, unrelated to the strike.'*

Quite unexpectedly the dismal gloom lifted. On the following day, Fredo's despair for his family's livelihood eased. He was delighted to read that the unions had received certain assurances and guarantees from the government. The general strike was called off and at long last the miners were returning to work.

"It's over, it's over," Fredo exclaimed at the top of his voice. "Business as usual, carts out, come on everybody."

***

Thereafter Fredo became an avid reader of the broadsheets. He strived to maintain contact with any events in Italy. He was keen to ascertain whether Mussolini's efforts to introduce his socialist ideas had been successful. His experiences in Montecino four years previously when Mr Mussolini first introduced himself to the world were still uppermost in his mind. On his rare visits to Stanley, Fredo routinely asked for

Vincenzo's views on the Italian political scene. He had learned that one of his cousins and co-worker in Stanley, Benny Mocogni, had become the Secretary of the Italian *Fascio* in Newcastle. The so called *Fasc*io, literally a bundle of rods tied together, had become the emblem of the new Italian state. This was the symbol of the new Italy, strength through unity, the idea being that each rod on its known was fragile whereas tied together in a bundle the whole was stronger.

But the news about Mussolini's actions had disturbed Fredo greatly.

Mr Mocogni, on the other hand, maintained that Mussolini was doing a great job. The charismatic leader had made national heroes of those who fell during the war. He had promised that the feudal system where the peasants served as vassals to their masters would end. He had guaranteed that the Italian trains would run on time. These were the headlines appeasing the general population. In the four years since Mussolini's socialist introduction to power, Italy had seen some other significant developments which displeased Fredo.

Firstly, Mussolini had re-invented the calendar. Nineteen twenty-two, the year he assumed power, was deemed the new year one. It was obligatory that all public documents be dated in two ways, *anno domini* and in the new Italian calendar, *era fascista* alias *anno Mussolini*. Thus nineteen twenty-six had become year four. '*Mussolini regarded in the same breath as Jesus Christ, not for me*,' Fredo thought. Secondly, laws had been passed in parliament to assure Mussolini's absolute power in Italy. Opposing views were effectively being banned. And a new state police had been formed. It was clear to Fredo the leader's aims were more sinister, to eliminate any form of democracy.

'Top quality propaganda, this is. I wish I could explain it to my boys,' he thought. *'Calls himself a socialist, is that what they do, these people? He presents himself as a benign dictator, promising his people a land of riches and plenty, while simultaneously censoring and eradicating people power and even worse, eliminating opposition. Now I understand why he needs a new state police.'*

The debate and discussion with Mr Mocogni was fruitless. Benny was part of the propaganda. There was no common ground with Fredo.

"Now Benny, I definitely will obtain those naturalisation papers," said Fredo attempting to end the debate.

"You will be betraying your motherland, betraying your ancestors and your children's legacy if you do that."

Vincenzo was the friendly arbiter, and he refrained from entering a fully blown discussion. Before parting he proposed the customary last glass of wine to toast Italy's future.

Chapter 15

1931

Catherine closed over her magazine, the *'People's Friend',* and placed it on the floor beside the bed.

"Fredo, please sit up, listen a moment," she said, "Edward's fascination with the army has never waned. Last night he told me he wants to join. You know, from time to time, I still see him staring at that glengarry, Ida made for him. Next week he wants to go to Leeds to the army office with a couple of other boys in the town. They want to stay the weekend, leaving on the first train on Saturday and back on last train on Sunday."

"Is he not too old for the army, he is nearly twenty one now?"

"He says he doesn't want to sell ice cream all his life. He's been doing it for ten years, after all."

"Ten years, that's nothing. Nowadays these lads, they just don't like work."

"He's not a kid, anymore. Maybe he needs some time away from us, from our routine, from our way of life. He aspires to see the world. Is that not what you would want for him?"

"What about Lewis, do you think he is happy?"

"Of course, he is. He's more mature. He's the eldest, feels more responsible. Look how he constantly watches out for his younger brothers. He kept tabs on Edward all the time and now he's doing the same with

Alfred. He is capable. He knows he will run the business after us."

"But he has a fondness for the ladies, I can see they like him too."

Catherine laughed loudly, "Oh shut up, you macho types are all the same, women in your little brains all the time."

***

Edward's plan for the weekend included a visit to the Carlton Barracks in Leeds with his three friends. This was the base of the Prince of Wales' West Yorkshire Rifles Regiment. Here the boys had planned to receive a four hour introduction to army life. The fact that the royal prince, himself, was his namesake had made a strong connection with Edward. His affinity with the prince had grown after seeing his photograph elegantly dressed in splendid military uniform on the front page of dad's newspaper. Edward wanted to be like him.

The four arrived at the barracks promptly at noon. A dozen other lads had arrived from other parts of the country. The group spent the afternoon on discipline, fitness drills and practicing elementary rifle shooting. At the end of proceedings they participated in an interactive workshop and question and answer session.

The pals from Errington were awash with adrenaline as they departed with recruitment forms and information folders safely tucked under their arms. They set off for the centre of Leeds to locate their guest house lodgings for the night.

The evening was warm and sultry, the perfect environment for exploring the streets and alleyways of the town centre. They needed some nourishment before the pub crawl. Edward was given the job to choose where to eat. He searched out the fish and chip shop with the longest queue as he knew that the busier shops signified fresher produce. "Strange," Edward said, "this is the first time I have walked down the street eating fish and chips. I have always been at the other side of the counter."

The lads strolled along the Headrow, the main shopping thoroughfare, fascinated by the fashion styles of the mannequins in the shop windows. Female bodies were so eerily lifelike dressed in long pencil thin floral frocks, satin blouses and cardigans with large frilly bows. Matching handbag and shoes coordinated perfectly.

"Look, the hat on that female dummy looks like a miner's cap," said one of Edward's friends, pointing to the stylish boudoir cap hat, laced in silk.

Male mannequins were equally elegant, mostly displaying double breasted suits with large collars and wide trousers. Shirts and breast pocket silk handkerchiefs accessorized the suit sublimely as did the two toned brogue shoes and fedora hat. The illusion was complete. The gentleman on show could step out into the street at any given moment.

"Imagine somebody coming into our café dressed like that," Edward said encouraging laughter from the others. "They would look ridiculous!"

The main street was swarming with people, trams filled with passengers passing by every two minutes. At the corner of Headrow and Brigate the boys stood against the iron railings for several minutes happily watching the world go by before they ventured into the first of many pubs.

At the guest house the following morning the boys were amazed at the fry up served up by Bessie. They never had so much on a single plate before, eggs, bacon, beans, sausages, black pudding and round chips.

"Are you sure, Edward, you don't pay extra for this," one remarked.

The bill paid, they set off into the morning sunshine. Shops were closed and traffic was light. The boys couldn't help but notice the posh folk proudly heading towards church in their Sunday best frocks and hats.

"You don't see people like dressed that in Errington," Edward said.

"We'll look smart too," said the eldest of the quartet, "when we stroll down some foreign city street in our fancy uniforms. Think of those lovely ladies who will swoon at our feet."

"Speak for yourself," Edward replied.

There were few cars about and the boys took to zigzagging down the street in between the tram lines. Their spirits were high, their bellies were full and the air was warm. The lads were doing what lads do. Edward heard a loud voice shouting at him, "Eddie, Eddie, watch out."

Edward froze and gazed into the direction of the warning. All he could see was the yellow glow of a huge rising sun completely blocking out the sky. His eyes were blinded by the glare. He heard the sound of screeching wheels metal against metal. The screeching sounded louder. Suddenly he heard no more screaming, no more screeching. Then nothing!

The boys immediately rushed to Edward. He was motionless on the ground in between the tram tracks. The sight was horrific. Only one of Edward's legs was clearly visible. It was obvious the other lay underneath the tram. He appeared unconscious.

"Quick, ambulance," one of the boys shouted, in a state of panic. Frantically the boys surveyed the scene while a small crowd quickly gathered. Fortunately an off duty nurse was on hand to take control.

"You, rush to the police box at the gushet, call an ambulance!"

"You, find a policeman!"

"You, find me a rag, or anything just so I can stop this bleeding!"

"You, stop all the cars and the trams! Don't allow any traffic to pass!"

"You, find me something soft that I can put under his head!"

Two hours later as Edward lay on a hospital bed at the Leeds Union Infirmary he was able to glance at the damage on his left leg. Now conscious he saw the huge gash in his partly severed left foot. The doctor started to bandage his foot and tightly. But he felt nothing in either leg as his three pals watched anxiously.

"Right boys, Edward is fine. He'll recover the strength in his good leg soon. However he won't be able to support himself, so you guys need to help him home. You are big lads so you should have no problem with that."

"And then what," Edward asked.

"See your doctor and he'll check for any further damage. He'll know what to do."

Edward sighed and gazed at the ceiling. He was wondering about his fledgling army career. He closed his eyes to the catastrophe that was before him. *'What has happened to me? What I have done? When can I walk again,'* he thought.

"The sun blinded me, I saw nothing," he mumbled, a solitary tear disappearing into the hair covering his ears.

"You were hit from behind," said the doctor. "The sun must have blinded the tram driver too. Your left foot was very badly gashed. We managed to get a few stitches in there straight away but you might need more repairs. You need to get home fast and see your own doctor."

The journey home seemed to take forever. The boys took turns at supporting Edward. His pain was sporadic and it was only when he sat down on the train that he obtained any degree of relief. The change of trains at York and Durham stations, especially limping up and down stairs, was painful. Edward grimaced the whole way.

At home Fredo and Catherine were startled at the sight. Edward's bandage was soaked completely and tiny droplets of blood scattered to the floor.

"Give me one of your belts, Fredo, we need to stop the bleeding, and then call Mrs Rooney fast."

Edward felt more excruciating pain as the belt was tightly wound round his ankle. He screamed.

"Edward, we have to do this. We need the wound to stop bleeding."

Mrs Rooney arrived with her large bag of medical supplies. She untied the bandage. The stitches were loosening. "Edward, I need to replace your stitches. I'll give you chloroform so you won't feel anything. You must have already had some earlier, so no need to worry."

"Just do what you need to do," Edward replied as he saw Mrs Rooney edge closer. "I just need to get back to normal as fast…. as possible. The army's ………waiting for me…………" Edward's slurred speech slowly came to a halt as he fell into a deep doze.

"Oh my God, what's going on?" Catherine blurted out.

"He's fine," Mrs Rooney said. "Edward just needs

some sleep. I'll be back first thing tomorrow morning. You should take him to a doctor as soon as you can, but I am certain in a few weeks he will be back to normal again."

Two days later Dr Murray examined Edward's leg.

"I don't feel anything down there, doctor, what can be wrong?" Edward asked.

"Please wait a moment, I need to call your mother and father here so I can explain."

Edward's parents held their breath as Dr Murray voiced his concern.

"I am afraid this accident has created more damage than you first thought. You can see here," the doctor lifting up Edward's leg, "that the foot has turned black and the tissue has died due to the lack of blood supply. Also see the blisters here, they are filled with fluid and the smell, it's putrid. The foot had been very badly infected. I am thinking gangrene has set in."

"What does that mean now, Doctor, can you be very clear?" asked Catherine worryingly.

"My fear is that we will need to amputate the foot as soon as possible. The bacteria in the infection may already have travelled through into the leg."

"Then what," Fredo said.

"It could be very serious, it could very well be that the leg needs to be amputated too."

Drifting in and out of drowsy consciousness, Edward was attempting to listen. "Soldier......army....," he repeated softly, again drifting into sleep.

The doctor continued, "The tissues in the skin have been destroyed around the wound. It's clear too, Edward has been running a fever for some time. Simply put, germs seem to have invaded the wound and are spreading fast through his body. The only hope is to sever his foot immediately."

Fredo put his arms around Catherine. "Are there any drugs which you can give, we will find the money," he said.

"No, Mr Baldini, there are no drugs to cure this disease and return the foot to normal. Amputation is the only option. The question is whether to amputate at the ankle or at the knee. With luck the disease hasn't spread any further."

Catherine burst into tears and ran outside to obtain some comfort from the girls, who were anxiously waiting for updates.

"Mr Baldini, I was warned by Mrs Rooney. Her diagnosis was absolutely correct. I have my equipment with me today. I can call Mrs Rooney to assist if you want me to proceed immediately. I can only repeat again that delaying the amputation may make the situation a lot worse."

Fredo walked out and spent ten minutes in deep conversation with his distraught wife.

"We have to do it," he said. "There is no option. The doctor took me to one side. There's the risk, if we don't ask fast, we might lose him completely."

"My poor Edward, he was so looking forward to his army career."

"Look, Catherine, so many of the old soldiers returned from the war without a limb. They survived. We see them in the town all the time, leading lives best they can. They are coping. Nowadays I have been reading in the papers that you can get wooden legs too which can help."

"Yes, only if you are rich."

Fredo continued to console his wife. "Don't worry, he's a strong boy, he will manage afterwards. We'll support him."

Later in the day the deed was done. With the able assistance of Mrs Rooney, Dr Murray amputated Edward's left leg at the knee joint.

For days Edward was unable to escape from his sick bed. He dosed in and out of drowsy sleep many times a day and his fever continued. Mrs Rooney returned every morning to check on her patient and to renew his bandages. Dr Murray visited every second day.

"The prognosis doesn't look good," Dr Murray said more than a week after the amputation. Edward isn't able to feel any of his left side. It's very worrying, Mrs Baldini."

Exactly two weeks following the amputation Edward fell into a final sleep from which he never returned. The family watched helplessly from his bedside as Edward struggled more and more with his breathing. His only display of any awareness was to pull the glengarry from underneath the bedsheet and hand it to Lewis. Edward had sensed his ending.

Lewis took the cap and placed it close to his heart. Young Alfred, already laden with tears, stretched his hands across and insisted on taking it. "Let me have it Lewis, please. I will look after it forever," he said.

That night before bedtime, Catherine gathered her little ones to explain about life and death. "Sometimes these things happen when we never expect it. Now is the time when we all need to stick together and be brave as a family. Edward will always be in our hearts and we must pray for him. This will test our love in God. However we shouldn't ever break that love. We all have to die at some time in our lives, even mama and papa."

Christine and Cora cuddled themselves to sleep. "Can I sleep in beside you tonight, mama," sobbed six year old Thomas. For the first time in his life since he was a baby, Alfred, at thirteen years old, slept all alone in his bed.

The funeral Mass at the new church of Our Lady was full to the brim. Many miners' families were represented. Edward had been most popular at the pit. He was constantly the joker who made light of his job. He joked with the children waiting for their dads. He was the jovial salesman effortlessly able to coax his friendly customers to spend some of their money with him. Edward never made a secret of his army dreams to them. For the pitmen his presence at the gates of the pit was as bright as the sunlight.

The miners arranged for a collection. They presented Fredo and Catherine with a carved wooden plaque which read, "Edward, the army missed out on this brave and happy young man."

After the funeral Fredo and Catherine cancelled the double celebration party which had been planned for later in the summer. It was twenty five years since they first fell in love and almost twenty years since they arrived in Errington. They had already booked The King's Head for their celebration. The notion of a celebration after Edward's untimely death didn't seem right.

"Let's have the party in a few years' time," Catherine said. "I am sure times will be better then."

Fredo wrote a letter to his very elderly parents that there was no need for them to travel for the celebrations.

"The train trip would have been too difficult for them anyway," he said, as he licked the edge of the envelope.

"Don't forget to write to Dino as well," said

Catherine.

***

Fredo's big brother Dino had settled with his wife Emilia in the countryside near Marseille. Dino had acquired several acres of land when he first arrived on the French coast. He exploited his farming skills in the rich and very fertile plains adjacent to the Mediterranean. The temperate climate meant that growing seasons were short and Dino had little difficulty in ensuring his large family was well fed. Furthermore, unlike the obligation of his father, there was no need to provide half his produce to the *padrone,* so life for Dino and Emilia was good.

Dino's family was complete with three daughters and three sons. Ida had married soldier John and they were living in Durham. Her middle sister Olga had little interest in male relationships and she was perfectly happy assisting her parents and assuming the responsibility for household domestic duties. Younger sister Luisa's life mirrored that of Ida. A few years previously she, too had met a young English soldier, this time from Yorkshire and they married in Marseille. Luisa's husband Cuthbert left the army when they married and both worked the farm together. Luisa and Cuthbert had two boys of their own. But Fredo had learnt that Cuthbert was homesick and eager to return home.

"If Cuthbert were to leave and take his family to England, would you support Ida and John to help them settle," Dino had asked Fredo in his last letter.

In Marseille there were three boys also. Louis, Franck and Josep were now in their late teens. They ran the farm with their dad with military precision. The three boys had developed skills well beyond traditional farming expertise. With little outside assistance they had built impressive stable blocks for the thoroughbred horses they were breeding. From the rusting chassis of an old bread delivery van they had built a multipurpose tractor unit to plough fields and to spray seed afterwards. They had even contrived to build a primitive irrigation system for their large greenhouse using old barrels and discarded pipes to optimise the use of valuable rainfall.

"You would love it if you were able to visit for a week or two to enjoy the sunshine and help us on the farm," Dino had written. "Please try to come, we would love to see you. I will convince you to come when we are with you at your celebration."

"It would have been great to accept the invite but we can't go any time soon," Catherine said. "With all the money we spent for the doctor and on the funeral we can't afford it. We all need to work a little harder, especially now we don't have Edward to help either."

"Yes, I know, in any case we can't leave the children behind. I'm not sure Lewis can really run the business on his own."

***

A week later Fredo received a letter from the Italian consul in Newcastle. It stated that Prime Minister Mussolini had introduced an organisation aimed specifically at Italy's youths, the *Opera Nazionale Balilla*. This was, the letter explained, a school to encourage physical prowess and patriotism. Summer camps had been developed to prepare children for Italy's golden future. Six boys from the age of fourteen to eighteen were to be chosen from the Italian community in the North East and they would be invited to spend the summer in Italy at one of the camps to learn about

Italian-ness and Mussolini's new doctrine of socialist fascism. The trips were being funded by the Italian government. Each boy would be prescribed to wear the standard *balilla* uniform, which was similar to the internationally renowned boys scout uniform except that the *balilla* shirt was black. The consul's letter was accompanied by a photograph of an unnamed boy, fully uniformed, his right arm thrust high in salute. *"Viva Il Duce,"* the caption below indicated.

"The consul is asking whether we would like to propose Alfred for this rubbish," Fredo said, throwing the letter onto the table in disgust. "What nonsense! They want our kids now too. Remember last year, we received the letter, asking, in fact it sounded like demanding, we contribute to Mussolini coffers by donating gold for the *'Motherland'.* What motherland baloney!"

"Calm down, high blood pressure is no good for you," said Catherine.

"Who does this guy think he is, this Mussolini? Over there he has abolished elections, God knows what's happening in Tripolitania since he took over, he wanted our wedding rings and now he wants our children."

"It's not compulsory that we send our children to these camps, is it? How did the consul know about us anyway?"

"Compulsory? Never in a million years. Edward gave his life for a potential career in the army, and that was the British army, not the Italian army. That's a fact. Our Alfred's not going anywhere."

Fredo continued after pausing for a short breath. "They know everything, these guys. They've snooped on us. People must have talked. Don't tell me we Italians are spying on each other now."

Fredo stood up and threw the letter, including the photograph of the innocent child, into the fire. He watched it burn.

Chapter 16

1933

Lewis's hands were covered in batter when the two policeman entered the shop.

"Mr Baldini," the elder policeman said, holding a crimpled piece of paper in his hand.

"Yes, what can I do for you?" Lewis grabbed the rag at his side and swept his hands clean. He recognised the contents of the piece of paper.

"Are you the owner of this establishment and do you rent the billiards salon on Station Road?"

"Well not me, but my father, yes," replied Lewis. "I'll call my father."

A moment later Fredo arrived from upstairs and motioned the officers to sit in one of the booths.

"Tea, lemonade, gentlemen?" Lewis asked.

The policemen nodded, "no, thanks," and placed the piece of paper on the table.

"Somebody has told us that this notice was pinned to the back of the door at your billiards salon. Can you confirm this, Sir?"

"Well, yes, officer?" Fredo replied, slightly bemused. "Yes, I wrote it."

The notice read *'Sunderland FA cup replay versus Derby - Go to Roker in luxury by motor car – there and back – five shillings only.'*

"Do you have a licence, Mr Baldini, for a public

carriage?" said the elder policeman, clearly trying to impress his junior colleague.

"Not really, sir. You need a licence? I didn't know, sir."

"I'm sorry, but ignorance of the law is no excuse, Mr Baldini. I require to book you. In due course you will receive notice to appear in court."

The policemen scribbled the necessary details in their notebooks and they departed.

The Sunderland football stadium at Roker Park was no more than thirteen miles away and Lewis had sparked on the idea of earning some extra money after Sunderland drew against high flying Derby County in the fifth round of the FA Cup. The replay at Roker Park was expecting its biggest crowd of the season and Lewis sensed the buzz in the town with the excitement of the replay. It was Lewis who pinned the notice to the door but it was Fredo who had the job to drive three lucky football fans to and from the match in his car.

"What will happen now?" Lewis asked his dad.

"I don't know, we've never been in trouble before."

"What about your naturalisation," interrupted Catherine. "You still haven't sorted that out, you old fool. What are you waiting for? If you go to court and are found guilty, it might go against you. You'll have a black mark against your name"

"We've all been busy. I just never found the time yet."

"Dad, what if I say I did the driving. Then it would be me who goes to jail. Then it wouldn't affect you."

"No, Lewis, I don't want any more trouble than I have right now. Let's not make this any worse. We are doing this properly. I want to be able sleep at night. I don't want any policeman ever at my door again."

Catherine nodded in agreement and took Lewis' hand. "It'll be fine, don't worry. My brothers and my dad were always in scraps with the police when they were drunk. None of them has ever been near a jail. Hopefully this might be nothing more than a fine. Don't worry."

"What if I would have had an accident?" Fredo said.

"Shut up, old man, the fact is you didn't," Catherine replied. "Anyway Sunderland lost the match, so it won't happen again. Now let's get the shop ready for today."

A few weeks later Fredo received the news.

"See, I told you it was going to be fine," said Catherine. "A ten shilling fine, overall you even made money on the deal. It was still good business, no."

"Now don't forget, you must get your naturalisation sorted out," said Lewis. "You never know what the future has in store for us."

"You're right. I was reading the other day about another guy in Germany, a dictator just like Mussolini, who seems to want to rule all by himself, without proper government. They say his supporters set fire to the parliament building. His name is Hitler, same first name, Adolfo, as Vera's father in law."

Lewis listened attentively. He let his dad ramble on.

"Looks like this Hitler guy has worked the same trick as all those socialists do, promising the people great and rosy futures in return for votes. It seems to have worked and he certainly has the country behind him now. According to the papers he has blamed Britain and America for humiliating Germany after they lost the war. It's rhetoric his people seem to love. His intent is to make the country great again. What nonsense!"

"Great again, meaning what?" Lewis asked.

"Don't know really."

"At the Empress, in between the movies, they project newsreels of what's going on over there. Maybe I should go and see sometimes."

"If only you had the time, dear boy. No doubt he will make his country great again in some shape or form. Next week, I'll see about the naturalisation. Promise."

Fredo continued. "Never mind that! I am more interested in the rumours I'm hearing about a plan to close the main seam of the pit. Can you find out if these rumours are true? That seam stretches far out to sea. I still cannot believe how these guys can work out there underground below the sea. Why doesn't it flood? I just don't understand."

"Dad, stop being an old git. Of course it won't flood, even if it does stretch five or six miles away from the coast. The men are safe down there, at least from flooding. It's the other dangers they need to worry about. These guys are really brave, just like our soldiers." Lewis continued, "I'm not brave like those miners, but at least maybe I can be brave like a soldier and follow Edward into the army. What do you think, papa?"

"Mama won't like that, son. We lost Tony, we lost Edward, for heaven's sake we don't want to lose you as well."

"Just a thought," murmured Lewis. "Okay, I will find out about this closure and whether it means any job losses. I hope not, the town relies on that colliery. If the closure talk is serious, it will affect all of us."

Catherine strolled downstairs with a large smile on her face. "By the way, Lewis, how are you getting on with Ethel? Do we have to put aside some time and some money for a celebration soon? It would be nice to know."

"Mama, just friends for the moment. We'll let you know well in advance, don't you worry."

"Did you hear that, Fredo? Lewis is serious about Ethel. You will need to have that black suit of yours cleaned soon."

"Oh be quiet, mama. I have work to do."

Lewis returned to the shop to prepare the batter for the days frying.

***

Initially Fredo and Catherine had found it difficult to come to terms with Edward's untimely death but normal life had to continue. Their other four younger children still needed care and attention. Vera, meanwhile, was happy with her lot in Seaham with Charlie. Their small ice cream business was doing well, and Charlie had just purchased a shiny black second hand car, a Ford Model T, which he managed to convert into a sophisticated ice cream cart. The car looked particularly splendid in Seaham where there were less vehicles on the streets.

But it was Lewis who was affected more by Edward's death. He insisted on tending Edward's glengarry. He wrapped it carefully and stored it under his bed.

When the colliery band marched on Station Road, Lewis would leap outside into the street to watch. He was fascinated not only by the precision and uniformity of the marching rhythms but also by the colours and patterns of the glengarries on view. Increasingly during these marches he felt Edward's presence and a calling to serve in the army. But at the moment he had other priorities.

On Sunday morning after Mass, as had been the habit for several months, Ethel met Lewis outside the church. Ethel was protestant and some of her friends has teased her about her boyfriend being a *'papist'*. As they walked home in the sunshine, Lewis made a jovial gesture to stoop to his knees, "It's now three years, let's get married," he said.

"Forget that," replied Ethel. "Of course, you silly romantic old fool." They kissed each other. "Enough Lewis, in public like this, no, we'll get arrested."

The pair had known each for over three years and at the workhouse their mothers chatted constantly together. For some time they had considered a marriage might be on the horizon.

Lewis and Ethel frequently discussed a future together so his latest gesture really made little impact on Ethel. Both mothers seemed to be keen, but whether her father would be just as enthusiastic, Ethel couldn't be sure. Her dad was the one branding the *'papist'* word around the home. Her friends had become aware of her father's true feelings. Ethel was in her early twenties and she worked at the local grocers shop. Most of her customers were already aware she was attracted to the handsome Italian fellow at the fish and chip shop. But to some he was the wrong type.

Later in the day as the colliery band were marching Lewis and Ethel watched on.

"One day I would like to join the army," he said. "I have a dilemma, my dear. Question is, should I go before or after we have children? I want to sign up but I also want to be at home with you and all my children. Can you understand or am I being stupid?"

"Edward's death had a very big impact on you. Are you not too old for guns and war?"

"Maybe so, I will ask papa. See what he thinks."

"Fine, Lewis, the army, weddings, your mum and dad. We have talked enough about all this. All my friends are already mothers. The last thing we need is an accident. That would really mess things up. I am not sure how my dad would react with an illegitimate grandchild and a catholic one as well, wow, that would be too much for him. He might even throw me out. I might never get back home. Come on, let's go." Ethel said quickening her pace home.

"You're right, no more sillliness. Our wedding must come first. The army can wait. Let's tell our parents this week. Let me talk to your dad, in private though."

The following day Ethel's parents were surprised when Lewis knocked on the door alone. Ethel, as planned, was out and about, nowhere to be seen. At first Lewis felt a very frosty atmosphere but he wasted little time in spluttering out his intentions. He sensed that her parents were not overly joyous that their precious daughter would want to marry a catholic and a foreigner. But after several cups of tea, Lewis reckoned his charm had won them over. Ethel's parents were gracious and courteous and when they started offering suggestions for the wedding, Lewis figured his job was done.

Lewis and Ethel decided to marry during springtime the following year.

"Isn't it great, Fredo that Lewis has finally decided?" Catherine said. "Great news all round. Vera tells me we may soon have another grandchild."

"Never mind another grandchild, let's have the first."

"Don't be so heartless," said Catherine, "we've already had our first."

Five years previously shortly after their marriage Vera had become pregnant for the first time. She had declared well in advance that the baby would be named after her parents. In due course she had given birth to little Charles but tragically he never managed to survive his first night. Vera and Charlie were devastated so much that it took them another five years before they tried for another child. Now she was pregnant a second time. The perpetual excuse was that they were just too busy with the business.

***

The couple were visiting her parents on the last Sunday in September for their usual Sunday lunch.

"I am not sure we can come again to see you until after the baby arrives," Vera said to her mother. "I can't move much these days."

"By the way, Fredo," interrupted Charlie, "did you receive one of those letters from the Consul?"

"What letters?"

"The one where they are asking for all our personal details. The consul is collating a census of all the Italians in the country. He says it's been demanded by Mussolini. You must have received one too."

"Oh that, I paid little attention to it. The consul is always asking, for this, for that. He's already urged we send our kids to Italy to those summer camps. I remember even we received a letter pleading, no, actually begging, that we give him our gold jewellery. To rebuild our country, he said. For God's sake, we don't have any gold, and now this, a what, a census? We already did the census two years ago."

"That was the English census, Fredo," Charlie said. "The consul says, if we need, he can send round one of his guys to help us to do this. They say it will be used to calculate our pension when we retire."

"First Mussolini, now this guy Hitler, dominating our lives. Where do these people come from? They pontificate they care for us, that they want to provide for us. I am not so sure. I'm doing nothing. I'll wait to see if the consul's man actually turns up at the door."

Fredo continued. "I still remember the day before the war when I went to see the consul for some reason, I can't remember. The arrogant guy looked at me, *'Mr Baldini, you have been called up to fight, you need to return home,'* he said. Then look what happened, hundreds of thousands dead, millions wounded. I didn't trust them then and I don't trust them now."

At that moment young Thomas ran in to the room, "Daddy, daddy look what Alfred made for me."

Thomas showed his dad the cardboard gun which Alfred had cut out from the box which the man from the chocolate company had left behind. Alfred had cut out a gun for himself too, a larger one. Both boys ran out into the backyard where their friends were waiting. The boys needed to play out the battle which had started earlier.

***

Eventually Lewis returned with news of the main pit seam. Indeed the owners had decided to close it, the reason supposedly that the depression of recent years had reduced the demand for coal. Other local pits had been similarly affected and many jobs were lost in the area. Lewis knew the consequences, he had seen it before. Job losses at the pit meant reduced takings in the business and immediately. But what Lewis did not know was that at the same time there were other events stirring on the horizon across mainland Europe which were about to reinvigorate production at the pit. The business was destined to be reprieved.

In the meantime Lewis had put his army plans on hold and he began earnestly planning his upcoming marriage to Ethel. He insisted on marrying in Our Lady's

Church so it meant Ethel would have to think about her conversion to the catholic faith. Errington was a town split in half by religion and the local priest was more than happy to proceed with yet another spouse conversion. But this wasn't unusual. The vast majority of mixed marriages in the town took place at the catholic church.

Despite some early misgivings Ethel's family eventually agreed to her daughter's conversion. Some friends had previously gone through the same experience with little by way of consequence. In fact they had concluded that the whole conversion affair was a sham, just another bureaucratic process. In their eyes Ethel wasn't ever becoming a fully emblazoned catholic but she was just converting for convenience to ensure her special day would be a great success.

***

Fredo continued to receive more letters from the consul in Newcastle. All lauded the greatness and glory of Mr Mussolini. One letter, in particular, explained in detail the concept of the *'fascio'*, Latin for a 'bundle of rods'. The symbolism of the *'fascio'*, rods when bound together signified strength through unity, without weakness. The Italian population in Britain was being reminded of the man's great achievements and philosophies. Mussolini's views were clearly spelled out. His observations were that across Europe new national identities had emerged, including in Germany, where power was returning to the common people. New politics were now being forged from the bitter experiences of the war and especially so from the communist revolution in Russia. This meant, he said, that his own socialist ideals had been converted to a unique socialism which required strong leadership. This he called fascism, or alternatively as his message proclaimed, socialism with a national identity.

"He has certainly stirred things up over there," Fredo said. "Gold, the *balilla*, a census, what next?"

"I think this guy Hitler in Germany shares the same doctrine. He must have been inspired by the same events," Lewis replied. "He's managed to get the population behind him in quick time. His movement is a type of National Socialism too. I saw the power of his speeches in the newsreels at the cinema. You should see some of those meetings. Masses and masses of people cheering, their arms thrust skywards in unison, thousands waving flags. Even the buildings are covered in huge displays of regalia. Mighty impressive it looks to me!"

"Let's hope for all our sakes, son, that these guys with their great national socialist beliefs are well intentioned."

Chapter 17

1936

Thomas ran out of the Empress cinema, gun in hand shooting at the passers-by. He returned the gun to his holster and he skipped along with a make believe limp in his leg. Christine and Cora strolled behind pretending to pay little attention to their young brother continually aiming his gun at the old ladies. The three of them had spent the afternoon at the cinema watching a recently released movie, starring Hopalong Cassidy.

Thomas barged into the shop and proclaimed, "Hands up, everybody." A customer buying tobacco for her husband was startled sufficiently she dropped her shopping bag to the ground. She turned round slowly and realised that the intruder was nothing more than a little kid. "Oh, pet, you gave me such a fright! Next time you do that I'll give you a clout round your ear."

"Don't worry, Mrs Stoddart, it's just my little brother," said Vera from behind the counter. "He's back from the pictures. It's obvious he had a great time."

"My children were seen and never heard," said Mrs Stoddart and she stormed out of the shop tutting and sighing.

Thomas darted upstairs to the bedroom, stuffed his gun and holster inside his cowboy hat and he placed them on the bed. "I wish I had a horse," he said to Alfred who was lying on his bed, trying to concoct smoke rings from his cigarette.

"I don't think you would like that," Alfred said. "A long time ago when I was even younger than you are now, it was my job to clean up the manure which the horse left behind."

"What, we had a horse!" Thomas said in amazement.

"Yes, a real horse. We called him Brandy. It was before we had a car. But he was old and useless in the end, and we had to send him to the slaughter house."

"Was he shot?" asked Thomas as he dived on the bed to grab his gun. "Did dad shoot him?"

"No, you little idiot, not dad, somebody else shot him. He probably ended up at the butchers."

"One day I will have a horse. I want to be like Hopalong. I want to kill all the bad guys."

"Be quiet, Thomas, stop dreaming. When the rag man next comes along, away and look at his horse. You'll see its hair is shaggy and dirty, not clean and beautiful like the one you saw at the movies," said Alfred, "and it's smelly too."

***

The cramped conditions at the house had eased a little during the previous year. After Lewis married Ethel they managed to find a rented room not far from the shop where they could enjoy their own privacy. However they shared a toilet with the occupants of twelve other rooms. So the pair were forever at the shop taking advantage of cleaner toilet facilities.

"I can accept family poo," Lewis repeatedly said, "but others' poo, well, that's something different."

Ethel had just recently announced she was pregnant with their first child and they had returned for celebratory tea and cake which was arranged by her mother-in-law. As usual Catherine had set a beautiful table. She had taken out the Sunday best but little used linen tablecloth.

Meanwhile Fredo was settling on his favourite chair in the corner reading his newspaper amongst clouds of pipe smoke.

"You should really give up that smoking," Catherine said. "It stinks the whole place out."

"Oh please shoosh, my dear, it's the only pleasure I have left."

Vera and Charlie, too had been invited. Their little girl was two years old. Charlie's shop in Seaham was much smaller and less busy than Fredo's, so Vera spent much of her time helping out her mama and papa. She had taken years to come to terms with baby Charles junior's untimely death within days of his birth, but in contrast little Ines was a bundle of joy and in good health. Grandpa Fredo doted on his grand-daughter and he was thrilled that there was now another one on the way.

At eighteen years of age Alfred was undertaking more manly roles in the business. He organised and managed relationships with suppliers. He formed the daily timetable of tasks, who was on shop duty and who was on the cart around town and at the pit. Increasingly Thomas was becoming more involved especially at weekends when he was not at school.

Christine and Cora, as young teenagers, were never out of each other's sight. There was less than two years between them but from afar they appeared as twins, similar hairstyles, similar clothes, always together. Outside of school their lives were consumed totally in the business. They stuck obediently to Alfred's timetables including taking their turns with the cart together. And at weekends it was their responsibility to renew the flowers at Edward's grave.

The previous Sunday the inseparable sisters had visited cousins from Montecino, the Rinaldi's, who had their own Ice Cream business in Wallsend, near Newcastle. Matilde was the same age as Christine and since they first met several years before they had struck up a close bond together. But they could only get together two or three times a year. This latest visit was the first where the girls were allowed to visit alone without their parents.

"Mind, don't speak to anyone at the train station." Catherine had repeatedly drilled to them to ensure the message was clear.

Christine had taken a liking to Matilde's big brother, Joe who looked smart and tidy in his new uniform. His parents were delighted that he had no interest in working the long hours of the family business. They had more ambitious prospects for him and he looked great dressed as a young police cadet. Joe earned great respect as he patrolled the streets of Wallsend. He knew the streets well. Most of the passing pedestrians were his parents' customers. One day, he was used to saying, he wanted to be the one who solved the big crimes in Newcastle.

"Speak to your mama when you girls get back," said an excitable Matilde. "They want to send me to the *Avanguardisti Giovanni Italiani,* a summer camp for young Italians in Italy. Why don't you both come as well?" She continued. "My mama and papa want me to learn Italian. They don't want me to lose my roots. They say the whole camp is being paid by the Italian government anyway, please come."

The following day Christine broached the subject

with her mum who iterated that any Italian stuff had to be discussed with her dad.

"Are you sure, Christine, your dad has always hated these initiatives. He thinks the indoctrination in the camps is wrong, certainly not right for a summer holiday. There will be lots of exercise, lots of marching and lots of schooling. It will be like being in the army. That's not what you want, surely?" her mum continued. "And in any case we still need you here. If both of you were to go, we would never manage."

"Oh, mama, please."

"As I said you need to speak with your dad when he returns from his rounds."

That evening Fredo and his daughters spoke freely. He exchanged a couple of letters with Mr Rinaldi. It transpired the Rinaldi's too had become suspicious of the real intentions at the summer camp and that Matilde wouldn't be allowed to go after all. They had received word that in addition to physical education and language learning, the girls would be heavily preached of their *Italianita,* Italian-ness, in particular of the need, in fact, of their responsibility and duty, to bring many more little baby Italians into the world as soon as possible. "*A quindici anni, non e Italianita, e la innocenza violata.* At fifteen years of age, it's not Italian-ness, it's a young innocence completely spoiled," Mr Rinaldi had written.

As Fredo reflected on Rinaldi's new perspective, he recalled his teenage years and his sister Rosa's wedding in Montecino. "Our children, the property of the state, is that all our girls are good for, having babies!" he yelled to Catherine. "God help me, this is why I left Italy, to get away from such abuse." He put Mr Rinaldi's letter back into his envelope. "I never want to go back!"

"Quiet now, calm down. Forget it. The girls already understand why they cannot go. In any case I think it's Joe, the young policeman whom Christine has her eyes on, really."

The girls were none too bothered about Mr Rinaldi's concerns, especially since they knew Matilde wasn't going either. "That's okay, papa, said Christine, "next time I'm in Newcastle and when I am with Joe, I'll need to find a handsome young boy for Cora."

***

Thomas was Catherine's little bundle of joy. His effervescent energy was plain for all to see. He never kept himself still for a moment. At school he was the shortest in the class, so tiny in stature for an eleven year old. He was everybody's pal and he knew it. He was also the class clown and often got himself into mischief. But as far as Mrs Thomson was concerned, his antics were just laddish behaviour. She wasn't able to castigate such a loveable tiny little rascal.

Catherine planned to bake a cake for Thomas' birthday, so the following Sunday another family gathering beckoned.

This time Ida was accompanied by her husband, John, who was on home leave. She brought with her the latest news of her folks in Marseille.

"I received a letter from papa the other day. Would you believe it, my two youngest brothers, Franck and Cristophe have become policemen," she said, "and Josep is taking over the farm. Olga and Louisa are helping out with Josep. Don't you find it strange, Catherine, I am the only one married. All of them are about thirty years of age and there seem to be no signs of any wedding bells anywhere."

"Still plenty of time, Ida dear. Maybe life's too good

for them, no kids around. They're having a ball, probably lots of money around too. Perhaps the right partners haven't turned up for them yet."

Catherine had baked a large Battenburg cake. She knew this was a favourite with the boys.

"How do you manage to bake those different colours exactly in those shapes," Fredo asked. She couldn't remember how many times her husband had asked this same question during the years of her marriage.

"I am not going to tell you again. Are you going senile? I bet you, even Thomas knows."

Although he still considered himself fit and healthy, Fredo was content in the evenings spending more time in his favourite chair reading the newspapers. In recent years the events across the water on mainland Europe had continued to bother him. But this year the newspapers had other more important matters on which to report. Earlier in the year the King passed away and the crown passed to Edward, his eldest son.

"What do you make of all this stuff with Wallis Simpson," Fredo said, trying to prompt a response from anybody listening.

Following a few moments of silence it was John who piped up, "Good on him, got himself a beautiful woman and an American too."

"But she's divorced," Ida interrupted. "You men are all the same. Beauty first before anything else. This is the King. You cannot have him marrying a loose woman and a divorced one as well. What about the children?"

"What about the children, they'll still be children," replied John.

"Yes, but this is the royal family. Royal blood and purity and all that. In my opinion they should marry their own kind. That's the way it works," replied Fredo.

"Look what happened in Russia, we don't need any revolution here. They killed off their kings and they're no better off now."

"Yes, exactly, Fredo, if they had married ordinary folk, they might still be alive."

"Yes, but still. It wouldn't be the same. Somehow Queen Wallis just isn't right."

The jovial chit chat of what the new king should or shouldn't do continued for several minutes until Catherine restored some order. "Come on, enough of this. The royal family should stay royal. And to celebrate we are going to enjoy this Battenburg cake. In fact, if I am not wrong one of the royal princes is a Battenburg, Prince Louis, I think. I am sure Thomas won't mind sharing his celebration."

Ethel had sat very quietly through the whole King and Wallis discussion.

"Catherine, is it a coincidence or are you just clever," she said. You baked a Battenburg cake, you say there is a Prince Louis of Battenburg, so perhaps Lewis and I can share the celebration too. Did you plan this on purpose?"

"Well, if you must know," Catherine paused for few moments, "well I am not going to tell you."

The family were only slightly amused at the irony.

"Can I have the first piece, mama?" Thomas jumped up, gun in hand.

"You need to ask your big brother, the new Prince Lewis of Battenburg. What do you think Lewis, if you were a prince, would you have this beautiful Ethel for your wife or would you rather have a loose floozy from America?"

"You know, mama, there is no need for me to answer that," Lewis put his arms around Ethel's waist and he patted her bulging stomach very gently.

***

The following morning Alfred awoke early to prepare for his day's duties. His mum took the opportunity to ask him what had been bothering her for a few months.

"You spent a lot of time speaking to John last night."

"He looked smart in his uniform. He said he might be off again on another tour. His infantry have indicated they need to be ready in case there are any troubles ahead."

"What did he mean, troubles ahead, do you know?"

"This guy, Hitler, in Germany, John says, the newsreels never show him without all his military regalia. His regiment thinks he must be building up his army again."

"Recently you've been obsessed with the army. You aren't serious, are you," said Catherine as she gestured to give her son a cuddle.

"Listen, mama, I am eighteen now, and I can't sell ice cream all my life."

"But the army, it's about war, fighting, death, families split apart, that's no future," she pleaded. "Why would you want that?"

"Mama, remember all those people who died in the war, look at the cemetery now with all those names. Even Mira has never come to terms with losing Tony. John told me these guys in Germany and Italy might want to fight it out all over again. So stupid, I know. Even Lewis agrees we need to stand up to them."

"What, Lewis as well," said Catherine exasperated.

"I heard many boys in the town are joining the Territorial Army. It's not the real army. They have a great time together at their training camps, it seems like great fun."

"Did Lewis put you up to this," she said clenching her right fist.

"No, Lewis knows nothing about that, but I want be ready. I can make new friends. Forget the Italian camps, I've no interest in those."

"But the Territorial Army will train you to fight." Catherine's voice sounded louder. "What if there was another war, you would have to leave us. I'm sure Lewis would never fight."

"You're wrong, mama. He told me he would fight as well. Once he even told me he thought every single boy in the country should spend a couple of the years in the army, to be ready, just in case. Sometimes, he said, he regrets not having signed up when he was eighteen," said Alfred walking back towards his room.

"I heard all that," said Fredo. "Don't worry, Catherine, boys will be boys. You have to let go, dear. They need to grow up, make their own decisions. They need to live their own lives."

Catherine grabbed a handkerchief from the pocket of her apron and wiped her moistening eyes.

"Listen, my dear, we had these discussions with Lewis and he is a fine lad. God, he will be a father soon. The same with Alfred, we have to let him go. We should concentrate now on Thomas, the little scallywag, he wants to be a cowboy, but I don't see any indians round here. It will all work out well, don't fret. Look at Vera, she and Charlie are still in love. And as for Christine and Cora they will soon mature into fine ladies so we need to be ready for them too. I think, maybe my dear, the shock of losing Edward is still with you."

"Perhaps you're right, but what happens if there is another stupid war?"

"No, there won't be another, this country won't let it

happen."

"You still haven't been to see about your British citizen papers, have you?"

"I was going to talk to you about that," said Fredo sitting on his customary chair. "I received a letter today from a Mr Crolla in Edinburgh, who is the secretary of the Italian something or other. He says Mussolini wants yet another census of all the Italians resident in the country including the names of family members as well. Crolla seems incensed that we never sent the information the last time. He is insisting we complete it this time."

"Whatever for."

"He claims to understand why we never filled it in before. He says he knows that we are proud Britons but he wants us to be proud Italians as well. He affirms we can be both. He reminds us of our traditions and heritage. Maybe there isn't any harm in completing the form this time."

"What's come over you? You've gone soft. How many damn letters have we received over the years? Why don't they just leave us in peace? Remember they suggested we send our kids to Italian classes, they urged we send them back to Italy for summer camps, they said they wanted us to give them our gold, now they want our names and addresses. What next, how many times we go to the toilet every day!"

"I know you are upset. I'll just do it. Then they might leave us in peace."

* * *

Fredo was following as much as he could of Mussolini's progress in Italy. On his visits to Newcastle he had observed that there seemed to be a renewed pride amongst the Italians he met. Most were supporting the actions of the leader, and indeed had accepted the invitation to send their children to the summer camps. Fredo had been informed that the local Italian language classes were always well attended and more children were speaking Italian at home. His fellow nationals, he had concluded, were no longer embarrassed by their origins of street peddlers and itinerants. In the community they had ceased feeling inferior citizens. He had noticed more Italian flags and other symbols of his compatriots' *Italianita,* Italian-ness, as they called it. Social events were varied and attendances, he was told, were high, especially more so where both parents were Italian. Fredo had been particularly taken aback by the so called *Sabato Fascista,* the Fascism Saturday initiative whereby on Saturday afternoons the children of the Italian community gathered in a public park, listening to speeches and taking part in mock military drills organised by the consul.

"We made the right decision with the kids, not to let them go to the camps," Fredo confirmed to Catherine.

Back home in Errington, far away from the big city, Fredo was better able to reflect. He felt the outsider when he visited Newcastle. He wasn't convinced the community events were well intentioned. He contemplated that these were indoctrination by default and he didn't like that idea. Additionally he was very conscious, of course, that he himself hadn't married an Italian and that his children had grown up truly British. His family had very little *Italianita,* if any at all. This isolated him further from the Italian community. He had no intention to send Thomas or his girls to the *Sabato Fascista,* even though he suspected Thomas would have loved it, playing soldiers with toy guns with other kids of his age.

In the meantime Fredo's fascination of all things Mussolini remained constant. He endeavoured to read between the lines in newspaper reports. What was really happening? Was he really making his country stronger? Positive or negative for the Italians? Fredo had never become a fan of Mussolini, and his views solidified firmly when he read that the Italian army had made advances into Africa. It seemed their military forays into Abyssinia were a plan to cement a new Italian empire in East Africa. Indeed if there was to be another global conflict Fredo pondered as to where Mussolini's loyalties would lie. For sure, a conflict would mean Britain and Germany at arms again. But for Mussolini, would his loyalties be with Britain or would his loyalties be elsewhere? But one thing was for sure, if Italy were to side with Germany, then he would surrender his *Italianita* fully. In his mind he was clear. And of course, he knew his boys were intent on joining the army and the British one at that.

Nevertheless being the diligent citizen he was, and despite his minor reservations, Fredo completed the Italian census form. At the same time he made a mental note yet again to obtain the forms to become a British citizen.

***

Every Saturday afternoon Thomas spent his pocket money at the Empress cinema. His passion was with the cowboy movies and he saw them all, Hopalong Cassidy, Custer's Last Stand and The Last of the Mohicans. Usually two cowboy movies were on show and he was never without his leather holster, gun and hat. When leaving the cinema he never forgot to arm himself with holster round his waist, hat on head and simulate riding down the street on his imaginary horse.

Newsreels were projected between the cowboy movies. Thomas was equally captivated by the drama and spectacle of the Olympic Games. He marvelled at the huge stadium bowl filled to capacity and draped in long red swastika flags. He was dumbfounded when the man in a tiny black moustache rose from his seat and waved to the crowd. He noticed how in unison everybody in the stadium rose to their feet and placed their right hand into the air in a loud chant which he couldn't make out. Even the athletes, as they walked around the stadium marched past, right arms in the air.

"That man must be very important," he said to his dad when he arrived back home. "Then they released all those pigeons, the sky was filled with them. Then they shot them."

"I don't really think they shot them, son. I think that must have been cannon fire, just for show."

"When I grow up, after I have killed all the indians, I want to be a fastest runner ever."

***

Later in the year, much to his mum's disappointment, Alfred passed the territorial medical. On the first night under canvas he wondered what he was really doing in the middle of a wet and miserable night somewhere in Wales. Comfortingly, however, in his bell tent there were three other feeble looking eighteen year olds from Errington and they shared his misery. They had known each other from school and they travelled to the drill together. The three were just thankful they were spending two whole weeks away from the dirty, dusty, and dank conditions down at the coal face underneath the sea.

"Mind, you guys, don't step on me if any of you need to relieve yourselves in the middle of the night," said

Alfred anxiously as he placed the flap of his blanket under his body to ensure he was fully covered.

Alfred was bewildered the following morning in the canteen. For breakfast he had been used to a light snack of coffee and bread. No such thing, here, as porridge was unceremoniously scooped out of a large rusty pot into well used tin bowls. On that first morning he was glad his bowl was the smallest. However during the course of the fortnight and particularly before the strenuous exercises and activities of the day ahead, Alfred came to appreciate the bowl of morning gruel. By the end of the drill one portion in a little bowl was never enough.

The second evening in, Alfred returned to his tent after the day's torturing events finding that one of his blankets had been stolen. On reporting the incident, he was promptly told, "Well, boy, you just have to steal somebody else's in return." Alfred looked rather sullen faced at the lack of concern, at which the sergeant cried out, "that's an order, do it!" Initially the response shocked him, but to avoid a frozen night's sleep Alfred found the courage to carry out the order. After that his confidence picked up a pace. And it grew day by day as the training became tougher.

Within the group Alfred's leadership qualities emerged through and he wasn't slow in cementing his proud status as leader to arouse enthusiasm from those around him.

"You know, Alf, I would have jumped off a cliff if you had asked me to," said Jack, one of the pals from Errington as the four boys lay in their tent on the last night of their training reminiscing on their experiences.

At the closing parade, Alfred was nominated as 'the best recruit' from the North East and he returned home proudly, his two weeks army pay safe in his pocket and with his crisp and shiny new uniform carefully folded in his bag.

His mum was relieved to see Alfred walk through the door.

"Come here, I missed you," she said.

"Mama, I am fine, it was great," Alfred replied slightly holding back. He was desperate to avoid the embarrassment of being cuddled by his mum in front of the customers.

Alfred remained exhilarated for weeks from the emotional highs of the experiences at the camp. He failed to understand why his mum and dad never showed any enthusiasm whilst listening to his adventures. Ultimately he came to realise, of course, that he was the only one feeling any exhilaration. It had been two weeks when nothing else mattered in the world, total isolation from the daily routineness of work, newspapers and ice cream. In the meantime, however, his mum and dad were just carrying on with their daily routine, oblivious to Alfred's exciting adventures. They were having no exhilarating experiences. It was he, and he alone, who was thrilling at sitting high in the clouds.

Chapter 18

1939

Fredo sat in his favourite armchair, pipe in hand and he gazed aimlessly at his nicotine stained palm and fingers. He couldn't work out what was happening.

He had completed the building of the shelter in the corner of the yard and he was exhausted. He had covered it with soil and gravel to shield it from bomb blasts. It was just as well, he thought, that Alfred and Thomas were there to help him. On the previous Sunday they had dug out a huge hole and then placed corrugated sheeting at the sides to act as walls. Half the sheeting lay underground and small wooden planks were placed at the entrance in order to step down inside. Flat sheets of metal served as a floor. Another corrugated sheet was bolted on top to serve as a roof. There was enough room for the six of them but even so they would feel crammed inside. He figured they couldn't spend too much time in the shelter and if it rained, well, would the thing be of any use at all?

"But this is what the government wants us to do," Fredo said to his boys. When they were finished he was glad Alfred and Thomas offered to go over to Seaham to help build Charlie's shelter. *'At least Vera and the kids will be safe,'* he thought. Lewis and Ethel lived nearby in a flat so they would have to use the public shelter.

The previous year Fredo had purchased a wireless

radio set. It was decorated in deep shades of mahogany exactly matching his pipe. He placed the wireless in the corner of the café so that his customers could listen to the latest BBC bulletins. In the evenings when the café closed Fredo was in the habit of taking the wireless upstairs to listen to dance band music and hot jazz whilst chatting to his wife about the darkening clouds sweeping across the continent.

"Surely, Catherine, it won't happen, will it?"

"You know more about this than me. We just need to make sure all our kids are safe."

Fredo had become deeply concerned. After years of struggle trying to etch a living for his family, finally he felt he had some degree of financial security. He had paid off his loans and his business was generating sufficiently to enable the family to enjoy a few more luxuries. He had purchased his second car, a brand new two toned black and green Austin Ten. Typically on Sundays he took his wife, Thomas, squashed between his two girls in the back seat on a day trip around the hills and dales in Durham.

But since the King abdicated, it seemed that the world was forever in turmoil. Fredo sucked long and hard on his pipe. Catherine knew when he sucked long and hard, he was in deep thought.

"Come on, what's troubling you?" she asked.

"Why do you think they've given us all these stupid gas masks? They must think something is about to happen."

"Just in case, I suppose. It's the smell of the rubber and disinfectant which is awful. Remember when I tried it on, it made me sick."

"The whole world is crazy. It's bound to end in disaster. Germany, Italy, France, Spain, Japan, us here in

Britain. Where's the common sense. There isn't any anymore."

"Fredo, dear, don't worry, come to bed now."

"They're still killing themselves on the streets in Spain right now. At this very moment, young men from Britain are fighting there. Your friend and mine Mussolini marched into Africa and hundreds were killed in his conquest of Abyssinia and of the Arabs. Now the man seems to want Albania as well. Then this guy in Germany, Hitler, has taken over Austria and Czechoslovakia and he is threatening to cause trouble for Poland."

"It's all too complicated for me, dear, I'm off to bed. You can talk to the wall, if you want."

"And Japan, they've invaded China. The government haven't been able to stop them. Worse still, I'm reading that Britain and America have stopped taking any more Jewish refugees from the continent. What have they done, these poor Jews, that Hitler wants them all out. You know, Catherine, they've burnt all their synagogues, as well. What is this thing about Jews, everybody hates them. I don't understand it."

By now Fredo was indeed talking to the wall. Catherine had disappeared and the bedroom door was firmly closed.

Form his inside pocket of his jacket, Fredo took out the letter which his brother had sent him from Marseille and he re-read it.

'The French government is very serious about the German threat. For years we have been building a line of defences on our border with Germany. The Maginot line, they call it. It's continually manned with troops and heavy artillery. The Germans will not be allowed to pass.'

Fredo carried on reading the letter.

'Here in Marseille, the French have allowed Britain to station a garrison in the town. In the event of a war...'

"See the French do think there will be a war," he remarked.

'In the event of a war the British will use this as their base for operations across the Mediterranean. There are thousands of British soldiers already here. Josep has now signed up as a reservist and has joined Franck and Cristophe in the police force. I am horrified to believe, dear brother, that we might all be at war soon. It seems inevitable, there seems little more which governments can do. Here in France we are concerned, not just from Germany but also from Italy. These two madmen have become allies. Mussolini admires Mr Hitler's icon status in Germany where nobody dares speak against him.'

Fredo placed the letter down and sat quietly contemplating his situation. He reflected back to the gatherings of his fellow Italians in Newcastle. Some of them, even those who were born in England, made no secret of their regular salute to Mussolini. *'Viva Il Duce'*, right arms outstretched in the air, to open and close meetings. Were these people just blindly following their Italian heritage or indeed were they full supporters of Mussolini in the impending war? He couldn't bear to think, even, that any of his countrymen, for example, might have taken an active part in the anti-Jewish riots which Oswald Mosley had orchestrated a few years previously in London.

He remained in deep thought. If there was to be a war, whose side would Mussolini choose? Surely not Hitler's, he wondered, whose military regime in Germany, it seemed, was trying to eliminate itself of all those who didn't agree with their leader. He pondered on the new race laws in Germany where Germans were banned from using any Jewish shops, any Jewish services, doctors or dentists. And perish the thought even that a German should marry a Jew. Was the night referred to in the newspapers as '*Kristallnacht*', the night of broken glass, really true? Surely, he thought, nobody would knowingly bring about a new war in a modern country which only recently had experienced the horrors of a horrifying global war. Surely Italy would never have any anti-Jewish laws like those. After all, he had never heard of any conflict with the Jews living in Valbona. He recalled to memory one family in particular, the Abramis who lived close to Montecino. Everybody knew they were Jews, who had escaped from persecution elsewhere. The family had inter-married with the locals, but there was no conflict, no tension, no trouble nor any concern. Also at the coast in Livorno he knew of the huge contingent of Jews who centuries earlier had arrived from North Africa. Surely the Italians wouldn't betray them now.

Mussolini could not possibly side with Hitler, Fredo concluded. The Italians, he reminded himself, were a passive people, for whom as long as the sun shone, as long as there were beautiful women around, and as long as there was homemade bread, cheese, ham and a bottle of wine on the table then the world was fine. Seems Mussolini had little option but to deliver himself as a strong, charismatic and table thumping leader. The Italians had never had one before. *'I am sure, at the end of the day, Mussolini, too, likes his bread and wine, as well as his beautiful women.'* Fredo fell asleep in his chair.

***

'Are you alright," Catherine said anxiously the following

morning as she stomped downstairs when it occurred to her that her husband hadn't come to bed. He was still asleep in his chair. She shook him on the shoulder as he opened his eyes with a sleepy glaze. Dino's letter and the newspaper pages were scattered on the floor. "You fool," she said, "just as well your pipe was no longer lit. Your way of avoiding the war, maybe," she continued with a sarcastic laugh. "We need to talk about the children."

"What's the matter today, dearest?"

"I have been thinking about what you were saying. What if there was to be a war? What do we do? Where do the kids stand in all this?"

"The situation is very clear, they are British, and we will be fine. I am the only Italian here. In any case, who really cares about me, an old man of nearly sixty." replied Fredo. "Alfred's been in the territorials for over three years. He is as British as anybody else."

He continued, "Lewis and Vera have their own families, the girls are almost fully grown women and little Thomas, well little Thomas will be little Thomas."

"Main thing for him, is that we need to stop him getting into trouble at school." Catherine replied.

"He might be being bullied because of his height, but they tell me he can look after himself pretty well. He isn't scared to square up with the big boys. His weekly jaunts to the movies has turned him into a tough little guy. He must have been inspired by Jimmy Cagney, that movie star."

"He's in his own little fantasyland. First he targeted the indians, he wanted to kill them all. God knows where he'll find them. Now he's fascinated with the Germans. He has been watching them in the newsreels. Masses of people, masses of soldiers marching with their guns. I don't know if he's with them or against them. Seems he's taking out all his frustrations at school. He wants to be a wee toughie but I know he's a softy at heart."

"Catherine, he's still only a boy, let's talk to him about school."

On cue, Thomas barged the door open and stormed into the back shop. "Papa, we've started a gang at school. When we are eighteen we are going to join the army to fight the Germans. And Mr Morton, the headmaster is going to help us. He told us his dad came back from the war with both legs missing. He spends his whole life in a wheelchair, so Mr Morton want us to take revenge for him, and we all agreed."

"What, are you making this up, Thomas?" asked his mum. "It sounds a bit far-fetched that he wants you boys to take revenge. It was a long time ago."

"No, mama, this is serious. Big Andy, George and Jack, we've all agreed."

"Okay, son, I believe you. Don't forget to take that sandwich with you today," his mum replied. "And no more trouble today, I'm warning you."

"Right, mama, bye."

"Boys will be boys," Catherine said glimpsing at her husband who was behind the counter listing what he had to buy that day. "Fredo, our little boy will be a man soon."

***

The inevitable finally happened and Fredo stooped down in his chair as he listened to the radio.

'....... and I have to tell you that no such undertaking has been received, and that consequently this country is at war with Germany.'

He took another deep draw on his pipe and he

glanced over at Catherine.

"We are here again, my dear. These people refuse to learn any lessons from the past."

"What does all this mean for us, now, for our family, for the town and for our business?" She glanced at her husband despairingly, hoping for some inspiration.

"I really don't know, at least we are with France, but Italy, I don't know. Mussolini and Hitler have had many meetings and spend lots of time together. It all depends on what the Italians do. I have my fears."

"We should all go to evening Mass today. It's a long time since we were at the church together," Catherine suggested. "We might obtain some inspiration from high above. He never lets us down. Let's try again, Fredo, every Sunday to Mass."

"That's it, from now on we'll need to black out our windows. And I guess there will no more gaslights in the street. I just hope, Catherine, that the six boxes of candles we bought will be enough. We also need to gather everybody round the table to establish some family rules. We can't have anybody go missing."

"Just as well you bought the radio. At least we should be able to follow what's happening."

PART TWO

BRITISH HEART

Chapter 19

World War 2 – Alfred's Story

Alfred consulted his dad when he needed some serious answers about the state of the world. He knew his dad was absorbed in the detail of Prime Minister Chamberlain's peace venture with Hitler in Munich. But although he felt a yearning to go out there and tangle with the enemy, today he didn't really care about the politics. He was looking for some solace from his mama.

"Mama, I have something to tell you," he said.

She sensed this was personal.

"You know Gladys, she worked here in the summer. They sent her back to her grandma in Cumberland to stay for the winter."

"So what, son. Just now lots of kids are being sent to their grandma's to be safe. Everything is so uncertain. Nobody knows from one day to the next what is going to happen." She wiped her hands and threw the dish cloths in the sink.

"But, mama, it's not that," whispered Alfred. "I think she's.......................I think she's having my baby."

Mama sighed and replied softly. "She is only seventeen, son, what are you talking about." She understood instantly but she didn't want the whole world to know before she obtained the facts. "Are you absolutely sure, Alfred?"

"So she says, mama. That's why they sent her away.

She says she'll not be back until after the baby's birth."

"Oh, Alfred, what have you done, you silly boy." Mama slapped a towel on her son's head. "Come on, tell me, when is it due."

"In the new year."

"But's that's in a few weeks. Then what are you going to do, dear boy." She grabbed him by the arm and together they went upstairs.

Mama came up with the plan. "Tell me. You're an adult now. Do you love Gladys? No larking around now, the truth," mama asked in her stern matron sounding voice.

"Yes, I think so."

"What do you mean you think so, yes or no?"

Alfred paused for a few moments. "Yes, yes, definitely."

"Good, does Gladys love you now, really love you? You know what I mean."

"Yes, of course," was Alfred's firm reply.

The pair crouched down on the bed, Alfred's head in his hands.

"I know how much this army stuff means to you, son. I'll talk to your dad and we'll both discuss it with Gladys' mother."

Gladys' dad was no longer around. A few years previously he had lost his life tragically in an accident at the mine. As a result the pit authorities had evicted Gladys and her mother from their home. The house was needed for another miner. So the pair had spent the last three years boarding with Gladys' uncle and his wife in a small single room.

"We'll see if you can get you married after the baby is born."

***

Catherine invited Gladys' mother for tea and Christmas pie and together they sorted out the arrangements. Fredo was unfazed. "Just you fix it, Catherine. We don't need anything major or special. Gladys only has her mum, there's little by way of family. So we can do something quick. With little Dino around the place another kid won't make too much difference."

The ladies went to the church and together they set the date, the last weekend before Lent. The priests were never keen to have weddings during Lent. This was the solemn six weeks period to prepare for the passion and death of Jesus, so joyous celebrations in Lent never seemed right for the church.

All agreed that Alfred's new family, Gladys and baby would live above the café. "We have some space," said Catherine, "particularly since Lewis moved out to his new flat with Ethel."

Baby Richard was born in the New Year and as planned Gladys returned to Station Road with her newborn infant. "Come on Gladys, let's fix your room up," said Catherine. "Your little boy seems so content. You're a natural."

"Thanks ever so much, Mrs Baldini."

"My dear Gladys, you still look like the little girl of last year, little pigtails, short socks and pretty fresh face. Call me mama, now. I'll always be here for you."

Although Alfred was desperate to be the caring and affectionate dad it was clear his mind was increasingly preoccupied with other thoughts.

He had completed four summer camps at the territorials since his first involvement just before the Olympics. Dutifully he attended the local drill hall one night per week to supplement and keep his training fresh. He knew that in the event of war his name would be one of the first on the army recruitment muster.

Alfred had noticed that since the Munich crisis of the previous year recruitment into the territorials had increased sharply. It was being reported that the prime minister had probably been duped by Hitler and as a result the country was on alert. Alfred recognised at least half a dozen boys from the school, only fifteen or sixteen years of age, who had recruited and were attending the drill. Alfred was the experienced one.

'You boys want to fight, yet a couple of years ago you were still wearing short trousers.' By comparison, he felt manly and mature.

"You gotta go home and tell your mums. You shouldn't be here," he repeated.

"Come on, Alf, just a few more sessions, one more, come on."

***

Alfred had become an expert marksman. But at shooting practice hitting the target was easy. He yearned to try it for real.

Soon afterwards, as the skies blackened over Europe, after Chamberlain's infamous *'we are at war'* address, Alfred was enlisted into the ninth battalion of the Northumberland Fusiliers.

Catherine was well aware of Alfred's determination. Her son was going to fight and that was it. Each year she had seen him return from his training stints on huge emotional highs lasting for weeks. She knew her boy was ready for any war. There seemed no way she could persuade Alfred otherwise. In her heart she had sensed that in some weird manner he was determined to live out big brother Edward's dream of the soldier's life.

"Don't forget," she said, "you now have two more lives that depend on you."

"I have talked this over with Gladys. She's just as concerned as you are, mama, but she understands. She knows I must do this. In any case she'll have too much on her hands with little Richard than to worry about me."

Baby Richard was four months old when his dad set off. Alfred had no idea when he would be back.

"Alfred, just make sure………….," his mum said as they stood on the street outside the shop to wave her boy off, "make sure you come back healthy and strong. Don't forget, Richard and Gladys will be waiting for you." She was sobbing.

"I will, mama, I'll be careful. They won't get me, don't worry. Please help me. Watch over them."

"That's what Tony said last time, and he never came back."

"Bye, mama, papa, I will write when I can, bye."

Fredo pulled a tearful Catherine back into the shop. "Come on now, we have things to do today."

At the barracks in Berwick Alfred's training was more intense than at the territorial camps. He had been assigned to a group of about fifty soldiers who were training separately from the main body of men at the camp. This was a group, he had been informed later, chosen for extra endurance training and particularly in man to man combat. During cold winter days the group had been deployed in additional outdoors exercises and when the first flurries of snow appeared on the Cheviots they had camped out in the open.

It all seemed unreal to Alfred. Yes, weeks previously Britain had declared war but nothing seemed to be happening. He listened to the bulletins on the camp radio, but life in the country was continuing as normal.

Each day before drill the commanding officers

reaffirmed their mantra. *'Careless talk costs lives. Where we are from, where we are going, how many ships, how many guns, how many shells? Mr Hitler has spies everywhere. He is desperate for knowledge. Silence at all times. You don't know who is listening.'*

During the winter staggered breaks had been arranged to allow soldiers to return home to their families for short periods. None of them had any idea how long their training would last, what would happen next, even whether in fact the war might already be over. Alfred received his break just after Christmas, and he was able to usher in the New Year back home with his family.

"Alfred, come here, let me see you," said his mama as they sat down after warmly embracing each other. Gladys rushed in, baby Richard in her arms. "It's great to see you." She gave Alfred a huge long kiss. Alfred stepped back and took his son into his arms. "You are so big, now, and all that hair. You're so beautiful."

Richard started to cry, "ma……ma, ma…ma." Instantly Gladys took her baby back into her arms. He stopped crying.

Christine and Cora sat either side of Alfred in the cubicles and they held his hands, not wishing to let go. "You can see things have changed a little here. We open only during lunch time. It's dark by about four o'clock and we are blacked out then. We can only use candles."

Alfred was oblivious to what the girls were saying. He kept his eyes transfixed on Richard. "He's so beautiful, Gladys."

From upstairs Ethel and her son Dino appeared. "Where's Lewis?" Alfred asked taking his attention away from Richard.

"Lewis has signed up too, the Royal Army Service

Corps. He left about two months ago. He has written a few letters. Thankfully he won't be on the front line. I guess you men have little option, you have to go when and where you are assigned," replied Ethel.

Catherine interrupted. "Soon, just three of us will be left, me, your papa and Thomas. Christine and Cora have decided they want to join in this crazy jamboree as well. Tell him, Christine, what you've done."

"We've registered with the ATS, the Auxiliary Territorial Service. Many girls around here have done the same. We don't know what this involves yet or what will happen, but we both need to help too. We can't have all the boys take the glory, can we, Cora."

"What about Vera, I'd love to see her tomorrow," said Alfred. "I assume Charlie will be signing up, too."

"Remember, son, Charlie is Italian. Soon they're coming back to stay with us. Business is bad up there in Seaham and Vera is slightly worried about Charlie. He's fit and capable but he's not interested in any fighting. She's not sure where his loyalties lie."

"Surely, papa, they can't touch Charlie what with a wife and a seven year old little girl."

"I wish I could be as sure as you are," replied Fredo. "Now, let's all have some cake and tea. I think there's a large slice of *panettone* left over from Christmas."

***

Back at the barracks Alfred and eleven others were summoned to a meeting with Colonel Jackson. The colonel's uniform was spotlessly clean, with razor sharp trouser pleats which could carve the Sunday roast and black shoes which bounced back the early spring sun streaming through the window. His thick bushy moustache gave him an air of arrogance and superiority. Alfred reckoned this meeting was serious, so he, too, had to look serious.

"Your winter training will serve you well," said Jackson. "You have been selected for a vital mission. Success could mean an early end to the war. Be packed and ready, tomorrow morning when we will brief you as a group. Tomorrow afternoon the ship sails. You'll all be heroes."

That evening Alfred found great difficulty in sleeping. *'What could be so important, and me, Alfred, the ice cream man from Errington, why am I so special?'*

Jackson and his troop of twelve remained close together on the voyage across the North Sea. They conversed with the crew only when necessary. The Royal Navy destroyer was heading northwards towards the Norwegian coast. The intelligence was that Germany was dispatching an invasion fleet to occupy Norway, so it was vital the ship reach its destination before any of the German fleet land on Norwegian soil. The destroyer was armed and ready in the event that any U-boat submarines threaten its safety.

Alfred finally received the detail of the group's mission. He was conscious that his personal war had begun.

The town of Narvik lay on the west coast of Norway and was considered very valuable strategically. There were two reasons for this, Alfred learned. A few months previously the Soviet Union had invaded Finland. The Allies had considered Narvik as the potential base for a naval fleet from which a counter offensive could be launched against the Russians in the event that they exercised any further ambitions further west. Secondly and more importantly, Jackson had mentioned in his briefing that the British had gained intelligence Germans destroyers were their way to the port as well.

"You see," Jackson informed the group, "We are told that Germany's war effort depends entirely on iron ore mined in Kiruna in Sweden. During summer, Swedish ore reaches Germany by cargo ship through the Baltic Sea but in winter the Baltic freezes. Therefore the only route for the iron ore to reach Germany's factories is by railway to Narvik and then by ship down the North Sea."

"New prime minister Churchill has further ambitious plans for the navy to ward off any German threat," continued Jackson, "which I can't discuss with you. However your mission will be to secure the railway which transports the ore. When the time is right you will destroy the railway line just outside of Narvik. The Norwegian army and the Royal Air Force will provide you with local support."

After a restful night's sleep in primitive army barracks on the Ofotfjord coast, Alfred and his group were transported to the town of Bogen. A tender had been provided by Norwegian locals. The tiny town, with a population in the low hundreds and the temporary base for Jackson and his troop was already swarming with Norwegian soldiers. It was directly across the fjord from Narvik about forty miles away by a road which zigzagged around the fjord. Alfred and his team were informed that the group's resources would be supplemented in their mission in the Norwegian hinterland by French and Polish soldiers. He knew now the mission was serious.

Jackson addressed his group. "The French and Poles will have other assignments but your task remains the same. Tomorrow six of you, and you already know who you are, will leave here by truck. Our friends will be waiting for you when we reach your destination at Straumsnes. There is a small train station there. You will conduct your operation there when you obtain the green light."

Alfred was one of the six.

As the truck made its way along the single track dirt track road, Alfred was awestruck at the glorious contrast in scenery. On the right hand side of the road were the glistening waters of the Ofotfjord, on the left were mountains covered in crisp, virgin snow. *'Why would we fight a war up here in this wilderness?'* he thought.

The truck arrived at the small railway station. The waiting room resembled an old shed, and beside it lay the single track line. *'How could this place be critical to the war effort?'* Alfred thought. The group scanned the surroundings briefly and marched into the shed where they were met by three locals. In pigeon English they introduced themselves. One of the locals grabbed a bottle of aquavit from inside his bag.

However before any toast could be shared Alfred heard a noise from outside. "Quiet, quiet," he whispered. Indisputable, the sound of rifle clicks. He gazed through the window of the shed. No need for any more silence. "Guys, the huns are here. Quick, get ready."

The group crowded around the two windows of the shed and were aghast at the sight before them.

There were at least twenty soldiers, rifles directly pointing to the shed. Soldiers in thick coats, steel helmets and dark sunglasses, their faces hidden by white woolen balaclavas. The eagle emblem on the lapels was the giveaway. The men were German. They were the enemy.

"Ole, what should we do, is there another way out?" shouted Alfred.

Before Ole could answer, the bellowing noise of a loudhailer vibrated against the walls of the shed.

"Achtung, Britisher, Achtung."

Instantly one of the group, Billy with the red hair, smashed a window with the butt of his rifle and fired a round of shots. The Germans took cover behind large boulders. They suddenly seemed to multiply in number.

"There's no other way out, we have to surrender," said Ole, "or we all die."

Billy gave Ole a stern, furious glare but within moments he too realised that there was no way to survive the trap which had been set. Alfred noticed Billy's facial expression morph from anger to despair. Both knew there was no alternative. Nine sitting ducks with half a dozen rifles against fifty well prepared German soldiers.

There was little agonising or resistance. Ole ventured forward to open the door. Slowly he walked out ensuring the German soldiers could see his hands were high in the air. The two other Norwegians followed but Alfred and his troop hesitated.

After a few seconds, "British Soldiers, *kommen sie, bitte, kommen sie bitte,* please come out." Alfred sensed the hopelessness of their situation. The German's tone of voice made it very clear. In silence and in humiliation, Alfred ushered his colleagues to drop their rifles to the floor and leave the shed.

Back at base camp Colonel Jackson hadn't been aware that in the previous weeks, over a thousand German soldiers had been dropped into the area and furthermore that hundreds had travelled through Sweden on their way to Narvik posing as health workers. Hitler had already acknowledged the strategic importance of the remote Norwegian outpost.

But Jackson's group had not been the only ones laired into German traps. Virtually all allied operations in those spring weeks in the Norwegian fjords had been compromised. The German high command had managed to infiltrate a female spy, amongst others, in the British military headquarters at Tromso, further north on the coast. Reputed to have been the Nazi sympathiser and ballerina, Marina Lee, she had made good use of her Red Cross uniform and her physical attributes, too, to obtain specifics of the Allied plans.

The following day, Alfred, Billy and the other failed saboteurs were summoned for interrogation at the German headquarters in Narvik. Alfred reminded Billy of the instructions the group had been given on the ship. If they were captured and interrogated, they were give just name and rank, nothing else.

"Fusilier Alfred Baldini." He repeated his name umpteen times and fixed his eyes to the corner of the room, where a spider was weaving its web. In turn Billy feigned loss of memory pointing to the cuts on his head from him breaking the window at the train station.

"I will tell Mr Churchill your war is over," said the German with a sarcastic laugh. Alfred had sensed fear in the sentry guards when they gave their *'Heil Hitler'* salutes. *'This guy really is the boss.'*

"Norway now belongs to the German Reich and soon your friends in your little navy will leave. They will not return for you."

The group's interrogation was short and nothing was revealed. Silence had been maintained.

Two days later the six were locked in a dark and damp mess room in the bowels of a German ship, destination unknown. Alfred and his team were lucky. The merchant ship had left just hours before the harbour in Narvik turned into a graveyard of destroyed ships. In a bloody battle to control the area many British and German destroyers had sunk to the bottom. The crisp cool waters of the harbour had become a watery graveyard of numerous helpless seamen.

***

The train was already parked at the edge of the shipyard as the battleship, no longer disguised as a merchant vessel, slowed down to dock. It consisted on ten carriages, four of which were cattle trucks. The last carriage was the private quarters of the train commandant, the senior officer responsible for the delivery of the cargo.

The six British men were led out from the ship's bowels and into the spring sunshine. It took them a time to adjust their eyes to the sun's glare. For days all they had experienced were watery glints of sun rays through a tiny porthole. The docks were patrolled by sentries and mouth foaming Alsatian dogs desperate for work. Edward sensed this was an important place. He saw dozens of ships, huge cranes as far as the eye could see, officers, soldiers impeccably dressed in German regalia, moving to and fro. Red banners and flags emblazoned with the swastika hung from buildings in the distance, these colourfully contrasting the black smoke emitted from hundreds of small tugs in the harbour.

After a gratefully received bowl of thin soup and rye bread, the six were motioned into the empty cattle truck at the rear of the train. The door was bolted firmly shut and Edward glanced at the two bales of straw and the dirty pig trough inside. The only source of light and air was through four six inch square vents at each corner of the truck.

"Remember everything you see," said Edward. "We need to find out where we are. It'll be vital when we're home. So many ships here, our guys will be able to bomb the harbour. Any of you know anything about Germany, names of cities, the lingo." There was silence, nodding heads only.

Soon the train moved off and the huge port disappeared from view. From Bremerhaven, then Loxstedt, Lunestedt and Stubben. A few stations on and the boys could no longer remember any names. They abandoned the quest to remember any detail.

"Guys, what about escape, any ideas?" said Billy with the red hair.

"Maybe at the next stop we should try. Or what about trying to get out when the train slows down."

"I reckon it's too soon now," replied Alfred. "There will be thousands of soldiers travelling to and from that port. Better wait until we get deeper into the countryside. When we escape we can hide in barns or sheds far away from busy towns."

"Then what," said Billy. "We eat grass, say moo and grow a tail. We've got no chance. We are at war with this lot. At the port they wanted to shoot us down if we as much as sneezed. Better let's wait a while and see where we end up."

The group remained silent. Soon the rhythmic and monotonous sound of the slowly moving train drove them to sleep.

***

The train made its final stop in Thorn, a town in occupied Poland. Stalag XX-A was one of a series of fortified forts built in the nineteenth century in the traditional style, with moat, drawbridge and portcullis.

Inside the fort the group were fingerprinted and

photographed holding a piece of slate bearing a prisoner of war number. Each was given a small metal tag perforated in the centre with the camp number. The prisoner of war number was stamped on both sides.

"You boys don't look too good. If you die here one half goes with you to the devil, the other half to your whore of a mother at home," sniggered the German soldier in a white overcoat, pretending to be the camp physician. "Now I shall send you to the next part of the process. Please enjoy your stay here with us."

The prisoners were escorted into another room where their heads were shaved. Billy with the red hair was no longer Billy with the red hair. "Easy on, mate," he shouted as the barber's blade scraped flesh from his skull. Blood rolled down Billy's cheek but the barber ignored the remark, motioned Billy to move on while Alfred stood next in line.

Yet another room and more instructions. "You," the soldier pointing to Alfred, "cut the loaf equally for all of you, six pieces. Last slice is yours. And each of you take your bowl now."

As the group picked away at the meagre rations the soldier in charge bellowed further instructions, "After this, you will be given a postcard each which you can send home. You can tell your wives and girlfriends we are caring for you. And soon, after we destroy your Spitfires, we will be able to tell them personally. Imagine, your Englisher roses becoming beautiful German frauleins."

Billy made a motion to confront the solder, but Alfred held him back. "Billy, not now, later, when the time's right." Billy sat down uncaring that the blood from his shaved head was dripping into his bread and soup mush.

In due course the six were marched to where the British contingent were lodged, camp number eleven. They were accommodated in a vault like room with a twelve inch wide door, the only light shining was through a small window. Mattresses covered with loose straw were spread on the floor. On the way to their room, Alfred grimaced at the damp corridors, water dripping from the roof and running down the walls.

Alfred and Billy stared at each other. "We need to stay strong and healthy," said Alfred.

"Yes, we must do all the hard labour they give us, otherwise we'll go nuts. We might even get some proper nosh on the outside."

The food was grim, a ladle of thin soup at midday and a piece of bread which seemed to get smaller and more dirt infested by the day.

The only thing plentiful was lice. The group spent many hours picking out the egg lice from the seams of their shirts trying to kill them off. "We need to break out of here soon," said Alfred.

There was no hard labour. Every day for an hour prisoners were marshalled around a courtyard surrounded by patrolling soldiers armed with rapid fire rifles.

"Get me one of those," said Billy, "and I'll wipe out the lot. I don't care what gets in the way."

He continued, "Look, guys, the camp just has a wire fence, If we could find some tools to cut it, then we could be out and away. It'll be easy at night."

"Then what, man, you don't even know where we are. There are Germans everywhere."

"Hey, you with the machine gun. Where are we? Can you order me a cab? I wanna be out of here." said Billy as he squared up to the nearest soldier.

Instantly the guard grabbed his gun from his shoulder and pointed it directly at Billy. Within seconds three other soldiers ran to the scene, with equally threatening manoeuvres.

"Okay, okay," he said hands in the air. "You boys are serious, just checking."

The group rallied round Billy and moved him back to the centre of the yard where he disappeared into the crowd.

***

Days passed into weeks. Alfred appreciated that Billy was just an impulsive hothead. His nature was bravado. He didn't really have the guts to attempt an escape.

"It will not be long," said a German sentry. "Our soldiers are already in England. They have taken over. Your country forms part of our Reich."

The prisoners had accepted their fate. They knew they were remaining in the camp until the war was over.

The miserable conditions worsened at a pace. Red Cross parcels with clothes and food arrived from home but deliveries were infrequent. Alfred reckoned they were being intercepted and pilfered by their captors. The bastards had first pick at the goodies. Even they had to survive, he figured.

The prisoners' days were long and tedious. Occasionally sporadic gunfire was heard, from futile or desperate escape attempts. The guards were never in a rush to help the wounded or even collect dead bodies. Clearly, Alfred understood, the rush through the fence and the hope of a quick suicide had become irresistible.

Regularly the camp commandant stood in front of the camp inmates declaring the stupidity of escape attempts. The perpetrators of impulsive lone wolf escapes, he said, would be shot instantly. Even any large scale attempt to escape from the middle of Germanic Poland, he further affirmed, was futile as there would no help from the population in the towns and villages around. Locals had no sympathy for escapees. Even on the outside chance an escapee made it and they assisted, he said with even more authority, the locals understood there would no leniency. Women and children regardless, they would be regarded as traitors, and shot on the spot. Of the twenty one escapees so far, he continued in a now arrogant tone of voice, ten had been shot, eight sent to more secure camps and three returned. He emphasised, "There is no escape."

***

Soon the days were shortening, in the far distance the leaves were falling from the trees and the air was perceptively chiller.

"Come on boys, we need to do more than stand around and wonder," said Alfred. "There's a cold winter ahead and we need to be ready. Let's organise ourselves, we need to make sure we survive. We must stave off as much of the cold as we can. We must share all we have. No selfishness. Let's be nice to the bastards at least until the winter is over."

The winter indeed was severe. Snow fell from mid-November onwards and according to the three thermometers nailed to boundary gateposts the temperature never rose above zero for over thirty days.

Illnesses were common, dysentery, scabies and diphtheria. Medical supplies were sporadic. Those prisoners who served as camp doctors used every trick in the book to scrounge medicines from their captors. Frost bite was frequent and many were not able to survive the harsh winter.

Escape attempts were becoming more desperate. Two guys from the air force found an abandoned tunnel and they had crawled through only to find a machine gun facing them at the other end. Luckily the guards weren't trigger happy. They survived the ordeal and were duly marched back to their hut. An Englishman camouflaged himself underneath a cartful of manure but the threatening pitchfork of a diligent German sentry forced him to surrender. Another inmate had constructed a makeshift ladder made out of bed clothing and he too was caught, in the glare of a wandering searchlight.

Consequently from such abysmal and amateur failures, the English contingent decided to form an escape committee. It strongly suggested all ideas for escape should be coordinated centrally. The committee was convinced that a properly organised escape attempt offered escapees greater chances of success. All the while the German sentries were upping their own security measures.

Poor Billy, he couldn't hack it. His red hair had grown, and so did his capacity to self-destruct. Just as the winter cold was dissipating into spring he approached a guard at the main gate and decided to relieve himself on the guard's left leg. None too pleased the guard grabbed Billy by the arm, whilst his manhood dangled in midstream. By the time any of his pals could reach him, the commotion had been witnessed by several guards who quickly restored calm to avoid a threatening riot. Billy was not seen again for two days, until the camp commandant, before his next lecture to the crowd, had his lifeless body dumped in full view of the whole camp. Billy was laid to rest by his pals in a hastily dug out grave at the makeshift camp cemetery.

***

"Surely you can do something, any special skill?" Alfred was asked by the posh speaking British Officer at a meeting of the escape committee.

"I worked in an ice cream shop. My parents had little practical skills, but my mum made our clothes."

"Right, fusilier Alfred, you will be in the tailoring team," retorted Lieutenant Colonel Airey Neave, satisfied that he had found a job for the young fusilier. "We must raise the stakes in here. It's everybody's duty to escape. Or at least help others to escape."

Alfred registered that this was a man of importance. He was reluctant to have him disappointed. As he lay in his bed, he desperately tried to recall those evenings when mama sat by the fireside stitching, sewing and mending clothes. He was surprised at the detail he remembered. He felt a renewed sense of great responsibility. *'My duty, now they are depending on me,'* he thought and without the wavering rants of his now departed best friend, Alfred focussed his efforts on doing what he had to do.

The camp scroungers found material for Alfred. His full time job was altering, mending any textiles and uniforms which came his way. He used ink and boot polish to dye the clothes and eventually his sewing and embroidery skills were renowned as the best in the camp.

In the months that followed, Alfred's tailoring process became as sophisticated as the escape process itself. Better quality materials were sourced. Even the Red Cross parcels, when they did manage to arrive, mysteriously contained particular tailoring supplies he knew he couldn't obtain from within the camp. The effort certainly was worth it. He knew then that some escapees were indeed making it home.

As chief tailor Alfred was a vital cog in the escape routine. Known as *'The Stitcher'* there was no other prisoner who matched his quality and improvisation. He took great pride when a successful escape was announced and he was conscious he couldn't volunteer himself. His job was too important. Other than the obligatory forays to the nearby labour camps pounding rocks into ballast for roads being built for a Polish aristocrat sympathetic to the Nazis there was little time for anything else. Tailoring kept Alfred focussed.

Winters were bitterly cold. At night icicles formed inside Alfred's hut from water dripping through holes in the roof. During the day when the temperature did rise above zero, the ice melted slowly, constantly dripping droplets onto Alfred's single bed sheet. Obtaining some warmth was essential and eventually Alfred bunked up with Stevie from Berwick, another fusilier from the Northumberland regiment. He was left behind on the French coast at St Valery after the evacuation at Dunkirk. Stevie's body heat was indispensable. Dossing together and with an extra sheet made for a little more comfort.

Outside latrines overflowed during the day but at night when doors were locked the prisoners used buckets instead. Alfred and Stevie knew it was vital to stay well above ground level at night, to avoid any mishaps with urine swishing on the ground.

Time marched on. Same routine as always. New prisoners arrived, mainly British, French and American. They replaced the odd few who escaped and those who never made it back from hard labour forays. A death in the camp was usually followed by a mad scramble to grab anything useful from the cadaver, even filthy, torn shirts covered in excrement.

The camp was situated in a remote part of Poland. Little by way of news was received from the outside world. *'Kaput London, kaput Glasgow, kaput Liverpool, kaput Churchill'*, the German guards continually and proudly reiterated. Only gossip from newly arrived prisoners could be relied upon. Permitted and rare medical visits to external doctors yielded nothing.

By the end of nineteen forty-four and after more than four years at the camp, Alfred's bulk had reduced to half his pre-war healthy weight of thirteen stones. Bones were visible through his skin fighting desperately hard to keep the skeleton in one piece.

During the summer hundreds of new prisoners had arrived at the camp from the east. The new rumour was that the Germans were moving out prisoners from the Baltic states of Lithuania and Latvia. The word was positive. The Russians seemed to be approaching from the east and the Americans were moving in from the west.

"Hey, Stevie, do you think it might be over soon? I don't know if I can get through another one of these winters."

"Remember, Alf, what we agreed, if we do manage to get out of here and if we are separated, we meet under the new Tyne Bridge on midsummers' day, June twenty-first. We'll have a few beers and then it's off to the Hoppings on the Town Moor."

"We can only dream, man. I can't remember what a beer tastes like. And I'll need a few bacon sandwiches with my beer," replied Alfred.

***

The increasing number of inmates made conditions at

the camp even more severe. At the same time, however, it was evident the Germans seemed to be losing motivation. They appeared demoralised. No longer were they carefully arranging the rations as they did before. No longer were they trying to maintain their camp in a state of good order. On occasions in the evenings they were even failing to lock down the huts.

On a cold and snowy winter morning Alfred and Stevie awoke with the sound of commotion. Yet again they stepped into their urine mud bath and they ventured out. There were no signs of any German soldiers. They noticed some prisoners had managed to break through the main gate and to walk through to the outside. Hands in the air, they were shouting, *'Free, free.'*

"Stevie, look, they've gone."

"Yeh, free, but nowhere to go," replied Stevie.

Soon hand in hand, and after scrounging the unlocked office buildings for anything useful left behind, the pair, too, walked through the gates.

In the forest to the west of camp the party of prisoners thinned out quickly. "Looks like each man for himself," said Alfred. At the first crossroads beyond the forest, some ventured right and some proceeded straight on.

"One thing's for sure," said Stevie, "we need to go west, right back through Germany."

Slowly the pair trudged on in the falling snow and freezing temperatures. Numerous dead bodies were strewn in their path, so little left to purloin. But now they came across a body yet untampered. Survival was vital. They took what they could, the coat, boots, and a hat but they didn't neglect, however, to leave the corpse with its basic dignity.

In the fields they ate whatever they could find. Remnants of nuts, flowers, fruit, anything which they thought edible. Moles and rats crossed their path but they had little strength to capture them. Their first night free was spent cuddled up with a wild pig. There was little option. This was the only barn they had come across which could protect them from the cold. "This pig is moving west, too," said Stevie. "Looks like he's looking for some warmth as well."

The next morning as they stepped out into the daylight with the other four souls who also bedded overnight in the barn, the full nature of the crisis was before them. A column of people, mainly women, children, laden with bags, some with rickety carts, was walking slowly in single file, like skeletons on parade, all aimlessly moving west.

Evacuation was taking place, big style. *'The Russians, indeed, are coming'* thought Alfred. *'Seems there are no Germans to halt them in their tracks, the war might just be over.'*

Alfred and Stevie joined the march, and the trail moved on in silence. For any unfortunate falling in the snow, unable to take that extra step, there was no commotion, no attempt to help, no emotion. Trance like, the column moved on oblivious to the fact that one of their company had stumbled and destined to remain there to die in the freeze.

Occasionally booms of falling mortar shells were heard from behind in the far distance but the march continued nevertheless. It seemed like the marchers' destiny was being left in the hands of the Almighty, who would decide who survives and who would die. From time to time a plane flew overhead only to quickly disappear again.

"On reconnaissance duty, what the hell for." said Stevie. Alfred nodded and they silently continued on their way. Keep moving, find something to eat, to drink, to shelter and survive.

This time the plane in the distance approached from the front. It seemed more threatening. It was descending towards the column at an alarmingly fast speed. As it neared the ground the front of the plane suddenly pulled up and a hail of bullets littered the ground. Instinctively Alfred and Stevie fell. They glanced up and noticed the plane arcing round. Presumably it would re-litter the ground. "Quick, into the ditch," Alfred shouted. The plane repeated its actions, again pelleting the road with bullets but this time it didn't arc around. They saw it disappear into the distance.

As Alfred and Stevie stood up to continue their march, they witnessed the carnage. Half the group remained motionless. Others lay on the ground screaming. Blood pools were scattered all over the road. The able bodies wasted little time to scrounge and fight over additional clothing.

"Seems like the end of the world," said Stevie. "Let's move on. We need to avoid these main roads."

The pair decided to go it alone and to veer away from the mass refugee march. After two days in unremarkable forests the pair came across an abandoned farmhouse. "Shelter at last," said Stevie. They broke down the brittle door and entered. Inside there were two rooms which could alleviate the worst of the cold. Walls and roof were intact. "Let's camp for a day or two to recover some strength before continuing on," suggested Stevie.

***

Alfred walked into the saloon with his young brother

Thomas. He was dressed in his British army uniform and Thomas in his leather waistcoat, chaps and cowboy hat. They noticed that the two Germans they had been searching were at the bar. Together they each grabbed the enemy from behind and before either of them could react, Thomas had guns in each hand pointing directly at the Germans' temples. Double click, double click again. Nothing. The guns didn't have any bullets. Suddenly Alfred awoke, drips of sweat on the brow of his head.

"Damn it, Stevie. That was Thomas, my wee brother. Last time I saw him he was just fourteen. I hope he isn't mixed up in this shit."

Alfred looked through the space where there was once a window pane and was aghast at what was in full view. Two tanks were moving swiftly towards the house. A shell whizzed past, beyond and behind the house.

"Stevie, come on, get up, They're here. They're our boys."

"Go on……. I'll…. be behind you… soon," came Stevie's reply, every word forced out through his wheezing.

'Was there shelling from behind the house?' Alfred couldn't be sure. He raced out towards the nearest tree.

"Hey you, get behind us, go!" boomed out the guy high above on the front tank.

Alfred didn't hesitate and ran like crazy. He fell into the arms of a soldier with a gentle voice. "Hi, buddy." He was American.

"Stevie's in there. You need to get him."

"Yep, soldier, we'll rescue him. Now back, right back, and fast."

His mind completely confused and dazed, his feeble

body aching with pain at every movement, Alfred scampered along, on hands and knees, away from the tank.

Within minutes the shelling ceased and Alfred was lying in the back of a support jeep, verging on unconsciousness.

"Stevie, Thomas, Stevie,..........!" He drifted into sleep.

***

Alfred lay in a hospital tent bed. He felt the amazing sensation of a chilled, damp towel on his cheek. He thrust his tongue out to absorb moisture from the edge of the towel. He was overwhelmed with its freshness. He knew at that moment his nightmare was over.

For several years after the war on the three days of midsummer Alfred made his annual pilgrimage to the Tyne Bridge and to the Hoppings. However he never ever saw Stevie from Berwick.

Chapter 20

World War 2 – Lewis' Story

Mama and papa were of the old school. Lewis was regarded as the responsible one. Being the eldest of their children he was to set the example to his siblings. As a kid his mum wanted him always clean and tidy. He was forever being scolded for being mucky.

"Come here, Lewis, let me wipe the dirt from your face," his mum would say. She would grab a handkerchief from inside her apron pocket, dampen it with her tongue and wipe Lewis' face. He hated it, especially when he whiffed the scent of her perfume. Worse still, occasionally when his mum smoked a cigarette, the combined smell of perfume and cigarette would make him feel like vomiting.

Lewis felt the burden of responsibility. Indeed he was the diligent child, mostly well behaved, rarely disappointing his parents. As time passed, he was conscious, sometimes jealous, that all his younger brothers, including the young livewire sprat that was Thomas, somehow avoided the wrath of his parents. He knew that gradually, one by one, they were relaxing their grip on their children. In his eyes, his siblings had a more happy and carefree childhood.

Many years before he had been envious of Edward's enthusiasm at joining the army and similarly of Alfred when he signed up for the territorials.

"I wish I had joined many years ago. You are so lucky," he complained to Alfred on the night before his first training camp. "Years ago I am sure mum and dad would have persuaded me not to go."

"You can still join. You just have to do it. You can't sell ice cream all your life."

"Too late for me now. Ethel is pregnant and I can't leave her. And in any case I am too old, I am nearly thirty. Can you imagine me, middle aged with child, playing toy soldiers and larking about with you lot. I would be the grumpy old git."

Alfred shrugged his shoulders and Thomas ran into the room. He was fully holstered as per normal. "When I grow up I am going with you too, wherever it is you're going, Alf. I want to know everything when you return."

"I am proud of you, Alfred, make sure you enjoy a great experience, and Thomas it's time you went off to bed."

Thomas fired the last shot from his pistol at Lewis and he hopped out of the room.

***

After Alfred departed for his mission with the Northumberland fusiliers at the outbreak of war Lewis and his two sisters were a great source of comfort to their mum and dad. They knew it was right that Alfred participate in the national effort and they thought it important for the country's young men to show strength and solidarity. Fredo particularly so. He was insightful to the unsavoury events occurring on mainland Europe.

"God help us all, if Mussolini eventually sides up with Hitler, and I think he will," said a worried Fredo. "That Nazi needs to be stopped too. He wants to conquer us all. First Austria, then Czechoslovakia, now Poland. I am sure he'll come west as well. I hope the British and French can hold him back."

"Do you think Alfred is really up to this, I mean this fighting," Catherine replied. "All he has done in his life is to stand up to a few drunks, who want to steal a packet of cigarettes or a few bars of chocolate. Big difference to facing a machine gun."

"They'll train him well, don't worry, mama," said Lewis. "It was his duty, he had little option."

Lewis continued. "In fact it's our duty, for all of us, to defend ourselves. We can't just sit back and let others fight on our behalf. The town now seems desolate as so many of our boys have signed up. That shows real guts and bravery."

The girls were anticipating what Lewis was ready to announce. Although still in their teens Christine and Cora were mature for their years.

"Mama, we've all got to play our part. Lewis might have to be involved too but if the war continues for any length of time, who knows, we might have to be involved as well," said Christine.

"Holy Mother of God, what's happening to us," said Catherine, tears swelling in her eyes. "Don't they remember what happened the last time?"

"Mum, Dad, I need to tell you. I am ready for it. I have looked into this, there will be no fighting, so I will be fine," said Lewis assertively. "I am signing up for the Service Corps."

"Yes, I know, son. I thought this might be coming." Fredo stood up and put his arms around his wife's shoulders. "He's a grown man now and he won't do anything stupid. He has a beautiful little boy to return to," he said glancing over at Lewis, "correct, Lewis?"

Lewis nodded in agreement.

Returning the handkerchief to her apron pocket Catherine sighed and said, "Lewis, dear, tell me again, what is the role of the Service Corps?"

"We'll be behind the lines at all times. We cook the meals, provide supplies, and generally ensure the boys are well equipped. In fact anything the soldiers require. It's our job, too, to bring back the injured to the field hospital. Lots of different tasks, really, but no fighting."

Mum and dad cuddled their girls and Lewis joined in. On seeing the group huddle Thomas took Dino by the hand and the two boys squeezed themselves through Lewis' legs to the centre of the huddle.

***

Lewis duly enrolled at the Northumbrian Brigade in Hartlepool. This was located close to home. Initially he was keen to avoid any extended periods away from his family. Training included spending weekends in Kielder forest where he mastered the skills of gun handling and of danger awareness. After a short period of basic training he was formally enlisted into the Royal Army Service Corp as a Driver.

He was assigned to the North East Anti-Aircraft division. The experiences of the Hartlepool bombing during the first war, had led the authorities to believe that the Germans might be planning similar bombing missions on the heavy industrial sites in the region. Shipbuilding yards, steel plants, coal mines, they were all legitimate targets. Damage would cause havoc to the British war effort.

Despite Hitler's belligerent rhetoric in the first few months of the war aimed specifically at the British, and further inflammatory rhetoric claiming his ability to fight on two fronts, there were no hostile incidents of note in the North East during the first six months. Lewis had spent the first winter of the war travelling backwards and forwards to his station at Hartlepool casually wondering what all the fuss was about.

But in early spring all changed. The Germans entered the previously demilitarised Rhine area in mainland Europe with battalions of troops. This was a red flag to the Allies. Officially the Rhineland had been a protected arms free zone, internationally agreed after the first war to prevent future German incursions into Belgium or France. Hitler had just smashed the vital treaty which had evolved from the chaos of the first war. Belgium and France had flagged serious concerns and the British understood that now Hitler was serious. Churchill had no option but to provide the necessary military support to their Belgian and French allies.

As a consequence Lewis' cosy lifestyle was transformed. His war was about to begin.

"When you have time, Lewis, please don't forget to write. We'll take care of Ethel and Dino. We need to know you are all right. Alfred has already sent us a card and a letter. It helps greatly when you keep in touch," said his mum.

Lewis was in no more mood for tears. He had witnessed Ethel's tormented goodbye a few minutes earlier. "I will," he said. He closed the shop door and walked out.

The phoney war had ended. Lewis' service corps unit was dispatched immediately to the new western front.

Lewis and his troop of service personnel found themselves supporting a Northumberland Infantry division and tank brigade on the Pas de Calais in Northern France. They were still working on defensive strategies with their French counterparts when the news from hell arrived. Germany had invaded Belgium and Luxembourg and they threatened direct incursions into France.

Following the first war the French had built their impressive Maginot fortifications across the entire border with Germany. These had been built to keep their traditional enemy at bay. But the French had failed to anticipate Hitler's alternative strategy, to launch an offensive on France by means of an invasion of Belgium and Luxembourg. The French had been entirely dependent on their Belgian friends to the north being able to defend themselves against any German incursion. But they had calculated wrongly. Belgium offered little resistance and within days Hitler's panzer divisions had crossed the French border.

Lewis' support unit was reassigned to a new front line near Arras, about fifty miles from the Belgian border. On route from the Pas de Calais he remarked on the numerous military cemeteries which dotted the landscape.

"Remnants from the first war," he related to Jack, his colleague. "Ironic that we should be here again."

"This time it might be worse, more destruction. It'll be tank versus tank now, not soldier against soldier," replied Jack.

At their camp station Lewis and Jack understood immediately the gravity of the situation. The high and mighty of the respective French and British armies were racing backwards and forwards to the billet station of General Gamelin. Rumours were emerging that arrangements were to be made to face the enemy straight on.

The colonel bellowed, "Lewis, Jack, both of you on ambulance duty. Your job is to rescue the wounded. Bring them back behind the lines. To the hospital. Got that."

The convoy of tanks and support vehicles rolled out in the early morning. It was already warm. It was sure to be another hot day. In little time they were at the front near the small village of Duisans.

In the near distance Lewis could see the effects of the conflict. Obviously random destruction. Houses with huge holes, sides ripped off buildings and churches no longer with steeples intact. He and Jack cautiously moved closer to the action armed with stretcher and a bagful of supplies. They came across their first casualty, a French soldier wounded in the shoulder, blooding streaming out of his right collar bone.

"Quick, stop the bleeding," Jack shouted as both scuttled nervously into their bags for bandages and tourniquet equipment.

Within a few minutes, the Frenchman was lying in the relative safety of a camp bed, "*Merci, vite, il y a beaucoup,* Hurry, there are many more out there."

"Jack, he's dead. We'll come back for him later. We need to rescue the injured first." Lewis said coming across their first lifeless body.

For the remainder of the day and into the balmy evening Lewis and Jack continued the rescue routine, at the same time dodging tank fire.

In the darkness of night there was little opportunity for rest. The sound of sporadic tank fire was constantly piercing the night silence. But the injured still needed tending, for them there was no longer day, no longer night.

"We can't see out in the field. But they're still bombing. When dawn breaks, no doubt, we'll see more carnage." Lewis whispered to Jack as they sat there sipping their tea.

"I heard the Sergeant say we might have to move back, the Germans seem to be making advances."

The next morning in the dawn of daylight they scanned the landscape towards Duisans. Nothing had changed. The pair scampered out into the open fields searching their first casualty of the day. He was British and he appeared to be still breathing.

"Grab his arms," said Lewis. They grabbed an arm each. Lewis screamed. As he tried to lift the soldier's arm, he was taken aback. It separated from the rest of the body. Jolted he let it go and the arm dropped ungraciously onto the man's stomach. No sound, no movement any more, the man was already gone.

"We'll come back for this one, come on let's go," said Jack.

There were bodies everywhere and teams of body carriers as far as the eye could see. The magnitude of the rescue mission had multiplied overnight.

"We need more carriers, Sarge," said Lewis after returning with the latest casualty.

"There are no more," he said. "Just keep going, keep bringing them in."

And off they went again, almost thirty six hours non-stop with little more than a sixty minute nap and cup of tea. Yet more dead bodies, yet more blood, yet more missing limbs, yet more skulls caved in.

As he raced out yet again, Lewis thought momentarily of his family back home. '*They have no idea, holes in bodies, arms and legs hanging off, hearing screaming pain, and we have to carry on, just feel numb and dumb. No time to think, no time to sympathise, no time to care, just carry on.*'

The pair came across another two bodies, hands held together, both in French uniform. One was dead, the other struggling for breath, limbless. His left arm and leg were missing, nowhere to be seen. The soil all around was a deep red. Further tank blast noise, more sound of machine gun fire in the distance. Oblivious to his surroundings, Lewis ignored the commotion and concentrated on the job at hand. "Jack, quick, let's lift this one out."

A two second eerie silence ensued. "Jack, down here, help." Still no response. A dreadful thought instinctively flashed through Lewis' mind. He looked around. His instinct was correct. There was Jack lying on the ground lifeless. "Jack, no, Jack!"

Jack's head was a bloody mess of flesh and bone. Lewis recognised him only from what he was wearing. Jack lay on top of his shoulder bag, his blood now also colouring the soil red.

Lewis quickly composed himself, lifted the French soldier and hobbled back with him to the hospital camp. He remained oblivious to the noise in the background.

***

The battle for Arras was short lived. Lewis later learned that the enemy panzer tanks were too powerful for the lightweight tanks of the French and British. Soon the Allies were in retreat.

"The enemy have surrounded us completely. We have to get back to the ports," announced Colonel Ramsay. His message was perfectly clear, just get back. Abandon everything, tanks, vehicles, equipment. "We are heading for Calais. The ships are waiting there to take us home."

At the admiralty in London, Churchill had already been preparing for the worst. Intelligence reports had indicated that the British army was now surrounded, north and south by the German panzers. How could he arrange for half a million men to return home, while at the same time maintain high spirits when morale was quickly deteriorating? He had decided. To avoid further disaster the only strategy was the immediate evacuation of every British soldier on the western front through the port of Dunkirk.

The country was mobilized into action. Every sailing vessel stationed along the south and east coasts of England which could transport soldiers was called to action. From Plymouth to Ramsgate to Hull hundreds of small ships, trawlers, pleasure craft, rowing boats, barges, tugs, ventured into the dangerous waters of the English Channel to take part in the rescue. Smaller boats had to battle against the waves as well as the German Luftwaffe. But fortunately it was summer, the sea was calm and the winds were light. However there were other unknown dangers lurking in the English Channel ahead for the rescue fleet. The Germans had mined the Channel and the rumour mill suggested U-boat submarines were lying in wait. But with the Royal Air Force in support the convoy of boats proceeded nevertheless. The smaller crafts, as instructed, headed for the beaches north of Dunkirk and the larger vessels headed directly to Dunkirk harbour.

Meanwhile Lewis was still forty miles away. "Straight to the coast, boys, fast as you can. Leave all your personal stuff behind. There is only a corridor ten miles wide. Germans are closing in from both sides. Time is against us. They will be waiting, the ships at the coast." Colonel Ramsay stressed.

The hospital camp descended into chaos. Trucks, carts, jeeps, and roadworthy tanks moved out in convoy. Every vehicle was crowded with anxious servicemen on permanent watch for approaching

Germans. As his vehicle hit the main trunk road towards the coast, Lewis feared the worst. He envisaged an imaginary scene from the air. *'A passing Stuka bomber would cause enormous carnage. It would be like watching thousands of ants scampering after each other to the safety of the mole hill,'* he thought. *'Easy target, no defence.'* Through good fortune there were no Stukas in sight.

Progress was slow and as Lewis made out the imposing church steeple of St Omer in the distance, the word was passed along the convoy. *'The Germans have Calais, we need to get to Dunkirk.'* The sound of shell fire in the distance continued. From Germans or British, nobody knew.

When his truck reached the elevated town of Bergues, a couple of miles from the coast, Lewis witnessed the panorama before him. On his right he saw the beach scattered with smoldering debris. People were moving to and from the beach in a chaos. Small boats littered the sea. On his left he saw the buildings of the town, presumably Dunkirk, virtually in ruins. The harbour was visible and he could make out the profile of larger ships, funnels belching out plumes of black smoke. In the sky above several planes were crisscrossing through the light evening mist like drunken seagulls.

"You lot, head for the harbour," Lewis heard an authoritative voice through the cacophony of distant noise.

By the time Lewis' transport had reached the outskirts of the town the strategy was clear. Every man for himself, find a boat and with luck make it home.

Evening had turned into night as Lewis made for the long queue for the tender to board the destroyer HMS

Grenade, anchored a hundred yards out at sea. Through the darkness, Lewis could see that the tender was weighed down by the quantity of men on board. But he knew he had little option. This ship, that ship, in the midst of the chaos and noise it was all the same. Ships with huge flashlights were pumping shells into the air at passing Stuka bombers. Whether they were hitting their targets or whether the shells were merely falling back to the sea in the distance, nobody had any idea.

The tender slowly made its way anonymously to the destroyer. Lewis was on board.

Rumours persisted that waiting U-boats in the channel had already fatally damaged another destroyer. But the evacuees didn't care. For the moment they were safe. They were delighted to be on board. They just wanted the boat to start moving. When all seemed quiet the unique drone of Stuka bombers was heard again. The flashlight roamed the night sky. Nothing. Then the fireball. Lewis felt severe pains all over his body. He had little time to react. With the force of the blast, he was plunged into the sea, hundreds of others too. He bobbled underneath the sea holding his breath. He saw that parts of the sea above were alight. For a moment he felt no pain. His thoughts were on surfacing for air, otherwise he knew he was going down. He found a spot between the burning spills, and he broke through. Gulping for air he heard the cries of those around. The fires lit the gloom and he grasped the full horror of the scene. Some men obviously dead, some struggling to swim and others floating around aimlessly like dancing bottle corks. *'Get to shore',* as the severe pains in his body ached once more.

The destroyer had suffered a direct hit. A bomb had completely destroyed a funnel and its boiler room underneath. The stokers and those below deck stood no chance.

***

As dawn broke, Lewis felt a slap on his face and he awoke from his trauma. He was lying on a sandy beach. He observed soldiers running around with stretchers, others tending the injured nearby.

"I am sore all over," Lewis said to his helper, noticing his torn white armband with a red cross inked on the cloth. Lewis' sodden clothes were ripped to shreds.

"The blast has left bits of metal and shrapnel all over your body. We'll bandage these up and see if we can find you a boat again. Can you walk?"

Bandages were rapidly applied to the worst of Lewis' injuries and they helped him to his feet.

"Next beach along there are about two dozen small boats. Off you go. Hurry."

The samaritans with the red cross on their sleeves moved on to their next body and Lewis slowly walked in the direction of the other beach, his left leg leaving behind a score in a sand. As he ambled along he witnessed the devastation first hand. A torso, without lower limbs and a lone leg a few feet to the side covered in blood. *'Was that his?'* Lewis thought. *'Shall I place the leg near the body? No, let me plod on'*. There were more dead bodies, more stretcher bearers, other soldiers running aimlessly. *'Where to, where from?'* Lewis felt alone. He saw upturned hulls, blackened vehicles abandoned and in the distance a town whose buildings were in ruins. Yet the sky was a shade of pure blue and the sand glistened pure white in the sunshine. *'How can we do this to each other?'* he thought.

Ahead he witnessed a flurry of people, a queue of worn out desperate men spiritlessly wading out into the sea. Off shore he saw several trawlers, lifeboats and other smaller craft. *'Today there are no Stukas in the sky, yet! Maybe this is the way home',* Lewis thought, his body still aching with pain. He joined the long queue and he too waded into the calm sea. Everyone speechless.

All of a sudden his legs gave way and Lewis fell into the sea. In agonizing pain he lay on the sea floor, waves gently lapping over his body. Silhouettes of those passing buy faded from black to light grey. He felt numb, his life was ebbing away, he saw images of his little boy, saying his first words, *'da........da, dada'.*

'Am I alive, am I already in another place?'

Suddenly a big fella with a Scots accent grabbed Lewis round the waist and scooped him out of the water. "Mon son, wur takin' ye hame."

Lewis found himself on board a fishing trawler, crammed so full like sardines that there was no room to sit. "Third crossing, so far," said the captain, "Just hold on to each other, and we'll be fine." The captain's twelve year old son opened up a box containing loaves of bread and bottles of water. Sustenance was welcome. Each passenger took his share and passed it along. There was little communication.

"Just all pray that the Stukas and the U-Boats are after the bigger boys," said the Captain as the trawler ventured into the open sea.

Lewis never noticed that the big guy with the Scots accent was staying behind. He had returned to the shore on the lookout for others desperate for help.

Indeed during the crossing Stukas did play cat and mouse with the Spitfires. When a plane fell into the sea an eerie silence enveloped the trawler. The evacuees continued pondering their fate as they peered at the sky above. One broke the silence, "Maybe the bombers have their sights on bigger, easier targets." Momentarily when planes disappeared from view, instead they glared anxiously at the sea. *Would the U-boats surface first or would they fire their torpedoes first?*

The scene was identical for all boats that day. Filled to the brim with weary soldiers, in anxious silence, eyes towards the sky, and eyes down to the sea.

The trawler reached Dover harbour safely. Teas and biscuits were plentiful as women and children swarmed around caring for the beleaguered. Lewis looked to heaven and screamed out the Lord's Prayer before he accepted the cup of tea. In an instant the whole harbour area were praying in unison.

***

The conflict seemed light years away as Lewis stepped off the coach which brought him from the railway station. To his waiting family in Errington he was in every sense the brave soldier. He was dressed in the new uniform he had received, but deep inside his body hurt. He found difficulty in swallowing water and he felt feverish constantly. His brain hurt too, '*what stupidity war is? I'm so lucky.*' On the train northwards he had prayed constantly. '*I just want to see my little boy. Please, Lord, let him be healthy. Let him never experience what I have gone through.*'

Lewis grabbed Ethel and Dino and he didn't release them for fully five minutes, tears rolling down his face. Dino was wedged in, he couldn't move. Then Fredo and Catherine joined in.

"Lewis, Lewis, it's wonderful to have you back. We have heard such terrible stories from France." Mum and dad left the room to enable the couple to have some privacy.

"Ethel, I missed you so much. Have they looked after you well?"

"If it wasn't for your sisters and little Thomas, it would have been difficult. They were great, helped with Dino and they kept my morale high especially with all the bad news around. Never mind me. We need to get you to see a doctor. Those wounds look bad, let me see."

Lewis turned away, "Where are the girls, where's Thomas?"

"Let me see, Lewis, the wounds," said Ethel pulling his arm back gently. "I guess they are down at the coast. Christine's best pal joined the auxiliaries and she is on patrol on the beach watching out for enemy aircraft. They should be home soon."

Lewis didn't flinch as Ethel removed Lewis' jacket and shirt. Bandages, plasters covered his body. "Oh my God," she said. "Tomorrow we go to the doctors." Lewis made an awkward movement arching his right shoulder upwards and away from his right pelvis. "Just need to get some comfort from this pain," he said.

Later in the evening Christine and Cora ran through the door of the shop and raced through to find their big brother. "Lewis, Lewis, we heard you're back."

He stood upright, almost emotionless, as the girls wrapped their arms around him. "Thomas, where is he?" The girls sensed all was not okay and they stepped back. Mum intervened. "He's had a bad time, he'll be fine tomorrow."

The following day at the pharmacy Ethel and Lewis bought a variety of ointments and creams. "There will be no charge for our brave soldiers," the pharmacist insisted as the pair walked out with four different bottles of cures.

***

The remedies had little effect and Lewis continued in pain for several months. He had been formally de-mobbed on the grounds of ill health but he found great difficulty in returning to his previously busy life.

"I am really worried now, especially with a new baby on the way, Catherine," said Ethel. "Lewis has been back nearly a year and I rarely see him smile any more. Sometimes we don't talk. It's as if he is in his own world. He seems to be in perpetual pain."

"Obviously he hasn't wanted to talk about his bad experiences. Maybe it's time we obtained some help elsewhere. There's a place up in the Durham moors. Some injured soldiers are there already. I think the hospital is really for tuberculosis sufferers but a long period of fresh air might do a lot of good."

"One of the women at the bath-house mentioned it, Wolsingham, I think, the place is called. Her husband, she says, had some huge trauma when he came back from the war and he's up there two days a week. We should check it out, will you come with us, please, Catherine."

"Yes, of course."

Ethel wasn't yet convinced about the hospital. She had consulted with everybody and anybody to try to establish what was happening to Lewis. Often he awoke in the middle of the night in a sweaty panic screaming, *"No, not again, another one, sergeant!"* Ethel kept a diary and she had noted the pattern, two or three nights of nightmares, then followed by two or three weeks of calm. She was almost able to predict the next incident. She was concerned also that Lewis' contortions of pain and muscle spasms had been continuing unabated. She decided to pay a visit to the Wolsingham Sanatorium.

"This is a facility for long term illness," the administrator said. "Most of the patients here are suffering from tuberculosis. The fresh air here assists with their recovery. The coal mines and all that dust, well it's in the air down there at the colliery."

The administrator continued, "We also have patients with other infectious diseases. The muscle spasms, you mention, sounds to me as if your husband has tetanus. Does he often have a fever, often sweat, trouble swallowing, for example?"

"Yes, exactly," Ethel replied.

"From what you have told me of his experiences I suspect Lewis' wounds have been severely infected, perhaps from the salty water on the beach. The water itself would have been contaminated from dead bodies and congealed blood all around. Nevertheless I do think that after a year his body ought to have healed. But it's not just about the body, you know, there's a lot about the human brain which is still mysterious. Maybe it's the trauma he suffered, who knows."

Ethel sat confused.

"A period of convalescence here will certainly help Lewis greatly. I suggest you think about it."

Ethel mulled over the situation. Her husband was clearly in pain, but whether it was serious enough to keep him away from his little four year old boy, she wasn't yet sure. And now with another child on the way, Ethel decided to wait until after her second was born.

Lewis junior arrived healthily and his dad doted on his second son. But the nightmares and pains rarely eased. When Lewis heard the latest war bulletins on the radio, he relapsed into his personal despair.

Ethel convinced herself that the war would never be blocked out from Lewis' consciousness. It was everywhere, air raid sirens, black outs, gas masks, military uniforms in the streets. Customers in the shop searched for their own sympathy after losing loved ones.

Lewis, too, had the fate of his brother, Alfred, permanently on his mind. He was in a prisoner of war camp somewhere out there in war torn Europe. Was he still there? Was he still alive, even? His dad had recently returned from his own horrific trauma. Thankfully he seemed fine. And now the girls Christine and Cora were signing up. And little Thomas, his hotheaded anger was never far away, when he was old enough he '*was going to run the hun out of Europe*,' he had declared with conviction.

Ethel delayed her decision for as long as she could. But Lewis' trauma had waned little during the previous three years. His pains seemed to be compounded in the smoky and grimy dampness of winter, so after Lewis junior's second birthday party in the autumn of 1943, she urged her husband to spend the winter at the sanatorium in the crisp freshness of the Durham moors.

Sadly, during seven months at the sanatorium Lewis never made the recovery which Ethel was desperate for. As the summer flowers were beginning to bloom whilst at the same time there was renewed hope that the war was ending soon, Lewis passed away peacefully. His war had come to an end on the peaceful and beautiful Durham moors.

Lewis was a Dunkirk survivor who never survived.

Chapter 21

World War 2 – Fredo's Story

Before the war Fredo was in a state of continual anxiety. Faithfully and regularly he listened to the news bulletins and read the newspapers cover to cover. He had never trusted Hitler from the outset and he reckoned something serious was afoot even before he read about the anti-Jewish propaganda streaming out of Germany. He was afraid also of Mussolini. He knew many of his countrymen from Valbona, admired the great man and followed his every move. They had declared that Mussolini would never side with Hitler. *'Dai Fredo, Mussolini mai con Hitler.'*

He had deliberated often on Mussolini's desire for *'an outlet for the surplus Italian population.'* He had read of his invasion into Abyssinia, his belligerent forays into Albania and his assistance to Franco to try to end the civil war in Spain. Fredo's real concern was Mussolini's desire that Italy should become an imperial power. Mussolini had to be an admirer of Hitler, he thought, for they shared the same visions. At the Munich peace conference had Mussolini been an active participant, or had he been Hitler's puppet? Fredo even considered the more hopeful scenario. Might Mussolini have been Chamberlain's puppet? But it didn't matter anymore. The conference had failed catastrophically and Mussolini had been present.

Ominously Hitler had annexed Austria and trampled over Czechoslovakia and Poland but now that he had overrun the allied armies of Belgium and Holland, Fredo was sure these acts would call Mussolini's hand. In the meantime, Britain was in despair and the country's humiliation at Dunkirk was complete. Fredo was awaiting the homecoming of his eldest son from the humiliation, a beleaguered and injured soldier. His other son had been captured in Norway, now likely to be rotting away in some work camp in the new greater Germany. What next, he couldn't imagine and Mussolini held the key.

Only days after Lewis returned home, Fredo received his answer. Following Hitler's excursions into France, the French government fled into exile at Bordeaux on the west coast. Mussolini grasped the opportunity. Hitler's opponents had been swiftly conceding defeat. Mussolini calculated that the conflict would be over soon. He had visions of a new Italian empire in control of the Mediterranean from Southern France to Northern Africa. In addition with Germany as an ally, Italy would inherit the French colonies in Africa and without doubt when Hitler defeated Britain, the British colonies too. So he gambled his country's future and declared his hand. Mussolini sided with Hitler.

It was on the tenth of June, 1940 when Italy declared war on Britain and France.

Fredo had no opportunity to consider the ramifications of this declaration of war. The impact for him and his family was rapid and unexpected.

That very evening the family were sitting after their evening meal contemplating the future.

"Switch on the wireless," said Catherine. "There might some more news from Italy."

The rumble seemed distant. *'Can't be a band tonight,'* thought Fredo. The noise was intensifying by the second, they seemed to be banging on drums. *'Can't make out a tune.'* But the objective of the commotion soon became clear. *'Eyeties out, eyeties out!'*

Fredo sprang from his chair. "Catherine, quick, get the children upstairs," he shouted.

Apprehensively he opened his door and he peeked out into the street. The mob were armed with boulders, sticks and bricks, metal bin lids. Some had rifles. *'Heil Hitler'* they shouted in unison and mimicking the Nazi salute, followed by the very threatening, *'Eyeties out'.*

Fredo bolted the door and ordered his family upstairs. The glass of one window shattered. "Mama, mama," squealed Christine. "Upstairs, quick." Fortunately the brick missed. Then a second window. The family was under attack.

They were terrified. Fredo ran to the back door to ensure it was locked. "What is they set fire to the shop," Lewis yelled as the group scampered upstairs.

Fredo turned around and he froze with fear. The mob were inside. The shouting continued, *'Eyeties out.'* But they didn't come for him alone. They were after the chocolate bars, the bottles of pop on display and the cakes inside the glass cabinets. Fredo remained transfixed, it was as if his feet were nailed to the floor. From fear to disgust as one spat at him. He recognized the villain as a customer. Catherine knew his wife well. He noticed that outside two policeman were struggling to maintain control. He bolted upstairs to join his family. From the first floor window he watched as the crowd outside continued to gesticulate.

"How could they," Catherine said in tears, tightly

holding onto Ethel and Dino.

From upstairs they heard it all. "Grab it, get it." A pause. "Let's go. There's four more." Fredo made a motion to return downstairs, but Lewis intervened. "They'll attack you, leave them to it, there's nothing much down there anyway." He grabbed his dad by the arm holding him back. In the few days since his return Lewis had seemed distant. This night he regained his spark.

Minutes later the commotion halted. The shop seemed to be empty. From the window Fredo noticed that police constables had restored some order. He saw the crowd moving on.

There were four other shops nearby owned by Italians, The Chiappas, the Fioris, the Mocognis and the café of Fredo's son in law, Charlie Gonnella. That night their windows too were smashed and the contents on display looted. Thankfully nobody was injured.

At midnight, the streets were empty and Fredo and Lewis surveyed the scene. Front and back doors were still locked. Confectionery and cakes were gone. The mob had missed the odd chocolate bar strewn on the floor. Damage to furniture had been minimal. They had entered and exited from the shop windows. "How do we get over this," Fredo said.

"Let's sleep on it. We'll worry about tomorrow," replied Lewis.

At precisely six o'clock the next morning, Fredo woke to the sound of fists banging at the front door. 'Please, not again. What now?" he gasped to his wife. By the time Fredo reached his front door, everybody was awake and in a fearful panic.

Credentials were displayed. *'Special Branch.'*

"Mr Fredo Baldini, you are an enemy alien. You are

under arrest. You have five minutes to pack a small bag."

He was flabbergasted. 'Hold on a minute. You're joking." He clasped his head in his hands. "Can't you see what hell we had last night?"

The two men remained stubbornly focussed. "Five minutes, Mr Baldini."

"An enemy! I don't understand. God, my son is just back from Dunkirk, he's here. You can speak to him. My other son is a prisoner of war in Germany, Poland, I don't know where."

They brushed past him and marched into the shop. Meanwhile Catherine and Lewis, who had little sleep were still in their clothes of the previous day.

"This can't be right! We were attacked last night," Lewis pleaded.

"We repeat, Mr Baldini for the last time, five minutes to pack your bag. Or else we take you by force. I guarantee you won't like that."

Catherine burst into tears. "Fredo, tell them, I am British, our kids are British, you're British. Tell them Fredo, please. What's happening? You're over sixty years of age. What harm can you do? Tell them."

Fredo pleaded but their abrupt reply was the same. "Please hurry, Mr Baldini."

"What's happening mum, dad?" said Thomas. The girls too were downstairs and pulled their young brother back.

"It's about the events of last night, son. Dad is going to the police station to identify the culprits. He'll be back soon," replied his mum trying to maintain some calm.

"That's not true, mama, he's Italian, that's why, isn't it?" Christine was well aware.

The girls tried to comfort their tearful mum as Fredo stomped gloomily downstairs with his suitcase.

Thomas ran over to his dad. He knew something was wrong. "A suitcase for the police station, mum, dad, tell us what's going on."

"I'll be back soon, son," he continued. "Catherine, call Joe Rinaldi in Wallsend. See if he can help, that is, if he's still a policeman. Perhaps they've arrested him as well."

The two officers ushered Fredo out of the door and pushed him into the back seat of the waiting car outside. The car sped off.

Catherine took control. Her tears vanished. "Thomas, away down the road and check on the others, especially Charlie and Vera. See what's happening also at Chiappas and Mocognis. Christine, call Joe, maybe he'll know what's going on."

Meanwhile Lewis remained frozen in a daze, his body pains making it difficult for him to move. "Mum, should I get a joiner to board up the shop?"

"Of course, unless you are prepared to do it yourself."

An hour later Thomas returned with big sister Vera and her kids with the news. Charlie's windows had remained intact, maybe his shop was slightly off the beaten track but he had been picked up too. He was taken by the police just minutes before Thomas arrived. Mr Chiappa, Mr Mocogni, both were gone, their windows too had been smashed the previous night. The families were equally terrified what would happen next.

Christine made the call from the telephone box at the corner of the next street. "It's as we live in a different planet now. Mrs Bennett, Mrs Thompson, both walked off the pavement when they saw me. They never acknowledged me. Mama, what are we going to do?"

"Never mind that, what about Joe Rinaldi?"

"I managed to get through to the police station in Wallsend. Joe sounded angry. His papa was taken too. He says there is nothing he or anybody else can do. He doesn't know what's going on. He's been told to carry on with his job as normal otherwise he will lose it. He's seen lists of people for his area. They are full of Italians."

The family sat round the table in total silence, anxious, fearful and desperate.

Thomas broke the stillness, "Come on Lewis, I'll help you find the joiner."

The town appeared transformed overnight, the pair discovered. There were no more good mornings. Old ladies crossed the street to avoid them, a few men spat at the ground as they passed. They could see Lewis' army trousers, they knew about his escape from Dunkirk, but it made no difference. Clearly the Italian family with the ice cream parlour and chip shop was now the enemy.

Eventually they found a willing joiner. To their surprise, his conditions were made clear at the outset, "I will do it, but cash only, and definitely up front."

"But you know us, my dad has given your wife credit, for God's sake. You probably still owe us money." replied an angry Thomas.

"That's the deal. I'm out on a limb here, you know. I could become the scab who helped the enemy," the joiner retorted ensuring his message was understood.

They knew the guy was serious. They raced back home.

"We need to watch every single penny now, our

money might run out soon," Catherine said to her family as she firmly closed the safe, notes in hand.

***

Fredo was transported to Newcastle central police station, where several bus coaches were already parked. Son-in-law Charlie Gonnella was already at the station and Mr Chiappa and Mr Mocogni from Errington too. He embraced his cousin, Pepe Rinaldi from Wallsend and he was taken aback that old friend Vincenzo from Stanley was there too. "They've arrested all of us," said Vincenzo. "Even our boys, too. I wish I could find out what's going on."

Soon the convoy of coaches filled with Italian men left Newcastle. There were all types. Some were fresh faced teenagers, with boyish looks, who should still be at school. Some were like Fredo, bald or balding with grey hair, clearly in retirement. And there was every age in between. They didn't discriminate. They were all enemies of the state.

A couple of pit stops later the coaches came to a halt somewhere in Lancashire at a huge austere looking building with bricked up windows. Fredo noted the faded lettering on the façade, Warth Mills, it said. They were ushered inside. Playtime for the rats had been interrupted and they scurried back into their rat-holes. The men were tossed blankets and bits of canvas. "Collect some straw for your mattress at the store and find a place to sleep," they were told. In each corner of the huge space, Fredo noticed rows of buckets. *'Presumably they're for us to keep the dirty floors clean of excrement and urine,'* he thought. Water ran down the walls, daylight shone through from the holes in the roof. The floor remained full of oils and grease from the building's former glory as a cotton mill.

During the course of the day the coaches continued to arrive, not only more Italians, but groups of Germans, then reportedly a busload of Jews. Supposedly they were refugees kicked out by Hitler. All enemies.

By the end of the day, each of the detainees had collected their tin mug, fork, knife and spoon from the makeshift canteen. Rations were meagre. Just hard bread, soup, offal and some vegetables.

In the following days the population at Warth Mills rapidly increased and the misery worsened. Overcrowding meant filthier sanitation and the rations thinned as they had to be divided across a larger number of people. *'Old men, young boys, surely we can't all be enemies,'* thought Fredo.

The coach arrivals continued. Every single space in the building was occupied and every piece of bread had to be fought for. Sanitation arrangements no longer functioned and the smell was intoxicating. Every breath of fresh air, too, had to be fought for. Only the rats found the environment anywhere near comfortable.

Rumours spread among the internees. *'They're sending us to Canada, they're sending us to Australia.'* Coaches now began to arrive empty. The grapevine had been accurate. The prisoners were being moved on. Fredo found his name on the notice board. He had been assigned to coach number twenty.

'Thank God, the coach is clean,' Fredo thought as he speculated what was happening back home. There had been no opportunities to write a letter. He reflected on the newspaper article he read a few months previously about Hitler's *'Kristallnacht'* and recalled his own *kristallnacht* of the previous week. *'How can this be possible, I've been here nearly fifty years, one son lost in some German work camp, another rescued from*

Dunkirk, both fighting for Britain and I am supposed to be the enemy? What about my wife and children, are they safe, are they being looked after, have they been taken too? Have they stolen our shop too? Where am I going now? If only I had applied for my naturalization? No, that would have made no difference. Some of them are here, I know for definite. British citizens. Some even born here. Maybe it was that damn census which Mussolini demanded. They insisted I complete it, those madman at the consul, those fascists. They thought Mussolini would be great for Italy, yet they are here, too, in this stupid chaos. The British government must have had access to all those census documents, that's why we were rounded up so fast. Mussolini announces war on Britain and within hours we are arrested. No coincidence. This was planned in advance. No time to question who's the real fascist, who's not.'

Fredo's sobering instincts had hit the mark. None of those arrested, none of the internees had been aware of the aggressive stance by Churchill. *'Collar the Lot,'* he had ordered his cabinet colleagues. There was no time to be concerned about the welfare of the Italians. Britain was at war. The disastrous fall of France and the British evacuation at Dunkirk had left the Prime Minister with few options. And now Mussolini had entered the fray and Fredo and his compatriots were the enemy too.

The coach made its way through Liverpool city centre and Fredo peered out at the columns of marching menfolk, flanked by soldiers, ordinary looking men of all ages just like him, dressed in trench coat and trilby. Each carried a single suitcase. It soon became apparent their destination was the same.

At the port Fredo was ushered past the huge liners,

Arandora Star and Ettrick, no doubt the ones destined for Canada or Australia, he thought. He was assigned to a smaller vessel beyond the next quay, destination Douglas, on the Isle of Man.

On the approach to the pier in Douglas it was clear this was no longer the fashionable seaside resort of old. The beautiful Victorian mansions overlooking the shore were separated from the promenade by rows of barbed wire fences. This was to be his prison, Fredo deduced, free from escape.

He was assigned to the Metropole Mansions, previously used as a hotel, which he later discovered were the lodgings for low risk detainees. Approximately fifty men had been assigned to the Metropole. Fredo was pleasantly surprised as he walked through the door. No leaking roofs, no dampness on the walls, furniture appeared in good condition and he detected an air of general cleanliness. The hotel's new guests were given a friendly welcome, they were shown the kitchens in the basement, the dining room on the ground floor, complete with piano and the bedrooms and toilets upstairs. Each member of the group was given a card containing instructions, rules and regulations, including where to report regularly for roll call. They were informed in very clear language of the punishment for any misdemeanors. Each prisoner was given a pencil, paper and an envelope to write home.

Before settling down into his new environment, Fredo had to take care of an urgent need. Very slowly he washed every crevice of his hands and face. It was the first time in three weeks he was able to feel the crisp freshness of running water.

Fredo bunked with Peter Cecchini, another emigrant from Montecino, who had a fish and chip shop in

Glasgow. Peter was ten years younger. Shortly after the first war he had brought his young wife to Glasgow in order to earn the fortune others had made before him.

"I have a son in the British army," he said. "George is with the Gordon Highlanders. No doubt he'll be fighting Mr Hitler somewhere. He's only eighteen, still a boy. His mum was in an awful state when they picked me up, especially after the riot. Fredo, how do you think will this end?"

"They looted your shop too."

"There was nothing to loot. We don't sell cigarettes or chocolates, only fish and chips. But the windows were smashed and then they relieved themselves in the fish fryer. They came with cricket bats and they did a fair bit of damage before the police arrived."

"Peter, tell me, are you a *fascista?*"

"I don't even know what a *fascista* is. In Glasgow we went along with all the hype. This *credere, obedire, combattere,* believe, obey, fight slogan is a load of mumbo jumbo. It's propaganda. The top guy maintains it's all about people, follow me, believe in me, obey me, fight with me and we'll make it all good. Then the ego takes over and everybody's the enemy. It's clearly brainwashing."

"I agree with you. And then they'll need a secret police to make sure everybody stays in line."

"We're here in this country for no other reason than to earn a living. Back home we couldn't feed our families. Here up to now it was great, we made some money. We're not involved in any politics. We're are just happy to sit around the table on a Sunday, away from all that greasy and smelly fish and chip stuff. We chat in Italian amongst ourselves while we can enjoy a plate of pasta with our home made sauce. You know,

Fredo, over there in Montecino, we didn't care who was running the stupid country. Even then we didn't want those damned politicians interfering in our lives. If that's being a *fascista,* fine, but it's not right."

"This whole fascist thing is a huge mess and we Italians are right in the middle of the mess," replied Fredo as they hugged each other. "Let's stick together."

The following day were the interviews. Fredo was summoned to the small office at the back of the dining room. The only shaft of light in an otherwise very austere room was a tiny window just below ceiling level which faced out into the back yard. A uniformed officer, spick and span, sat on one side of the table, chain smoking full strength cigarettes.

"Mr Baldini, I want your stay here to be as comfortable as possible. Britain is at war with your country and it's in your interest to answer my questions very truthfully," said the officer.

'*My country is Britain*,' Fredo thought but thought it better not to antagonize the officer. "Yes, sir, I will."

Fredo wasted no time in answering the routine questions, name, family members, where he was born, where his family was born, what did he do, whom did he work with.

"Have any of your family been in the military?" Fredo reeled off the little he knew about Alfred and he explained that Lewis had just arrived back in a bad way from Dunkirk. Then about Tony in the first war. "Oh yes, my brother's daughter married a British soldier too. My wife is British, and she has, I don't how many relatives in the British military, some even died in the first war. Do you want all their names? My wife and I are both sixty years of age, for goodness sake. Between us we're bound to have family in the military."

The officer remained stern and he made no comment.

"Have you or your family ever been to Germany."

"Yes, as I told you my son is somewhere in the new greater Germany at the service of Mr Hitler, no doubt being tortured or doing hard labour," replied Fredo angrily.

The officer continued to scribble frantically and he made no effort to acknowledge Fredo's reply.

"Have you or any of your family sent your children to Italy on the Fascist summer camps?"

"Absolutely not. Would never have sanctioned that."

"Have you ever attended Mr Mussolini's fascist gatherings in England?"

Again another firm no.

"Can you give me the names of friends and colleagues who have attended Mr Mussolini's fascist gatherings in England?"

"I have never attended these gatherings so how would I know who was there."

The officer looked up, lit another cigarette. "Thank you, that's all for now. You can return to your room."

Fredo searched out Peter.

"My questions were the same. I guess they're looking for the real fascists," he said. "Of course, I could have given him some names, but they were there only for the social stuff, *Italianita*, I'm sure none of them had any other motive. They're weren't Mussolini's spies, for heaven's sake."

***

The camp descended into its own monotonous routine. Roll call was twice daily, before breakfast and before lockdown at night. Meals were taken in a galley canteen room next to the kitchen in the basement. The internees kept themselves busy with recreational and educational activities. Younger prisoners organized football tournaments in the back yard, while Fredo himself arranged English classes for those who couldn't speak or write as well as he could. Some prisoners had converted one of the smaller rooms into a makeshift chapel for Sunday Mass. They had managed to borrow an internee priest from another camp on the island for the weekly service. Eventually the authorities allowed the Italian priest to devise his own rota of camp hotels for confessions and Mass.

Fredo received mail from Catherine. He knew the letters were being read by prying eyes. In her first letter she explained the events following his round up. Lewis and Thomas had arranged to board up the windows. There had been no further riots. Catherine was agitated that the family, just like the other Italians in the town, were regarded as outcasts. On the street the locals were crossing to the other side. The girls were running the shop but takings had decreased drastically. Only a very loyal few continued to bring their business. Thomas, virtually single handed, had converted the backyard into a sizeable vegetable plot. With little source of income, they were struggling for money. They couldn't wait to see the results of Thomas' efforts in the autumn. "………………………. *slowly but surely I hope and think, the customers might come back. It will take time,*" she wrote.

***

Six months into the internment, rumours were spreading like wildfire.

"They say one of the ships was torpedoed in the Atlantic. Some of our people have disappeared, never made it to Canada," said Peter as he sat in the breakfast room next to Fredo. At the same table were other internees from Valbona.

"Yeh, Freddie Pieri and Gino Casci made it to Canada. They are in a camp there, but nothing has been heard from Santino from Motherwell or from Cesare in Ayr. They were on another ship," said Leo who was seated next to Peter.

Another piped up, "My wife wrote to me. She informed me that Guido Marchi had made it home to his family in Glasgow. He says he survived, had to jump into the sea. He managed to pull himself into a lifeboat. He witnessed the awful sight of so many disappearing under the water, never to be seen again. They couldn't swim, the poor souls. He was on the Arandora Star supposedly on its way to Canada. He says it must have been a torpedo attack. Probably a German submarine. Mostly everybody drowned but he made it to one of the few lifeboats they dropped into the water."

"The Arandora Star," said Fredo. "God, I saw that ship at Liverpool. That was over six months ago. We need to ask the priest if he can find out what happened to the ship."

"And did you know about Sergio Cardosi from Valbona," said Leo. "He was thrown out of a second floor window in the middle of the night at one of the other hotel camps. They said he was a diehard fascist, and that he marched side by side with Oswald Mosley at the Cable Street riots."

"Serves him right," said another at the table. "Those people on the ship were innocent. But this guy never stopped ranting about the future British fascist state. The others become so irritated they took matters into their own hands. Sergio never stood a chance, it seems he was beaten up and then thrown out to become a healthy diet for passing vermin and hungry seagulls."

"Good for them," said Peter. "We don't need scum like that mixing with us.

In due course the officers at the camp were asked about the Arandora Star. They denied emphatically any knowledge of a sinking of a ship full of internees.

***

Fredo and the rest of the internees had resigned themselves to their new life. From afar they kept in some touch with the outside world. They were able to write and receive letters, although it was obvious the letters were being censored. In the camp itself he was conscious they were being closely watched. They were foreign aliens, regarded as the enemy. Conditions were bearable, the internees were given basic provisions and apart from the twice daily roll call, they were mostly left alone to their private thoughts and hopes.

Fredo was losing weight, several pounds a month. He had no inkling whatsoever that his namesake son, Alfred, was also shedding pounds fast in another far away camp, and in entirely different conditions.

Christmas came and went and there was were small signs the authorities were thinking again about the mass incarceration. Some of the over sixties had been released. Gigi Nardini was over seventy when he was sent packing just before the festive season. '*A seventy year old,*' Fredo thought, '*a threat to national security. Maybe common sense will prevail soon.*'

"Some people have already been released. With any luck we might be next. I hope we've still our businesses to return to. That's all we've got." Fredo said to Peter after Sunday Mass. "I wonder how the priest knows but he says they're still bombing the cities. And the papers are reporting that Hitler seems to have his eye on opening up a new front in the east towards Russia. The whole thing has gone global. They might realize now, finally, that we oldies, we pose no threat."

"You're alright up there in Errington, the bombers won't know where that is. But Glasgow's different, I've been told they blitzed Clydebank, hundreds dead. My shop's in nearby Maryhill. Hopefully it's still standing."

By the spring it was clear the authorities were adopting a different approach. There had been no more ships sailing to Canada or to Australia and there had been no more new internees. It seemed the paranoid sweep of the country for enemies had terminated. Gradually throughout the spring and summer, one by one, a few each day, most of the internees were released and allowed to return home to their families. Nobody could figure out the logic for their release but they didn't care. They were desperate to return home.

Fredo and Peter were set free within a week of each other.

However there was no release for another of Fredo's many cousins. Lino Mazzolini, who had a Fish and Chip shop in Paisley had the misfortune of being the only one in his family to be born in Dusseldorf in Germany. His parents had gone there at the turn of the century to sell their plaster cast figurines. Without any great success in Germany the family had returned to Valbona for a short period before joining the gravy train in Glasgow. Lino was the double whammy, born in Germany and an Italian. So his release never came. It was only when the war was virtually over that he was able to return home.

Meanwhile Peter himself had safely arrived home. His shop had remained boarded up since the riots of the previous year. The blitz didn't make it to Maryhill. His wife had been cared for by their daughter Nina who worked at the local bakery. He discovered his son George had been assigned to fight against Rommel's troops in the North Africa campaign. He never made it. He was one of the numerous British casualties in the Battle for Tunisia. Ironically he had been fighting against an Italian battalion, some of whose soldiers were born and bred in Valbona. Cousin against cousin, if only they had known!

Ultimately Fredo too made it home to discover that Christine, Cora and a sprightly Thomas were in charge of the business. The locals seemed to have forgotten about the night Mussolini declared war. It helped, no doubt, that when the German air force was attempting to bomb the coal mine which their engineers had commissioned thirty years previously, the Baldinis had provided free tea and cake for the residents whose homes had suffered some collateral damage.

"After all," Catherine said to Fredo after he returned home, "they knew exactly where the mine was, they knew its weaknesses, they had the plans. It was only by good fortune the bombs mostly missed, nobody was hurt."

"That's some good news amidst all this carnage," he replied wearily.

"But, Catherine, I can stay here only this evening. I have to report tomorrow to a proper work camp, near Crook. As long as I don't cause any trouble with the farmer, for whom I'll be working, they'll grant me leave to return home every so often."

"And you definitely won't cause them any trouble, Fredo."

Chapter 22

World War 2 – Christine and Cora's Story

Christine and Cora were inseparable. They were born just seventeen months apart. Same clothing and hairstyle, same height and build, same expressions, from afar they looked like twins. The girls had started school at the same time big sister Vera married. With big sister gone from the home they were domesticated very early in their lives. Mama had taught them how to cook, how to keep house as well as how to run the business. Now as mature teenagers in the midst of the turmoil of war they were crucial in maintaining the family's morale. They were the solid rocks on which their mum depended after Alfred and Lewis conscripted. In particular they were the comfort after the traumatic events of June of the previous year when Mussolini had declared war. The girls had kept their mum's spirits alive and hopeful after dad was snatched. Together with Thomas at the helm they were instrumental in keeping the business as a going concern. The shop was the family's only source of income after the billiards saloon was closed.

The girls figured that the anti-Italian protest in their town was just a one-off. On reflection they had concluded that the angry response to the family after Mussolini's declaration of war had been expected.

However they were optimistic that in the course of time, the anti-Italian sentiment would all but disappear. Some of the rioters were their friends after all. Indeed now they aimed their anger not at the locals who disowned them temporarily but at the disloyal Italians who supported the pact with the German dictator.

After their dad had been released from his nightmare, the girls' concern was with Alfred. In their prayers they never missed their nightly petitioning to have him return safely. Was he healthy, was he being properly cared for at the prisoner of war camp? On the grapevine the girls had heard of horrific stories of concentration camp conditions. But whether they were true, there was no way they could know.

***

One night in August, just three days before Cora's eighteen birthday the girls were baking when they heard the news. A former school pal ran into the shop.

"Christine, they bombed Hartlepool again. You need to get to your shelters," she shouted.

The family would have expected a warning siren but this time there was none. Nevertheless they crammed into their shelter. They felt the ground rumbling as the shells fell. They remained inside in quiet contemplation until the rumbling ceased.

Next morning the extent of the damage became apparent. More than twenty people dead and over a hundred injured.

Now was the time to inform their parents. They had decided that as the elder, Christine should break the news.

"Mama, papa, now that Cora is eighteen years of age, we want to join the auxiliary service. We talked about this, haven't we, Cora? We want to do out bit too," she said.

"Oh, girls," mama was tearful. "Both of you too, please no."

Thomas piped up, pumping his chest out of his little five feet high body, "And when I'm eighteen, I'll be out there as well. I'll finish this bloody war."

"Be quiet, Thomas, it will be all over by then," papa replied. "You're too tiny anyway. They won't let you in."

"I am ready to go now, I'll let those Germans know who's boss."

The girls were determined. Within days they were in Catterick at the recruitment offices of the Auxiliary Territorial Service, the women's branch of the army. Their course of intensive training lasted six weeks during which time the girls were tested for fitness, hearing, eyesight, mental prowess and aptitude.

They volunteered for anti-aircraft duty and to qualify it was necessary to pass all the stringent final tests and with flying colours.

"Christine, what happens if I fail and you pass," Cora asked at the end of another day's training.

"You won't fail. We're like twins, remember. You and me together, we are inseparable. We'll pass. Don't you worry, dear sister. I'll make sure we are both successful."

Training was tough. At the end of each day the girls were drained both mentally and physically. Constantly gazing through the telescope and maintaining imaginary targets on the horizon line demanded steady nerves. Teamwork between the sisters was impressive. Christine set the target line on the telescope while Cora inserted the shells. As a team the chemistry worked. In addition, the training instructors had witnessed some leadership potential.

The girls duly passed the tests with distinction. After being kitted out, receiving their gas mask drill, inoculations and smallpox vaccinations they returned home for a short break. How proudly they marched, heads held high, down Station Road in their new uniform.

"Hello girls, we are so thrilled for you," remarked Mrs Thompson, who met the girls half way between the bus stop and home.

"This time she never crossed the road to avoid us. Did you see that?" said Cora.

"We are home for two days, mama. We'll be assigned to a defence battery along the east coast somewhere. We'll be safe, mama. This work is not dangerous. We'll be searching out planes in the sky to shoot them down," said Christine trying to ease her mum's anxieties.

"Good on you, I wish it was me doing that," interrupted Thomas.

"Thomas, be quiet, you're needed here at home. Anyway you're only sixteen."

***

The services' administration team was aware of the close bond between the sisters. Since they had trained together, it was decided they would be assigned together too. Christine and Cora were entrusted with anti-aircraft gunnery duty on the Norfolk coast at Great Yarmouth.

Corporal Anne Blythe was the senior official at the first meeting of the latest batch of auxiliary recruits. "This area is of critical extreme importance to the war effort. The Anglian bulge in the British map means that any enemy aircraft targeting the North of England requires to fly close to or over the Norfolk coast. We have to find and destroy them before they can cause any damage to us." She continued, "You are the elite group. You have the best equipment, the best guns. Don't disappoint us."

The sisters were billeted at a former workhouse commandeered by the army on the edge of town. The building was set in impressively landscaped grounds where the auxiliaries exercised and trained. Initially the sisters covered the evening shift. They manned the huge Bren gun mounted on a tripod at the end of Britannia pier. While on duty they owned the impressive vantage point.

East Anglia was more than an enormous bulge on the map to defend the North. The surrounding flat lands made the area ideal for airfield bases, from where the British launched attacks on the enemy in mainland Europe. Now it was full of Americans. After the United States entered the European war, the majority of their contingent in the European theatre were stationed on the bulge. The area was strategically vital for Britain, and of course, the enemy knew this. So the girls had to remain on constant alert for enemy aircraft, especially when the sun disappeared into the twilight.

During the first week of their patrol they observed six planes approaching the coast, Focke Wulf bombers, they had been told the following day. Together with the other batteries in the area, they saturated the sky with shell bursts. The strategy was to fill the sky with so much lethal ammunition in order to increase the chances of the formation of bomber planes flying through would hit the projectiles. In addition the enemy planes would be so disrupted in their attack that they might be less accurate in their bombing. In the noise and confusion and frenzy of shellfire, the girls were never fully sure of any successful hits.

When the enemy planes disappeared from sight the girls rested to reflect.

"Do you really think we brought any down tonight," asked Cora.

"I'm not so sure. We'll have to wait to see what we are told at breakfast roll call."

**

Just as in the previous day, the girls awoke to another beautiful spring day. They saw that the early morning fret in the North Sea was blanking out the glare of the slowly rising sun to the east. They knew that later in the day the moisture in the fret would burn itself out when the sun warmed the air. At lunch time they would be free to enjoy a crisp and cloudless light blue sky. This was their day off. Breakfast was over and the girls planned some physical recreation in the grounds.

They joined a group of fellow auxiliaries. It felt invigorating, stretching limbs in the light breeze. The group heard the reverberation, they sensed it was originating from beyond the fret. Momentarily they froze. The rumble intensified. At the precise moment it dawned that there might be danger, the planes broke through the fret. The deafening sound of repetitive gunfire ignited the senses, the girls ran in all directions, some trying to seek sanctuary at the house, some behind the trees, and some falling exactly where they stood. Nowhere to run. Unimaginable chaos had shattered the calm. Hell had arrived.

"The tree, the tree, fast," Christine pushed her little sister towards the large oak nearby. Tightly holding on to each other they crouched down and watched the carnage unfold. The first pair of planes were followed by further pairs of planes, arcing downwards, machine gunning in tandem, and then arcing back upwards.

After several minutes the planes had disappeared back into the fret and the girls carefully stepped out from behind their hiding place. They surveyed the scene. The sky was empty. Women were racing out of the main building with stretchers, flapping shoulder bags filled with supplies. "Let's go help," said Christine. Their first aid training was made to good use.

For the rest of the day the only duty was to tend the injured. For the thirty servicewomen who died on the field there was nothing in the first aid box which could have helped them.

"It was awful we had to go through this for real," said Christine. "You're still a child, Cora."

"You too, dear sister, how can we recover with this. We could never have imagined it, limbs blasted apart, bullets boring holes randomly in these young and delicate bodies. It could have been us. Why, why, what's this world coming to?"

That night the sisters fell asleep in each other's arms.

The following day they heard the news of the destruction in the town. More dead. Buildings destroyed. Bewildered citizens walking the streets aimlessly. In the evening nevertheless the sisters were at their station manning the Bren gun again at the end of the pier. The planes might be returning.

***

Following the blitz attack in the spring, further forays by the German Luftwaffe were rare. The sisters' initial enthusiasm to fight the enemy appeared to be waning. There seemed to be no enemy to fight. They were delighted at their occasional home leave.

Lewis' health was deteriorating rapidly, and the girls helped Ethel convince him that he should convalesce at the sanatorium in Durham. Lewis agreed with his wife's wish, "I am sure I will recover better in the fresh air," he said. Seeing how the war had damaged their beloved big brother, the girls' commitment to defeat the enemy was revitalized.

Still there was little word about Alfred. The family had resigned themselves for the worst. Would he return home and if so, in what state?

After his internment Charlie had returned safely to Vera and the experiences at Warth Mills and in the Isle of Man seemed long forgotten. In addition to the work obligations assigned to him with a local farmer he had his two small children to care for and he needed his wife to keep his business running in order to pay the bills. "The anti-Italian taunts have all but disappeared," he had remarked to the girls.

In contrast, however, Fredo was finding it tougher to recover from the internment. The nightmares were recurring and he was being forced to confront his demons. With the war over, uniformed German soldiers in shiny black jackboots strode arrogantly down Station Road on the lookout for fresh and tender young females. His two precious daughters fitted the bill perfectly and at gunpoint he had no option to let the soldiers have them. Before he could witness any further trauma, he always awoke.

He considered the nightmares were giving him a message. It was time the girls were told. They were old enough to understand. And Christine and Cora were shocked.

"Prima notte, are you crazy, papa, surely not," said Cora.

"That's the way it was in those days, there was nothing you could do, you just went along with it, or else you starved."

"What horrific nightmares too," said Christine. "If any dirty scum ever came near me like that, I'd make sure they would never use it again, no doubt about that."

Thomas was listening intently. He didn't hesitate, "I can't wait to get out there. I'll fight them with everything I have. I'm definitely going, mama."

"I know, son, you've said so too many times. Looks like I won't be able to stop you. When your time comes you just have to be careful. But you'll promise me you'll come back. We need to be a family again."

***

Back at Great Yarmouth, Corporal Blythe called Christine and Cora into her office.

"Sit down, have some tea, I guess I won't be able to separate you girls. You've been together like bread and butter since you arrived."

Christine clasped her sister's hand.

The corporal continued, "The tide is turning against Germany and something major may occur soon. I need you girls to be involved, but it is top secret. I can trust you, can't I?"

The girls nodded. "Of course, yes," Christine said, "we are in this until the end, aren't we, sister?"

They sat back to listen.

"As you know, there are many airfields in East Anglia. At one of these airfields we are planning something which will be key to our success in defeating the Germans. Top secret, remember."

The following day the girls were summoned to a huge hangar filled with all sorts of debris, crates of wooden planks and a variety of equipment and tools.

A soldier in an American accent stepped forward,

"Christine, Cora, follow me." They marched towards an office in the corner of the hangar. Soldiers in the office were stretching over a huge table littered with paper, pencils, slide rules and a variety of small instruments. Christine recognised some from her maths class at school.

"Girls, you will be our guests for a week. Your memory and powers of recollection are vital. We need you to describe to us every single detail of the Bren gun at the end of the pier. My men tell me you have been manning the thing for over a year. We need to know every detail, and I mean every detail."

The girls knew not to ask why. This was top secret after all.

"You know, we could obtain the drawings from army command. That would mean them knowing about our mission. We don't know who we can trust. Careless talk and all that stuff. Do you understand? Every detail?"

Cora was first to respond. "Of course, yes, where do you want to start?"

"By the way, the only people in the know on this are inside this hangar right now. Nobody else knows. Classified. *Capish*?

"I guess you know what that means, *capish*. There's no need for me to explain."

"*Si, si*," joked Christine. The American gave her a stern look.

A drawing of the Bren gun quickly took shape as the girls described it using an array of arm movements and gestures. When the girls were satisfied with parts of the drawings, others in the hangar began the build. The grinding noise of the sawing machine soon drowned out the sound of hammer to nail.

At the end of the week the girls were astonished.

After paint had been applied the three Bren guns looked as magnificent as the real thing. The circular movements on the central axis and movement mechanism skywards were extraordinarily precise. Even the seat felt real. But they were well aware these guns would never fire any shot in anger.

They had witnessed other artefacts being made inside the huge hangar. There were planes, tanks, jeeps, some made of wood and some of rigid cardboard.

"Ladies, *Grazie,* Thanks for your help," the American said on their final day as they boarded the bus to return to Great Yarmouth. "Don't forget, silence, top secret, or else."

The American made a movement across his throat with his right hand, fist clenched as if holding a knife. The girls knew exactly what that signified.

At the barracks the girls whispered to each other underneath the bedsheets before dozing off, "Looks like they are trying to fool Hitler, before this something major happens. Those dummy planes can't fly anywhere, the guns can't shoot. I guess it's to fool the enemy's reconnaissance. Or maybe even any spies who can't get close enough to the airfield. Do you really think the Germans will be duped?"

"Perhaps the Americans will photograph the setup themselves and deliberately allow the photos to fall into the hands of the Germans, who knows? The objective, I guess is to let them think we've more artillery than we actually have."

"We need to forget about it. In any case, we'll never know if the plan is successful, whatever it is."

***

The girls' next leave was a sudden and sad one. They were allowed home to attend Lewis' funeral. In the church they broke down unashamedly when seven year old Dino lifted his two year old little brother Lewis high on his shoulders to place a bunch of flowers on top of the coffin.

"Poor little Lewis! He will never know his father." Ethel wept incessantly as the family crowded round at the cemetery.

Fredo tried to maintain some composure, "He never made it and his wounds were too severe. The doctor had insisted he must have picked up the disease as he fled on the boats at Dunkirk. The water's bacteria and germs must have seeped through into his wounds, and his body never recovered, poor man."

The coffin was gently lowered into the ground and Lewis' army cap was thrown in on top. The hole was filled in by the grave diggers.

***

Within a few days Christine and Cora were back on duty at their base. They discovered the objective of their secret mission. In early June East Anglia had emptied itself of the American soldiers. Simultaneous landings of Allied troops and equipment on four nondescript beaches in Normandy began the operation to roll back the Nazi enemy back into Germany.

Days previously Hitler had convinced his generals that the anticipated Allied invasion would likely occur further north near Calais or indeed in Belgium. After all, he argued, why would the Allies have had all that equipment at all those airfields in East Anglia ready for warfare if they didn't have a strategy to invade at the nearest shoreline of mainland Europe?

Chapter 23

World War 2 – Dino's Story

Life in the North East of England was never going to be easy for Ida. Husband John was frequently away on army assignments and she didn't care much for John's family. The couple's social life centered on the local pub in Durham. John's mother Lizzie was something of a celebrity in the ladies lounge. She knew everybody and anybody. She smoked like a trooper and she was able to handle her whisky and Newcastle Brown with great aplomb. Like most of her family she drank more than she could eat. Lizzie was forever trying to induce Ida into her social circle.

"Come on, Ida, have a dram, pet, it's good for you!" But Ida hated the smell of the pub which masqueraded as a hotel. She loathed the sight of ash trays at the bar washed in the same sink as the beer dregs. Lipstick coated cigarette butts squished around the sink too. Disgusting! And the sawdust on the floor. She never understood why the men in the pub consistently missed the spittoon on the floor. Ida loved John, but not his family. When John was on assignment, Ida decamped to spend most of her time with Catherine. Occasionally she spent the weekend with her sister Louisa and husband Cuthbert in Yorkshire. Louisa, too have left the South of France to live near her husband's family. The pair had met in Marseille and after a short romance they married there before setting up home in Yorkshire. He was doing well as a sales representative in the rag trade selling thread and zip fasteners to the textile factories in and around Leeds.

"Let's go to the coast for a walk along the beach." John said to Ida.

It was a bright summer day amidst the gloom of the coming war. They grabbed deck chairs and they gaped out across the North Sea. The sea was calm, the beach was alive with families, children and scampering dogs. Some were playing football, others enjoying homemade lard filled sandwiches interspersed with unwelcome grains of sand.

"We are both in our late thirties now. You would love to have children, Ida. It's not too late you know."

"Yes, of course, but you are never here. It's no way to bring up children, you not around."

"If I left the army, what would we do, I've been in the thing nearly twenty years."

Ida was unsure what was coming. "What about money, what other job can you do," she replied.

"Here's an idea, why don't we return to Marseilles, stay with your folks on the farm. I'm sure they wouldn't mind that either. I loved it there before, great weather, sunshine every day. There was always great excitement at the port."

Ida glanced over, "Yes, and......."

"I don't want to bring up kids here. There's nothing but these damn mines here. Work, drink, sleep and a struggle for food in a dingy miner's house, it's no life for a young family. In Marseille is different. With your two brothers in the police your dad will need help."

Ida was overjoyed. "You mean then we could have children."

"Yes, I am ready to leave this place for good, that's if your dad will agree. He could put us up for a couple of years and then we would find our own little place. You don't need much to live there. And anyway, there'll always be work at the port."

"Are you really sure about this? We'll manage, won't we?"

"Of course, my dear." They stood up and cuddled. The kids around stopped kicking their ball. Rarely had they seen a middle aged couple kissing so passionately together.

Within weeks letters had been exchanged between John and Dino and he was mustered out. The couple were on their way.

They reached Dino's farm in the hills above La Ciotat, about twenty miles east of Marseille two months before France's declaration of war against Hitler's Germany.

In the midst of the phoney war where life continued much as usual, John and Ida thrilled themselves with the experience. The couple lovingly lapped up the warm glow of the Mediterranean sun whilst threshing the wheat at harvest time and trampling the grapes at *La Vendemmia.*

"This is the highlight for me as a farmer," said Dino. "*La Vendemmia*". Although he spoke perfect French, he never used *La Recolte*, the French equivalent. The Italian word sounded more exciting, more exhilarating. Wine production was important to him. There could be no other term. Only *La Vendemmia* would do.

"*Beviamo alla Vendemmia,* let's drink to a great wine this year.*" Dino didn't take no for an answer.

***

All changed in the spring of 1940. Hitler had decided to move west. His army invaded Belgium, crossed the

French border and he himself proudly and defiantly marched into Paris. France had succumbed easily to their traditional enemy. The country was split into two zones, the first zone occupied and run by Germany, whilst the second zone, the so called 'free zone', remained under French control. Its capital was Vichy, a small town in Central France. The French zone had been declared fully autonomous from Germany, but it didn't take long for so called Vichy France to adopt legislation of which Hitler himself would have been extremely proud. In fact Vichy France was a German puppet state in disguise. The legislation targeted the Jewish community. Jews were banned everywhere, in the professions, teachers, journalists and their businesses were confiscated. For them there was no sanctuary in the 'free zone'. The government had commissioned the immediate construction of makeshift concentration camps. When Jewish refugees and other undesirables crossed the demarcation line from the German occupied zone to the apparent 'free zone', there was still no freedom. Jews realised their only hope of escape from Nazi terror meant somehow reaching the coast by whatever means in order to seek a safe passage to any destination and on any ship which was prepared to take them.

Consequently Marseille, as the only major port in the south, became the strategic transit destination for thousands of refugees of all nationalities from occupied Europe in search of passage elsewhere. Largely through the collaboration of his two policemen sons, Dino had become an active participator in the French resistance. He was a cog in the chain of alternative land based escape routes through the Alps into Switzerland and to Spain via the Pyrenees. He had knowledge of the adjacent safe houses in the chain. And soon John too, by utilising his network with the British military at the port, became part of the resistant movement.

"Another British soldier arrived this week," said Franck as the family sat together for Sunday brunch. During weekends in the summer they always skipped lunch. A large Sunday spread of baguettes, crepes and croissants loaded with fresh butter and chocolate hazelnut sauce was enough to last until evening dinner.

"He escaped right under German noses at St Valery. His unit never made to Dunkirk for the evacuation. They were left as sitting ducks on the coast up there and the Germans moved in for them. He says it was brutal. Some of his pals were captured, no doubt tortured too. They'll be in a concentration camp somewhere. He needs to return to England."

"Not another who's supposed to have vital information," replied Cristophe. "Why don't they be honest? They are desperate for home. We'll help them all no matter what. It makes little difference to us."

John's part in the operation was ensuring his contacts at the British garrison produced the relevant paperwork. "Remember, guys, the Spanish are getting tougher now, even if our guys do have documents which look genuine. The border at the coast is more dangerous and if our boys don't make it to the consul in Barcelona, their number's up. They'll be sent to Miranda prison and that's a hell hole of a camp. There will be no escape from there. My guys have informed me that the mountain route is the best way out. The escapees need to be in groups, six at a time and they'll need a guide to cross the Pyrenees. The guides know who can be bribed and who can't. Our new arrival will have to wait until we reach a compliment of six."

Franck and Cristophe, too, were playing for high stakes. They were trained gendarme officers and it was their obligation to obey their superiors. But they didn't have much respect for Marshall Petain, the man in charge of Vichy France and they knew many other police officers who were disillusioned also. The majority view was that Petain had sold the country out to the hated Germans. The relationship between France and Germany had never been reconciled following the first war and the French had never forgotten the brutality in the Franco Prussian war seventy years previously.

"As always," said Dino, "we have to be careful. We take nothing for granted. We worked hard to arrange these escape routes. We need to do everything and anything to keep them safe."

Dino placed his right hand on the table and his three sons followed suit. John, too, placed his right hand on top of the others. "*Fraternite*, brotherhood, we're in this together." Promptly they nodded in approval. *"Fraternite!"*

Errant British soldiers continued to arrive and most were directed towards Spain via the Pyrenees, while some were expertly smuggled on rare cargo ships heading further afield through the Mediterranean. However Dino's work multiplied from a huge increase in Jewish families seeking refuge. Those with funds were pursuing passage to Switzerland.

"Josep, John we need your help even more now. We need to ensure the escape routes to the Swiss border are still sound and safe," said Dino. "In the coming weeks it looks like we'll need all of them readily available. Remember there are numerous Italian families, like us, living near the paths of the escape routes. Now that Mussolini has sided with Hitler we can't tell which of them we can trust. Let's stick to our proven schedules and proven contacts. If there are any changes, I need to clear them myself first!"

"Yes, pops, we are with you all the way," replied John.

"*Bien sur,* of course" said Josep, the youngest of the brothers.

Meanwhile British soldiers continued arriving, seeking an escape route, as did increasing numbers of Jewish families, crippled grandparents, malnourished children, boys, girls and babies. "Those bastards, how can they do this to ordinary human beings?" Dino whispered to his wife, Emilia, away from listening ears.

Dino's farm had evolved into a clandestine transit station for Jewish refugees. When it was considered safe to do so Dino arranged passage for the refugees to the next transit station. He always had to assume that the unfortunates had made it to their final destination. It was not his business to find out otherwise.

The number of refugees passing through Dino's network was increasing substantially. He and his boys had built well disguised accommodation facilities in the attic of the barn and in the basement of an outhouse, fifty yards from the farmhouse. Typically they held their guests for several days before moving them on. Dino had lost count of the number. There was no paper trail nor were there any records maintained. The operation was based entirely on word of mouth. It was too dangerous. While they were in his care, Dino kept the refugees nourished and little was said to them. They complied with all instructions, no questions asked, until they were passed on.

***

"The Allies have landed in Algeria. What do you think

that means for us here in France," asked Franck.

"With luck the British and Americans will sweep across North Africa and push on through the Mediterranean to Italy and Greece," said John. "The war will be over soon."

"No," said Dino, "it's not going to be that easy. But if it were to happen the Nazis would take over Vichy. There's no way they would leave the South undefended. I'm sure they'll fight to the bitter end in Africa, otherwise they'll be seriously weakened. And that means they would need Vichy." Dino paused to take a sip of his coffee. "The Nazis could be here soon. It might be necessary to re-think our tactics."

At the end of the meal the boys placed their right hands on the table, one on top of the other, '*Fraternite*!'

"We continue," said Cristophe.

***

Dino was right. Hitler had sensed his vulnerability at the Mediterranean coast and in due course Vichy France was overrun by the German military machine. A small part of the country in the South East was ceded to Mussolini. Since this area was critical for the escape route to the Swiss border, the danger in Dino's operation increased exponentially overnight.

***

In the new year, Cristophe and Franck raced into the kitchen where Emilia was cooking dinner. "Where's papa, we need to talk."

"He's on his rounds locking away the chickens."

The boys ran out to find Dino. "We just heard today at the gendarmerie. The Gestapo are planning the clear out of the old port in Marseille, all of it, house by house. Trains are arriving soon to transport everybody up north, who knows where."

"Slow down, boy, slow down."

"They say the whole area is full of enemies and terrorists. That means Jews, us, *la resistance*, anybody in their way.

"Do you know when the clearance will start," asked Dino. "We need to organize ourselves."

"Immediately, you know how ruthless they can be, papa."

The grapevine in the city was already alive with rumours of the destruction that might lie ahead. The message was clear when Dino's contact arrived. They had to multiply their efforts. Dino's operation was a small cog in a large wheel and the wheel was about to turn much faster. If any cog wasn't functioning then the wheel couldn't operate. There was no choice. Despite constantly increasing danger he knew his family had to continue the operation. They couldn't let these people down, especially now, with the ruthless Gestapo closer to home.

The family were prepared to risk all.

"We take one family per night, maximum eight people, no more, and we move them on the following day. This we can manage," he said to his contact.

***

The escape routine had to be identical for all escapees. Travel by night, hide by day. Sometimes they arrived by truck, sometimes by cart. Families were often separated. During their stay the escapees were accommodated in the barn or in the outhouse. Younger children always in the outhouse so crying or baby noises couldn't be heard from the farmhouse. Thankfully for all concerned it was wintertime. In the hideouts the intense heat of summer would have been another insufferable obstacle.

***

A week into Dino's newly accelerated operation SS Colonel Lubeck visited the farm. He was accompanied by half a dozen soldiers. Dino instructed his wife and three daughters to remain indoors. "Stay here, nobody speak unless you are asked."

"Herr, colonel, how can I help you today," said Dino stepping out onto the porch to welcome his guest.

The colonel loosened the buttons on his long double breasted leather coat and they sparkled in the winter sun.

"Help is an interesting word, Mr Baldini. It's not about helping me. Indeed are you, Mr Baldini, or any of your family helping anybody else here today," replied the colonel, his steely eyes firmly fixed on Dino's motionless stare.

"The only help I am giving is to you, Herr Colonel."

"Are you inviting me inside your home, Mr Baldini? I would like a glass of water." The colonel headed towards the porch without waiting for Dino's response.

Dino ushered the officer into the kitchen. One of the colonel's soldiers followed. Emilia and the girls gazed out of the window paying little attention. They were hoping none of the other soldiers would be venturing anywhere near the outhouse.

"A glass of water for the colonel, please, Emilia," said Dino.

The colonel sat and placed his hat and leather gloves on the table. For several seconds nobody spoke. He was scanning the scene very carefully no doubt ears perked for the slightest sound. After two minutes had passed he broke the silence.

"I have been hearing rumours, Mr Baldini." He

sipped his water. "Could they possibly be true?"

Dino thought about making a joke about his zucchini flowers which were best sellers at the vegetable market in Marseille but he refrained from doing so. "Can you tell me what rumours you are referring to?"

Another period of silence. Emilia and the girls remained rooted to the spot. The silence seemed eternal.

"Will you invite me, Mr Baldini, to show me around your home?"

"Why, of course. Right now." Dino stood up and gestured the colonel to the kitchen door.

Dino moved from room to room with the colonel and his bodyguard. No words were spoken. Then they went outside.

"Search all the buildings," the colonel ordered his men. Immediately soldiers scurried off in all directions. Meanwhile the girls resumed their gaze at the window.

The conversation between Dino and the colonel continued.

"Where are your boys, today, Mr Baldini?"

"I assume they are working. You know the gendarmerie is very busy these days. There is so much stealing and the looting, it's a terrible crime."

"Yes, those Jews and those French terrorists will stop at nothing for a loaf of bread. We can assist your gendarmerie to fix this problem, don't you think?"

"Of course, Herr Colonel. The problem does need to be fixed."

"And the Englisher?"

"I assume you mean John, Herr Colonel. He comes and goes. He sells our fruit and vegetables at the market. He married my daughter many, many years ago," replied Dino.

"Maybe next time you invite me into your home, Mr Baldini, I might meet him too." Colonel Lubeck slapped his gloves across the palm of his hand and motioned the guard towards his car. With synchronized timing the other soldiers returned. "*Niemand,* nobody, Herr Colonel."

A few moments later the huge black car, Nazi flags fluttering in the wind, and the truck of soldiers were out of sight.

"That was close, Emilia. We were lucky," said Dino as he shuffled back into the kitchen.

When the boys returned home they discussed the motive behind Colonel Lubeck's visit. Coincidence or did he have information about their operation? The truth didn't matter. They considered it prudent to take more precautions before they passed their seven guests on. Nearing midnight, the boys scoured the main road, one hundred yards in each direction in search of prying eyes. Josep travelled alone to the next transit station.

"We cannot deliver tonight. It's too dangerous." He said to his contact. "We try again tomorrow night."

The following morning at breakfast Dino needed to make sure yet again.

One by one the boys placed their right hand on the table, one on top of the other. "*Fraternite!*"

That night the family's activities resumed as normal.

***

In the meantime Franck and Cristophe had been introduced to their new bosses at the gendarmerie. Overnight their activities were reprioritised. The hunt was on for Jews, French terrorists, and other undesirables. Nobody was to be spared, the brothers were told.

The brothers, however, needed to establish what

the Gestapo had in store for those captured.

"They are loaded onto filthy cattle trucks, hundreds at a time and sent to extermination camps in the east," said Franck. "Some say they are being gassed to death in huge gas ovens. Unbelievable!"

"Impossible," said Dino, "even those ruthless bastards couldn't invent such a horrible way to die."

"Papa, yes, this is what's happening, I heard it said from another officer," interjected Cristophe. "Their plan is to cleanse the whole of Europe of these people."

"*Non, Ce n'est pas posible,* no, not possible. The Jews built the port, for God's sake, they've been in the city since the beginning."

***

Sunday morning was the first occasion since Colonel Lubeck's first visit, that the family were all together at the same time. Only John was absent. As far as Dino knew, he was transiting to and from Tunisia on intelligence and surveillance duty relating to the allied campaign In North Africa. He wasn't expected back for another week.

This time Colonel Lubeck was accompanied by two trucks full of soldiers.

It was the same routine as the previous visit, little eye to eye contact and sparse communication. Long moments of silence.

"I see, Mr Baldini, you have your sons with you today."

"Franck, Cristophe, I do hope my officers at the gendarmerie are looking after you well," said the Colonel. "Your assistance is so valuable to us."

This time the colonel's two bodyguards at the kitchen door were armed with automatic rifles.

Cristophe looked up from his bowl of coffee, full to

the brim with soaked bread. "Yes, Herr Colonel, indeed they are very good to us especially when we carry out our orders well."

"Why, of course, we all have to follow orders, don't we, Mr Baldini, even if we don't approve of these orders. This is what makes us good citizens and good soldiers. Following orders! Correct?" The colonel gazed at Dino, motioning a reply.

"Yes, correct, Herr Colonel."

The boys continued eating their breakfast. The girls stood in a huddle at the window with their mother.

"Will you invite me again to look round your farm, Mr Baldini? As you will see outside I have many more men to carry out the orders which I have been given. May I ask them to proceed?"

Dino stood up and motioned the colonel to the door.

In the yard the colonel gave the signal and the soldiers made for the barns and other buildings.

Meanwhile Dino stepped outside and he was followed by his three boys. They waited in silence. Colonel Lubeck inserted a cigarette into his gold plated cigarette holder and he lit it.

The faint ringing of church bells was heard in the distance, calling the congregation to Sunday Mass. Just as the bells seemed to increase in intensity a soldier sprinted back.

"Colonel, *kommen zie, kommen zie, wir haben die menshen gefunden,* come, we have found some people," he screamed.

The colonel stubbed his cigarette on the ground and marched at a rapid pace towards the outhouse. People were already climbing out of a hole in the ground by the side of the outhouse. "Of course, a cellar!" the colonel muttered.

Soldiers stood motionless, their guns aimed directly at them. A man, a woman holding a baby, three children and an old woman surfaced. They stood pitifully in front of the gathering, the children trying to hide behind their mother's torn and tattered long skirt.

"Take them away, get them out of my sight," the colonel barked angrily to his bodyguard.

"Yes, Herr Colonel, *sofort,* immediately."

The group were led to the truck and ungraciously manhandled inside. No dignity was spared. The baby remained asleep oblivious to its family's predicament.

The colonel and the remaining soldiers slowly made their way back to the farmhouse where Dino and his boys were waiting.

"Mr Baldini, you never mentioned that you had guests today."

"Today you didn't ask, Herr Colonel."

"And what shall we do with you, Mr Baldini, let me think."

Another wave of the hand and a soldier ran towards one of the trucks. Several machine guns were already pointed directly at the four standing on the porch. The church bells had stopped ringing. The soldier returned with a bundle of towels.

The colonel gestured over to the barn at the trough where the family did their washing. By its side was a water tap.

"Pails of water, as many as you can," he shouted.

Soon the torture began. The four were forced to lie on their backs. Towels were placed over their heads and when instructed, the soldiers poured ice cold water into the cavity of their mouths.

"Tell me your contacts," the colonel barked. Their heads were lifted so they could answer.

Silence.

Their heads were let go and the more water poured. The four coughed and spluttered.

"Tell me your contacts," the colonel snarled louder than before. Again their heads were lifted.

Yet more silence.

More water, more coughs and more spluttering.

The process continued for several minutes. Suddenly Dino motioned that he might want to say something.

"Stop, stop," cried the colonel bending down to listen.

"Fr....Fr......Fraternite," Dino managed to ensure his word was clearly heard.

The colonel crashed Dino's head back to the ground. Immediately a small pool of blood emerged but nevertheless the soldiers moved forward to continue the torture.

Suddenly the colonel signalled to pause the punishment. He crouched down to the four miserable souls on the ground.

Meanwhile, Emilia had urged her daughters to remain in the house. They had no reason to witness the proceedings. There was nothing they could do.

"Mr Baldini, Franck, Cristophe, Josep, I will give you one last chance." The colonel paused to light another cigarette. He took a long draw and in a softer voice he asked, "Where is the Englisher?"

Stubborn silence again.

The colonel stood up and gestured for more water.

"Maybe you misunderstand, Mr Baldini, help me find the Englisher and we will leave immediately. Then you can all go to your church to pray."

Continuing silence.

More water, more desperate coughs and even more

desperate splutters.

The process continued for a few rounds.

"You sacrifice all for an Englisher. You crazy people, you French. You leave me with no option."

The soldiers lifted the three sons and dragged them over towards the barn. The soldiers attempted to maintain them erect against the wall. But their efforts were in vain. They kept falling over, their limbs too weak to support themselves. Eventually the soldiers were ordered to step back.

"Mr Baldini, your contact, the Englisher!," the colonel shouted at the top of his voice.

Again total silence.

Desperately pleading for his sons' lives Dino grabbed the colonel's right leg. "Please, Herr Colonel….."

Finally the colonel's patience expired. He raised his right hand into the air. A round of machine gun fire rained at the ground where the group were lying.

Dino let out a huge scream. "*No, no, bastardi." figlie di puttane,* you animals. Burn in hell!"

Emilia and the girls had emerged from the house and they collapsed on top of the group, screaming and crying.

Dino dragged himself well away from the colonel. His anger, his indignation gave him strength. He stood up and faced up to the devil. "I will come after you, kill you, I will."

Then he collapsed again back to the ground.

"Mr Baldini, thank you for your hospitality. Your fate will be different. Your punishment will be to bury your sons and to console and care for your wife and daughters."

The Colonel glanced at his troops, "The women are yours, but we leave in fifteen minutes. Be quick!"

The group of refugees inside the truck could do nothing. All that was heard was the Mourners Kaddish, the Jewish prayer for the dead.

Chapter 24

World War 2 – Thomas' Story

After his sojourn in Tunisia, assisting the allies with military intelligence for the North Africa campaign, John returned to Marseille incognito. "It's too dangerous for you to stay in Marseille now," his commander had said. "Take your wife, I suggest, you return to England as soon as possible. We'll provide the transport."

Fredo was on weekend leave from the work camp at Crook. He stared at the raging fire in the grate, stunned at John's version of the events on the farm. He cowered in shock. His fingers gripped his forehead, his nails drawing blood. Catherine comforted him. John had been used to seeing some horrific sites but he remained steadfast as he narrated the circumstances of the shootings at Dino's farm.

Eventually Thomas broke the silence, "Are you telling us, John, they just shot my cousins in cold blood, all three of them."

"Yes, when they found the refugees, it was curtains. These Nazis have no tolerance for anyone helping the Jews. Your cousins didn't relent, they remained silent, gave nothing away. It was about our *'fraternite'*, you know. Poor Dino, not only was he keeping the escape route alive he was protecting me as well. Had I been there at the time, I wouldn't have been able to help them. I would be dead too. No doubt."

341

Catherine butted in. "When this damn war is over, Fredo, you need to find time to visit Dino and all those poor women. What an ordeal for them."

She glanced over at John, "What about the women, how are they managing now?"

"They are really suffering. Only God knows how they are really coping. You know, Catherine, this raping and pillaging, it's happening everywhere across there. Thank God those bastards never made it here to our island."

Thomas stood and smashed his glass of pop into the sink. "This family has been torn apart, Lewis is up there in the sanatorium, Alfred, who knows how he is, the girls shooting planes out of the sky, this thing with Dino. I'm off as well, no doubt about that. I'm eighteen now. Papa, too, he's not the same since he came back from his prison."

"I know in my heart there's no stopping you now. Come over and give me a cuddle," his mama replied, holding back her tears, after which she ran upstairs and slammed the bedroom door shut.

***

Within days Thomas had signed up with the cadet force in nearby Durham. He enlisted with three other lads from Errington. Three times a week, they attended drill, weapon training and map reading. In between training the boys assisted with the Home Guard. Thomas felt his induction was too long. He was impatient. He was desperate for the real thing. He knew he was ready for the fight. He wanted revenge. For his family, for his country, for himself.

Thomas was kitted in battledress and at Easter he travelled to the sanatorium proudly wearing his cadet uniform. Although there was an eighteen year gap between them, Lewis and he were close. It was Lewis who had encouraged his young brother to act the naughty little boy, to deliberately jump into puddles, to get his hands dirty filling tin cans with muck, to build bogies with old planks of wood and discarded pram wheels. Lewis had bought him his first cowboy outfit, complete with gun and rifle. The pair had a special bond, oldest and youngest.

"Thomas, you look great. When are you off for the real thing," said Lewis.

"Big pal, not sure, but I hope it's soon. I'm doing my training now."

"I wish I was back there. You know if it wasn't for that big Scottish bloke who carried me onto that boat I wouldn't have made it. Those Scots guys are tough old men, you know. I wish I could remember his name."

He didn't know it, but this was the last time Thomas saw his big brother. Lewis' wounds had failed to heal and his body was weakening. The fresh air on the Durham moors had made no difference to his health. Sadly Lewis never lived to see the beginning of the end of the conflict. Just a few weeks after his demise the Allies landed on the French beaches in Normandy.

Thomas had little inkling of the impact of the Normandy landings. He had taken inspiration from his big brother. A Scot had saved his favourite brother at Dunkirk and his young focus and determination was to fight with the Scots. Lewis had witnessed Scots' bravery at first hand and Thomas hadn't forgotten about his talking times at night in bed with his dad when he was a boy. His dad himself had been inspired by the Scots' fearsomeness when he was in Glasgow. "They were tough especially when they were determined. You never want to cross them," his dad had often said.

***

Thomas listened attentively at the Royal Scots Fusiliers camp at the Churchill Barracks in Ayr.

"We might have landed on those beaches," said the officer, "but the war is far from over, son. Hitler will fight to the last man, you can be sure of that."

"Seems you passed all the tests. I think you are ready, son. For a wee man, all five feet of you, you're tough and feisty, just the way we like our soldiers."

***

Following the landings on the Normandy beaches a new western front had been opened. Within three months Paris had been liberated and the allied advance continued towards the Rhine. Strategically the Rhine was critical. It marked an effective border between Germany and its neighbours to the west. The river was deemed a significant barrier. For the Allies to cross the Rhine would signify humiliation for the Germans. They were well aware that the German military machine wouldn't allow that to happen too easily. And so it proved all the way from Holland in the north to Alsace in the south.

In autumn the Allies attempted to breach the river in the Netherlands in Operation Market Garden. It failed. The objective had been to capture several bridges near Arnhem but despite huge aerial support the powerful Panzer divisions of the German army resisted and any thoughts of the Allies that the war would be over before Christmas had been completely extinguished. After that disastrous campaign Thomas' training intensified.

"No more mamsy pamsy from now on. You know how to shoot, you know to defend yourself. Now it's about strategy, tactics and teamwork. We need to be more astute to beat the hun," said Sergeant McFadzean at the morning roll call. "In our next mission we'll have the weather to beat as well. Let's be ready."

Thomas and his battalion were put through their paces on tactics, attacking, defending and supporting colleagues.

"No surrender, we cannot be defeated. We are close to the end. We have to win," was the constant message of the sergeant.

Thomas bunked up with his new pal Davie who had enrolled on the same day. Davie, too, was desperate to join the Scots battalion. He was eighteen years of age, soon turning nineteen. Their backgrounds were similar, uncles lost in the first war and brothers and relatives dispersed in this war. In the next bunk were two lads from Glasgow, Willie and Jack. Theirs was an odd combination, Willie with his broad accent and Jack, a polite and softly spoken posh lad who seemed out of place in the boisterous environment.

"Are you looking forward to sticking your bayonet into some jerry belly?" Davie asked Jack.

"Aye, he will," said Willie before Jack could reply. "I'll be right 'rer 'wae 'um. Dinne worry. We'll dae it re 'gether."

For his small eighteen year old frame, Willie acted tough. His demeanor was similar to that of Thomas.

Thomas proposed. "Guys, let's all stick together as pals, the four of us," he said. "Let's support each other and we'll all survive."

Davie thumped his hand against the wall of the barracks. "Shit, shit, shit, one of us is bound to die. The odds are against us. We can't all make it."

Thomas let loose his rage. "Come on, Davie, we're here to win this bloody war. Those damn Nazi bastards have messed up our lives, our families, good and proper. We'll search them out and we'll kill them, no bother."

"All re 'gether, right boys," said Willie.

The laddish banter continued a time after which the four dozed off into sleep.

***

During the winter the Allies' worst fears were realized. The enemy were fighting back. They had taken strength from the successful resistance at the bridge at Arnhem. The German army machine had been revitalized and it embarked on a major new offensive in the Belgian Ardennes forest. They had attacked a weakly defended section of the allied line and they were in no mood to surrender. The Battle of the Bulge had been set in motion.

Sergeant McFadzean called his battalion to order. "The Germans have launched an offensive in Belgium which our American friends are dealing with. We need to stay resolved. Soon we may have the opportunity to create our own counter offensive. They'll make mistakes. They'll become desperate. That's when we move in."

The winter remained cold and at the turn of the year the weather turned more extreme. Consistently clear blue skies made for little snow but frosts were hard. And the frosts were good for the tanks. Any thaw would turn the fields and roads into mulch.

The battalion of the Royals Scots Fusiliers had crossed the channel and they were billeted in Eastern Holland. They were safe from the German offensive occurring further south. Finally the unit received its orders and Sergeant McFadzean called his troop together. He hung a sketch map on the wall. The German Dutch border was traced in a thick red line.

"This is it, boys" he said. "You've all been waiting on

this for weeks. This is our operation."

They rallied round the table to ensure they understood the mission.

"See on the map, there are three rivers, which form a triangle, the Maas, the Roer and the Wurm. There are three towns, Roermond here to the north, Sittard to the south and Heinsberg here to the east all about fifteen miles apart. The border crosses right here." McFadzean traced his pointer the full length of the border and glanced to ensure everybody was paying attention. "The German army are defending the area in the triangle. Our objective is simple, to drive them back into Germany across to the other side of the Roer and Wurm rivers. Then we push on towards the Rhine. We are coordinating the attack with other battalions. We succeed and it's all ours. Later we cross the Rhine and the war will be over."

The sergeant continued. "The German front line is here on the Maas. Our intelligence tells us there are three lines of trench defences. Pill boxes and gun positions connect their trenches. They have laid trip wires and mines, so the area is well defended. They know we're coming. But we think their resources have been badly mauled and their morale is low. We have support from the Americans in the north and our own infantry divisions further down here."

Again the sergeant looked up.

"It's likely to be very foggy, so there'll be no air support. There are few roads, just a few dirt tracks. They are intersected by streams and culverts so cross country conditions are difficult. As the enemy retreat, I'm am sure they'll blow up any bridges too."

"Our own D-day is tomorrow the sixteenth. The artillery move out first thing. We wait for our turn. Get a good night sleep."

***

The boys barely slept.

"Tomorrow we're gonna meet the hun. I'll be fine. I'll look him straight in the eyes and pull the trigger," said an anxious Davie.

"Nae time for 'rat," said Willie. "You'll no get that close. Look intae his eyes when he's deed."

"When you see him, shoot first, think about it later," said Thomas. "I want to see them running back to their mammies. And I'll be there racing after them."

The bravado receded slightly when Jack spoke his first words of the night. "These Germans are young boys as well, just like us, teenagers."

Willie, the fearless Scot, said, "Shut the fuck up, Jack. I'll help you pull that trigger, dinnae worry about that."

Eventually the four lapsed into sleep, excited and anxious at what they might have to face in the following days. Thomas dreamt of picnics in pastures and meadows with his brothers and sisters around. His papa was toasting his ancestors and his mother was lamenting the lives in her family lost in the mines.

***

The following day the fusiliers were transported close to the front line. Base camp was in the town of Sittard close to the border. To McFadzean's shock the weather had changed. A thaw had taken hold overnight and it seemed the day might turn milder by the hour. The boys noticed that the road tracks and flat fields were rapidly being rutted in the thaw. They knew that movement of bigger artillery would be more difficult.

Blast booms and gunfire were heard in the distance.

The sergeant brought the group together again. He had a large piece of paper and a pencil in his hand.

"Our task will be to capture the Isenbruch to Breberen road her at Hongen." The sergeant sketched out the scene. "We think the fields here are mined. The enemy's trenches are behind the Saeffler Beek, here. We are relying on the flail tanks sweeping up the mines and the crocodile flame throwers will follow behind. You need to find your way through the minefield in front of the beek. You build two assault bridges over the canal here near Stein. And then we push those huns back. Good luck."

There was little wind and it was likely that the drizzle brought by the dark clouds would continue for the rest of the day.

"At least we won't freeze to death today," piped up Jack. The other three remained silent as they trudged through the flat landscape ever watchful for a straying enemy machine gun. Up ahead they saw the flail tanks moving forward. Behind them were the crocodiles.

They had reached the battleground. The offensive was in full flow. The sounds were increasingly deafening. Smoke and debris filled the air. The whining noise of falling shells were edging closer. The little villages of Lind and Stein, previously anonymous and peaceful, were under threat of obliteration.

"Get down," shouted Thomas. A blast exploded twenty yards to his right.

"There's the beek ahead," said Willie. "The infantry are assaulting the towns. Let's keep going."

Thomas assumed the role of leader and he was first to reach the beek. The other three walked carefully behind him. The fields were churning over fast. The scene resembled a bog. Progress was slow. One assault bridge was already in place. The boys had to build the other. One of the flail tanks was inactive. It had been mined. Another made it over the bridge but was bogged down in the mud. Behind Thomas observed that one of the crocodiles was stuck also.

Thomas spotted the silhouette of Sergeant McFadzean. "Boys, never mind the second bridge. They're running scared," the sergeant screamed. "C'mon, let's get across, let's go."

Shells continued to fall. Some tanks were moving, some were stuck, some smoking and damaged, no longer useful. Voices balling out orders were faint amidst the noise and smoke. *"Hell on earth,"* Thomas thought. *"We need to push on, get these huns out."*

Ahead through the foggy chaos Thomas saw the fighting on the main road. He noticed some Germans taking shelter in the houses of the village. All the while machine gun fire continued relentlessly and the grenades kept coming.

Thomas fell into a ditch behind some barbed wire to avoid another shell whining through the wind. Momentarily he was out of sight of any German bullets. The others fell beside him. He looked behind. "All our fucking tanks are stuck in the fucking mud." He looked ahead. "Our guys are down. Their snipers are picking us off one by one. We'll never make it." He was assessing the situation. He glanced to his left hand side. "Sarge, sarge," he screamed. McFadzean lay in the mud, blood oozing from his body.

"Just a scrape," said McFadzean. "On you go, I'll be behind you."

Their eyes came together. The sergeant's glare was enough. His message was clear. Thomas knew his next move. He had no option, otherwise the mission was lost.

He and his pals were at the most advanced position.

Behind him the tanks were immobile. Several soldiers were scurrying towards the temporary safety of the ditch. He knew it had to be man to man. And he had to take the initiative. From his trench he studied the road ahead. His target was clear. The house where most of the firing was coming from. "Cover me, guys, come on."

In a flash Thomas was on the move and the other three followed. Other soldiers behind followed too. Machine gun fire continued relentlessly. Within moments Thomas fell to the ground. "Thomas' been hit," said Willie. "Let's pull him back."

Momentarily Thomas' world went black. His brain was in overdrive. He was in a dark tunnel with a fleeting light. His last memory was standing up from the trench and rallying the charge forward. Suddenly the light was switched on.

"For Christ's sake, leave me, Willie." he shouted to his pal.

Thomas lashed at Willie as he made it to his feet. Instinctively his charge continued. He threw a grenade through the window of his target house. He fell to the ground awaiting the explosion. He glanced round, his pals were on the ground too, rifles cocked ready to fire at anything that moved. Further back towards the trench, support was following. There was an explosion at the target. He stood, tossed another grenade through a second window of the target. Another explosion. Momentarily there was silence. Now he felt the pain, but he knew the house was no longer sniping. His pain had eased. He wiped the blood from his face.

Behind the houses he saw them fleeing. They were running scared through the back gardens. The noise was intensifying, bullets continued to whizz by. In the distance the booms of the battle raged on. Body carnage and relentless chaos everywhere.

He ran to a birch tree, Willie and Davie, too, but Jack was nowhere to be seen.

"He must have been hit," said Davie. He glanced at Thomas. "You're soaked in blood, pal, ye cannae see."

"I'm fine, man. That barn over there," shouted Thomas. "Go!"

As they ran across the open space heavy fire continued to rain on them. He was bleeding profusely but he made it, Willie too. Again he swiped the blood away from his eyes and glanced back. Davie was lying in the mud. He was still moving, he was still alive. Thomas dropped his rifle. He zigzagged out into the space. He scooped up his pal. He carried him to the safety of the barn. "You're only five fit tall, but wae the strength of an ox, ye can dae anythin'", shouted Willie.

His adrenaline pumping, he made himself ready. Bren gun in his right hand and his grenades within easy reach, Thomas looked out from the side window. The enemy trenches were just a few yards away. They were there, a squad of snipers. He noticed McFadzean limping towards the barn with his own squad. "Ready, Willie. One chance only!" Thomas never waited for any response. Armed with his rifle and grenades he ran out, Willie behind him covering. He tossed the grenades one after the other, Willie fired relentlessly.

From behind, McFadzean seized the moment. Thomas' intentions were clear. There was only one response. "The machine guns at either end, now, get them, now!" he screamed to the rest of the men.

His grenades launched, Thomas sprayed the trench with bullets. But his world went black again. He had been hit. He fell to the ground. He muttered to his pal, "Willie, come on." But Willie wasn't there. A spark of light and he staggered up again, his Bren gun still firing at the trench. He felt into his left pocket, one more grenade. He retrieved it. As he put his hand skywards to release it, his world went black again. This time he collapsed in stages. Firstly his ankles gave way. He sank to his knees in defiance. Thomas was an easy target and a final flurry of bullets followed. His young obliterated body, completely immersed in blood and now minus a right arm, finally collapsed to the ground. The light in Thomas' tunnel never switched on again.

***

In his report of the battle, Sergeant McFadzean wrote,

"Fusilier Thomas Baldini was an extraordinary soldier. Despite his small stature he was tough, brave and demanding. He assumed the leadership role to his other young colleagues, he defied the odds and sacrificed his young life. In and around the villages of Lind and Stein the enemy had twice as many soldiers defending their positions. As a result of his determined actions, he drew the enemy away from their positions that enabled the remainder of the platoon to capture the villages mentioned. This was vital to the eventual success of Operation Blackcock. The fighting was at point blank range, man to man. He even had the courage to return one of his colleagues to safety before proceeding with his task. This young man exemplified the spirit of The Royal Scots Fusiliers."

Chapter 25

World War 2 – The Final Story

Eventually Fredo was assessed by government officials at the internment camp on the Isle of Man. Although he had retained the status of an enemy alien he was considered to pose no threat to national security. After a year on incarceration he was released. But he still was not truly a free man. He had been assigned to spend the remainder of the war at an agricultural work camp near Crook. His family were able to visit and he was allowed home periodically under license and as the war progressed the restrictions on his movements eased.

Fredo was at home when the telegram arrived. Catherine placed the envelope on the table. She dared not open it. Her dream of Thomas' return might be shattered. She had lost one son to this war, another was dispersed elsewhere, maybe already dead, and now there was the nightmare her baby boy might be gone too.

"Fredo, it seemed only yesterday when he started walking, first day at school, Holy Communion in church, cowboys and indians. When the war began all those years ago he had just started secondary school, first time he wore long trousers. Surely, it can't be, not another gone." Catherine burst into tears.

He stood to comfort his wife. "We need to open it. Let's be brave. Come on, let me do it."

The message was clear. Both collapsed to their knees inconsolably.

The telegram ended with an ice cold sentiment. "………………sorry for your loss." No doubt the typist had written the words that often that they no longer carried any significance.

"We need to inform Vera. I'll go to Seaham later," said Fredo.

The couple were alone. Before the war six children had flitted in and out of their lives every day. Now it was only Vera who was there to comfort them. And it was over two months since Christine and Cora had been home.

"Are Christine and Cora in any danger? Tell me, no, please Fredo," pleaded Catherine.

"I really don't know, dear. I don't know what they are doing now. We'll have to wait."

"I am exhausted and washed out. I have been waiting over five years. I'll never forget the night of the riot when they took you away. You can't even guess what it was like here without you."

Catherine took out her handkerchief again.

"If it hadn't been for Thomas…………," Catherine sobbed again. "……………he was my little rock. I never thought The Lord would take him away as well. Oh Fredo, what has happened to us?"

He managed to grab hold of his wife before she could collapse to the floor.

For several minutes they sobbed.

Finally Fredo relented. "Come on, let's bring Vera here. We'll go to church, light a candle and say a few more prayers."

"What about his body. He's out there all alone. Will they bring him back?"

"I don't think so, dear. I don't know if they can bring any bodies back, there are so many who have lost their lives. They say thousands, millions dead."

"But he'll be all alone, my little baby Tommy,……. why Thomas, why did you go?"

***

It was usual in the royal household that the King hold his daily conference with his Private Secretary at the breakfast table. In recent weeks the King had been grumpy. He was frustrated the Allies still seemed no closer to winning the damned war. During the previous autumn he had been advised by both Churchill and Eisenhower that it was likely the war would be over during the winter. They had said the Germans were too weak, they wouldn't be able to hold out, especially since the Russians were moving in from the East at the same time. The King's continuing anxiety was obvious to his Private Secretary.

"Your Majesty, there is one final item on the agenda today. May I inform you that we have received a nomination from the Royal Scots Fusiliers resulting from an act of gallantry and bravery. It's with regard to the award of the Victoria Cross medal to a young English soldier. The documents are in order and the nomination has been duly supported by three witnesses, Your Majesty."

"Have the documents been countersigned fully by the military hierarchy and have they been approved by the Minister of Defence?"

"Yes, indeed, Your Majesty, you can view the signatures here."

The document folder was placed on the table. "The nomination concerns a youngster, aged nineteen, Your Majesty. A remarkable case."

"During war, my man, youngsters become men. Even they have to kill or be killed. Please let me read the detail."

The King opened the folder and scanned its contents. The Private Secretary moved to the corner of the room and stood at his desk awaiting further instructions. After several minutes the King looked across and said, "Sir Alan, can you ensure Her Highness, the Princess Elizabeth reviews the file too."

***

Since the war started Catherine had faithfully attended Mass every day during Lent. Losing Thomas had hit her hard. This Lent she was praying with more fervour, more belief. '*Please Lord, let them rest in peace, not just Thomas, Lewis, but all those who will not be returning. Please Lord, watch over Alfred and others whose fates are yet unknown, Amen,*'

On her way home she reflected on her family's Easter Sunday lunches. How special they were before the war, family around the table, joyous occasions. Catherine was in no mood this year for any such gathering. She returned home and a letter was lying on the shop counter. It was stamped with a strange square motif. To the left a lion stood on its hind legs, to the right a unicorn. Both animals held a shield with Latin inscriptions on the front legs. Anxiously she opened the envelope and read its contents.

'To be published by Authority in The London Gazette of FRIDAY, the 16th of MARCH, 1945

War Office, 20th March, 1945
The KING has been graciously approved the posthumous award of the VICTORIA CROSS to:-

No, 14768011 Fusilier Thomas Baldini, The Royal Scots Fusiliers (Errington, Co. Durham).

In North-West Europe on 18th January 1945, a Battalion of The Royal Scots Fusiliers supported by tanks was the leading battalion in the assault of the German position between the Rivers Roer and Maas. This consisted of a broad belt of minefields and wire on the other side of a stream.

As a result of a thaw the armour was unable to cross the stream and the infantry had to continue the assault without the support of the tanks. Fusilier Baldini's platoon was ordered to attack a small village.

As they left their trenches the platoon came under concentrated machine gun and rifle fire from the houses and Fusilier Baldini was hit by a bullet in the head. After a few minutes he recovered consciousness, charged down thirty yards of open road and threw a grenade into the nearest window.

The enemy fled through the gardens of four houses, closely pursued by Fusilier Baldini and the survivors of the platoon. Under heavy fire at seventy yards range Fusilier Baldini and two companions crossed an open space and reached the cover of a wooden barn, thirty yards from the enemy trenches.

Fusilier Baldini, still bleeding profusely from his wound, went into the open under intense close range fire and carried one of his companions, who had been wounded, into the barn. Taking a Bren gun he again went into the open, firing as he went.

He was wounded a second time but recovered and went on firing until a third bullet hit a grenade which he was carrying and killed him.

The superb gallantry and self-sacrifice of Fusilier Baldini drew the enemy fire away from his companions on to himself. As the result of this, the platoon were able to capture the position, accounting for thirty Germans and two machine guns.

Throughout the action, fought from beginning to end at point blank range, the dash, determination and magnificent courage of Fusilier Baldini enabled his comrades to overcome an enemy more than twice their own number.'

Catherine placed the letter to her chest and placed the soiled handkerchief back inside her sleeve. '*What does this mean*," she wondered. '*I need to go see Vera.'*

The walk to Seaham seemed much longer than usual. Vera was still in her auxiliary service uniform when Catherine arrived.

"Do you always have to wear that stupid uniform," she said.

"Oh mama, shoosh."

Vera read the letter. "Oh mama, your little boy has done something remarkable. The King wants to honour him with a special medal. I don't think many are awarded with this medal, The Victoria Cross, it's called. Thomas really achieved something wonderful. He must have been so brave."

"But it won't bring him back. I wish I could hold him one more time, Vera. He was my little baby."

"Mama, we were all your little babies once. Now we need to care for other little babies which have come along. Lewis has two, I have my own little baby. Alfred has his two also. When the girls return they'll have their own little babies too." Vera continued. "You know, mama, when I was in the kitchen at the mess in Catterick, I saw all these young soldiers, those fresh innocent faces. I fed them dinner, I gave them tea and I knew some of them would never return. I comforted some of the other mums who lost their boys. Terrible, heartbreaking for a time, but even they had to come to terms with what happened to their babies. Life has to carry on. You have to be strong, mama. Soon this damned war will be over. Thomas won't be returning, but Alfred, who knows? We're still a family, a strong family. We've all had it tough. If we have to start again, we will."

Indeed Vera had suffered too. She had experienced the trauma of Charlie's internment and she had many dark thoughts when she was alone at night. *Where was he, was he locked up like a murderer, was he being cared for, would he ever return?* Her little girl couldn't comprehend why daddy was no longer at home.

In Charlie's absence she had boarded up her small shop and returned home to care for her mother. It had bothered Vera's conscience when Christine and Cora signed up for the auxiliaries. So she had decided to sign up too. She had requested an assignment closer to home. She never desired that her family be separated further than was necessary. Fortunately an opportunity had arisen locally in the staff kitchen at the nearby barracks in Catterick.

After the Allies landed on the French beaches Vera's work had diminished somewhat due to the reduced number of new soldiers training at the barracks. Thomas too had been at the barracks. He was in one of the last groups in the war to be trained before experiencing action in the field.

***

At home Catherine proudly placed the letter from the War Office on the mantelpiece above the fireplace in the little sitting room upstairs. She promised to herself to remain calm and collected. Fredo's visits home had become more frequent as did Charlie's too. For years, the pair, released on parole, had been assigned each to a local farmer. As part of their release conditions from internment they had been required to report and work on the farm under the farmer's personal supervision. With little pay, all they had to do was to demonstrate they were model British citizens, no disturbances, no fuss and no threat.

When at home, although still prohibited to do so, Fredo listened to the news broadcasts. He was horrified at what he was hearing. "Listen, Catherine, I have heard of prison camps, of diseases, starvation, gas chambers. This is worse than any of us could have imagined."

"It's even worse than that, my dearest," she replied. "I've been to the cinema to see for myself. On the newsreels the images are right in front of you. There are no words to explain it. It's terrible what the movie reveals. It's horrific." Catherine paused to pull the handkerchief from her sleeve. "Now I only go there, to see if I can spot Alfred anywhere. It's been over a year since we heard from him."

"*Dio mio, Alfredino, dov'e sei*, where are you, Alfred? I wish I could go to the cinema with you," said Fredo.

"You know you're not allowed to be there. I don't want them taking you away again. It's bad enough you are listening to the wireless when you are not supposed to. In any case trust me. You wouldn't even want to see the pictures of those camps. They're awful. Once you've seen the pictures, you can't un-see them. Heartbreaking it is. It's crazy what these people have done to these poor Jews. Whole communities destroyed!"

"I guess that's what happened to the family Dino was hiding in Marseilles."

"And then all the images of those poor refugees plodding hopelessly along those roads covered with snow. Mainly women and children, freezing to death and at the mercy of soldiers on the prowl. How awful the devastation is over there."

"So many wasted lives everywhere. Us too, Lewis first, Dino's boys, our own Thomas, what next?"

"They're saying it will all over soon. Let's pray to God they are right."

***

There was little to celebrate at the family assembly for Easter lunch. It was low key and sombre. The little kids ran around, joyously playing, oblivious to the trauma of their parents. Christine and Cora were on leave. Still there was no word from Alfred. According to the newsreels some camps in the east had been liberated.

"Maybe we can salvage something from this horrible mess," said Catherine. "If only we could hear from Alfred."

"I've some more awful news," said Fredo. "For a few days I've been meaning to tell you about by sister but I suppose I never found the time, I'm not sure you want to know."

"Come on, tell us. It can't be any worse, really."

Fredo pulled an envelope out from his inside pocket. "I don't know how the letter has managed to reach us but it's from Elisa, you know my young sister. Remember, Catherine, when we were in Italy all those years ago you met her. Well she never left Montecino. She married another guy from the village, Mario Casci was his name. It seems he was called to the army too. He was with the Italians when they invaded Albania. He was badly wounded there and they sent him home to recover."

The family sat motionless in anticipation. Fredo shuffled the flimsy paper around pondering on the translation. He knew nothing about how the war was affecting his family in Italy.

"Well, as Elisa says, Montecino was right in the middle of a battle zone between Germans and Americans. The front was called the Gothic Line, she says. The Germans had built a wall in the valley south of Valbona supposedly to prevent the advancing Americans from breaking through. However a bunch of black American soldiers penetrated the wall and the Germans retreated to the mountains. Unfortunately for us back home they retreated to Lama further up the hills above Montecino. These American soldiers made it to Valbona where they camped just before Christmas. But a unit was sent up to Montecino to hold the fort as a defensive measure should the Germans think of attacking. It seems there were some skirmishes between Lama and Montecino and some locals were wounded in the crossfire. But on Christmas night, it seems, a battle ensued. Bombs and rockets lit up the sky between Lama and Valbona."

Fredo paused to turn over the page and he noticed that his family were engrossed.

"Where was I?....... Remember, Catherine, where Elisa's house was. It was the first house you reach in Montecino if you were to walk down the mule track from Lama. Well, Elisa says, that at the crack of dawn whilst the Americans were still sobering off from Christmas Day, all of a sudden, a group of six or seven Germans knocked on Elisa's door. Her husband Mario answered. She says he had his army trousers on when he opened the door. She heard the Germans shout out, *'paesano o partigiano,'* in other words, are you a paesano, a friend of theirs,' the Germans, or a partisan, an enemy. Elisa never heard Mario's response but next thing she heard was a gunshot. The bastards had shot him dead on the spot."

"My God, it must have been horrible for the poor woman," cried Christine. Catherine's eyes were swelling up and Christine stretched across to her. "Mama, it's just another story amongst millions. These people are evil. That's why in the end good will triumph."

"Elisa goes on to say that the Germans emptied the house. She and Mario's invalid mum and their two little girls aged seven and five were forced out, manhandled to step over Mario's body like he didn't exist. They were ushered to move down the mule track. At the next house Elisa was right there as the Germans fired several shots through the wooden door. They didn't know that Bruna, petrified, was standing behind the door, holding her little son, Giuliano by the hand. He was only four years of age. When they barged through the door, Elisa saw little Giuliano on the floor, already dead. Bruna, blood streaming from her right shoulder was screaming inconsolably. The Germans grabbed and pulled her away. The bastards coldly stepped over Giuliano's little body and searched the house. By this time most people in the village were running down the street to try to reach the safety of the American soldiers at the other end of the village."

The girls were shocked at the events and comforted each other, Christine, Cora and Vera with their mum. Gladys and Ethel weren't sure how to react. Charlie remained composed. "How can they do those things to our people, how could they?"

"Gladys, come on, help me make some tea," Ethel said. "Let's leave them alone for a moment. It was their family, their people. Kiddies, come here, let's all go downstairs." The two ladies went downstairs into the shop and filled the urn. "Do you really think, Ethel, Edward will return after all this mess. It has been so long since we heard," said Gladys in her soft childlike voice.

"Of course, he will, I'm sure. Is there still some fresh milk around? Can you see?"

Upstairs Fredo continued to translate the latter.

"It transpired that the whole village was cleared, all the villagers were forced out of their homes. The Germans and Americans fought it out between them. It seems afterwards there were bodies of soldiers strewn everywhere. The battle continued for two days. Finally the Germans were forced out and the Americans regained control of the village. Elisa says that a couple of days later when she returned, Mario was still laying on the ground exactly where he died and little Giuliano too. Some villagers, she says, even today apparently have refused to return. Those who did return helped Elisa and Bruna to carry the two bodies directly to the cemetery. The church in Montecino was completely destroyed in the bombing so the cemetery was the only place where they could take the bodies. The priest and villagers dug some holes there and then. On that day six villagers were known to have lost their lives."

Fredo folded up the letter and put it back into his inside pocket. "Horrific, isn't it."

Total silence around the table.

***

The gossip spread through Errington like wildfire. Was it really possible, was it true? They were saying Hitler had committed suicide in Berlin. PC Robinson was on his rounds as usual that morning. "I have no idea, I've heard the same rumour as you. Now be on your way." But the constable had noticed a change. People felt happier, there was a little more laughter around. On that spring day it seemed also that the birds were singing louder. The buds on the leaves seemed to be larger and the leaves themselves seemed to be a deeper shade of green. Even the smoke from the factories and the soot from the mines didn't seem so nasty. *'The Mayday celebration will be a great one if this rumour is correct,'* thought the constable.

At home Fredo was used to being upstairs on his own. The wireless was set to the lowest possible volume. He was fearful to venture downstairs to the café in case a passing policeman dropped in. He wasn't allowed to work there, just at the camp. He heard the news. Nazi concentration camps were being liberated, German forces were retreating back towards Berlin. He heard of the death of Mussolini and then of German forces surrendering in Italy. Maybe it really was all over, he thought, especially when the newsreader announced the suicide of Hitler.

Finally the message from Winston Churchill was heard loud and clear. *'Hostilities will end officially at one minute after midnight tonight, the cease fire on the front has already begun, and our dear Channel Islands are also to be freed today.'*

Fredo sat down, put his head into his hands and cried. *'Lewis dead, Thomas dead, Where is my Alfred? Dino's boys, Elisa's husband. Please, God, please just let me be free.'*

The streets in Errington throbbed into life. Even the pouring rain didn't stand in the way. There was singing and dancing everywhere. But Catherine was in little mood to sing and dance. Her heartache was still alive and present. She knew the merriment in the streets was temporary. There were few males in the streets. She had witnessed scenes like this before. And just like the first time she knew many of the missing males would never make it back.

***

The following weekend another telegram arrived. Fredo and Catherine were having breakfast.

'Arrive at Durham, noon tomorrow, stop. Please meet me, stop. Love you all, stop. Alfred.'

Catherine shouted upstairs. "Gladys, come down, quick. Great news."

The family gathered round. There were tears of joy and endless embraces, the children couldn't figure out was going on.

Gladys called over her two little children and she knelt down in front of them. "Daddy will be here tomorrow, Richard. Aren't you happy? And Teresa, your daddy has never seen you, my love. He didn't know when he left that you were in my tummy." The two children groaned and scampered off to play together.

They opened one of the last two bottles of wine they had in the kitchen cabinet. "We will keep this last one special. This is for Alfred tomorrow," said Catherine.

At Durham station the group were in their Sunday best clothes, Fredo, Catherine, Gladys and Vera. The train steamed in and several passengers alighted. There was nobody they recognised.

"Mama, he's not here," said Gladys in despair.

Suddenly in the distance she noticed a frail man carrying a small bag over his shoulder. He was waving frantically.

"Alfred?" screamed Catherine. "Alfred?" Gladys dropped her handbag and ran as fact as her legs could take her. Catherine walked briskly behind her.

"Gladys, not so much, it still aches all over," Alfred tried to push away the cuddles and kisses.

Alfred was fragile. The family hadn't counted on this.

Although delighted at his safe return, they were shocked when he removed his overcoat. He left a sturdy twelve stone frame, now Alfred was barely seven stone.

"We'll soon build you back up, isn't that right, Gladys?" said Catherine.

"Mama, I've been told to go easy with food. My body is not used to having food regularly. Little and often, please, mama," Alfred whispered. "It's so great to see you all."

"You must have had it tough," said Fredo.

"I don't really want to talk about it. It's just great to be home. I heard about Thomas, why the hell did he go as well, that stupid kid. They told me how brave he was. The guys down there were toasting him and then toasting me because I was his brother. What a load of nonsense, waste of a young life."

"Yes, poor Thomas, just a kid he was," said Catherine.

"He was still an idiot. He was my little brother, still a wee boy. The last time I saw him he had that silly toy gun and holster with him. Out there against those Nazis the guns have real bullets. You only get one chance. He's lying somewhere out there in some rotten battlefield."

"Forget that for now, Alfred, let's just celebrate you're back. With your two kids, as well. Aren't they beautiful, my dear? Think about it. You missed all that nappy shit stuff," said Gladys cuddling her husband ever so gently.

***

The letter of invitation to Buckingham Palace was addressed solely to Fredo. Details were scant. Thomas had been awarded the Victoria Cross posthumously. Fredo was invited to attend on the seventeenth of July, along with one other relative, whose name required to be provided in advance.

"Catherine, what do we wear, what do we do? I assume the people at the camp will let me go."

"Stop fussing, of course they will."

Ever since the announcement in the London Gazette journalists from the local newspapers had visited the shop in order to obtain any further snippets of information about Thomas and to put some flesh on the bones of the story. The Hartlepool Mail, the Sunderland Echo, the Newcastle Journal all sent journalists.

But their visits to the shop were largely in vain. Fredo and Catherine knew no more what already had been written and published.

"We don't get many local heroes in this part of world," said the journalist from the Journal. "Here's my card, Mr Baldini. Call me when you leave for the palace. I would like a photograph for our front page."

The family prepared for their big day.

"Fredo, I don't think I can face the journey and all that pomp. I need to stay here and look after our Alfred and the kids," said Catherine.

"You're coming with me. This is our boy, our Thomas, our hero. You must come, you should be very proud."

"Yes, very proud but also very sad. Thomas was full of fun and I miss him so much. I really don't wish to go. It's too much for me. Please, you go. Take the girls, ask Charlie, I'm sure he'll go. You can all go as a family. Tell them Christine will attend on my behalf. She will look the part in her Auxiliary Service uniform."

"Really, Catherine, this will be special. Please, dear, think again." But Fredo knew his wife was a strong and determined woman. When she was committed and she had made up her mind, well that was it.

The family felt elegant and important at Newcastle railway station. The journalist from the Journal was there as he had promised. Fredo looked the city gent, with detachable stiff Newmarket collar and black tie, fedora hat tilted to one side. His two daughters, Private Christine and Private Cora, were at his side, proudly wearing Auxiliaries' attire. Eldest daughter Vera, arm in arm with husband Charlie, appeared the professional couple intent on having lunch at the Ritz.

The following morning they reached the Palace gates well in advance of their noon ceremony.

A handful of tourists were already milling around watching the beefeaters on sentinel duty at the gates.

The group walked up to the main gate and Fredo presented the formal invitation letter. Christine was at his side whilst the three others stood behind.

The guard read the letter and shouted unceremoniously, "Personal Identification Documents, please."

They handed over their documents.

The guard examined them and responded in a similarly brisk fashion.

"Excuse me, Sir, I cannot let you enter. Wait here, I will be back shortly."

The guard summoned over one of his colleagues to replace him at the gates. He duly disappeared into the palace with the documents.

"Sir, can you let us know what is happening," said Christine to one of the two guards.

"Madam, please step aside." Christine noticed a movement towards his rifle.

All five huddled around wondering what would happen next. What was wrong? Why couldn't they enter the palace to collect Thomas' medal?

"Must be our documents," said Fredo. "Remember Charlie and I are still aliens."

"Probably." Charlie uttered. "I knew it was pointless me being here." He lit another cigarette. The sky was cloudless. "And just as well it's not raining. Wouldn't we look great if we went in with sodden clothes?"

About thirty minutes later the first guard returned. "Please wait here a few more minutes, a member of the King's staff will collect you."

Soon a gentleman dressed in Savile Row best flanked by two soldiers exited the main door of the palace and made their way towards the public entrance.

"Mr Baldini and party," he exclaimed from inside the railings. Fredo raised his hand. "Guard, please check the remaining documents. Please follow me, all of you."

The group were awestruck at their surroundings as they followed the guide. The soldiers escorted the group. They noticed the areas of the palace damaged by enemy bombs. '*This place suffered some large hits, also,*' thought Fredo. They were led into a large room and they were asked to sit and wait. The elegantly dressed gentleman left the room and the soldiers remained outside the door.

As they sat contemplating the next move, a maidservant entered the room with a tray, cups of tea and a plate of plain biscuits.

Moments later another formally dressed gentleman entered the room. To his astonishment Fredo immediately recognised the person walking behind from her newspaper photographs. "Her Royal Highness, The Princess Elizabeth," the gentleman said.

In unison the family stood to attention. They froze. None of them knew whether to bow, to courtesy or to shake hands.

"Please remain seated," said the Princess. "We don't require any formalities today."

The Princess had a bundle of papers in her hand.

"I shall get straight to the point, Mr Baldini. Thirty minutes ago His Majesty the King called me. You see, officially you are still an enemy alien of Great Britain, and as such, protocol dictates you should not have entered the Palace today."

Fredo motioned to stand up but the Princess waved her right hand for him to remain seated.

"His Majesty has asked me to intervene. Last week, he asked me to review the case surrounding this award. Mr Baldini, very few of our brave soldiers are nominated to receive the Victoria Cross, and certainly it's very rare for a young man of Thomas' age. Your son was extraordinary and he is a worthy recipient."

Charlie noticed the girls' eyes swelling and he motioned to collect a handkerchief from his trouser pocket. "May I, Your Highness."

"Indeed, Mr Baldini, your whole family has been extraordinary. You have a son who survived the evacuation at Dunkirk, when our country was in its most vulnerable period during our war. You have a son who spent his own personal war in a German prisoner of war camp. I am glad he has been returned to you safely."

The Princess glanced over at the uniformed girls.

"Mr Baldini, you have two daughters who so bravely participated at the front in the Auxiliary Territorial Service. Are you aware, Mr Baldini, that I, too, served time in the Service? Your daughters were renowned. In the Service they were called '*the inseparables*' and I see here today they remain inseparable. You, yourself, Mr Baldini, you had the misfortune to be caught up in the politics of war, interned just like all your fellow Italians. The war has had tragic consequences for us all."

The Princess paused. The family regained their composure.

"May I inform you, Mr Baldini, that His Majesty the King has requested the authorities to waive all the restrictions which have been placed on you as an enemy alien. You can consider yourself a free man. You can return home to your family, a very proud man."

The Princess gathered her papers and stood up.

"Now please, my secretary will escort you to the main order of the day. The Victoria Cross will be awarded to you, Mr Baldini, on behalf of your son, Thomas, by His Majesty the King. All of you should feel very proud. You have provided a great service to this nation."

***

The journey home was bitter sweet. They had the train compartment all to themselves. Fredo felt it was appropriate the family should be together for this special occasion. He was regretful Catherine was not sitting in the unoccupied sixth seat.

The Flying Scotsman steamed slowly out of the King's Cross station. With a huge smile across his face and with a touch of irony Fredo said, "Isn't it strange we have just left the King's Cross but I have the real King's Cross, or Queen's Cross, if you like, close to my heart." Fredo patted the inside pocket of his coat to ensure the box was safely in its place.

With a few wispy clouds in the sky and the majestic

Durham cathedral landscaping the horizon the train pulled into the station. The bus journey home to Errington seemed to take forever.

When the party finally arrived back home they were taken aback. On Station Road, about a hundred yards to either side of the shop and on both sides of the road, bunting hung from lamppost to lamppost. The grapevine had become alive. Townsfolk emerged from their homes and from shops. A crowd had quickly formed. Fredo's thoughts raced back to the terrifying ordeal the last time he had seen a crowd in Station Road. But on this occasion they were clapping, they were cheering, they were raising their hats, including the policemen who had been alerted to the commotion. Today the throng wasn't threatening. It was wholeheartedly welcoming.

The crowd formed an impromptu passageway to the front door of the shop, where Catherine was waiting, overcome with emotion. *'Now we are back in the fold, back in the community,'* she thought.

The group lapped it up, waving in all directions, "Thank you, thank you," they repeated. Fredo and Charlie, hats off, bowed in acknowledgement. The door of the shop closed behind them and the crowd slowly dispersed.

Inside the rest of the family were waiting, in laws, children, all survivors of the horrific war. The table had been set for a family meal.

Catherine carefully took the medal from inside its box, kissed it several times and placed it proudly in the centre of the mantelpiece between two photographs. On one side was a photograph of Lewis looking splendid in military uniform. On the other the smiling face of Thomas with rosy cheeks sparkling in the light, his glengarry tilted perfectly to one side.

Soon the meal was ready. Catherine smiled at Fredo at the other end of the table. The family held hands. "We are a different family now, a bigger family with grandchildren too," she said, "we have been battered in this war but now we are stronger. We must never forget, and our grandchildren must never forget the huge sacrifice our family has made. Lewis and Thomas will remain forever in our hearts.

Next in the Blood Heart Trilogy

Jewish Blood Italian Heart

Italian Blood American Heart

Authors Note

The village of Montecino and the town of Valbona cannot be found on any map. They exist in my imagination, although they are closely based on hamlets and hill towns in Garfagnana in Tuscany which I have visited so often and which have impacted greatly in my life.

The town of Errington is also in my imagination and it is typical of many coal mining towns in Scotland and the North East of England.

Acknowledgements

My thanks to Jerome Donnini whose ancestors' experiences provided the inspiration for me to proceed with the project.

My thanks also to Davina, Natalie and Paul, Michelle and Mauro for their love and support throughout this journey.

I also acknowledge my debt to the following publicly available resources:
    The Victoria Cross Citation in the Supplement to the London Gazette, Friday, 16th March, 1945.
    Report on Operation Blackcock at the Ike Skelton Combined Arms Digital Library.

Printed in Great Britain
by Amazon

56485596R00225